DATE DUE NOV 0 6

DEC 2 3 2008			
MAR 1 4 2007			
9-27			
GAYLORD			PRINTED IN U.S.A.

The PINHOE EGG

Also by Diana Wynne Jones

Diana Wynne Jones

The PINHOE EGG

A CHRESTOMANCI BOOK

Greenwillow Books
An Imprint of HarperCollins*Publishers*

The Pinhoe Egg
Copyright © 2006 by Diana Wynne Jones

The right of Diana Wynne Jones to be identified as the author of this work has been asserted by her.

The text of this book is set in 13-point Granjon.
Book design by Paul Zakris

Library of Congress Cataloging-in-Publication Data
Jones, Diana Wynne.
The Pinhoe egg / by Diana Wynne Jones.
   p. cm.
"Greenwillow Books."
Summary: Two powerful young enchanters, Cat, the future Chrestomanci, and Marianne, who is being trained to be Gammer of the Pinhoes, work together as friends to try to end an illegal witches' war and, in the process, right some old wrongs.
ISBN-10: 0-06-113124-5 (trade bdg.) ISBN-13: 978-0-06-113124-0 (trade bdg.)
ISBN-10: 0-06-113125-3 (lib. bdg.) ISBN-13: 978-0-06-113125-7 (lib. bdg.)
[1. Magic—Fiction. 2. Witchcraft—Fiction. 3. Fantasy.] I. Title.
PZ7.J684Pin 2006 [Fic]—dc22 2005046794

First American Edition 10 9 8 7 6 5 4 3 2 1

 GREENWILLOW BOOKS

To Greer Gilman

The PINHOE EGG

Chapter One

At the beginning of the Summer holidays, while Chrestomanci and his family were still in the south of France, Marianne Pinhoe and her brother, Joe, walked reluctantly up the steep main street of Ulverscote. They had been summoned by Gammer Pinhoe. Gammer was head of Pinhoe witchcraft in Ulverscote and wherever Pinhoes were, from Bowbridge to Hopton, and from Uphelm to Helm St. Mary. You did not disobey Gammer's commands.

"I wonder what the old bat wants this time," Joe said gloomily, as they passed the church. "Some new stupid thing, I bet."

"Hush," said Marianne. Uphill from the church, the Reverend Pinhoe was in the vicarage garden spraying his roses. She could smell the acid odor of the spell and hear the *hoosh* of the vicar's spray. It was true that Gammer's commands had lately become more and more exacting and peculiar, but no adult Pinhoe liked to hear you say so.

Joe bent his head and put on his most sulky look. "But it doesn't make sense," he grumbled as they passed the vicarage gate. "Why does she want me too?"

Marianne grinned. Joe was considered "a disappointment" by the Pinhoes. Only Marianne knew how hard Joe worked at being disappointing—though she thought Mum suspected it. Joe's heart was in machines. He had no patience with the traditional sort of witchcraft or the way magic was done by the Pinhoes—or the Farleighs over in Helm St. Mary, or for that matter the Cleeves in Underhelm, on the other side of Ulverscote. As far as that kind of magic went, Joe wanted to be a failure. They left him in peace then.

"It makes sense she wants *you*," Joe continued

as they climbed the last stretch of hill up to Woods House, where Gammer lived. "You being the next Gammer and all."

Marianne sighed and made a face. The fact was that no girls except Marianne had been born to Gammer's branch of the Pinhoes for two generations now. Everyone knew that Marianne would have to follow in Gammer's footsteps. Marianne had two great-uncles and six uncles, ten boy cousins, and weekly instructions from Gammer on the witchcraft that was expected of her. It weighed on her rather. "I'll live," she said. "I expect we both will."

They turned up the weedy drive of Woods House. The gates had been broken ever since Old Gaffer died when Marianne was quite small. Their father, Harry Pinhoe, was Gaffer now, being Gammer's eldest son. But it said something about their father's personality, Marianne always thought, that everyone called him Dad, and never Gaffer.

They took two steps up the drive and sniffed. There was a powerful smell of wild animal there.

"Fox?" Joe said doubtfully. "Tomcat?"

Marianne shook her head. The smell was strong, but it was much pleasanter than either of those. A powdery, herby scent, a bit like Mum's famous foot powder.

Joe laughed. "It's not Nutcase anyway. He's been done."

They went up the three worn steps and pushed on the peeling front door. There was no one to open it to them. Gammer insisted on living quite alone in the huge old house, with only old Miss Callow to come and clean for her twice a week. And Miss Callow didn't do much of a job, Marianne thought, as they came into the wide entrance hall. Sunlight from the window halfway up the dusty oak staircase made slices of light filled thick with dust motes, and shone murkily off the glass cases of stuffed animals that stood on tables round the walls. Marianne hated these. The animals had all been stuffed with savage snarls on their faces. Even through the dust, you saw red open mouths, sharp white teeth, and glaring glass eyes. She tried not to look at them as she and Joe crossed the hall over the wall-to-wall spread of grubby coconut matting and knocked on the door of the front room.

"Oh, come in, do," Gammer said. "I've been waiting half the morning for you."

"No, you haven't," Joe muttered. Marianne hoped this was too quiet for Gammer to hear, true though it was. She and Joe had set off the moment Aunt Joy brought the message down from the Post Office.

Gammer was sitting in her tattered armchair, wearing the layers of black clothing she always wore, with her black cat, Nutcase, on her bony knees and her stick propped up by the chair. She did not seem to have heard Joe. "It's holidays now, isn't it?" she said. "How long have you got? Six weeks?"

"Nearly seven," Marianne admitted. She looked down into the ruins of Gammer's big, square, handsome face and wondered if she would look like this when she was this old herself. Everyone said that Gammer had once had thick chestnutty hair, like Marianne had, and

Gammer's eyes were the same wide brown ones that Marianne saw in the mirror when she stared at herself and worried about her looks. The only square thing about Marianne was her unusually broad forehead. This was always a great relief to Marianne.

"Good," said Gammer. "Well, here's my plans for you both. Can't have the pair of you doing nothing for seven weeks. Joe first, you're the eldest. We've got you a job, a live-in job. You're going to go and be boot boy to the Big Man in You-Know-Where."

Joe stared at her, horrified. "In Chrestomanci Castle, you mean?"

"Be quiet," his grandmother said sharply. "You don't say that name here. Do you want to have them notice us? They're only ten miles away in Helm St. Mary."

"But," said Joe, "I'd got plans of my own for these holidays."

"Too bad," said Gammer. "Idle plans, stupid plans. You know you're a disappointment to us all, Joseph Pinhoe, so here's your chance to be useful for once. You can go and be our inside eyes and ears in That Castle, and send me word back by Joss Callow if they show the slightest signs of knowing us Pinhoes exist—or Farleighs or Cleeves for that matter."

"Of course they know we exist," Joe said scornfully. "They can't think there's no one living in Ulverscote or—"

Gammer stopped him with a skinny pointing finger. "Joe Pinhoe, you know what I mean. They don't know and can't know that we're all of us witches. They'd step in and make rules and laws for us as soon as they knew and stop us from working at our craft. For two hundred years now —ever since they put a Big Man in That Castle—we've stopped them finding out about us, and I intend for us to go *on* stopping them. And you are going to help me do that, Joe."

"No, I'm not," Joe said. "What's wrong with Joss Callow? *He's* there."

"But he's an outside man," Gammer said. "We want you *inside*. That's where all the secrets are."

"I'm not—" Joe began.

"Yes, you *are!*" Gammer snapped. "Joss has you all fixed up and recommended to that harpy Bessemer that they call Housekeeper there, and go there you will, until you start school again." She snatched up her stick and pointed it at Joe's chest. "I so order it," she said.

Marianne felt the jolt of magic and heard Joe gasp at whatever the stick did to him. He looked from his chest to the end of the stick, dazed and sulky. "You'd no call to do that," he said.

"It won't kill you," Gammer said. "Now, Marianne, I want you with me from breakfast to supper every day. I want help in the house and errands run, but we'll give out that you're my apprentice. I don't want people thinking I need looking after."

Marianne, seeing her holidays being swallowed up and taken away, just like Joe's, cast around for something—anything!—that might let her off. "I promised Mum to help with the herbs," she said. "There's been a bumper crop—"

"Then Cecily can just do her own stewing and distilling alone, like she always does," Gammer said. "I want you *here*, Marianne. Or do I have to point my stick at you?"

"Oh, no. Don't—" Marianne began.

She was interrupted by the crunch of wheels and hoofbeats on the drive outside. Without waiting for Gammer's sharp command to "See who's there!" Marianne and Joe raced to the window. Nutcase jumped off Gammer's knee and beat them to it. He took one look through the grimy glass and fled, with his tail all bushed out. Marianne looked out to see a smart wicker-work pony carriage with a well-groomed piebald pony in its shafts just drawing up by the front steps. Its driver was Gaffer Farleigh, whom Marianne had always disliked, in his best tweed suit and cloth cap, and looking grim even for him. Behind him in the wicker carriage seat sat Gammer Norah Farleigh. Gammer Norah had long thin eyes and a short thin mouth, which made her look grim at the best of times. Today she looked even grimmer.

"Who is it?" Gammer demanded urgently.

"Gaffer Farleigh. In his best," Joe said. "And Gammer Norah. State visit, Gammer. She's got that horrible hat on, with the poppies."

"And they all look horribly angry," Marianne added. She watched a Farleigh cousin jump out of the carriage and go to the pony's head. He was in a suit too. She watched Gaffer Farleigh hand the whip and the reins to the cousin and climb stiffly down, where he stood smoothing his peppery whiskers and waiting for Gammer Norah, who was making the carriage dip and creak as she stood up and got down too. Gammer Norah was a large lady. Poor pony, Marianne thought, even with a light carriage like that.

"Go and let them in. Show them in here and then wait in the hall," Gammer commanded. "I want *some* Pinhoes on call while I speak to them." Marianne thought Gammer was quite as much surprised by this visit as they were.

She and Joe scurried out past the stuffed animals, Joe with his sulkiest, most head-down, mulish look. The cracked old doorbell jangled, and Gaffer Farleigh pushed the front door open as they reached it.

"Come all the way from Helm St. Mary," he said, glowering at them, "and I find two children who can't even be bothered to come to the door. She in, your Gammer? Or pretending she's out?"

"She's in the front room," Marianne said politely. "Shall I show—?"

But Gaffer Farleigh pushed rudely past and tramped toward the front room, followed by Gammer Norah, who practically shoved Joe against the nearest stuffed animal case getting her bulk indoors. She was followed by her acid-faced daughter Dorothea, who said to Marianne, "Show some manners, child. They'll need a cup of tea and biscuits at *once*. Hurry it up."

"Well, I like that!" Joe said, and made a face at Dorothea's back as Dorothea shut the front-room door with a slam. "Let's just go home."

Raised voices were already coming from behind the slammed door. "No, stay," Marianne said. "I want to know what they're so angry about."

"Me too," Joe admitted. He grinned at Marianne and quietly directed a small, sly spell at the front-room door, with the result that the door shortly came open an inch or so. Gaffer Farleigh's voice boomed through the gap. "Don't deny it, woman! You let it out!"

"I did *not*!" Gammer more or less screamed, and was then drowned out by the voices of Norah and Dorothea, both yelling.

Marianne went to the kitchen to put the kettle on, leaving Joe to listen. Nutcase was there, sitting in the middle of the enormous old table, staring ardently at a tin of cat food someone had left there. Marianne sighed. Gammer always said Nutcase had only two brain cells, both of them devoted to food, but it did rather look as if Gammer had forgotten to feed him again. She opened the tin for him and put the food in his dish. Nutcase was so ecstatically grateful that Marianne wondered how long it was since Gammer had remembered that cats need to eat. There were no biscuits in any of the cupboards. Marianne began to wonder if

Gammer had forgotten to feed herself, too.

As the kettle was still only singing, Marianne went into the hall again. The screaming in the front room had died down. Dorothea's voice said, "And I nearly walked into it. I was lucky not to be hurt."

"Pity it didn't eat you," Gammer said.

This caused more screaming and made Joe giggle. He was standing over the glass case that held the twisted, snarling ferret, looking at it much as Nutcase had looked at the tin of cat food. "Have you found out what it's about yet?" Marianne whispered.

Joe shrugged. "Not really. They say Gammer did something and she says she didn't."

At this moment the noise in the front room died down enough for them to hear Gaffer Farleigh saying, "Our sacred trust, Pinhoes and Farleighs both, not to speak of Cleeves. And you, Edith Pinhoe, have failed in that trust."

"Nonsense," came Gammer's voice. "You're a pompous fool, Jed Farleigh."

"And the very fact that you deny it," Gaffer

Farleigh continued, "shows that you have lost all sense of duty, all sense of truth and untruth, in your work and in your life."

"I never heard anything so absurd," Gammer began.

Norah's voice cut across Gammer's. "Yes, you have, Edith. That's what we're here to say. You've lost it. You're past it. You make mistakes."

"We think you should retire," Dorothea joined in priggishly.

"Before you do any more harm," Gaffer Farleigh said.

He sounded as if he was going to say more, but whatever this was, it was lost in the immense scream Gammer gave. "What nonsense, what cheek, what an *insult*!" she screamed. "Get out of here, all of you! *Get out of my house, this instant!*" She backed this up with such a huge gust of magic that Joe and Marianne reeled where they stood, even though it was not aimed at them. The Farleighs must have gotten it right in their faces. They came staggering backward out of the front room and across the hall. At the front door, they managed to turn themselves around. Gaffer Farleigh, more furiously angry than either Joe or Marianne had ever seen him, shook his fist and roared out, "I tell you you've *lost* it, Edith!" Marianne could have sworn that, mixed in with Gammer's gust of magic, was the sharp stab of a spell from Gaffer Farleigh, too.

Before she could be sure, all three Farleighs bolted for their carriage, jumped into it, and drove off, helter-skelter, as if Chrestomanci himself was after them.

In the front room, Gammer was still screaming. Marianne rushed in to find her rocking back and forth in her chair and screaming, screaming. Her hair was coming down and dribble was running off her chin. "Joe! Help me stop her!" Marianne shouted.

Joe came close to Gammer and bawled at her, "I'm *not going* to Chrestomanci Castle! Whatever you say!" He said afterward that it was the only thing he could think of that Gammer might attend to.

It certainly stopped Gammer screaming. She stared at Joe, all wild and shaky and panting. "Filberts of halibuts is twisted out of all porringers," she said.

"Gammer!" Marianne implored her. "Talk *sense*!"

"Henbane," said Gammer. "Beauticians' holiday. Makes a crumbfest."

Marianne turned to Joe. "Run and get Mum," she said. "Quickly. I think her mind's gone."

By nightfall, Marianne's verdict was the official one.

Well before Joe actually reached Furze Cottage to fetch Mum, word seemed to get round that something had happened to Gammer. Dad and Uncle Richard were already rushing up the street from the shed behind the cottage where they worked making furniture; Uncle Arthur was racing uphill from the Pinhoe Arms; Uncle Charles arrived on his bicycle, and Uncle Cedric rattled in soon after on his farm cart; Uncle Simeon's builder's van stormed up next; and Uncle Isaac pelted over the fields from his smallholding, followed by his wife, Aunt Dinah, and an accidental herd of goats. Soon after that came the two great-uncles. Uncle Edgar, who was a real estate agent, spanked up the drive in his carriage and pair; and Uncle Lester, who was a lawyer, came in his smart car all the way from Hopton, leaving his office to take care of itself.

The aunts and great-aunts were not far behind. They paused only to make sandwiches first—except for Aunt Dinah, who went back to the Dell to pen the goats before she too made sandwiches. This, it seemed to Marianne, was an unchanging Pinhoe custom. Show them a crisis, and Pinhoe aunts made sandwiches. Even her own mother arrived with a basket smelling of bread, egg, and cress. The great table in the Woods House kitchen was shortly piled with sandwiches of all sizes and flavors. Marianne and Joe were kept busy carrying pots of tea and sandwiches to the solemn meeting in the front room, where they had to tell each new arrival exactly what happened.

Marianne got sick of telling it. Every time she got to the part where Gaffer Farleigh shook his fist and shouted, she explained, "Gaffer Farleigh cast a spell on Gammer then. I felt it." And every time, the uncle or aunt would say, "I can't see Jed Farleigh doing a thing like that!" and they would turn to Joe and ask if Joe had felt a spell too. And Joe was forced to shake his head and say he hadn't. "But there was such a lot of stuff coming from Gammer," he said, "I could have missed it."

But the aunts and uncles attended to Joe no more than they attended to Marianne. They turned to Gammer then. Mum had arrived first, being the only Pinhoe lady to think of throwing sandwiches together by witchcraft, and she had found Gammer in such a state that her first act had been to send Gammer to sleep. Gammer was most of the time lying on the shabby sofa, snoring. "She was screaming the place down," Mum explained to each newcomer. "It seemed the best thing to do."

"Better wake her up, then, Cecily," said the

uncle or aunt. "She'll be calmer by this time."

So Mum would take the spell off and Gammer would sit up with a shriek. "Pheasant pie, I tell you!" she would shout. "Tell me something I don't know. Get the fire brigade. There's balloons coming." And all manner of such strange things. After a bit, the uncle or aunt would say, "On second thoughts, I think she'll be better for a bit of a sleep. Pretty upset, isn't she?" So Mum would put the sleep spell back on again and solemn peace would descend until the next Pinhoe arrived.

The only one who did not go through this routine was Uncle Charles. Marianne *liked* Uncle Charles. For one thing—apart from silent Uncle Simeon—he was her only thin uncle. Most of the Pinhoe uncles ran to a sort of wideness, even if most of them were not actually fat. And Uncle Charles had a humorous twitch to his thin face, quite unlike the rest. He was held to be "a disappointment," just like Joe. Knowing Joe, Marianne suspected that Uncle Charles had worked at being disappointing, just as hard as

Joe did—although she did think that Uncle Charles had gone a bit far when he married Aunt Joy at the Post Office. Uncle Charles arrived in his paint-blotched old overalls, being a house-painter by trade, and he looked at Gammer, snoring gently on the sofa with her mouth open. "No need to disturb her for me," he said. "Lost her marbles at last, has she? What happened?"

When Marianne had explained once more, Uncle Charles stroked his raspy chin with his paint-streaked hand and said, "I don't see Jed Farleigh doing *that* to her, little as I like the man. What was the row about?"

Marianne and Joe had to confess that they had not the least idea, not really. "They said she'd let a sacred trust get out and it ran into their Dorothea. I *think*," Marianne said. "But Gammer said she never did."

Uncle Charles raised his eyebrows and opened his eyes wide. "Eh?"

"Let it be, Charles. It's not important," Uncle Arthur told him impatiently. "The important thing is that poor Gammer isn't making sense anymore."

"Overtaxed herself, poor thing," Marianne's father said. "It was that Dorothea making trouble again, I'll bet. I could throttle the woman, frankly."

"Should have been strangled at birth," Uncle Isaac agreed. "But what do we do now?"

Uncle Charles looked across at Marianne, joking and sympathetic at the same time. "Did she ever get round to naming you Gammer after her, Marianne? Should *you* be in charge now?"

"I hope *not*!" Marianne said.

"Oh, do talk *sense*, Charles!" all the others said. To which Dad added, "I'm not having my little girl stuck with that, even for a joke. We'll wait for Edgar and Lester to get here. See what they say. They're Gammer's brothers, after all."

But when first Great-Uncle Edgar and then Great-Uncle Lester arrived, and Marianne had gone through the tale twice more, and Gammer had been woken up to scream, "We're infested with porcupines!" at Uncle Edgar and "I *told* everyone it was twisted cheese!" at Uncle Lester, neither great-uncle seemed at all sure what to do. Both pulled at their whiskers uncertainly and finally sent Joe and Marianne out to the kitchen so that the adults could have a serious talk.

"I don't like Edgar," Joe said, moodily eating leftover sandwiches. "He's bossy. What does he wear that tweed hat for?"

Marianne was occupied with Nutcase. Nutcase rushed out from under the great table demanding food. "It's what real estate agents wear, I suppose," she said. "Like Lester wears a black coat and striped trousers because he's a lawyer. Joe, I can't find any more cat food."

Joe looked a little guiltily at the last of Great-Aunt Sue's sandwiches. They had been fat and moist and tasty and he had eaten all but one. "This one's sardine," he said. "Give him that. Or—" He lifted the cloth over the one untouched plateful. These were thin and dry and almost certainly Aunt Joy's. "Or there's these. Do cats eat meat paste?"

"They sometimes have to," Marianne said.

She dismantled sandwiches into Nutcase's dish, and Nutcase fell on them as if he had not been fed for a week. And perhaps he hadn't, Marianne thought. Gammer had neglected almost everything lately.

"You know," Joe said, watching Nutcase guzzle, "I'm not saying you *didn't* feel Gaffer Farleigh cast a spell—you're better at magic than I am—but it wouldn't have taken much. I think Gammer's mind was going anyway." Then, while Marianne was thinking Joe was probably right, Joe said coaxingly, "Can you do us a favor while we're here?"

"What's that?" Marianne asked as Nutcase backed away from the last of Aunt Joy's sandwiches and pretended to bury it. She was very used to Joe buttering her up and then asking a favor. But I think her mind *was* going, all the same, she thought.

"I need that stuffed ferret out there," Joe said. "If I take it, can you make it look as if it's still there?"

Marianne knew better than to ask what Joe

wanted with a horrid thing like that ferret. Boys! She said, "Joe! It's Gammer's!"

"*She's* not going to want it," Joe said. "And you're much better at illusion than me. Be a sport, Marianne. While they're all still in there talking."

Marianne sighed, but she went out into the hall with Joe, where they could hear the hushed, serious voices from the front room. Very quietly, they inspected the ferret under its glass dome. It had always struck Marianne as like a furry yellow snake with legs. All *squirmy*. Yuck. But the important thing, if you were going to do an illusion, was that this was probably just what everyone saw. Then you noticed the wide-open fanged mouth, too, and the ferocious beady eyes. The dome was so dusty that you really hardly saw anything else. You just had to get the shape right.

"Can you do it?" Joe asked eagerly.

She nodded. "I think so." She carefully lifted off the glass dome and stood it beside the stuffed badger. The ferret felt like a hard furry log when she picked it up. Yuck again. She passed the thing to Joe with a shudder. She put the glass dome back over the empty patch of false grass that was left and held both hands out toward it in as near ferret shape as she could. Bent and yellow and furry-squirmy, she thought at it. Glaring eyes, horrid little ears, pink mouth snarling and full of sharp white teeth. Further yuck. She took her hands away and there it was, exactly as she had thought it up, blurrily through the dust on the glass, a dim yellow snarling shape.

"Lush!" said Joe. "Apex! Thanks." He raced back into the kitchen with the real ferret cradled in his arms.

Marianne saw the print of her hands on the dust of the dome, four of them. She blew on them furiously, willing them to go away. They were slowly clearing, when the door to the front room banged importantly open and Great-Uncle Edgar strode out. Marianne stopped doing magic at once, because he was bound to notice. She made herself gaze innocently instead at Edgar's tweed hat, like a little tweed flower-pot on his head. It turned toward her.

"We've decided your grandmother must have professional care," Great-Uncle Edgar said. "I'm off to see to it."

Someone must have woken Gammer up again. Her voice echoed forth from inside the front room. "There's nothing so good as a stewed ferret, I always say."

Did Gammer read other people's minds now? Marianne held her breath and nodded and smiled at Great-Uncle Edgar. And Joe came back from the kitchen at that moment, carrying Aunt Helen's sandwich basket—which he must have thought was Mum's—with a cloth over it to hide the ferret. Great-Uncle Edgar said to him, "Where are you off to?"

Joe went hunched and sulky. "Home," he said. "Got to take the cat. Marianne's going to look after him now."

Unfortunately Nutcase spoiled this explanation by rushing out of the kitchen to rub himself against Marianne's legs.

"But he keeps getting out," Joe added without a blink.

Marianne took in a big breath, which made her quite dizzy after holding it for so long. "I'll bring him, Joe," she said, "when I come. You go on home and take Mum's basket back."

"Yes," said Great-Uncle Edgar. "You'll need to pack, Joseph. You have to be working in That Castle tomorrow, don't you?"

Joe's mouth opened and he stared at Edgar. Marianne stared too. They had both assumed that Gammer's plans for Joe had gone the way of Gammer's wits. "Who told you that?" Joe said.

"Gammer did, yesterday," Great-Uncle Edgar said. "They'll be expecting you. Off you go." And he strode out of the house, pushing Joe in front of him.

Chapter Two

Marianne meant to follow Joe home, but Mum came out into the hall then, saying, "Marianne, Joy says there's still her plate of sandwiches left. Can you bring them?"

When Marianne confessed that there were no sandwiches, she was sent down to the Pinhoe Arms to fetch some of Aunt Helen's pork pies. When she got back with the pies, Aunt Joy sent her off again to pin a note on the Post Office door saying CLOSED FOR FAMILY MATTERS, and when she got back from that, Dad sent her to fetch the Reverend Pinhoe. The Reverend Pinhoe came back to Woods House with Marianne, very serious and dismayed, wanting to know why no one had sent for Dr. Callow.

The reason was that Gammer had no opinion at all of Dr. Callow. She must have heard what the vicar said because she immediately began shouting. "Quack, quack, quack! Cold hands in the midriff. It's cabbages at dawn, I tell you!"

But the vicar insisted. Marianne was sent to the vicarage phone to ask Dr. Callow to visit, and when the doctor came, there was a further outbreak of shouting. As far as Marianne could tell from where she sat on the stairs with Nutcase on her knee, most of the noise was "No, no, no!" but some of it was insults like "You knitted squid, you!" and "I wouldn't trust you to skin a bunion!"

Dr. Callow came out into the hall with Mum, Dad, and most of the aunts, shaking his head and talking about "the need for long-term care." Everyone assured him that Edgar was seeing to that, so the doctor left, followed by the vicar, and the aunts came into the kitchen to make more sandwiches. Here they discovered that there was no bread and only one tin of sardines. So off Marianne was sent again, to the baker and the grocer and down to Aunt Dinah's to pick up some eggs. She remembered to buy some cat food, too, and came back heavily laden, and very envious of Joe for having made his getaway so easily.

Each time Marianne came back to Woods House, Nutcase greeted her as if she were the only person left in the world. While she was picking him up and comforting him, Marianne could not help stealing secret looks at the glass dome that had held the ferret. Each time she was highly relieved to see a yellow smear with a snarl on the end of it seemingly inside the dome.

At long last, near sunset, the hooves, wheels, and jingling of Great-Uncle Edgar's carriage sounded in the driveway. Great-Uncle Edgar shortly strode into the house, ushering two extremely sensible-looking nurses. Each had a neat navy overcoat and a little square suitcase. After Mum, Aunt Prue, and Aunt Polly had shown them where to sleep, the nurses looked into the kitchen, at the muddle of provisions heaped along the huge table there, and declared they were not here to cook. Mum assured them that the aunts would take turns at doing *that*—at which Aunt Prue and Aunt Polly looked at each other and glowered at Mum. Finally the nurses marched into the front room.

"Now, dear"—their firm voices floated out to Marianne on the stairs—"we'll just get you into your bed and then you can have a nice cup of cocoa."

Gammer at once started screaming again. Everyone somehow flooded out into the hall with Gammer struggling and yelling in their midst. No one, even the nurses, seemed to know what to do. Marianne sadly watched Dad and Mum looking quite helpless, Great-Uncle Lester wringing his hands, and Uncle Charles stealthily creeping away to his bicycle. The only person able to cope seemed to be solid, fair Aunt Dinah. Marianne had always thought Aunt Dinah was only good at wrestling goats and feeding chickens, but Aunt Dinah took hold of Gammer's arm, quite gently, and, quite as gently, cast a soothing spell on Gammer.

"Buck up, my old sausage," she said. "They're here to *help* you, you silly thing! Come on upstairs and let them get your nightie on you."

And Gammer came meekly upstairs past Marianne and Nutcase with Aunt Dinah and the nurses. She looked down at Marianne as she went, almost like her usual self. "Keep that cat in order for me, girl," she said. She sounded nearly normal.

Soon after that, Marianne was able to walk home between Mum and Dad, with Nutcase struggling a little in her arms.

"Phew!" said Dad. "Let's hope things settle down now."

Dad was a great one for peace. All he asked of life was to spend his time making beautiful solid furniture with Uncle Richard as his partner. In the shed behind Furze Cottage the two of them made chairs that worked to keep you comfortable, tables bespelled so that anyone who used them felt happy, cabinets that kept dust out, wardrobes that repelled moths, and many other things. For her last birthday, Dad had made

Marianne a wonderful heart-shaped writing desk with secret drawers in it that were *really* secret: no one could even find those drawers unless they knew the right spell.

Mum, however, was nothing like such a peace addict as Dad. "Huh!" she said. "She was born to make trouble as the sparks fly upward, Gammer was."

"Now, Cecily," said Dad. "I know you don't like my mother—"

"It's not a question of *like*," Mum said vigorously. "She's a Hopton Pinhoe. She was a giddy town girl before your father married her. Led him a proper dance, she did, *and* you know it, Harry! It was thanks to her that he took to going off into the wild and got himself done away with, if you ask—"

"Now, *now*, Cecily," Dad said, with a warning look at Marianne.

"Well, forget I said it," Mum said. "But I shall be very surprised if she settles down, mind or no mind."

Marianne thought about this conversation all

evening. When she went to bed, where Nutcase sat on her stomach and purred, she sleepily tried to remember her grandfather. Old Gaffer had never struck her as being led a dance. Of course she had been very young then, but he had always seemed like a strong person who went his own way. He was wiry and he smelled of earth. Marianne remembered him striding with his long legs, off into the woods, leading his beloved old horse, Molly, harnessed to the cart in which he collected all the strange plants and herbs for which he had been famous. She remembered his old felt hat. She remembered Gammer saying, "Oh, *do* take that horrible headgear *off*, Gaffer!" Gammer always called him Gaffer. Marianne still had no idea what his name had been.

She remembered how Old Gaffer seemed to love being surrounded by his sons and his grandchildren—all boys, except for Marianne— and the way she had a special place on his knee after Sunday lunch. They always went up to Woods House for Sunday lunch. Mum couldn't have enjoyed that, Marianne thought. She had very clear memories of Mum and Gammer snapping at each other in the kitchen, while old Miss Callow did the actual cooking. Mum loved to cook, but she was never allowed to in that house.

Just as she fell asleep, Marianne had the most vivid memory of all, of Old Gaffer calling at Furze Cottage with what he said was a special present for her. "Truffles," he said, holding out his big wiry hand heaped with what looked like little black lumps of earth. Marianne, who had been expecting chocolate, looked at the lumps in dismay. It was worse when Gaffer fetched out his knife—which had been sharpened so often that it was more like a spike than a knife—and carefully cut a slice off a lump and told her to eat it. It tasted like *earth*. Marianne spat it out. It really hurt her to remember Old Gaffer's disappointed look and the way he had said, "Ah, well. She's maybe too young for such things yet." Then she fell asleep.

Nutcase was missing in the morning. The door was shut and the window too, but Nutcase was gone all the same. Nor was he downstairs asking for breakfast.

Mum was busy rushing about finding socks and pants and shirts for Joe. She said over her shoulder, "He'll have gone back to Woods House, I expect. That's cats for you. Go and fetch him back when we've seen Joe off. Oh, God! I've forgotten Joe's nightshirts! Joe, here's two more pairs of socks—I *think* I darned them for you."

Joe received the socks and the other things and secretively packed them in his knapsack himself. Marianne knew this was because the stolen ferret was in the knapsack too. Joe had his very sulkiest look on. Marianne could not blame him. If it had been her, she knew she would have been dreading going to a place where they were all enchanters and out to stop anyone else doing witchcraft. But Joe, when she asked him, just grumbled, "It's not the magic, it's wasting a whole holiday. That's what I hate."

When at last Joe pedaled sulkily away, with a shirtsleeve escaping from his knapsack and fluttering beside his head, it felt as if a thunderstorm had passed. Marianne, not for the first time, thought that her brother had pretty powerful magic, even if it was not the usual sort.

"Thank goodness for that!" Mum said. "I hate him in this mood. Go and fetch Nutcase, Marianne."

Marianne arrived at Woods House to find the front door—most unusually—locked. She had to knock and ring the bell before the door was opened by a stone-faced angry nurse.

"What good are *you* going to do?" the nurse demanded. "We asked the vicar to phone for Mr. Pinhoe."

"You mean Uncle Edgar?" Marianne asked. "What's wrong?"

"She's poltergeisting us," said the nurse. "That's what's wrong." As she spoke, a big brass tray rose from the table beside the door and sliced its way toward the nurse's head. The nurse dodged. "See what I mean?" she said. "We're not going to stay here one more day."

Marianne watched the tray bounce past her

down the steps and clang to a stop in the driveway, rather dented. "I'll speak to her," she said.
"I really came to fetch the cat. May I come in?"

"With pleasure," said the nurse. "Come in and
make another target, do!"

As Marianne went into the hall, she could not
help snatching a look at the ferret's glass dome.
There still seemed to be something yellow inside
the glass, but it did not look so much like a ferret
today. Damn! she thought. It was fading.
Illusions did that.

But here Gammer distracted her by coming
rushing down the stairs in a frilly white night-
dress and a red flannel dressing gown, with the
other nurse pelting behind her. "Is that you,
Marianne?" Gammer shrieked.

Maybe she's all right again, Marianne
thought, a bit doubtfully. "Hallo, Gammer.
How are you?"

"Under sentence of thermometer," Gammer
said. "There's a worldwide epidemic." She
looked venomously from nurse to nurse. "Time
to leave," she said.

To Marianne's horror, the big longcase clock that always stood by the stairs rose up and launched itself like a battering ram at the nurse who had opened the door. The nurse screamed and ran sideways. The clock tried to follow her. It swung sideways across the hall, where it fell across the ferret's dome with a violent twanging and a crash of breaking glass.

Well, that takes care of that! Marianne thought. But Gammer was now running for the open front door. Marianne raced after her and caught her by one skinny arm as she stumbled over the brass tray at the bottom of the steps.

"Gammer," she said, "you can't go out in the street in your nightclothes."

Gammer only laughed crazily.

She isn't all right. Marianne thought. *But she's not so un-all right as all that.* She spoke sternly and shook Gammer's arm a little. "Gammer, you've got to stop *doing* this. Those nurses are trying to *help* you. And you've just broken a valuable clock. Dad always says it's worth hundreds of pounds. Aren't you *ashamed* of yourself?"

"Shame, shame," Gammer mumbled. She hung her head, wispy and uncombed. "I didn't *ask* for this, Marianne."

"No, no, of course not," Marianne said. She felt the kind of wincing, horrified pity that you would rather not feel. Gammer smelled as if she had wet herself, and she was almost crying. "This is only because Gaffer Farleigh put a spell on you—"

"Who's Gaffer Farleigh?" Gammer asked, sounding interested.

"Never mind," Marianne said. "But it means you've got to be *patient*, Gammer, and let people help you until we can make you better. And you've really *got* to stop throwing things at those poor nurses."

A wicked grin spread on Gammer's face. "They can't do magic," she said.

"That's why you've got to stop doing it to them," Marianne explained. "Because they can't fight back. Promise me, Gammer. Promise, or—" She thought about hastily for a threat that might work on Gammer. "Promise me, or I shan't even think of being Gammer after you. I shall wash my hands of you and go and work in London." This sounded like a really nice idea. Marianne thought wistfully of shops and red buses and streets everywhere instead of fields. But the threat seemed to have worked. Gammer was nodding her unkempt head.

"Promise," she mumbled. "Promise Marianne. That's you."

Marianne sighed at a life in London lost. "I should hope," she said. She led Gammer indoors again, where the nurses were both standing staring at the wreckage. "She's promised to be good," she said.

At this stage, Mum and Aunt Helen arrived hotfoot from the village, Aunt Polly came in by the back door, and Great-Aunt Sue alighted from the carriage behind Great-Uncle Edgar. Word had got round, as usual. The mess was cleared up, and to Marianne's enormous relief, nobody noticed that there was no stuffed ferret among the broken glass. The nurses were soothed and took Gammer away to be dressed.

More sandwiches were made, more Pinhoes arrived, and, once again, there was a solemn meeting in the front room about what to do now. Marianne sighed again and thought Joe was lucky to be out of it.

"It's not as if it was just anyone we're talking about, little girl," Dad said to her. "This is our head of the craft. It affects all of us in three villages and all the country that isn't under Farleighs or Cleeves. We've got to get it right and see her happy, or we'll *all* go to pot. Run and fetch your Aunt Joy here. She doesn't seem to have noticed there's a crisis on."

Aunt Joy, when Marianne fetched her from the Post Office, did not see things Dad's way at all. She walked up the street beside Marianne, pinning on her old blue hat as she went and grumbling the whole way. "So I have to leave my customers and lose my income—and it's no good believing your uncle Charles will earn enough to support the family—all because this spoiled old woman loses her marbles and starts throwing clocks around. What's wrong with putting her in a Home, I want to know."

"She'd probably throw things around in a Home too," Marianne suggested.

"Yes, but I wouldn't be dragged off to deal with it," Aunt Joy retorted. "Besides," she went on, stabbing her hat with her hatpin, "my Great-Aunt Callow was in a Home for years and did nothing but stare at the wall, and she was just as much of a witch as your Gammer."

When they got to Woods House, Marianne escaped from Aunt Joy by going to look for Nutcase in the garden, where, sure enough, he was, stalking birds in the overgrown vegetable plot. He seemed quite glad to be taken back to Furze Cottage and given breakfast.

"You stupid old thing!" Marianne said to him. "You have to have your meals here now. I don't think Gammer knows you exist anymore." To her surprise, Marianne found herself swallowing back a sob as she spoke. She had not realized that things were as upsetting as that. But they were. Gammer had never done anything but order Marianne about, nothing to make a person fond of her, but all the same it was awful to have her screaming and throwing things and being generally like a very small child. She hoped they were deciding on a way to make things more reasonable, up at Woods House.

It seemed as if it had not been easy to decide anything. Mum and Dad came home some hours later, with Uncle Richard, all of them exhausted. "Words with the nurses, words with Edgar and Lester," Mum said while Marianne was making them all cups of tea.

"Not to speak of Joy rabbiting on about that nursing home she stuck old Glenys Callow in," Uncle Richard added. "Three spoonfuls, Marianne, love. This is no time for a man to watch his weight."

"But what *did* you decide?" Marianne asked.

It seemed that the nurses had been persuaded to stay on another week, for twice the pay, provided one of the aunts was there all the time to protect them.

"So we take it in turns," Mum said, sighing. "I've drawn tonight's shift, so it's cold supper and rush off, I'm afraid. And after that—"

"It's my belief," Dad said peacefully, "that they'll settle in and she'll get used to them and there'll be no more need to worry."

"In your dreams!" Mum said. Unfortunately, she was right.

The nurses lasted two more nights and then, very firmly and finally, gave notice. They said the house was haunted. Though everyone was positive the haunting was Gammer's doing, no one could catch her at it and no one could persuade the nurses. They left. And there was yet another Pinhoe emergency meeting.

Marianne avoided this one. She told everyone, quite reasonably, that you had to keep a cat indoors for a fortnight in a new place or he would run away. So she sat in her room with Nutcase. This was not as boring as it sounded because, now that Joe was not there to jeer at her, she was able to open the secret drawer in her heart-shaped desk and fetch out the story she was writing. It was called "The Adventures of Princess Irene" and it seemed to be going to be

very exciting. She was quite sorry when everyone came back to Furze Cottage after what
Uncle Richard described as a Flaming Row and
even Dad described as "a bit of difficulty."

According to Mum, it took huge arguments
for them even to agree that Gammer was not
safe on her own, and more arguments to decide
Gammer had to live with someone. Great-Uncle
Edgar then cheerfully announced that he and
Great-Aunt Sue would live in Woods House
and Great-Aunt Sue would look after Gammer.
This had been news to Great-Aunt Sue. She did
not go for the idea at all. In fact, she had said she
would go and live with her sister on the other
side of Hopton, and Edgar could look after
Gammer himself and see how *he* liked it. So
everyone hastily thought again. And the only
possible thing, Mum said, was for Gammer to
come and live with one of Gammer's seven sons.

"Then," said Uncle Richard, "the fur really
flew. Cecily let rip like I've never seen her."

"It's all very well for *you*!" Mum said. "You're
not married and you live in that room over in

the Pinhoe Arms. Nobody was going to ask *you*, Richard, so take that smug look—"

"Now, Cecily," Dad said peaceably. "Don't start again."

"I wasn't the only one," said Mum.

"No, there was Joy and Helen and Prue and Polly all screeching that they'd got enough to do, and even your Great-Aunt Clarice, Marianne, saying that Lester couldn't have his proper respectable lifestyle if they had to harbor a madwoman. It put me out of patience," Dad said. "Then Dinah and Isaac offered. They said as they don't have children, they had the room and the time, and Gammer could be happy watching the goats and the ducks down in the Dell. Besides, Dinah can manage Gammer—"

"Gammer didn't think so," said Mum.

Gammer had somehow gotten wind of what was being decided. She appeared in the front room wrapped in a tablecloth and declared that the only way she would leave Woods House was feet first in her coffin. Or that was what most Pinhoes thought she meant when she kept saying, "Root first in a forcing bucket!"

"Dinah got her back to bed," Uncle Richard said. "We're moving Gammer out tomorrow. We put a general call out for all Pinhoes to help and—"

"Wait. There was Edgar's bit before that," Mum said. "Edgar was all set to move into Woods House as soon as Gammer was out of it. Your Great-Aunt Sue didn't disagree with him on *that*, surprise, surprise. The ancestral family home, they said, the big house of the village. As the oldest surviving Pinhoe, Edgar said, it was his *right* to live there. He'd rename it Pinhoe Manor, he thought."

Dad chuckled. "Pompous idiot, Edgar is. I told him to his face he couldn't. The house is mine. It came to me when Old Gaffer went, but Gammer set store by living there, so I let her."

Marianne had had no idea of this. She stared. "Are *we* going to live there, then?" And after all the trouble I've been to, training Nutcase to stay *here*! she thought.

"No, no," Dad said. "We'd rattle about in there as badly as Gammer did. No, my idea is to sell the place, make a bit of money to give to Isaac to support Gammer at the Dell. He and Dinah could use the cash."

"Further flaming row," said Uncle Richard. "You should have seen Edgar's face! And Lester saying that it should only be sold to a Pinhoe or not at all—and Joy screeching for a share of the money. Arthur and Charles shut her up by saying, 'Sell it to a Pinhoe, then.' Edgar looked fit to burst, thinking he was going to have to *pay* for the place, when he thought it was his own anyway."

Dad smiled. "I wouldn't sell to Edgar. His side of the family are Hopton born. He's going to sell it for *me*. I told him to get someone rich from London interested, get a really good price for it. Now let's have a bit of a rest, shall we? Something tells me it may be hard work moving Gammer out tomorrow."

Dad was always given to understating things. By the following night, Marianne was inclined to think this was Dad's understatement of the century.

Chapter Three

Everyone gathered soon after dawn in the yard of the Pinhoe Arms: Pinhoes, Callows, half-Pinhoes, and Pinhoes by marriage, old, young and middle-aged, they came from miles around. Uncle Richard was there, with Dolly the donkey harnessed to Dad's furniture delivery cart. Great-Uncle Edgar was drawn up outside in his carriage, alongside Great-Uncle Lester's big shiny motor car. There was not room for them in the yard, what with all the people and the mass of bicycles stacked up among the piles of broomsticks outside the beer shed, with Uncle Cedric's farm cart in front of those. Joe was there, looking sulky, beside Joss Callow from That Castle, alongside nearly a hundred distant relatives that Marianne had scarcely ever met. About the only people who were *not* there were Aunt Joy, who had to sort the post, and Aunt Dinah, who was getting the room ready for Gammer down in the Dell.

Marianne tried to edge up to Joe to find out how he was getting on among all the enemy enchanters, but before she could get near Joe, Uncle Arthur climbed onto Uncle Cedric's cart and, with Dad up there too to prompt him, began telling everyone what to do. It made sense to have Uncle Arthur do the announcing. He had a big booming voice, rather like Great-Uncle Edgar's. No one could say they had not heard him.

Everyone was divided into work parties. Some were to clear everything out of Woods House, to make it ready to be sold; some were to take Gammer's special things over to the Dell; and yet others were to help get Gammer's room ready there. Marianne found herself in the fourth group that was supposed to get Gammer herself down to the Dell. To her disappointment, Joe was in the work party that was sent to Aunt Dinah's.

"And we should be through by lunchtime," Uncle Arthur finished. "Special lunch for all, here at the Pinhoe Arms at one o'clock sharp. Free wine and beer."

While the Pinhoes were raising a cheer at this, the Reverend Pinhoe climbed up beside Uncle Arthur and blessed the undertaking. "And may many hands make light work," he said. It all sounded wonderfully efficient.

The first sign that things were not, perhaps, going to go that smoothly was when Great-Uncle Edgar stopped his carriage outside Woods House slap in the path of the farm cart and strode into the house, narrowly missing a sofa that was just coming out in the hands of six second cousins. Edgar strode up to Dad, who was in the middle of the hall, trying to explain which things were to go with Gammer and which things were to be stored in the shed outside the village.

"I say, Harry," he said in his most booming

and important way, "mind if I take that corner cupboard in the front room? It'll only deteriorate in storage."

Behind him came Great-Uncle Lester, asking for the cabinet in the dining room. Marianne could hardly hear him for shouts of "Get out of the *way*!" and "Lester, move your car! The sofa's *stuck*!" and Uncle Richard bawling, "I have to back the donkey there! *Move* that sofa!"

"Right royal pile-up, by the sound," Uncle Charles remarked, coming past with a bookshelf, two biscuit tins, and a stool. "I'll sort it out. You get upstairs, Harry. Polly and Sue and them are having a bit of trouble with Gammer."

"Go up and see, girl," Dad said to Marianne, and to Edgar and Lester, "Yes, *have* the blessed cupboard *and* the cabinet and then get out of the way. Though mind you," he panted, hurrying to catch up with Marianne on the stairs, "that cupboard's only made of plywood."

"I know. And the legs on the cabinet come off all the time," Marianne said.

"Whatever makes them happy," Dad panted.

The shouts outside rose to screams mixed with braying. They turned around and watched the sofa being levitated across the startled donkey. This was followed by a horrific crash as someone dropped the glass case with the badger in it. Then they had to turn the other way as Uncle Arthur came pelting down the stairs with a frilly bedside table hugged to his considerable belly, shouting, "Harry, you've *got* to come! Real trouble."

Marianne and Dad squeezed past him and rushed upstairs to Gammer's bedroom, where Joss Callow and another distant cousin were struggling to get the carpet out from under the feet of a crowd of agitated aunts. "Oh, thank goodness you've come!" Great-Aunt Clarice said, looking hot and wild-haired and most unlike her usual elegant self.

Great-Aunt Sue, who was still almost crisp and neat, added, "We don't know what to do."

All the aunts were holding armfuls of clothes. Evidently they had been trying to get Gammer dressed.

"Won't get dressed, eh?" Dad said.

"Worse than that!" said Great-Aunt Clarice. "Look."

The ladies crowded aside to give Dad and Marianne a view of the bed. Dad said, "My God!" and Marianne did not blame him.

Gammer had grown herself into the bed. She had sunk into the mattress, deep into it, and rooted herself, with little hairy nightdress-colored rootlets sticking out all round her. Her long toenails twined like transparent yellow creepers into the bars at the end of the bed. At the other end, her hair and her ears were impossibly grown into the pillow. Out of it her face stared, bony, defiant, and smug.

"Mother!" said Marianne's dad.

"Thought you could get the better of me, didn't you?" Gammer said. "I'm not going."

Marianne had almost never seen her father lose his temper, but he did then. His round amiable face went crimson and shiny. "Yes, you *are* going," he said. "You're moving to Dinah and Isaac's whatever tricks you play. Leave her be," he said to the aunts. "She'll get tired of this in the end. Let's get all the furniture moved out first."

This was easier said than done. No one had realized quite how much furniture there was. A house the size of Woods House, that was big enough to have held a family with seven children once, can hold massive quantities of furniture. And Woods House did. Joss Callow had to go and fetch Uncle Cedric's hay wain and then borrow the Reverend Pinhoe's old horse to pull it, because the farm cart was just not enough and they would have been at it all day. Great-Uncle Edgar prudently left at this point in case someone suggested they use his fine, spruce carriage too; but Great-Uncle Lester nobly stayed and offered to take the smaller items in his car. Even so, all three vehicles had to make several trips to the big barn out on the Hopton Road, while a crowd of younger Pinhoes rushed out there on bikes and broomsticks to unload the furniture, stack it safely, and surround it in their best spells of preservation. At the same time, so many things turned up that people thought Gammer would need in her new home, that Dolly the donkey was going backward and forward non-stop between Woods House and the Dell, with the cart loaded and creaking behind her.

"It's so *nice* to have things that you're used to around you in a strange place!" Great-Aunt Sue said. Marianne privately thought this was rather sentimental of Aunt Sue, since most of the stuff was things she had never once seen Gammer use.

"And we haven't touched the attics yet!" Uncle Charles groaned, while they waited for the donkey cart to come back again.

Everyone else had forgotten the attics. "Leave them till after lunch," Dad said hastily. "Or we could leave them for the new owner. There's nothing but junk up there."

"I had a toy fort once that must be up there," Uncle Simeon said wistfully.

But he was ignored, as he mostly was, because Uncle Richard brought the donkey cart back with a small Pinhoe girl who had a message from Mum. Evidently Mum was getting impatient to know what had become of Gammer.

"They're all ready," small Nicola announced. "They sprung clent."

"They *what?*" said all the aunts.

"They washed the floor and they dried and they polished and the carpet just fits," Nicola explained. "And they washed the windows and did the walls and put the new curtains up and started on all the furniture and the pictures and the stuffed trout and Stafford and Conway Callow teased a goat and it butted them and—"

"Oh, they spring cleaned," said Aunt Polly. "Now I understand."

"Thank you, Nicola. Run back and tell them Gammer's just coming," Dad said.

But Nicola was determined to finish her narrative first. "And they got sent home and that Joe Pinhoe got told off for being lazy. I was good. I helped," she concluded. Only then did she scamper off with Dad's message.

Dad began wearily climbing the stairs. "Let's hope Gammer's uprooted herself by now," he said.

But she hadn't. If anything, she was rooted to

the bed more firmly than ever. When Great-Aunt Sue said brightly, "Up we get, Gammer. Don't we want to see our lovely clean new home?" Gammer just stared, mutinously.

"Oh, come on, Mother. Cut it out!" Uncle Arthur said. "You look ridiculous like that."

"Shan't," said Gammer. "I said root downward and I meant it. I've lived in this house every single year of my life."

"No, you haven't. Don't talk nonsense!" Dad said, turning red and shiny again. "You lived opposite the Town Hall in Hopton for twenty years before you ever came here. One last time—do you get up, or do we carry you to the Dell bed and all?"

"Please yourself. I can't do with your tantrums, Harry—never could," Gammer said, and closed her eyes.

"Right!" said Dad, angrier than ever. "All of you get a grip on this bed and lift it when I count to three."

Gammer's reply to this was to make herself enormously heavy. The bare floor creaked under the weight of the bed. No one could shift it.

Marianne heard Dad's teeth grind. "Very well," he said. "Levitation spell, everyone."

Normally with a levitation spell, you could move almost anything with just one finger. This time, whatever Gammer was doing made that almost impossible. Everyone strained and sweated. Great-Aunt Clarice's hairstyle came apart in the effort. Pretty little combs and hairpins showered down on Gammer's roots. Great-Aunt Sue stopped looking neat at all. Marianne thought that, for herself, she could have lifted three elephants more easily. Uncle Charles and four cousins left off loading the donkey cart and ran upstairs to help, followed by Uncle Richard and then by Great-Uncle Lester. But the bed still would not move. Until, when every possible person was gathered round the bed, heaving and muttering the spell, Gammer smiled wickedly and let go.

The bed went up two feet and shot forward. Everyone stumbled and floundered. Great-Aunt Sue was carried along with the bed as it made for the doorway and then crushed against the doorpost as the bed jammed itself past her and swung sideways into the upstairs corridor. Great-Aunt Clarice rescued Aunt Sue with a quick spell and a tremendous *POP!* which jerked the bed on again. It sailed toward the stairs, leaving everyone behind except for Uncle Arthur. Uncle Arthur was holding on to the bars at the end of the bed and pushing mightily to stop it.

"Ridiculous, am I?" Gammer said to him, smiling peacefully. And the bed launched itself down the stairs with Uncle Arthur pelting backward in front of it for dear life. At the landing, it did a neat turn, threw Uncle Arthur off, bounced on his belly, and set off like a toboggan down the rest of the stairs. In the hall, Nutcase—who had somehow gotten out again— shot out of its way with a shriek. Everyone except Uncle Arthur leaned anxiously over the banisters and watched Gammer zoom through the front door and hit Great-Uncle Lester's car with a mighty *crunch*.

Great-Uncle Lester howled, "My car, my *car*!" and raced down after Gammer.

"At least it stopped her," Dad said as they all clattered after Great-Uncle Lester. "She hurt?" he asked, when they got there to find a large splintery dent in the side of the car and Gammer, still rooted, lying with her eyes shut and the same peaceful smile.

"Oh, I do hope so!" Great-Uncle Lester said, wringing his hands. "*Look* what she's done!"

"Serve you right," Gammer said, without opening her eyes. "You smashed my dollhouse."

"When I was *five*!" Great-Uncle Lester howled. "Sixty *years* ago, you dreadful old woman!"

Dad leaned over the bed and demanded, "Are you ready to get up and walk now?"

Gammer pretended not to hear him.

"All *right*!" Dad said fiercely. "Levitation again, everyone. I'm going to get her down to the Dell if it kills us all."

"Oh, it will," Gammer said sweetly.

Marianne's opinion was that the way they

were all going to die was from embarrassment. They swung the bed up again and, jostling for a handhold and treading on one another's heels, took it out through the gates and into the village street. There the Reverend Pinhoe, who had been standing in the churchyard, vaulted the wall and hurried over to help. "Dear, dear," he said. "What a very strange thing for old Mrs. Pinhoe to do!"

They wedged him in and jostled on, downhill through the village. As the hill got steeper, they were quite glad of the fact that the Reverend Pinhoe was no good at levitation. The bed went faster and faster and the vicar's efforts were actually holding it back. Despite the way they were now going at a brisk trot, people who were not witches or not Pinhoes came out of the houses and trotted alongside to stare at Gammer and her roots. Others leaned out of windows to get a look, too. "I never knew a person could *do* that!" they all said. "Will she be like that permanently?"

"*God* knows!" Dad snarled, redder and shinier than ever.

Gammer smiled. And it very soon appeared that she had at least one more thing she could do.

There were frantic shouts from behind. They twisted their heads around and saw Great-Uncle Lester, with Uncle Arthur running in great limping leaps behind him, racing down the street toward them. No one understood what they were shouting, but the way they were waving the bed carriers to one side was quite clear.

"Everyone go right," Dad said.

The bed and its crowd of carriers veered over toward the houses and, on Marianne's side, began stumbling over doorsteps and barking shins on foot-scrapers, just as Dolly the donkey appeared, with her cart of furniture bounding behind her, apparently running for her life.

"Oh, *no!*" groaned Uncle Richard.

The huge table from the kitchen in Woods House was chasing Dolly, gaining on her with every stride of its six massive wooden legs. Everyone else in the street screamed warnings and crowded to the sides. Uncle Arthur collapsed on the steps of the Pinhoe Arms. Great-

Uncle Lester fled the other way into the grocer's. Only Uncle Richard bravely let go of the bed and jumped forward to try to drag Dolly to safety. But Dolly, her eyes set with panic, swerved aside from him and pattered on frantically. Uncle Richard had to throw himself flat as the great table veered to charge at him, its six legs going like pistons. Gammer almost certainly meant the table to go for the bed and its carriers, but as it galloped near enough, Uncle Charles, Dad, Uncle Simeon, and the Reverend Pinhoe each put out a leg and kicked it hard in the side. That swung it back into the street again. It was after Dolly in a flash.

Dolly had gained a little when the table swerved, but the table went so fast that it looked as if, unless Dolly could turn right at the bottom of the hill toward Furze Cottage in time, or left toward the Dell, she was going to be squashed against the Post Office wall. Everyone except Marianne held their breath. Marianne said angrily, "Gammer, if you've killed poor Dolly I'll never forgive you!"

Gammer opened one eye. Marianne thought the look from it was slightly ashamed.

Dolly, seeing the wall coming up, uttered a braying scream. Somehow, no one knew how, she managed to throw herself and the cart sideways into Dell Lane. The cart rocked and shed a birdcage, a small table, and a towel rail, but it stayed upright. Dolly, cart and all, sped out of sight, still screaming.

The table thundered on and hit the Post Office wall like a battering ram. It went in among the bricks as if the bricks weighed nothing and plowed on, deep into the raised lawn behind the wall. There it stopped.

When the shaken bed carriers trotted up to the wreckage, Aunt Joy was standing above them on the ruins, with her arms folded ominously.

"You've done it now, haven't you, you horrible old woman?" she said, glaring down at Gammer's smug face. "Making everyone carry you around like this—you ought to be ashamed! Can you pay for all this? Can you? I don't see why *I* should have to."

"Abracadabra," Gammer said. "Rhubarb."

"That's right. Pretend to be balmy," said Aunt Joy. "And everyone will back you up, like they always do. If it was me, I'd dump you in the duck pond. *Curse* you, you old—!"

"That's enough, Joy!" Dad commanded. "You've every right to be annoyed, and we'll pay for the wall when we sell the house, but no cursing, please."

"Well, get this table out of here at least," Aunt Joy said. She turned her back and stalked away into the Post Office.

Everyone looked at the vast table, half buried in rubble and earth. "Should we take it down to the Dell?" a cousin asked doubtfully.

"How do you want it when it's there?" Uncle Charles asked. "Half outside in the duck pond, or on one end sticking up through the roof? That house is *small*. And they say this table was built inside Woods House. It couldn't have gotten in any other way."

"In that case," asked Great-Aunt Sue, "how did it get *out*?"

Dad and the other uncles exchanged alarmed looks. The bed dipped as Uncle Simeon dropped his part of it and raced off up the hill to see if Woods House was still standing. Marianne was fairly sure that Gammer grinned.

"Let's get on," Dad said.

They arrived at the Dell to find Dolly, still harnessed to the cart, standing in the duck pond shaking all over, while angry ducks honked at her from the bank. Uncle Richard, who was Dolly's adoring friend, dropped his part of the bed and galloped into the water to comfort her. Aunt Dinah, Mum, Nicola, Joe, and a crowd of other people rushed anxiously out of the little house to meet the rest of them.

Everyone gratefully lowered the bed to the grass. As soon as it was down, Gammer sat up and held a queenly hand out to Aunt Dinah. "Welcome," she said, "to your humble abode. And a cup of hot marmalade would be very welcome too."

"Come inside then, dear," Aunt Dinah said. "We've got your tea all ready for you." She took hold of Gammer's arm and, briskly and kindly, led Gammer away indoors.

"Lord!" said someone. "Did you know it's four o'clock already?"

"Table?" suggested Uncle Charles. Marianne could tell he was anxious not to annoy Aunt Joy any further.

"In one moment," Dad said. He stood staring at the little house, breathing heavily. Marianne could feel him building something around it in the same slow, careful way he made his furniture.

"Dear me," said the Reverend Pinhoe. "Strong measures, Harry."

Mum said, "You've stopped her from ever coming outside. Are you sure that's necessary?"

"Yes," said Dad. "She'll be out of here as soon as my back's turned, otherwise. And you all know what she can do when she's riled. We got her here, and here she'll stay—I've made sure of that. Now let's take that dratted table back."

They went back in a crowd to the Post Office, where everyone exclaimed at the damage. Joe said, "I *wish* I'd seen that happen!"

"You'd have run for your life like Dolly did," Dad snapped, tired and cross. "Everybody levitate."

With most of the spring-cleaning party to help, the table came loose from the Post Office wall quite quickly, in a cloud of brick dust, grass, earth, and broken bricks. But getting it back up the hill was not quick at all. It was *heavy*. People kept having to totter away and sit on doorsteps, exhausted. But Dad kept them all at it until they were level with the Pinhoe Arms. Uncle Simeon met them there, looking mightily relieved.

"Nothing I can't rebuild," he said cheerfully. "It took out half the kitchen wall, along with some cabinets and the back door. I'll get them on it next Monday. It'll be a doddle compared with the wall down there. That's going to take time, and money."

"Ah, well," said Dad.

Uncle Arthur came limping out of the yard, leaning on a stick, with one eye bright purple-black. "There you all are!" he said. "Helen's going mad in here about her lunch spoiling. Come in and eat, for heaven's sake!"

They left the table blocking the entrance to the yard, under the swinging sign of the unicorn and griffin, and flocked into the inn. There, although Aunt Helen looked unhappy, no one found anything wrong with the food. Even elegant Great-Aunt Clarice was seen to have two helpings of roast and four veg. Most people had three. And there was beer, mulled wine, and iced fruit drink—just what everyone felt was needed. Here at last Marianne managed to get a word with Joe.

"How are you getting on in That Castle?"

"Boring," said Joe. "I clean things and run errands. Mind you," he added, with a cautious look at Joss Callow's back, bulking at the next table, "I've never known anywhere easier to duck out from work in. I've been all over the Castle by now."

"Don't the Family mind?" Marianne asked.

"The main ones are not there," Joe said. "They come back tomorrow. Housekeeper was really hacked off with me and Joss for taking today off. We told her it was our grandmother's funeral—or Joss did."

With a bit of a shudder, hoping this was not an omen for poor Gammer, Marianne went on to the question she really wanted to ask. "And the children? They're all enchanters too, aren't they?"

"One of them is," Joe said. "Staff don't like it. They say it's not natural in a young lad. But the rest of them are just plain witches like us, from what they say. Are you going for more roast? Fetch me another lot, too, will you?"

Eating and drinking went on a long time, until nearly sunset. It was quite late when a cheery party of uncles and cousins took the table back to Woods House, to shove it in through the broken kitchen wall and patch up the damage until Monday. A second party roistered off down the hill to tidy up the bricks there.

Everyone clean forgot about the attics.

Chapter Four

On the way back from the south of France, Chrestomanci's daughter, Julia, bought a book to read on the train, called *A Pony Of My Own*. Halfway through France, Chrestomanci's ward, Janet, snatched the book off Julia and read it too. After that, neither of them could talk about anything but horses. Julia's brother, Roger, yawned. Cat, who was younger than any of them, tried not to listen and hoped they would get tired of the subject soon.

But the horse fever grew. By the time they were on the cross–Channel ferry, Julia and Janet had decided that both of them would die unless they had a horse each the moment they got home to the Castle.

"We've only got six weeks until we start lessons again," Julia sighed. "It has to be at *once*, or we'll miss all the gymkhanas."

"It would be a complete waste of the summer," Janet agreed. "But suppose your father says no?"

"You go and ask him now," Julia said.

"Why me?" Janet asked.

"Because he's always worried about the way he had to take you away from your own world," Julia explained. "He doesn't want you to be unhappy. Besides, you have blue eyes and golden hair—"

"So has Cat," Janet said quickly.

"But you can flutter your eyelashes at him," Julia said. "My eyelashes are too short."

But Janet, who was still very much in awe of Chrestomanci—who was, after all, the most powerful enchanter in the world—refused to talk to Chrestomanci unless Julia was there to hold her hand. Julia, now that owning a horse had stopped being just a lovely idea and become almost real, found she was quite frightened of her father too. She said she would go with Janet if the boys would come and back them up.

Neither Roger nor Cat was in the least anxious to help. They argued most of the way across the Channel. At last, when the white cliffs of Dover were well in sight, Julia said, "But if you *do* come and Daddy *does* agree, you won't have to listen to us talking about it anymore."

This made it seem worth it. Cat and Roger duly crowded into the cabin with the girls, where Chrestomanci lay, apparently fast asleep.

"Go away," Chrestomanci said, without seeming to wake up.

Chrestomanci's wife, Millie, was sitting on a bunk darning Julia's stockings. This must have been for something to pass the time with, because Millie, being an enchantress, could have mended most things just with a thought. "He's very tired, my loves," she said. "Remember he had to take a travel-sick Italian boy all the way back to Italy before we came home."

"Yes, but he's been resting ever since," Julia pointed out. "And this is urgent."

"All right," Chrestomanci said, half opening his bright black eyes. "What is it, then?"

Janet bravely cleared her throat. "Er, we need a horse each."

Chrestomanci groaned softly.

This was not promising, but, having started, both Janet and Julia suddenly became very eloquent about their desperate, urgent, crying need for horses, or at least ponies, and followed this up with a detailed description of the horse each of them would like to own. Chrestomanci kept groaning.

"I remember feeling like this," Millie said, fastening off her thread, "my second year at boarding school. I shall never forget how devastated I was when old Gabriel de Witt simply refused to listen to me. A horse won't do any harm."

"Wouldn't bicycles do instead?" Chrestomanci said.

"You don't under*stand*! It's not the *same*!" both girls said passionately.

Chrestomanci put his hands under his head and looked at the boys. "Do you all have this mania?" he asked. "Roger, are you yearning for a coal black stallion too?"

"I'd rather have a bicycle," Roger said.

Chrestomanci's eyes traveled up Roger's plump figure. "Done," he said. "You could use the exercise. And how about you, Cat? Are you too longing to speed about the countryside on wheels or hooves?"

Cat laughed. After all, he was a nine-lifed enchanter, too. "No," he said. "I can always teleport."

"Thank heavens! One of you is sane!" Chrestomanci said. He held up one hand before the girls could start talking again. "All right. I'll consider your request—on certain conditions. Horses, you see, require a lot of attention, and Jeremiah Carlow—"

"Joss Callow, love," Millie corrected him.

"The stableman, whatever his name is," Chrestomanci said, "has enough to do with the horses we already keep. So you girls will have to agree to do all the things they tell me these tiresome creatures need—mucking out, cleaning tack, grooming, and so forth. Promise me you'll do that, and I'll agree to one horse between the two of you, at least for a start."

Julia and Janet promised like a shot. They were ecstatic. They were in heaven. At that moment, anything to do with a horse, even mucking it out, seemed like poetry to them. And, to Roger's disgust, they still talked of nothing else all the way home to the Castle.

"At least I'll get a bicycle out of it," he said to Cat. "Don't you really want one too?"

Cat shook his head. He could not see the point.

Chrestomanci was as good as his word. As soon as they were back in Chrestomanci Castle, he summoned his secretary, Tom, and asked him to order a boy's bicycle and to bring him all the journals and papers that were likely to advertise horses for sale. And when he had dealt with all the work Tom had for him in turn, he called Joss Callow in and asked his advice on choosing and buying a suitable horse. Joss Callow, who was rather pale and tired that day, pulled himself

together and tried his best. They spread news-
papers and horsey journals out all over
Chrestomanci's study, and Joss did his best to
explain about size, breeding, and temperament,
and what sort of price a reasonable horse should
be. There was a mare for sale in the north of
Scotland that seemed perfect to Joss, but
Chrestomanci said that was much too far away.
On the other hand, a wizard called Prendergast
had a decent small horse for sale in the next
county. Its breeding was spectacular, its name
was Syracuse, and it cost rather less money. Joss
Callow wondered about it.

"Go and look at that one," Chrestomanci said.
"If it seems docile and anything like as good as
this Prendergast says, you can tell him we'll have
it and bring it back by rail to Bowbridge. You
can walk it on from there, can you?"

"Easily can, sir," Joss Callow said, a little dubiously. "But the fares for horse travel—"

"Money no object," Chrestomanci said. "I
need a horse and I need it now, or we'll have no
peace. Go and look at it today. Stay overnight—

I'll give you the money—and, if possible, get the creature here tomorrow. If it's no good, telephone the Castle and we'll try again."

"Yes, sir." Joss Callow went off, a little dazed at this suddenness, to tell the stableboy exactly what to do in his absence.

He reached the stableyard in time to discover Janet and Julia trying to open the big shed at the end. "Hey!" he said. "You can't go in there. That's Mr. Jason Yeldham's store, that is. He'll kill us all if you mess up the spells he's got in there!"

Julia said, "Oh, I didn't know. Sorry."

Janet said, "Who's Mr. Jason Yeldham?"

"He's Daddy's herb specialist," Julia said. "He's lovely. He's my favorite enchanter."

"And," Joss Callow added, "he's got ten thousand seeds in that shed, most of them from foreign worlds, and umpteen trays of plants under stasis spells. What did you think you wanted in there?"

Janet replied, with dignity, "We're looking for somewhere suitable for our horse to live."

"What's wrong with the stables?" Joss said.

"We looked in there," Julia said. "The loose box seems rather small."

"Our horse is special, you see," Janet told him.

Joss Callow smiled. "Special or not," he said kindly, "the loose box will be what he's used to. You don't want him to feel strange, do you? You cut along now. He'll be here tomorrow, with any luck."

"Really?" they both said.

"Just off to fetch him now," said Joss.

"Clothes!" Janet said, thoroughly dismayed. "Julia, we need riding clothes. *Now!*"

They went pelting off to find Millie.

Millie, who always enjoyed driving the big sleek Castle car, loaded Joss Callow into the car with the girls and dropped him at Bowbridge railway station before she took Julia and Janet shopping. Julia came back more madly excited than ever, with an armload of riding clothes. Janet, with another armload, was almost silent. Her parents, in her own world, had not been rich. She was appalled at how much riding gear *cost*.

"Just the hard hat on its own," she whispered to Cat, "was *ten years'* pocket money!"

Cat shrugged. Although it seemed to him to be a stupid fuss, he was glad Janet had new things to think about. It made a slight change from horses. Cat was feeling rather flat himself, after the south of France. Flat and dull. Even the sunlight on the green velvet stretch of the lawns seemed dimmer than it had been. The usual things to do did not feel interesting. He suspected that he had grown out of most of them.

Next morning, the Bowbridge carter arrived with Roger's gleaming new bicycle. Cat went down to the front steps with everyone else to admire it.

"This is something like!" Roger said, holding up the bike by its shiny handlebars. "Who wants a horse when they can have *this*?" Janet and Julia, naturally, glared at him. Roger grinned joyfully at them and turned back to the bicycle. The grin faded slowly to doubt. "There's a bar across," he said, "from the saddle to the handles. How do I—?"

Chrestomanci was standing with his hands in the pockets of a sky blue dressing gown with dazzling golden panels. "I believe," he said, "that you put your left foot on the near pedal and swing your right leg over the saddle."

"I do?" Roger said. Dubiously, he did as his father suggested.

After a moment of standing, wobbling and upright, Roger and the bicycle slowly keeled over together and landed on the drive with a crash. Cat winced.

"Not quite right," Roger said, standing up in a spatter of pebbles.

"I fancy you forgot to pedal," Chrestomanci said.

"But how does he pedal *and* balance?" Julia wanted to know.

"One of life's mysteries," Chrestomanci said. "But I have frequently seen it done."

"Shut up, all of you," Roger said. "I *will* do this!"

It took him three tries, but he got both feet on the pedals and pushed off, down the drive in a curvaceous swoop. The swoop ended in one of the big laurel bushes. Here Roger kept going and the bicycle mysteriously did not. Cat winced again. He was quite surprised when Roger emerged from the bush like a walrus out of deep water, picked up the bike, and grimly got on it again. This time his swoop ended on the other side of the drive in a prickly bush.

"It'll take him a while," Janet said. "I was three days learning."

"You mean you can *do* it?" Julia said. Janet nodded. "Then you'd better not tell Roger," Julia said. "It might hurt his pride."

The rest of the morning was filled with the sound of sliding gravel, followed by a crash, with, every so often, the hefty threshing sound of a plump body hitting another bush. Cat got bored and wandered away.

Syracuse arrived in the early afternoon. Cat was up in his room at the time, at the top of the Castle. But he clearly felt the exact moment when Joss Callow led Syracuse toward the stableyard gates and the spells around

Chrestomanci Castle canceled out whatever spells Wizard Prendergast had put on Syracuse. There was a kind of electric jolt. Cat was so interested that he started running downstairs at once. He did not hear the mighty hollow bang as Syracuse's front hooves hit the gates. Nor the slam as the gates flew open. He did not see how Syracuse then got away from Joss Callow. By the time Cat arrived on the famous velvety lawn, Syracuse was out there too being chased by Joss Callow, the stableboy, two footmen, and most of the gardeners. Syracuse was having the time of his life dodging them all, skipping this way and that with his lead rein wildly swinging, and, when any of them got near enough to catch him, throwing up his heels and galloping out of reach.

Syracuse was beautiful. This was what Cat mainly noticed. Syracuse was a dark brown that was nearly black, with a swatch of midnight for his mane and a flying silky black tail. His head was shapely and proud. He was a perfect slender, muscly build of a horse, and his legs were elegant, long, and deft. He was not very large, and he moved like a dancer as he jinked and dodged away from the running, shouting, clutching humans. Cat could see Syracuse was having enormous fun. Cat trotted nearer to the chase, quite fascinated. He could not help chuckling at the clever way Syracuse kept getting away.

Joss Callow, very red in the face, called instructions to the rest. Before long, instead of running every which way, they were organized into a softly walking circle that was moving slowly in on Syracuse. Cat saw they were going to catch him any second now.

Then into the circle came Roger on his bicycle, waving both arms and pedaling hard to stay upright. "Look, no hands!" he shouted. "I can do it! I can do it!" At this point, he saw Syracuse and the bicycle wagged about underneath him. "I can't steer!" he said.

He shot among the frantically scattering gardeners and fell off in front of Syracuse.

Syracuse reared up in surprise, came down, hurdled Roger and the bicycle, and raced off in quite a new direction.

"Keep him out of the rose garden!" the head gardener shouted desperately, and too late.

Cat was now the person nearest to the rose garden. As he sprinted toward the arched entry to it, he had a glimpse of Syracuse's gleaming brown rear turning left on the gravel path. Cat put on more speed, dived through the archway, and turned right. It stood to reason that Syracuse would circle the place on the widest path. And Cat was correct. He and Syracuse met about two-thirds of the way down the right-hand path.

Syracuse was gently trotting by then, with his head and ears turned slightly backward to listen to the pursuit rushing up the other side of the rose garden. He stopped dead when he saw Cat and nodded his head violently upward. Cat could almost hear Syracuse thinking, *Damn!*

"Yes, I know I'm a spoilsport," Cat said to him. "You were having real fun, weren't you? But they don't let people make holes in the lawn. That's what's annoyed them. They'll probably kill Roger. You made hoofprints. He's practically plowed it up."

Syracuse brought his head halfway down and considered Cat. Then, rather wonderingly, he stretched his neck out and nosed Cat's face. His nose felt very soft and whiskery, with just a hint of dribble. Cat, equally wonderingly, put one hand on Syracuse's firm, warm, gleaming neck. A definite thought came to him from Syracuse: *Peppermint?*

"Yes," Cat said. "I can get that." He conjured a peppermint from where he knew Julia had one of her stashes and held it out on the palm of his left hand. Syracuse, very gently, lipped it up.

While he did so, the pursuit skidded round the corner and piled to a halt, seeing Syracuse standing quietly with Cat. Joss Callow, who had been cunning too, and limping because Syracuse had trodden on him, came up behind Cat and said, "You got him, then?"

Cat quickly took hold of the dangling lead rein. "Yes," he said. "No trouble."

Joss Callow sniffed the air. "Ah," he said. "Peppermint's the secret, is it? Wish I'd known. I'll take the horse now. You better go and help your cousin. Got himself woven into that cycle somehow."

It took Cat quite serious magic to separate Roger from the bicycle, and then it took both of them working together to unplow the lawn where Roger had hit it, so Cat never saw how Joss got Syracuse back to the stables. He gathered it took a long time and a lot of peppermints. After that, Joss went to the Castle and asked to speak to Chrestomanci.

As a result, next morning when Janet and Julia came into the stableyard self-consciously wearing their new riding clothes, Chrestomanci was there too, in a dressing gown of tightly belted black silk with sprays of scarlet chrysanthemums down the back. Cat was with him because Chrestomanci had asked him to be there.

"It seems that Wizard Prendergast has sold us a very unreliable horse," Chrestomanci said to the girls. "My feeling is that we should sell Syracuse for dog meat and try again."

They were horrified. Janet said, "Not *dog*

meat!" and Julia said, "We ought to give him a *chance*, Daddy!" Cat said, "That's not fair."

"Then I rely on you, Cat," Chrestomanci said. "I suspect you are better at horse magics than I am."

Joss Callow led Syracuse out, saddled and bridled. Syracuse reeked of peppermint and looked utterly bored. In the morning sunlight he was sensationally good looking. Julia exclaimed. But Janet, to her own great shame, discovered there and then that she was one of those people who are simply terrified of horses. "He's *enormous*!" she said, backing away.

"Oh, nonsense!" said Julia. "His head's only a bit higher than yours is. Get on him. I'll give you first go."

"I—I can't," Janet said. Cat was surprised to see she was shaking.

Chrestomanci said, "Given the creature's exploits yesterday, I think you are very wise."

"I'm not wise," Janet said. "I'm just scared silly. Oh, what a *waste* of new riding clothes!" She burst into tears and ran away into the Castle, where she hid in an empty room.

Millie found her there, sitting on the unmade bed sobbing. "Don't take it so hard, my love," she said, sitting beside Janet. "A lot of people find they can't get on with horses. I don't think Chrestomanci can, you know. He always says he hates them because of the way they smell, but I think it's more than that."

"But I feel so ashamed!" Janet wept. "I went on and on about being a famous rider and now I can't even go *near* the horse!"

"But how could you possibly know that until you tried?" Millie asked. "No one can help the way they're made, my love. You just have to think of something you're good at doing instead."

"But," said Janet, coming to the heart of her shame, "I made such a fuss that I made Chrestomanci spend all that money on a horse, and all for *nothing*!"

"I think I heard Julia making quite as much fuss," Millie remarked. "We'd have bought the horse for her in the end, you know."

"And these clothes," Janet said. "So *expensive*.

And I shall never wear them again."

"Now that is silly," Millie told her. "Clothes can be given to someone else. It will take me five minutes and the very minimum of magic to make them into a second set for Julia—or for anyone else who wants to ride. Roger might decide he wants to, you know."

Janet found herself giving a weak giggle at the thought of Roger sitting on Syracuse in her clothes. It seemed the most impossible thing in all the Related Worlds.

"That's better," said Millie.

Meanwhile, Chrestomanci said, "Well, Julia? You seem to have this horse all to yourself."

Julia happily approached Syracuse. She attended carefully to the instructions Joss Callow gave her, gathered up the reins, put her foot in the stirrup, and managed to get herself into the saddle. "It feels awfully high up," she said.

Syracuse contrived to hump his back somehow, so that Julia was higher still.

Joss Callow jerked the bit to make Syracuse

behave and led Syracuse sedately round the yard with Julia crouching in a brave wobbly way on top. All went well until Syracuse stopped suddenly and ducked his head down. Cat only just prevented Julia from sliding off over Syracuse's ears, by throwing a spell like a sort of rope to hold her on. Syracuse looked at him reproachfully.

"Had enough, Julia?" Chrestomanci asked.

Julia clenched her teeth and said, "Not yet." She bravely managed another twenty minutes of walking round the yard, even though part of the time Syracuse was not walking regularly, but putting his feet down in a random scramble that had Julia tipping this way and that.

"It really does seem as if this animal does not wish to be ridden," Chrestomanci said. He went away indoors and quietly ordered two girl's bicycles.

Julia refused to give up. Some of it was pride and obstinacy. Some of it was the splendid knowledge that she now owned Syracuse all by herself. None of this stopped Syracuse making himself almost impossible to ride. Cat had to be in the yard whenever Julia sat on the horse, with his rope spell always ready. Two days later, Joss Callow opened the gate to the paddock and invited Julia to see if she—or Syracuse—did better in the wider space.

Syracuse promptly whipped round and made for the stables with Julia clinging madly to his mane. The stable doors were shut, so Syracuse aimed himself at the low open doorway of the tack room instead. Julia saw it coming up fast and realized that she was likely to be beheaded. Shrieking out the words of a spell, she managed to levitate herself right up onto the stable roof. There, while Cat and Joss hauled Syracuse out backward, draped in six bridles and one set of carriage reins, Julia sat with big tears rolling down her face and gave vent to her feelings.

"I *hate* this horse! He *deserves* to be dog meat! He's *horrible*!"

"I agree," Chrestomanci said, appearing beside Cat in fabulous charcoal gray suiting. "Would you like me to try to get you a real horse?"

"I hate you too!" Julia screamed. "You only got this one because you thought we were silly to want a horse at all!"

"Not true, Julia," Chrestomanci protested. "I did think you were silly, but I made an honest try and Prendergast diddled me. If you like, I'll try for something fat and placid and elderly, and this one can go to the vet. What's his name?" he asked Joss.

"Mr. Vastion," Joss said, untangling leather straps from Syracuse's tossing head.

"*No!*" said Julia. "I'm sick of *all* horses."

"Mr. Vastion, then," said Chrestomanci.

Cat could not bear to think of anything so beautiful and so much alive as Syracuse being turned into dog meat. "Can I have him?" he said.

Everyone looked at him in surprise, including Syracuse.

"You want the vet?" Chrestomanci said.

"No, Syracuse," said Cat.

"On your head be it, then." Chrestomanci shrugged and turned to help Julia down off the roof.

Cat found he owned a horse—just like that. Since everyone seemed to expect him to, he approached Syracuse and tried to remember the way Joss had told Julia to do things. He got his foot stretched up into the correct stirrup, collected the reins from Joss, and jumped himself vigorously up into the saddle. He would not have been surprised to find himself facing Syracuse's tail. Instead, he found himself looking forward across a pair of large, lively ears beyond a tossing black mane, into Julia's tearful face.

"Oh, this is just not *fair*!" Julia said.

Cat knew what she meant. As soon as he was in the saddle, a peculiar kind of magic happened, which was quite unlike the magic Cat usually dealt in. He knew just what to do. He knew how to adjust his weight and how to use every muscle in his body. He knew almost exactly how Syracuse felt—which was surprise, and triumph at having gotten the right rider at last—and just what Syracuse wanted to do. Together, like one animal that happened to be in two parts, they surged off across the yard, with Joss Callow in urgent pursuit, and through the open paddock gate. There Syracuse broke into a glad canter. It was the most wonderful feeling Cat had ever known.

It lasted about five minutes, and then Cat fell off. This was not Syracuse's fault. It was simply because muscles and bones that Cat had never much used before started first to ache, then to scream, and then gave up altogether. Syracuse was desperately anxious about it and stood over Cat nosing him until Joss Callow raced up and seized the reins. Cat tried to explain to him.

"I see that," Joss said. "There must be some other world where you and this horse are the two parts of a centaur."

"I don't think so," Cat said. He levered himself up off the grass like an old, old man. "They say I'm the only one there is in any world."

"Ah, yes, I forgot," said Joss. "That's why you're a nine-lifer like the Big Man." He always called Chrestomanci the Big Man.

"Congratulations," Chrestomanci called out,

leaning on the gate beside Julia. "It saves you having to teleport, I suppose."

Julia added, rather vengefully, "Remember you have to do the mucking out now." Then she smiled, a sighing, relieved sort of smile, and said, "Congratulations too."

Chapter Five

Cat ached all over that afternoon. He sat on his bed in his round turret room wondering what kind of magic might stop his legs and his behind and his back aching. Or one part of him anyway. He had decided that he would make himself numb from the neck down and was wondering what the best way was to do it, when there was a knock at his door. Thinking it must be Roger being more than usually polite, Cat said, "I'm here, but I'm performing nameless rites. Enter at your peril."

There was a feeling of hesitation outside the door. Then, very slowly and cautiously, the handle turned and the door was pushed open. A sulky-looking boy about Roger's age, wearing a smart blue uniform, stood there staring at him. "Eric Chant, are you?" this boy said.

Cat said, "Yes. Who are *you*?"

"Joe Pinhoe," said the boy. "Temporary boot boy."

"Oh." Now Cat thought about it, he had seen this boy out in the stableyard once or twice, talking to Joss Callow. "What do you want?"

Joe's head hunched. It was from embarrassment, Cat saw, but it made Joe look hostile and aggressive. Cat knew all about this. He had mulish times himself, quite often. He waited. At length Joe said, "Just to take a look at you, really. Enchanter, aren't you?"

"That's right," Cat said.

"You don't look big enough," Joe said.

Cat was thoroughly annoyed. His aching bones didn't help, but mostly he was simply fed up at the way *everyone* seemed to think he was too little. "You want me to prove it?" he asked.

"Yes," said Joe.

Cat cast about in his mind for something he could do. Quite apart from the fact that Cat was forbidden to work magic in the Castle, Joe had the look of someone who wouldn't easily be impressed. Most of the small, simple things Cat thought he could get away with doing without Chrestomanci noticing were, he was sure, things that Joe would call tricks or illusions. Still, Cat was annoyed enough to want to do *something*. He braced his sore legs against his bed and sent Joe up to the very middle of the room's round ceiling.

It was interesting. After an instant of total astonishment, when he found himself aloft with his uniformed legs dangling, Joe began casting a spell to bring himself down. It was quite a good spell. It would have worked if it had been Roger and not Cat who had put Joe up there.

Cat grinned. "You won't get down that way," he said, and he stuck Joe to the ceiling.

Joe wriggled his shoulders and kicked his legs. "Bet I can get down somehow," he said. "It must take you a lot of effort doing this."

"No it doesn't," Cat said. "And I can do this too." He slid Joe gently across the ceiling toward the windows. When Joe was dangling just above the largest window, Cat made the window spring open and began lowering Joe toward it.

Joe laughed in that hearty way you do when you are very nervous indeed. "All right. I believe you. You needn't drop me out."

Cat laughed too. "I wouldn't drop you. I'd levitate you into a tree. Haven't you ever wanted to fly?"

Joe stopped laughing and wriggling. "Haven't I just!" he said. "But boys can't use broomsticks. Go on. Fly me down to the village. I dare you."

"Er—*hem*," said someone in the doorway.

Both of them looked round to find Chrestomanci standing there. It was one of those times when he seemed so tall that he might have been staring straight into Joe's face, and Joe at that moment was a good fifteen feet in the air.

"I think," Chrestomanci said, "that you must achieve your ambition to fly by some other means, young man. Eric is strictly forbidden to perform magic inside the Castle. Aren't you, Cat?"

"Er—" said Cat.

Joe, very white in the face, said, "It wasn't his fault—er—sir. I told him to prove he was an enchanter, see."

"*Does* it need proving?" Chrestomanci asked.

"It does to me," Joe said. "Being new here and all. I mean, *look* at him. Do *you* think he looks like an enchanter?"

Chrestomanci turned his face meditatively down to Cat. "They come in all shapes and sizes," he said. "In Cat's case, eight other people just like him either failed to get born in the other worlds of our series, or they died at birth. Most of them would probably have been enchanters, too. Cat has nine people's magic."

"Sort of squidged together. I get you," Joe said. "No wonder it's this strong."

"Yes. Well. This vexed matter being settled," Chrestomanci said, "perhaps, Eric, you would be so good as to fetch our friend down so that he can go about his lawful business."

Cat grinned up at Joe and lowered him gently to the carpet.

"Off you go," Chrestomanci said to him.

"You mean you're not going to give me the sack?" Joe asked incredulously.

"Do you want to be sacked?" Chrestomanci said.

"Yes," said Joe.

"In that case, I imagine it will be punishment enough to you to be allowed to keep your doubt-less very boring job," Chrestomanci told him. "Now please leave."

"Rats!" said Joe, hunching himself.

Chrestomanci watched Joe slouch out of the room. "What an eccentric youth," he remarked when the door had finally shut. He turned to Cat, looking much less pleasant. "Cat—"

"I know," Cat said. "But he didn't believe—"

"Have you read the story of Puss in Boots?" Chrestomanci asked him.

"Yes," Cat said, puzzled.

"Then you'll remember that the ogre was killed by being tempted to turn into something very large and then something small enough to be eaten," Chrestomanci said. "Be warned, Cat."

"But—" said Cat.

"What I'm trying to tell you," Chrestomanci went on, "is that even the strongest enchanter can be defeated by using his own strength against him. I'm not saying this lad was—"

"He wasn't," said Cat. "He was just curious. He uses magic himself, and I think he thinks it goes by size, how strong you are."

"A magic user. *Is* he, now?" Chrestomanci said. "I must find out more about him. Come with me now for an extra magic theory lesson as a penalty for using magic indoors."

But Joe was all right, really, Cat thought mutinously as he limped down the spiral stairs after Chrestomanci. Joe had not been trying to tempt him, he knew that. He found he could hardly concentrate on the lesson. It was all about the kind of enchanter's magic called Performative Speech. *That* was easy enough to understand. It meant that you said something in such a way that it happened as you said it. Cat could do that, just about. But the *reason* why it happened was beyond him, in spite of Chrestomanci's explanations.

He was quite glad to see Joe the next morning on his way out to the stables. Joe dodged out of the boot room into Cat's path, in his shirtsleeves, with a boot clutched to his front. "Did you get into much trouble yesterday?" he asked anxiously.

"Not too bad," Cat said. "Just an extra lesson."

"That's good," said Joe. "I didn't mean to get you caught—really. The Big Man's pretty scary, isn't he? You look at him and you sort of drain away, wondering what's the worst he can do."

"I don't *know* the worst he can do," Cat said, "but I think it could be pretty awful. See you."

He went on out into the stableyard, where he could tell that Syracuse knew he was coming and was getting impatient to see him. That was a good feeling. But Joss Callow insisted that there were other duties that came first, such as mucking out. For someone with Cat's gifts, this was no trouble at all. He simply asked everything on the floor of the loose box to transfer itself to the muck heap. Then he asked new straw to arrive, watched enviously by the stableboy.

"I'll do it for the whole stables if you like," Cat offered.

The stableboy regretfully shook his head. "Mr. Callow'd kill me. He's a great believer in work and elbow grease and such, is Mr. Callow."

Cat found this was true. Looking after Syracuse himself, Joss Callow said, could never be done by magic. And Joss was in the right of it. Syracuse reacted very badly to the merest hint of magic. Cat had to do everything in the normal, time-consuming way and learn how to do it as he went.

The other part of the problem with Syracuse was boredom. When Cat, now wearing what had been Janet's riding gear, most artfully adapted by Millie, had gotten Syracuse tacked up ready to ride, Joss Callow decreed that they go into the paddock for a whole set of tame little exercises. Cat did not mind too much, because his aches from yesterday came back almost at once. Syracuse objected mightily.

"He wants to gallop," Cat said.

"Well he can't," said Joss. "Or not yet. Lord

knows what that wizard was up to with him, but he needs as much training as you do."

When he thought about it, Cat was as anxious to gallop across open country as Syracuse was. He told Syracuse, Behave now and we can do that soon. Soon? Syracuse asked. Soon, soon? Yes, Cat told him. Soon. Be bored now so that we can go out soon. Syracuse, to Cat's relief, believed him.

Cat went away afterward and considered. Since Syracuse hated magic so much, he was going to have to use the magic on himself instead. He was forbidden to use magic in the Castle, so he would have to use it where it didn't show. He used it, very quietly, to train and tame all the new muscles he seemed to need. He let Syracuse show him what was needed and then he used the strange unmagical magic that there seemed to be between himself and Syracuse to show Syracuse how to be patient in spite of being bored. It went slower than Cat hoped. It took longer than it took Janet, laughing hilariously, to teach Julia to ride her new bicycle. Roger, Julia, and Janet were all pedaling joyfully around the Castle grounds and down through the village long before Cat and Syracuse were able to satisfy Joss Callow.

But they did it quite soon. Sooner than Cat had believed possible, really, Joss allowed that they were now ready to go out for a real ride.

They set off, Joss on the big brown hack beside Cat on Syracuse. Syracuse was highly excited and inclined to dance. Cat prudently stuck himself to the saddle by magic, just in case, and Joss kept a stern hand on Cat's reins while they went up the main road and then up the steep track that led to Home Wood. Once they were on a ride between the trees, Joss let Cat take Syracuse for himself. Syracuse whirled off like a mad horse.

For two furlongs or so, until Syracuse calmed down, everything was a hardworking muddle to Cat, thudding hooves, loud horse breath, leaf mold kicked up to prick Cat on his face, and ferns, grass, and trees surging past the corners of his eyes, ears and mane in front of him. Then, finally, Syracuse consented to slow to a mere trot and Joss caught up. Cat had space to look around and to smell and see what a wood was like when it was in high summer, just passing toward autumn.

Cat had not been in many woods in his life. He had lived first in a town and then at the Castle. But, like most people, he had had a very clear idea of what a wood was like—tangled and dark and mysterious. Home Wood was not like this at all. Any bushes seemed to have been tidied away, leaving nothing but tall, dark-leaved trees, ferns, and a few burly holly trees, with long, straight paths in between. It smelled fresh and sweet and leafy. But the new kind of magic Cat had been learning through Syracuse told him that there should have been more to a wood than this. And there was no more. Even though he could see far off through the trees, there was no depth to the place. It only seemed to touch the front of his mind, like cardboard scenery.

He wondered, as they rode along, if his idea of a wood had been wrong after all. Then Syracuse surged suddenly sideways and stopped. Syracuse was always liable to do this. This was one reason why Cat stuck himself to the saddle by magic. He did not fall off—though it was a close thing—and when he had struggled upright again, he looked to see what had startled Syracuse *this* time.

It was the fluttering feathers of a dead magpie. The magpie had been nailed to a wooden framework standing beside the ride. Or maybe Syracuse had disliked the draggled wings of the dead crow nailed beside the magpie. Or perhaps it was the whole framework. Now that Cat looked, he saw dead creatures nailed all over the thing, stiff and withering and beyond even the stage when flies were interested in them. There were the twisted bodies of moles, stoats, weasels, toads, and a couple of long, blackened, tubelike things that might have been adders.

Cat shuddered. As Joss rode up, he turned and asked him, "What's this for?"

"Oh, it's nothing," Joss said. "It's just— Oh, good morning, Mr. Farleigh."

Cat looked back in the direction of the grisly framework. An elderly man with ferocious side whiskers was now standing beside it, holding a long gun that pointed downward from his right elbow toward his thick leather gaiters.

"It's my gibbet, this is," the man said, staring unlovingly up at Cat. "It's for a lesson. And an example. See?"

Cat could think of nothing to say. The long gun was truly alarming.

Mr. Farleigh looked over at Joss. He had pale, cruel eyes, overshadowed by mighty tufts of eyebrow. "What do you mean bringing one like him in my wood?" he demanded.

"He lives in the Castle," Joss said. "He's entitled."

"Not off the rides," Mr. Farleigh said. "Make sure he stays on the cleared rides. I'm not having him disturbing my game." He pointed another pale-eyed look at Cat and then swung around and trudged away among the trees, crushing leaves, grass, and twigs noisily with his heavy boots.

"Gamekeeper," Joss explained. "Walk on."

Feeling rather shaken, Cat induced Syracuse to move on down the ride.

Three paces on, Syracuse was walking through the missing depths that the wood should have had. It was very odd. There was no foreground, no smooth green bridle path, no big trees. Instead, everywhere was deep blue-green distance full of earthy, leafy smells—almost overpoweringly full of them. And although Cat and Syracuse were walking through distance with no foreground, Cat was fairly sure that Joss, riding beside them, was still riding on the bridlepath, through foreground.

Oh, please, said someone. *Please let us out!*

Cat looked up and around to find who was speaking and saw no one. But Syracuse was flicking his ears as if he, too, had heard the voice. "Where are you?" he asked.

Shut behind, said the voice—or maybe it was several voices. *Far inside. We've been good. We still don't know what we did wrong. Please let us out now. It's been so long.*

Cat looked and looked, trying to focus his witch sight as Chrestomanci had taught him. After a while, he *thought* some of the blue distance was moving, shifting cloudily about, but that was all he could see. He could feel, though. He felt misery from the cloudiness, and longing. There was such unhappiness that his eyes pricked and his throat ached.

"What's keeping you in?" he said.

That—sort of thing, said the voices.

Cat looked where his attention was directed and there, like a hard black portcullis, right in front of him, was the framework with the dead creatures nailed to it. It seemed enormous from this side. "I'll try," he said.

It took all his magic to move it. He had to shove so hard that he felt Syracuse drifting sideways beneath him. But at last he managed to swing it aside a little, like a rusty gate. Then he was able to ride Syracuse out round the splintery edge of it and on to the bridle path again.

"Keep your horse straight," Joss said. He had obviously not noticed anything beyond Syracuse moving sideways for a second or so. "Keep your mind on your road."

"Sorry," said Cat. As they rode on, he realized that he had really been saying sorry to the hidden voices. Even using all his strength, he had not been able to help them. He could have cried.

Or perhaps he had done something. Around them the wood was slowly and gently filling up with blue distance, as if it were leaking round the edge where Cat had pushed the framework of dead things aside. A few birds were, very cautiously, beginning to sing. But it was not enough. Cat knew it was not nearly enough.

He rode home, hugging the queer experience to him, the way you hug a disturbing dream. He thought about it a lot. But he was bad at telling people things, and particularly bad at telling something so peculiar. He did not mention it properly to anyone. The nearest he came to telling about it was when he said to Roger, "What's that wood like over on that hill? The one that's farthest away."

"No idea," Roger said. "Why?"

"I want to go there and see," Cat said.

"What's wrong with Home Wood?" Roger asked.

"There's a horrible gamekeeper," Cat said.

"Mr. Farleigh. Julia used to think he was an ogre," Roger said. "He's vile. I tell you what, why don't we both go to that wood on the hill? Ulverscote Wood, I think it's called. You ride and I'll go on my bike. It'll be fun."

"Yes!" said Cat.

Cat knew better than to mention this idea to Joss Callow. He knew Joss would say it was far too soon for Cat to take Syracuse out on his own. He and Roger agreed that they would wait until it was Joss's day off.

Chapter Six.

Cat was interested to see that Joss seemed to want to avoid Mr. Farleigh too. When they rode out after that, they went either along the river or out into the bare upland of Hopton Heath, both in directions well away from Home Wood. And here too, going both ways, Cat discovered the background felt as if it were missing. He found it sad, and puzzling.

Roger was hugely excited about going for a real long ride. He tried to interest Janet and Julia in the idea. They had now cycled everywhere possible in the Castle grounds and round and round the village green in Helm St. Mary too, so they were ripe for a long ride. The three of them made plans to cycle all of twelve miles, as far away as Hopton, although, as Julia pointed out, this made it twenty-four miles, there and back, which was quite a distance. Janet told her not to be feeble.

They were just setting out for this marathon, when a small blue car unexpectedly rattled up to the main door of the Castle.

Julia dropped her bike on the drive and ran toward the small blue car. "It's Jason!" she shrieked. "Jason's back!"

Millie and Chrestomanci arrived on the Castle steps while Julia was still yards away and shook hands delightedly with the man who climbed out of the car. He was just in time to turn around as Julia flung herself on him. He staggered a bit. "Lord love a duck!" he said. "Julia, you weigh a ton these days!"

Jason Yeldham was not very tall. He had contrived, even after years of living at the Castle, to keep a strong Cockney accent. "No surprise. I started out as boot boy here," he explained to Janet. He had a narrow, bony face, very brown from his foreign travels, topped by sun-whitened curls. His eyes were a bright blue and surrounded by lines from laughing or from staring into bright suns, or both.

Janet was fascinated by him. "Isn't it odd," she said to Cat, who came to see what the excitement was. "You hear about someone and then a few days later they turn up."

"It could be the Castle spells," Cat said. But he liked Jason too.

Roger morosely gathered up the three bicycles and put them away. The rest crowded into the main hall of the Castle, where Jason was telling Millie and Chrestomanci which strange worlds he had been to and saying he hoped that his storage shed was still undisturbed. "Because I've got this big hired van following on, full of some of the weirdest plants you ever saw," he said, with his voice echoing from the dome overhead. "Some need planting out straightaway. Can you spare me a gardener? Some I'll need to consult about—they need special soil and feed and so on. I'll talk to your head gardener. Is that still Mr. McDermot? But I've been thinking all the way

down from London that I need a real herb
expert. Is that old dwimmerman still around—
the one with the long legs and the beard—*you*
know? He always knew twice what I did. Had
an instinct, I think."

"Elijah Pinhoe, you mean?" Millie said. "No.
It was sad. He died about eight years ago now."

"I gather the poor fellow was found dead in a
wood," Chrestomanci said. "Hadn't you heard?"

"No!" Jason looked truly upset. "I must have
been away when they found him. Poor man! He
was always telling me that there was something
wrong in the woods round here. Must have had
a presentiment, I suppose. Perhaps I can talk
with his widow."

"She sold the house and moved, I heard," Millie
said. "There's some very silly stories about that."

Jason shrugged. "Ah, well. Mr. McDermot's
got a good head for plants."

Roger gloomed.

The van arrived, pulled by two cart horses,
and everyone from the temporary boot boy to
Miss Rosalie the librarian was roped in to deal

with Jason's plants. Janet, Julia, the footmen, and most of the Castle wizards and sorceresses carried bags and pots and boxes to the shed. Millie wrote labels. Jason told Roger where to put the labels. Cat was told, along with the butler and Miss Bessemer the housekeeper, to levitate little tender bundles of root and fuzzy leaves to places where Mr. McDermot thought they would do best, while Miss Rosalie followed everyone round with a list. Anyone left over unpacked and sorted queer-shaped bulbs to be planted later in the year. Roger knew there was no question of cycling anywhere that day.

He almost forgave Jason that evening at supper when Jason kept everyone fascinated by telling of the various worlds he had been on and the strange plants he had found there. There was a plant in World Nine B that had a huge flower once every hundred years, so beautiful that the people there worshipped it as a god.

"That was one of my failures," Jason told them. "They wouldn't let me take a cutting, whatever I said."

But he had done better in World Seven D, where there was a remote valley full of medicinal crocuses. At first the old man who owned the valley could not think of anything he wanted in exchange for the bulbs, and he warned Jason that the crocuses were very bad for your teeth. Jason got round the old man and got a sackful of the crocuses by enchanting sets of false teeth for the old man and his family. And then he told of the mountain in World One F that was the only place in all the worlds where a dark green ferny plant grew that actually cured colds. Naturally, the man who owned the mountain was very rich from selling these plants—minus their roots, so that no one else could grow any—and quite determined that nobody else was going to get hold of one. He had guard beasts and armed men patrolling the mountain night and day. Jason had sneaked in at night, under heavy spells, and dug up several before he was spotted and forced to run for it. The guards pursued him right through World Two A before Jason skipped to World Five C and they gave up.

There were now three of those plants at Chrestomanci Castle, in the care of Mr. McDermot.

"And we'll plant some of the rest tomorrow," Jason said gleefully.

Janet and Julia and most of the others were still helping Jason that next day. But that day was Joss Callow's day off. Roger looked at Cat. Cat went to the stables, where he fed Syracuse peppermints and saddled him up and led him through all the people busy around Jason and his shed. "I'm just going to ride him round the paddock," he explained. And he did that. He knew Syracuse would be unmanageable unless he had had a bit of exercise first.

Half an hour later, Cat and Roger were on the road to the distant hills.

Joss Callow meanwhile cycled down to Helm St. Mary, where he dropped in to see his mother, so that if anyone asked he could truthfully say he had been to visit his mother. But he only stayed half an hour before he pedaled on to Ulverscote.

In Ulverscote, Marianne's dad finished his work at mid-morning by packing the donkey cart with a set of kitchen chairs and sending Dolly the donkey and Uncle Richard off to deliver them in Crowhelm. Harry Pinhoe then walked up to the Pinhoe Arms to meet Joss. The two of them settled comfortably in the Private Snug with pints of beer. Arthur Pinhoe leaned amiably in through the hatch from the main bar, and Harry Pinhoe lit the pipe that he allowed himself on these occasions.

"So what's the news?" Harry Pinhoe asked, puffing fine blue clouds. "I hear the Family came back."

"Yes, and bought a horse," Joss Callow said. "Got diddled properly over it." Harry and Arthur laughed. "Me included," Joss admitted. "Wizard who sold it put half a hundred spells on it to make it seem manageable, see. About the only one who can ride it is the boy they're training up to be the next Big Man, and he gets on with it a treat. Odd, though. He doesn't seem to use any magic on it that I can see. But what I was

getting round to with this was about Gaffer
Farleigh. He turned up when I was out with the
boy in Home Wood and gave us both a proper
warning off. Seemed to think the boy was likely
to interfere with our work. What do you
think?"

Harry and Arthur exchanged looks. "Some of
that may be about the row he had with
Gammer," Arthur suggested, "before Gammer
got took strange. All us Pinhoes are dirt to the
Farleighs at the moment."

"They'll get over it," Harry said placidly. "But
we can't have that boy riding all over the country. We'll have to stop that."

"Oh, I will," Joss assured him. "He's not going
out without me any day soon."

Harry chuckled. "If he does, the road workings will take care of it." They drank beer peacefully for a while, until Harry asked, "Anything
else, Joss?"

"Not much. Usual stuff," said Joss. "The Big
Man got straight back to work when he wasn't
buying horses and bicycles—magical swindle in

London, some coven in the Midlands giving trouble, Scottish witches fussing about funds for Halloween, row of some kind two worlds away over the new tax on dragon's blood—business as usual. Oh, I nearly forgot! That enchanter's back from collecting plants all over the Related Worlds. The young one that used to be so thick with Old Gaffer. Jason Yeldham. He was asking after Gaffer. How much of an eye ought I to keep on him?"

"Shouldn't think he'd be much trouble," Harry said, emptying vile black dottle from his pipe into the ashtray. He scraped round the pipe bowl and thought about it. He shook his head. "Nah," he said. "He's not likely to come bothering us here, now Gaffer's gone all these years ago. I mean, it's all studying and book learning with him, isn't it? It's not like he *uses* the herbs the way we do. No need to interfere with him. But stay alert, if you follow me."

"Will do," said Joss.

They asked Arthur for more beer and refreshed themselves with pork pies and pickled onions for a while. After a bit, Harry remembered to ask, "How's Joe doing, then?"

Joss shrugged. "All right, I suppose. I scarcely ever see him."

"Good. Then he's not in trouble yet," Harry said.

Then Joss remembered to ask, "And how's Gammer settling in?"

"She's fine," Harry said. "Dinah looks after her a treat. She sits there and no one can get any sense out of her, not even our Marianne, but there you go, she's happy. She makes Marianne go round there every day and tells Marianne she has to look after that cat of hers every time, but that's all. It's all peace this end, really."

"I'd better go and pay my respects to her," Joss said. "She's bound to find out I was here if I don't." He drained off the rest of his beer and stood up. "See you later, Harry, Arthur."

He picked up his bicycle from the yard and coasted his way downhill through the village, nodding to the occasional Pinhoe who called out a greeting, shaking his head at the piles of brick and earth where the table had run into the Post Office wall. Wondering why nobody had done anything yet about mending that wall, he turned into Dell Lane and shortly arrived at the small-holding, where geese, ducks, and hens ran noisily out of his way as he went to knock at the front door.

"Come to see Gammer," he said to Dinah when she opened it.

"Now there's an odd thing!" Dinah exclaimed. "She's been on about you all this morning. She's said to me over and over, 'When Joss Callow comes, you're to show him straight in,' she said, and I'd no idea you were even coming to Ulverscote!" She dived back in and opened the door on the right of the tiny hallway. "Gammer, guess who! It's Joss Callow come to see you!"

"Well, they all say that," Gammer's voice answered. "They look and they spy on me all the time."

Joss Callow paused in the front doorway. Partly he was wondering what you said to that, and partly he was shaken by the strength of the spells Harry Pinhoe had put up to stop Gammer getting out. He pulled himself together and pushed his way through into the tiny front room, full of teapots and vases and boxes that people had thought Gammer might want. Gammer was sitting in an upright armchair with wings that almost hid her ruined face and tousled white hair, with her hands folded on the knee of her clean, clean skirt. "How are you today, then, Gammer?" he said heartily.

"Not so wide as a barn door, but enough to let chickens in," Gammer answered. "Thank you very much, Joss Callow. But it was Edgar and Lester who did it, you know."

"Oh?" said Joss. "Really?"

While he was wondering what else to say, whether to give her news from the Castle or talk about the weather, Gammer said sharply, "And now you're here at last, you can go and fetch me Joe here at once."

"Joe?" Joss said. "But I can give you news of the Castle just as well, Gammer."

"I don't want news, I want Joe," Gammer insisted. "I know as well as you do where he is and I want him *here*. Or don't you call me Gammer anymore?"

"Yes, of course I do," Joss said, and tried to change the subject. "It's a bit gray today, but—"

"Don't you try to put me off, Joss Callow," Gammer interrupted. "I've told you to fetch me Joe here and I mean it."

"But quite warm—a bit warm for cycling, really," Joss said.

"Who *cares* about the weather?" Gammer said. "I said to fetch Joe here. Go and get him at once and stop trying to humor me!"

This seemed quite definite and perfectly sane to Joss. He sighed at the thought of a lost afternoon at the Pinhoe Arms, chatting to Arthur and maybe playing darts with Charles. "You want me to cycle all the way back to Helm St. Mary and tell Joe to come here, do you?"

"Yes. You should have done it yesterday," Gammer said. "I don't know what you young ones are coming to, arguing with the orders I give. Go and fetch Joe. Now. Tell him I want to speak to him and he's not to tell anyone else. Go on. Off you go."

Such was the awe all the Pinhoe family felt for Gammer that Joss didn't argue and didn't dare mention the weather again. He said, "All right, then," and went.

With Syracuse fighting to go faster, *faster!* Cat rode along the grass verge, while Roger pedaled beside them on the road. They were quite evenly matched going along the level, but whenever they came to a hill, Syracuse sailed up it, shaking his head and trying to gallop, and Roger stood on his pedals and worked furiously, puffing like a train. Roger's chubby face became the color of raspberries, and he still got left far behind.

They could see the woods they were making for, tantalizingly only two hills away, a spill of dark green trees with already one or two dashes of pure, sunlit yellow that signaled autumn coming. Every time Cat looked—usually while he was at the top of a hill waiting for Roger—those trees seemed farther and farther off, and more away to the left, and *still* two hills away. Cat began to think they had missed a turning, or perhaps even taken the wrong road to start with.

When Roger caught up next time, with his face beyond raspberry into strawberry color, Cat said, "We ought to take the next left turn."

Roger was too much out of breath to do anything but nod. So Cat took the lead and swung Syracuse into a nice broad road leading away left. SHALLOWHELM, the signpost said. UPHELM.

About half a mile later, when he could speak, Roger said, "This road can't be right. It should take us back to the Castle."

Cat could still see the wood, still in the same place, so he kept on. The road bent about, among nothing but empty countryside for what seemed miles, up and down, until Roger was more the color of a peony than anything else. Then it swung round a corner and went up a truly enormous hill.

Roger let out a wail at the sight of it. "I *can't*! I'll have to get off and push."

"No, don't," Cat said. "Let me give you a tow."

He used the same spell he had used to keep Julia from falling off Syracuse and flung it round Roger's bicycle. They went on, fast at first, because Syracuse still regarded every hill as a challenge to gallop, then slower—even when Cat allowed Syracuse to try to gallop—and then slower still. Halfway up, when Syracuse's front hooves were digging and digging and his back ones were scrambling, it dawned on Syracuse what was going on. He looked across at Roger and the bicycle, so uncannily keeping beside him. Then he threw Cat in the ditch and scrambled through the hedge into the stubble field beyond.

Roger only just saved himself and the bicycle from falling in the ditch too. "That horse," he said, kneeling in the grass beside his spinning front wheel, "is too clever by half. Are you all right?"

"I think so," Cat said, but he stayed sitting in the squashy weeds at the bottom of the ditch. It was not so much the fall. It was that Syracuse had broken the spell quite violently. This had never happened to Cat before. He discovered that it hurt. "In a moment," he added.

Roger looked anxiously from Cat's white face to Syracuse pounding happily about in the field above them. "I wish I was old enough to drive a car," he said. "Or I wish that there was some way of moving this bike without having to pedal."

"Couldn't you invent a way?" Cat asked, to take his mind off hurting.

They were both sitting thinking about this, when a boy on a bicycle came past them up the hill. He was riding an ordinary bike, but he was humming smoothly upward at a good speed, and he was not pedaling at all. Roger and Cat stared after him with their mouths open. Cat was so amazed that it took him several seconds to recognize Joe Pinhoe. Roger was simply amazed. They both began shouting at once.

"Hey, Joe!" Cat shouted.

"Hey, you!" Roger shouted.

And they both yelled in chorus, "Can you stop a moment? Please!"

For a moment, it looked as if Joe was not going to stop. He had hummed his way about twenty yards uphill before he seemed to change his mind. He shrugged a bit. Then his hand went down to a box on his crossbar, where he appeared to move a switch of some kind, after which he turned in a smooth curve and came coasting back down the hill to them.

"What's the matter?" he asked, propping himself on the bank with one boot. "Want me to help catch the horse?" He nodded at Syracuse, who was now watching them across the hedge with great interest.

"No, no!" Cat and Roger said at once. "It's not the horse," Cat added.

Roger said, "We wanted to know how you make your bike go uphill without pedaling like that. It's *brilliant*!"

Joe was clearly very gratified. He grinned. But, being Joe, he also hung his head and looked sulky. "I only use it on hills," he said guardedly.

"That's what's so brilliant," Roger said. "How do you *do* it?"

Joe hesitated.

Roger could see Joe was very proud of his device, whatever it was, and was itching to show it off, really. He asked coaxingly, "Did you invent it yourself?"

Joe nodded, grinning his sulky grin again.

"Then you must be a brilliant inventor," Roger said. "I like inventing things too, but I've never come up with anything *this* useful. I'm Roger, by the way. Don't you work in the Castle? I know I've seen you there."

"Boot boy," said Joe. "I'm Joe." He nodded at Cat. "I've met him."

"Jason Yeldham used to be boot boy there too," Roger said. "It must go with brilliance."

"Herbs, I know," Joe said. "It's machines I like, really. But this box—it's more of a dwimmer-thing, see." His hand went out to the box on his crossbar, and stopped. "What's in it for me, if I do show you?" he asked suspiciously.

Roger was commercially minded too. He sympathized with Joe completely. The problem was that he had no money on him and he knew

Cat had none either. And Joe could be offended at being offered money anyway. "I wouldn't tell anyone else about it," he said while he thought. "And Cat won't either. I tell you what—when we get back to the Castle, I'll give you the address of the Magics Patent Office. You register your invention with them, and everyone has to pay you if they want to use it too."

Joe's face gleamed with cautious greed. "Don't I have to be grown up to do that?"

"No," said Roger. "I sent for the forms when I invented a magic mirror game last year, and they don't ask your age at all. They ask for a fifty-pound fee, though."

Cat wondered whether to point out that he, and not Roger, had invented the mirror game by accident. But he said nothing, because he was quite as interested in the box as Roger was.

Joe had a distant, calculating look. "I *could* be earning that much this summer," he decided. "They pay quite well at the Castle. All right. I'll show you."

Grinning his sulky grin, Joe carefully

unhooked the small latch that held the box on his crossbar shut. The hinged lid dropped downward to show—Cat craned out of the ditch and then recoiled—of all things, a stuffed ferret! The bent yellow body had bits of wire and twisted stalks of plants leading from its head and its paws to the place where the box met the crossbar.

"Metal to metal," Joe explained, pointing to the join. "That's machinery, see. The dwimmer part is to use the right herbs for life. You have to use something that has once been alive, see. Then you can get the life power running through the frame and turning the wheels."

"Brilliant!" Roger said reverently, peering in at the ferret. Its glass eyes seemed to glare sharply back at him. "But how do you get the life power to flow? Is that a spell, or what?"

"It's some old words we sometimes use in the woods," Joe said. "But the trick is the herbs that go with the wires. Took me ages to find the right ones. You got to *blend* them, see."

Roger bent even closer. "Oh, I see. Clever."

Cat got up out of the ditch and went to catch Syracuse. He knew, now he had seen the box, that he could almost certainly make Roger one this evening, probably without needing a stuffed ferret. But he knew Roger would hate that. Cat's kind of magic made some things too easy. Roger would be wanting to make a box by himself, however long it took. As Cat pushed his way through the hedge, he wondered exactly what Joe's word "dwimmer" meant. Was it an old word for magic? It sounded more specialized than that. It must mean a special *sort* of magic, probably.

Syracuse was not very hard to catch. He was quite tired after hauling Roger uphill, and a little bored by now in the wide, empty stubble field. But when Cat finally had the reins in his hands again, he discovered that Syracuse only had three shoes. One shoe must have torn off while Syracuse was plunging through the hedge.

Finding the shoe was not a problem. Cat simply held his hand out and *asked*. The missing horseshoe whirled up out of a clump of grass, where no one would have found it for years in the ordinary way, and slapped itself into Cat's hand. The real problem was that Cat knew Joss Callow would be outraged if Cat tried sticking the shoe back on by magic. It was bound to go on wrong somehow. And Joss would be truly angry if Cat tried to ride Syracuse with one uneven foot. Cat sighed. He was going to have to levitate Syracuse all the way home, or conjure him along in short bursts, or—knowing how much Syracuse hated magic—most likely just walk. Bother.

He found a gate and led Syracuse out through it and down the hill, where Joe and Roger were sitting side by side on the bank, talking eagerly. Cat could see they were now fast friends. Well, they clearly had a lot in common.

"That's *women's* work, a machine for washing dishes," Joe was saying. "We can do better than that. If you get any good notions, you better come and tell me. I get in trouble if I wander round the Castle. You can find me in the boot room." He looked up as he heard Syracuse's uneven footfalls. "I have to be going," he said. "I've an errand to run for our Gammer, down in Helm St. Mary." He got up off the bank and picked up his bicycle. "And you'll never guess what it is," he said. "Take a look." He pulled a large glass jar with a lid on out of the basket on the front of his bicycle and held it up. "I'm to tip this in their village pond there," he said.

Cat and Roger leaned to look at the murky, greenish water in the jar. A few fat black things with tails were wiggling slowly around in it.

"Tadpoles?" said Roger. "A bit late in the year, isn't it?"

"Quite big ones," Cat said.

"I know," Joe said. "I could only find six, and some of those have their legs already. Know what they're for?" They shook their heads. "This is not a jar of tadpoles," Joe said. "It's a declaration of war, this is." He put the jar back in his basket and got astride his bike.

"Wait a moment," Cat said. "Do you know how far it is to Chrestomanci Castle?"

Joe shot him a slightly guilty look. "You can

see it from the top of this hill," he said. "Got turned around, didn't you? Not my fault. But the Farleighs don't like people wandering around in their country, so they do this to the roads. See you."

He switched the toggle at the side of his box and went purring smoothly away up the hill.

Chapter Seven

Not surprisingly, Cat got back to the Castle a
long time after Joe or Roger did. Syracuse resisted
Cat's attempt to levitate him and started to stamp
and panic at the mere hint of teleportation. Cat
was too much afraid he would split the unshod
hoof to try either spell more than just the once. He
could hardly bear to think of what Joss Callow
would say if he brought Syracuse in with an
injury. So he was reduced to plodding along by the
grass verge, with Syracuse breathing playfully on
his hair, happy that Cat was not trying to use
magic anymore. That wizard who sold Syracuse,
Cat thought glumly, must have frightened the
horse badly by slamming spells on him. Cat would
have liked to slam a few spells back on the wizard.

After a while, however, Syracuse's happiness made Cat cheerful too. He began to notice things in that special way Syracuse seemed to be training him to do. He sniffed the smells of the grass, the ditches, and the hedges, and the dustier smell of the crops standing in the fields. He looked up to see birds teeming across the sky to roost for the night; and, like Syracuse, he jumped and then peered at a rustling in the hedge that was certainly a weasel. They both glimpsed the tiny, brown, almost snakelike body. They both raised their heads to see rabbits bounce away from the danger in the pasture on the other side of the hedge.

But Syracuse was puzzled, because there should have been *more* than just these smells and sights. Cat knew what Syracuse meant. There was an emptiness to the countryside, where it should have been full—though quite what should have filled it, neither Cat nor Syracuse knew. It reminded Cat a little of that time in Home Wood, where the distance was so strangely missing. Things were not here, where they should have been joyful and busy. Even so, it was peaceful. They plodded on, quietly enjoying the walk, until they topped the hill and turned the long corner, and there was Chrestomanci Castle in the distance on the next hill.

Oh dear, Cat thought. Walking was so *slow*. He was going to miss supper.

In fact, it was still only early evening when they reached the stableyard gates. When Cat pushed one gate open and led Syracuse through, the yard was full of long golden light, with two long shadows stretching across it. Unfortunately, these shadows belonged to Chrestomanci and Joss Callow. They were waiting side by side to meet him, looking as unlike as two men more or less the same height could look. Where Chrestomanci was rake thin, Joss was wide and heavy. Where Chrestomanci was dark, Joss was ruddy. Chrestomanci was wearing a narrow gray silk suit, while Joss was in his usual rough leather and green shirt. But they both looked powerful and they both looked far from pleased. Cat could hardly tell which of them he wanted less to meet.

"At last," Chrestomanci said. "As I understand it, you had no business to be out alone on this horse at all. What kept you?"

Joss Callow simply ran his hand down Syracuse's leg and picked up the shoeless foot. The look he gave Cat across it made Cat's stomach hurt. He could think of nothing else to do but hold the missing horseshoe out to Joss.

"How come?" Joss said.

"He threw me off and went through a hedge," Cat said, "but it was my fault."

"Is he lame?" Chrestomanci asked.

"No more than you would be, walking with one bare foot," Joss said. "The hoof's sound, by some kind of a miracle. I'll take him to the stable now, if you don't mind, sir."

"By all means," Chrestomanci said.

Cat watched Joss lead Syracuse off. Syracuse drooped his head as if he felt as much to blame as Cat. From Syracuse's point of view this was probably true, Cat thought. Syracuse had *loved* their illegal outing.

"I am going to ask Joss to exercise that

wretched horse himself for a while," Chrestomanci said. "I haven't decided yet if it's for a
week or a month or a year. I'll let you know. But
you are not to ride him until I say so, Cat. Is that
clear?"

"Yes," Cat said miserably.

Chrestomanci turned round and started to
walk away. Cat was relieved at first. Then he
realized there was something he ought to tell
Chrestomanci and ran after him.

"Did Roger tell you about the roads?"

Chrestomanci turned back. He did not look
pleased. "Roger seems to be keeping out of my
way. What about the roads?"

This made Cat see that, unless he was very
careful, he would get not only Roger but Joe too
into trouble. Joe should have been in the Castle,
not riding about with a jar of tadpoles. He said,
thinking about every word, "Well, Roger was
with me on his bike—"

"And it jumped a hedge as well and perhaps
lost a wheel?" Chrestomanci said.

"No, no," Cat said. Chrestomanci always

confused him when he got sarcastic. "No, he's fine. But we were trying to get to Ulverscote Woods and we couldn't. The roads kept turning us back toward the Castle all the time."

Chrestomanci dropped his sarcastic look at once. His head came up, like Syracuse when he heard Cat coming. "Really? A misdirection spell, you think?"

"Something like that—but it was one I didn't know," Cat said.

"I'll check," Chrestomanci said. "Meanwhile, you are in disgrace, Cat, and so is Roger, when I find him."

Roger of course knew he was likely to be in trouble. He met Cat on his way down to the very formal supper they always had at the Castle. "Is he very angry?" he asked, nervously straightening his smart velvet jacket.

"Yes," Cat said.

Roger shivered a little. "Then I'll go on keeping out of his way," he said. "Oh, and keep out of the girls' way too."

"Why?" said Cat.

"They're being a *pain*," Roger said. "Partic-ularly Janet."

The girls were already there, when Roger and Cat went into the anteroom where Chrestomanci, Millie, and all the wizards and sorcerers who made up the Castle staff were gathered before supper. Janet and Julia were pale and quiet but not particularly painful as far as Cat could see. Roger at once slid off along the walls, trying to keep a wizard or a sorceress always between himself and his father. It did not work. Wherever Roger slid, Chrestomanci turned and fixed him with a stare from those bright black eyes of his. At supper, it was worse. Roger had to be in plain view then, sitting at the table, since, being Roger, he seriously wanted to eat. Chrestomanci's vague, sarcastic look was on him most of the time. Jason Yeldham, for some reason, was not there that evening, so there was no one to distract Chrestomanci. Roger squirmed in his chair. He kept his head down. He pretended to look out of the long windows at the sunset over the gardens, but, whatever he did, that stare kept meeting his eyes.

"Oh *blast* it!" Roger muttered to Cat. "Anyone would think I'd murdered someone!"

As soon as supper was over, Roger jumped from his chair and rushed off. So too did Julia and Janet. Chrestomanci raised one of his eyebrows at Cat. "Aren't you going to run away as well?" he said.

"Not really. But I think I'll go," Cat said, getting up.

"Are you quite sure you won't join us for nuts and coffee?" Chrestomanci asked politely.

"You always talk about things I don't understand," Cat explained. "And I need to see Janet."

Whatever Roger said, Cat found this was one of the times when he felt a little responsible for Janet. She had been looking very pale. And she was only here in this world of Twelve A because Cat's sister Gwendolen had worked a thoroughly selfish spell and stranded Janet here. He knew there were still times when strangeness and loneliness overwhelmed Janet.

He thought, when he went into the playroom,

that this was one of those times. Janet was sitting sobbing on the battered sofa. Julia had both arms round her.

"What is it?" Cat said.

Julia looked up, and Cat saw she was almost as woebegone as Janet. "Jason's *married*!" Julia said tragically. "He got married in London before he came here."

"So?" said Cat.

Janet flung herself round on the sofa. "You don't *understand*!" she said sobbingly. "I was planning to marry him myself in about four years' time!"

"So was I," Julia put in. "But I think Janet's more in love with him than I am."

"I know I shall hate his wife!" Janet wept. "*Irene!* What an *awful* name!"

Julia said, judicious and gloomy, "She *was* Miss Irene Pinhoe, but at least Irene Yeldham makes a better name. He probably married her out of kindness."

"And," Janet wailed, "he's gone to fetch her *here*, so that they can look at houses. They'll be here for *ages*, and I know I won't be able to go near her!"

Julia added disgustedly, "She's an *artist*, you see. The house they buy is going to have to be just right."

Cat knew by now exactly what Roger had meant. He began backing out of the playroom.

"That's right! Slide away!" Janet shouted after him. "You've no more feelings than a— than a chair leg!"

Cat was quite hurt that Janet should say that. He knew he was full of feelings. He was wretched already at being forbidden to ride Syracuse.

The next day, he missed Syracuse more than ever. What made it worse was that he could feel Syracuse, turned out into the paddock, missing Cat too, and sad and puzzled when Cat did not appear. Cat moped about, avoiding Janet and Julia and not being able to see much of Roger either. Roger, possibly as a way of avoiding Chrestomanci, was spending most of his time with Joe. Whenever Joe was not working—

which seemed to be more than half the day—he and Roger were to be found with their heads together, talking machinery in the old garden shed behind the stables. At least, Cat could find them, being an enchanter, but nobody much else could. They had a surprisingly strong "Don't Notice" spell out around the shed. But Cat was bored by machinery and only went there once.

The day after that, Jason Yeldham's small blue car thundered up to the front door of Chrestomanci Castle. This time, Janet and Julia refused to go near it. But Millie rushed through the hall to meet it and Cat went with her out of boredom. Jason sprang out of the car in his usual energetic way and ran around it to open the other door and help Irene climb out.

As Irene stood up and smiled—just a little nervously—at Millie and Cat, Cat's instant thought was, Janet and Julia can't possibly hate *her*! Irene was slender and dark, with that proud, pale kind of profile that Cat always thought of as belonging to the Ancient Egyptians. On Irene, it was somehow very beautiful. Her eyes, like those of the wives of the Pharoahs, were huge and slanted and almond shaped, so that it came as quite a shock when Irene looked at Cat and he saw that her eyes were a deep, shining blue. Those eyes seemed to recognize Cat, and know him, and to take him in and warm to him, like a friend's. Millie's eyes had the same knack, now Cat came to think of it.

He did not blame Jason for smiling so proudly as he led Irene up the steps and into the hall, where Irene looked at the huge pentacle inlaid in the marble floor, and up into the glass dome where the chandelier hung, and round at the great clock over the library door. "Goodness gracious!" she said.

Jason laughed. "I told you it was grand," he said.

By this time, all the wizards and sorceresses of Chrestomanci's staff were streaming down the marble stairs to meet Irene. Chrestomanci himself came behind them. As usual at that hour of the morning, he was wearing a dressing gown. This one was bronzy gold and green and blue, and seemed to be made of peacock feathers. Irene blinked a little when she saw it, but held out her hand to him almost calmly. As Chrestomanci took it and shook it, Cat could tell that Chrestomanci liked Irene. He felt relieved about that.

Julia and Janet appeared at the top of the stairs, behind everyone's backs as they crowded round Irene. Janet took one look and rushed away, crying bitterly. But Julia stayed, watching Irene with a slight, interested smile. Cat was relieved about that, too.

Altogether, the arrival of Irene made Cat's separation from Syracuse easier to bear. She was as natural and warm as if she had known Cat for years. Jason allowed Cat to show her round the Castle—although he insisted on showing Irene the gardens himself—and Irene strolled beside Cat, marveling at the ridiculous size of the main rooms, at the miles of green carpeted corridors, and at the battered state of the schoolroom. She was so interested that Cat even showed her his own round room up in the turret.

Irene much admired it. "I've always wanted a tower room like this myself," she said. "You must love it up here. Do you think there's a house in the neighborhood that's big enough to have a tower like this one?"

Cat was quite ashamed to say he didn't know.

"Never mind," said Irene. "Jason's found several for sale that I might like. You see, it's got to be quite a big house. My father left me money when he died, but he left me his two old servants as well. We have to have room for them to live with us without being cramped. Jane James insists she doesn't mind where we live or how much room we have—but I know that's not true. She's a very particular person. And Adams has set his heart on living in the country and I simply can't disappoint him. If you knew him, you'd understand."

Later, Irene sat in the vast Small Saloon and showed Cat a portfolio of her drawings. Cat was surprised to find that they were more like patterns than drawings. They were all in neatly ruled shapes, long strips and elegant diamonds.

The strips had designs of ferns and honeysuckle inside them and the diamonds had fronds of graceful leaves. There were plaits of wild roses and panels of delicately drawn irises. It was a further surprise to Cat to find that each pattern sent out its own small, fragrant breath of magic. Each was full of a strange, gentle joy. Cat had had no idea that drawings could do this.

"I'm a designer really," Irene explained. "I do book decorations and fabrics, tiles and wallpaper and so forth. I do surprisingly well with them."

"But you're a witch too, aren't you?" Cat said. "These all have magic in."

Irene went the pink of the wild roses in the design she was showing Cat. "Not exactly," she said. "I always use real plants for my drawings, but I don't do anything else. The magic just comes out of them somehow. I've never thought of myself as a witch. My father, now, he could do real magic—I never knew quite what he did for a living, but Jason says he was a well-known enchanter—so maybe just a touch of it came down to me."

Later still, Cat overheard Irene asking Millie why Cat was so mournful. He went away before he had to hear Millie explain about Syracuse.

"Huh!" Janet said, catching him on the schoolroom stairs. "In love with Irene, aren't you? Now you know how I feel."

"I don't think I am," Cat said. He thought he probably wasn't. But it did strike him that when he was old enough to start being in love—pointless though that seemed—he would try to find someone not unlike Irene to be in love with. "She's just nice," he said, and went on up to his room.

Irene's niceness was real, and active. She must have spoken to Jason about Cat. The next morning, Jason came to find Cat in the schoolroom. "Irene thinks you need taking out of yourself, young nine-lifer," he said. "How do you feel about driving around with us this morning to look at a few houses for sale?"

"Won't I be in the way?" Cat asked, trying not to show how very much more cheerful this made him feel.

"She says she values your judgment," Jason said. "She assures me, hand on heart, that you'll only have to look at a house to know if we'll be happy there or not. Would you say that's true?"

"I don't know," Cat said. "It may be."

"Come along, then," Jason said. "It's a lovely day. It feels as if it's going to be important somehow."

Jason was right about this, although perhaps not quite in the way he or Cat thought.

Chapter Eight

Over in Ulverscote, Nutcase was being a perfect nuisance to Marianne. Nothing seemed to persuade him that he was now living in Furze Cottage. Dad changed all the locks, and the catches on the windows, but Nutcase still managed to get out at least once a day. No one knew how he did it. People from all over the village kept arriving at Furze Cottage with Nutcase struggling in their arms. Nicola found him prowling in Ulverscote Wood. Aunt Joy sourly brought him back from the Post Office. Aunt Helen arrived at least twice with him from the pub, explaining that Nutcase had been at the food in the kitchen there. And Uncle Charles repeatedly knocked at the door, carrying

Nutcase squirming under one paint-splashed arm, saying that Nutcase had turned up in Woods House yet *again*.

"He must think he still lives there," Uncle Charles said. "Probably looking for Gammer. Do try to keep him in. The wall's mended and I've nearly finished the painting. We put the back door in yesterday. He'll get locked in there when we leave and starve to death if you're not careful."

Mum's opinion was that Nutcase should go and live with Gammer in the Dell. Marianne would have agreed, except that Gammer was always saying to her, "You'll look after Nutcase for me, won't you, Marianne?"

Gammer insisted that Marianne walk over to see her every day. Marianne had no idea why. Often, Gammer simply stared at the wall and said nothing except that she was to look after Nutcase. Sometimes she would lean forward and say things that made no sense, like "It's the best way to get pink tomatoes." Most frequently Gammer just grumbled to herself. "They're out to get me," she would say. "I have to get a blow in first. They have spies everywhere, you know. They watch and they wait. And of course they have fangs and terrible teeth. The best way is to drain the spirit out of them."

Marianne grew to hate these visits. She could not understand how Aunt Dinah put up with these sinister grumbles of Gammer's. Aunt Dinah said cheerfully, "It's just her way, poor old thing. She's no idea what she's saying."

Nutcase must have learned the way to the Dell by following Marianne. He turned up there one day just after Marianne had left and got in among Aunt Dinah's day-old chicks. The slaughter he worked there was horrific. Uncle Isaac arrived at Furze Cottage, as Marianne was setting off to look for Nutcase, and threw Nutcase indoors so hard and far that Nutcase hit the kitchen sink, right at the other end of the house.

"Dinah's in tears," he said. "There's barely twenty chicks left out of the hundred. If that cat gets near the Dell one more time, I'll kill him.

Wring his neck. I warn you." And he slammed the front door and stalked away.

Mum and Marianne watched Nutcase pick himself up and lick his whiskers in a thoroughly satisfied way. "There's no way he can go and live with Gammer after *this*," Mum said, sighing. "*Do* try to keep him in, Marianne."

But Marianne couldn't. She doubted if anyone could. She tried putting twelve different confinement spells on Nutcase, but Nutcase seemed as immune to magic as he was to locks and bolts, and he kept getting out. The most Marianne could manage was a weak and simple directional spell that told her which way Nutcase had gone *this* time. If he had set off in any way that led toward the Dell, Marianne ran. Uncle Isaac very seldom made threats, but when he did he meant them. Marianne could not bear to think of Nutcase with his neck wrung, like a dead chicken.

Each time she found Nutcase was missing, Marianne's heart sank. That particular morning, when she got back from another useless visit to

Gammer and found that Nutcase had vanished yet again, she hastened to work her weak spell and did not feel comfortable until she had spun the kitchen knife three separate times and it had pointed uphill toward Woods House whenever it stopped.

That's a relief! she thought. But it's not fair! I never get any time to *myself*.

Upstairs, hidden in Marianne's heart-shaped desk, her story about the lovely Princess Irene was still hardly begun. She had made some headway. She knew what Princess Irene looked like now. But then she had to think of a Prince who was good enough for her and, with all these interruptions, she wondered if she ever would.

As she set off uphill to Woods House, Marianne thought about her story. Princess Irene had a pale Egyptian sort of profile, massive clusters of dark curls and fabulous almond-shaped blue eyes. Her favorite dress was made of delicate crinkly silk, printed all over with big blue irises that matched her eyes. Marianne was pleased about that dress. It was not your usual princess wear. But she could not for the life of her visualize a suitable Prince.

Typically, her thoughts were interrupted all the way up the street. Nicola leaned out of a window to shout, "Nutcase went that way, Marianne!" and point uphill.

Marianne's cousin Ron rode downhill on his bike, calling, "Your cat's just gone in the pub!"

And when Marianne came level with the Pinhoe Arms, her cousin Jim came out of the yard to say, "That cat of yours was in our larder. Our mum chased him off into the churchyard."

In the churchyard, the Reverend Pinhoe met Marianne, saying, "Nutcase seems to have gone home to Woods House again, I'm afraid. I saw him jump off my wall into the garden there."

"Thanks," Marianne said, and hastened on toward the decrepit old gates of Woods House.

The house was all locked up by this time. Uncle Simeon and Uncle Charles had repaired the damage and gone on to other work, leaving the windows bolted and the doors sealed.

Nutcase could not have gotten inside. Marianne gloomily searched all his favorite haunts in the garden instead. She wanted simply to go away. But then Nutcase might take it into his head to go down to the Dell by the back way, beside the fields, where Uncle Isaac would fulfill his threat.

Nutcase was not among the bushy, overgrown near-trees of the beech hedge. He was not sunning himself in the hayfield of the lawn, nor on the wall that hid the jungle of kitchen garden. He was not in the broken cucumber frame, or hiding in the garden shed. Nor was he lurking under the mass of green goosegrass that hid the gooseberry bushes by the back fence. Big, pale gooseberries lurked there instead. They had reached the stage when they were almost sweet. Marianne gathered a few and ate them while she went to inspect Old Gaffer's herb bed beside the house. This had once been the most lovingly tended part of the gardens, but it was now full of thistles and tired elderly plants struggling among clumps of grass. Nutcase often liked to bask in the bare patches here, usually beside the catmint.

He was not there either.

Marianne looked up and around, terribly afraid that Nutcase was now on his way to the Dell, and saw that the door to the conservatory was standing ajar.

"That's a relief— Oh, *bother*!" she said. Nutcase had almost certainly gone indoors. Now she had to search the house too.

She shoved the murky glass door wider and marched in over the dingy coconut matting on the floor. The massed Pinhoes had forgotten to clear the conservatory. Marianne marched past broken wicker chairs and dead trees in large pots and on down the passage to the hall.

There were four people in the hall—no, five. Great-Uncle Lester was just letting himself in through the front door. One of the other people was Great-Uncle Edgar in his tweed hat, looking unusually flustered and surprised. And as for the others—! Marianne stood there, charmed. There stood her Princess Irene, almost exactly, in her floating dress with the big irises printed on it to match her eyes. As she was a human lady and not part of Marianne's imagination, she was not quite as Marianne had thought. No one had the masses of hair that Marianne had dreamed up. But this Irene's hair *was* dark, though it was wavy rather than curly, and she had the right slender figure and exactly the right pale Egyptian profile. It was amazing.

Beside the Princess was a fair and cheerful young man with a twinkly sort of look to him that Marianne immediately took to. He was wearing a jaunty blazer and very smart, beautifully creased pale trousers, which struck Marianne as the sort of things a prince might put on for casual wear. He's just the Prince I ought to have given her! she thought.

There was a boy with them, who had that slightly deadened expression Joe often had when he was with adults he didn't like. Marianne concluded that he didn't care for Great-Uncle Edgar, just like Joe. Since the boy was fair haired, Marianne supposed he must be the son of

Irene and her Prince. Obviously the story had moved on a few years. Irene and her Prince were in the middle of living happily ever after and looking for a house to do it in.

Marianne walked toward them, smiling at this thought. As she did so, the boy said, "*This* one's the right house."

Irene turned toward him anxiously. "Are you quite sure, Cat? It's awfully run-down."

Cat was sure. They had visited two shockers, one of them damp and the other where the ceilings pressed down, like despair, on your mind. And then they had gone to look at what was advertised as a small castle, because Irene had hoped it would have a tower room like Cat's, only it had had no roof. This one felt— Well, Cat had been confused for a moment, when the bulky man with a hat like a tweed flowerpot had come striding up to them booming, "Good *morning*. I'm Edgar Pinhoe. Real estate agent, you know." This man had looked at Jason and Irene as if they were two lower beings—and they did seem sort of frail beside Edgar—and

Jason had looked quite dashed. But Irene had laughed and held out her hand.

"How extraordinary!" she said. "My maiden name was Pinhoe."

Edgar Pinhoe was astonished and dismayed. He stepped backward from Irene. "Pinhoe, Pinhoe?" he said. "I had instructions to sell this house to a Pinhoe if possible." Upon this, he remembered his manners and shook Irene's hand as if he were afraid it would burn him, and dropped his superior, pitying look entirely. Cat realized that the man had been using some kind of domination spell on them up to then. Once it was gone, Cat was free to think about the house.

Jason said, "You might do that—sell it to a Pinhoe. My wife is the one with the money, not me."

While he was speaking, Cat was feeling the shape of the house with his mind. It was all big, square, airy rooms, lots of them, and though it echoed with emptiness and neglect, underneath that it was warm and happy and eager to be lived in again. Over many, many years, people had lived here who were friendly and full of power—special people—and the house wanted to be full of such people again. It was glad to see Irene and Jason.

Cat let them know it was the right house at once. Then he saw the girl walking up to them, as glad to see them as the house was. She was wearing villager sort of clothes, with the pinafore over them to keep them clean, the way most country girls did, but Cat did not think of her as a country girl because she had such very strong magic. Cat noticed the magic particularly, being used to Julia with her medium-sized magic and Janet with almost none at all. It seemed to blaze off this girl. He wondered who she was.

Edgar Pinhoe saw her. "Not now, Marianne," he said. "I'm busy with prospective buyers. Run along home, there's a good girl." His domination spell was back, aimed at Marianne. Cat wondered what good Edgar Pinhoe thought it would do, when his magic was only about warlock level and this girl's was pretty well as strong as Millie's. And Millie, of course, was an enchantress.

Sure enough, the domination bounced off Marianne. Cat was not sure she even noticed it. "I'm looking for Nutcase, Uncle Edgar," she said. "I think he got in through the conservatory door. It was open."

"Of course it was open. I unlocked it so that these good people could look round the garden," Edgar Pinhoe said irritably. "Never mind your wretched cat. Go home."

Here the pinstriped man who had just come in said, in a fussy, nervous way. "Please, Marianne. You've no right to come into this house now, you know."

Marianne's wide brown eyes turned to him, steady and puzzled. "Of course I've got the right, Uncle Lester. I know Gammer lived here, but the house belongs to my dad." A very good idea struck her. She turned to Jason and Irene. She was longing to get to know them. "Can I help show you round? If we go into all the rooms, we're bound to find Nutcase somewhere. He used to live here with Gammer, you see, and he keeps coming back."

"When he's not slaughtering day-old chicks," Great-Uncle Lester murmured.

He was obviously about to say no, but Irene smiled and interrupted him before he could. "Of course you can help show us round, my dear. Someone who knows the house would be really useful."

"You'll know where the roof leaks and so on," Jason said.

Both older men looked shocked. "I assure you this house is absolutely sound," Edgar said. He added, with a slightly defiant look at Uncle Lester, "Shall we start with the kitchen, then?"

They all went along to the kitchen. It was newly painted, and Cat could see new cupboards down the far end. Irene stood looking down the length of the huge scrubbed table, which seemed to have been carefully mended and planed smooth at her end. "This is lovely and light," she said. "And so much space. This table's enormous, and it still doesn't nearly fill the room. I can see Jane James loving it. We'd need to put in a new stove for her, though."

She went over to the old black boiler and cautiously took up one of its rusty lids, shaking her head and sprinkling soot down her iris-patterned dress. Marianne knew that Gammer's old cooker was now stored in the shed on the Hopton road. She had never seen that stove used since the old days before Gaffer died. She shook her head too and made her way down the kitchen, opening all the cabinets to make sure that Nutcase had not gotten himself shut inside one, and then looking into the pantry. Nutcase was not there either.

Jason meanwhile was rubbing his hand vaguely across the damaged end of the huge table. Cat could tell he was using a divining spell, but to the two elderly men who were rather tensely watching him, Jason probably looked like a man bored with womanish things like kitchens and stoves. "Seems to have got a bit bashed here, this table," he said. "Was there some trouble getting it in here?"

Edgar and Lester both flinched. "No, no, no," Lester said, and Edgar added, "I am told—family tradition has it—that this table was actually made inside this room."

"Ah!" said Jason. Cat could feel him quivering, hot on the scent of something. "Someone else told me about this table, quite a few years ago now. A dwimmerman called Elijah Pinhoe."

Edgar and Lester both jumped, quite violently. Lester answered gravely, "Passed away. Passed away these eight years now."

"Yes, but am I right in thinking he actually lived in this house?" Jason said.

"That's right," Edgar admitted. "Marianne's grandfather, you know."

"Right! Great!" Jason said. He whirled round on Marianne as she came out of the empty pantry and seized her arm. "Young lady, come with me at once and show me where your grandfather's herb bed was."

"We-ell," said Marianne, who was wondering whether Nutcase had gone up to hide in the attics.

"You *do* know, don't you?" Jason said eagerly.

Good gracious, he's just like Gaffer, only young and Cockney! Marianne thought. And he has lovely bright blue eyes. "Yes, of course I do," she said. "It's outside the conservatory, so that he could take the weak ones inside. This way."

Jason cheered and rushed them all outside. Irene laughed heartily at his enthusiasm. "He's always like this about his herbs," she told Cat. "We have to humor him."

Jason stopped in dismay when he saw the thistles and the grass. "I suppose it *has* been eight years," he said, walking in among the weeds. Next moment he was down on his knees, quite forgetting his nice pale trousers, carefully parting a clump of nettles. "Hairy antimony!" he cried out. "Still alive! Well, I'll be—! And this is button lovage and here's wolfwort still going strong! This must be a strong spell on it, if it's alive after eight years! The ground's too dry for it, really. And here's— What's this?" he asked, looking up at Marianne.

"Gaffer always called it hare's paws," she said. "And the one by your foot— Oh, it's on the tip of my tongue! Do *you* know?" she asked Cat.

Cat surprised himself and everyone else by answering, "*Portulaca fulvia.* Scarlet purslane's the English name." Evidently some of the herb lore he had been made to learn must have stuck in his brain somewhere. He rather thought it was Marianne's strong magic that had brought the name up out of a very deep, bored sleep.

"Yes, yes! And very rare. You get the green and yellow all the time, but the scarlet's the really magic one and you almost never find it!" Jason cried out, crawling across to another clump of plants. "Pinwort, golden spindlemans, nun's pockets, fallgreen—this is a *treasure house*!"

Edgar and Lester were standing in the grass, looking helpless, prim, and irritated. "Wouldn't you like to see the rest of the house?" Edgar said at last.

"No, no!" Jason cried out. "I'll buy it even if the roof's fallen off! This is *wonderful*!"

"But *I'd* like to see it," Irene said, taking pity on them. "Come and show me round." She led the pair of them away through the conservatory.

Marianne left Jason wrestling with a thistle and came over to Cat. "Will you help me look for Nutcase?" she asked him.

"What does he look like?" Cat said.

Marianne approved of this practical question. "Black," she said. "Rather fat, and one eye greener than the other. His coat grows in a ruff round his neck but the rest of him is smooth, except his tail. That's bushy."

"Have you tried a directional spell?" Cat said. "Or divining?"

More practical questions, Marianne thought approvingly. There was no nonsense about Cat. "Nutcase is pretty well immune to magic," she said. "I suppose he had to be, living with Gammer."

"But I bet he's not immune to a spell making a luscious fish smell down in the hall," Cat said.

"Wouldn't that fetch him out?"

"Not fish. Bacon. He loves bacon," Marianne said. "Let's go and try."

They hurried through the house to the hall. It was empty, but they could hear hollow footsteps as Irene and the two great-uncles trod about on bare floorboards somewhere in the distance. Here Marianne set the bacon spell, going slowly and carefully, as if she did not quite trust her powers. Cat, while he waited, fixed the image of a black cat with odd eyes and a ruff in his mind and cast about for Nutcase.

"He went up," he said, pointing to the stairs when Marianne had finished. "We could go and catch him coming down."

"Yes," she said. "Let's."

They went up to the next floor. "This is nice," Cat said, looking through an open door into a square, comfortable bedroom.

The room was completely bare, but Marianne knew what Cat meant. "Isn't it?" she agreed. "You know, Gammer kept it all so dark and dusty that I never saw what a nice house this really is."

Cat found himself saying, "I think she kept *you* dark and dusty too. You do know your magic is pretty well enchanter standard, do you?" What made me say that? he thought.

Marianne stared at him. "*Is* it?"

"Yes, but you just don't trust it," Cat said.

Marianne turned away. Cat thought at first that she was upset, then that she didn't believe him, until she said, "I think you're right. It's hard to—to trust yourself when everyone's always telling you you're too young and to do what you're told. Thank you for telling me. I think Nutcase went to the attics. I've known he did all along really, but I didn't trust it."

They went along the bare passage to another set of stairs that were half hidden by a huge wooden hutch thing that must have had a hot-water tank inside. At any rate it was glopping and trickling as if it didn't work very well. The stairs were dark and splintery, and the door at the top was half open, on to brown dimness. Uncle Charles must have left it open, Marianne thought, as her foot knocked against a row of paint tins just inside.

Cat thought, There's been a really strong "Don't Notice" spell here! At least, it was more like a "Don't Want to Know" when he came to think about it—as if somebody had really disliked this place. He wondered why. Marianne seemed to have broken the spell as she went inside.

He followed Marianne into a glorious smell like the ghosts of mint sauce, turkey stuffing, and warm spiced wine. This came, he saw, from bundles and bundles of dry herbs hanging from the beams in the roof, most of them too old and dry to be any good now. Nearly all the floor space was filled with boxes, bundles, and old leather suitcases, but there were old-fashioned chairs and sofas there too, rows of pointed boots, tin trunks, and what looked like clumps of rusty garden tools. Everything was lit by a dim light coming in under the eaves of the house. Cat could see a dusty toy fort down by his feet, which made him feel sorry that he seemed to be too old for such things these days.

The place turned a corner, he saw, and went on out of sight. There was something exciting round there.

Cat was stepping forward in the narrow space between the piles of junk, to find out just what it was round that corner, when Marianne said, "Nutcase *was* here."

"How do you know?" said Cat.

Marianne pointed to what was left of a mouse, lying beside the paint cans. "He always only eats the front end and leaves the tail," she said.

This gave Cat the perfect excuse to explore the attic. He edged his way on along the strip of floor between the bundles and boxes.

"But he's not here now," Marianne said.

"I know, but I need an excuse," Cat said, and shuffled on. Marianne followed him.

The first recognizable thing they met as they turned the corner was a box of Christmas ornaments, really old-fashioned ones: carved wooden angels, heavy round glass balls, and masses of thick golden paper stamped into shapes and letters.

"Oh, I remember these!" Marianne cried out. "I used to help Gaffer put them on the tree in the hall."

She knelt by the box. Cat left her shaking out the gold paper, so that it fell into a long MERRY CHRISTMAS and an equally long YULETIDE IS COME, and groped his way onward. It was darker in this part of the attic and there were no more herbs, but Cat was now convinced that there was something truly precious and exciting stored down near the end. He shuffled and groped—and occasionally put an arm up over his face as something that did not seem quite real fluttered at his head. His feeling grew, and grew, that there was something enormously magical along there, something so important that it needed to be protected with nearly real illusions.

He found it right at the end, where it was so dark that he was in his own light and could barely see it at all. It was large and round and it sat in a nest of old moth-eaten blankets. At first Cat thought it was just a football. But when he put his hands on it, it seemed to be made of china. The moment Cat touched it, he knew it was very strange and valuable indeed. He picked it up—it was quite heavy—and shuffled carefully back to where Marianne was kneeling beside the box of decorations.

"Do you know what this is?" he asked her. He found his voice was shaking with hidden excitement, like Jason's when he knew that this was the herbman's house.

Marianne looked up from laying a row of golden bells out on the floor. "Oh, is that still here? I don't know what it is. Gammer always said it was one of Gaffer's silly jokes. She said he told her it was an elephant's egg."

It *could* be an egg, Cat supposed. He turned the thing round under what little light there was. It was *possibly* more pointed at one end. Its smooth, shiny surface was mauvish and speckled with darker mauve. It was not particularly lovely—just strange. And he knew he had to have it.

"Can—can I have it?" he said.

Marianne was doubtful. "Well, it's probably

Gammer's," she said. "Not mine to give." But if everyone hadn't forgotten the attics, she thought, it would have been cleared out with all the other things up here and probably thrown away. And the house was Dad's really, together with all the things left in it. In a *way*, Marianne had a perfect right to give some of the junk away, since nobody else was going to want it. "Oh, go on, take it," she said. "You're the only person who's ever been interested in the thing."

"Thanks!" Cat said. Marianne could have sworn that his face literally glowed, as if a strong light had been shone on it. For a second his hair looked the same gold as the Christmas bells.

Great-Uncle Edgar's voice floated up to them, peevish and distant, from somewhere downstairs. "Marianne! Marianne! Are you and the boy up there? We want to lock the house up."

Marianne bundled the bells back into the box, in a strong, high chiming. "Lord!" she said. "And I've still not found Nutcase! Let's hope that bacon spell fetched him down."

It had. When they clattered down the bare

stairway to the hall, Cat carefully carrying the strange object in both arms, the first thing they saw was Nutcase's smug face peering at them over Irene's shoulder. Nutcase's tail was wrapped contentedly over Irene's arm, and he was purring. Irene was walking about the hall with him, saying, "You big fat smug thing you! You have no morals at all, do you? You wicked cat!" Jason was watching her with an admiring smile and a brown patch of earth on both knees.

"I knew she was bound to be a cat person!" Marianne said, at which the faces of both great-uncles turned up to her, irritably. Cat put a good strong "Don't Notice" around the thing he was carrying.

Great-Uncle Lester had enough magic to know that Cat was carrying *something*, but he must have thought it was the box of Christmas decorations. "Has Marianne given you those?" he said. "Rubbishy old stuff. I wouldn't be seen dead with those on my tree." Then, while Cat and Marianne both went red trying not to laugh, Uncle Lester turned to Jason. "If you and your good lady can be at my office in Hopton at eleven tomorrow, Mr. Yeldham, we'll have the paperwork ready for you then. Marianne, collect your cat and I'll give you a lift down to Furze Cottage."

Chapter Nine

All the way back to Chrestomanci Castle, Jason and Irene were far too excited at having actually bought a real house, with a bed full of rare herbs, to pay much attention to Cat and the strange object he was holding on his knees. When they got to the Castle, there was no one to ask Cat what it was or to tell him he shouldn't have it. There was some kind of panic going on.

Staff were rushing anxiously around the hall and up and down the stairway. Tom, Chrestomanci's secretary, was with Millie beside the pentacle on the floor. As Cat went past carrying his object, Tom was saying, "No, *none* of the usual spells have been tripped. Not one!"

Millie replied, "And I'm quite certain he

didn't leave by this pentacle. Has Bernard finished checking the old garden yet?"

It seemed nothing to do with Cat. He carried the object carefully away by the back stairs and on up to his room. His room was in a mess, as if Mary, the maid who usually did the bedrooms, had been sucked into the panic too. Cat shrugged and took his new possession over to the windows to have a good look at it.

It was the chilly sort of mauve that his own skin went when he was too cold for too long. It was heavy and smooth and not at all pretty, but Cat still found it the most exciting thing he had ever owned in his life. Perhaps this feeling had something to do with the mysterious dark purple spots and squiggles all over its china surface. They were like a code. Cat thought that if only he knew this code, it would tell him something hugely important that nobody else in the world knew. He had never seen anything like this thing.

But the mauve color kept making him think it was too cold. He carefully put a spell of warmth around it. Then, because it looked as if it would break rather easily, and he knew how careless Mary could be, he surrounded the warmth with a strong protection. To keep it properly safe beyond that, he made a sort of nest for it out of his winter scarf and hat and put the lot on his chest of drawers so that he could look at it from wherever he was in the room. After that, he had to tear himself away from it and go down to the playroom for lunch.

Cat had meant to tell them all—or Roger at least—that he had just been given this amazing new object, but the three of them looked so worried that he said, "What's the matter?"

"Daddy's disappeared," Julia said.

"But he's *always* disappearing!" Cat said. "Whenever someone calls him."

"This is different," Roger said. "He has a whole string of spells set up so that the people here know who's called him and roughly where he's gone—"

"And," said Janet, who was still glum and red-eyed over Jason, "there are more spells to say if he's run into danger, and none of them have been set off."

"Mummy thinks he might not have had any clothes on when he went," Julia chipped in. "Today's dressing gown was thrown over a chair and none of the rest of his clothes seem to have gone."

"That's silly," Cat said. "He can always conjure clothes from somewhere."

"Oh, so he can," said Julia. "What a relief!"

"I think it's *all* silly," Cat told her. "He must have forgotten to set off the spells." He got on with his lunch. It was liver and bacon, and the smell reminded him of Marianne's spell. He thought about that cat, Nutcase. Cats were queer animals. This one had struck him as unusually magical.

"Oh, I wish you weren't so *calm* about things!" Janet said passionately. "You're even worse than Chrestomanci is! Can't you *see* when things are serious?"

"Yes," Cat said, "and this isn't."

But by suppertime, when Chrestomanci had

still not reappeared, even Cat was beginning to wonder. It was odd. When Cat thought about Chrestomanci, he had a calm, secure feeling, as if Chrestomanci was quite all right, wherever he was, but possibly wishing he could be there to supper; but when he looked at Millie, he saw desperate worry in her face, and in all the faces round the table, even Jason's. Cat almost began thinking he ought to worry too. But he knew that would make no difference.

Still, when he went to bed that night and lay staring proudly at the big speckled mauve sphere sitting in his scarf across the room, Cat found himself hanging a piece of his mind out to one side, so that he would know in his sleep if Chrestomanci came back in the night. But all that piece of his mind caught was Syracuse, out in the paddock under the moon, wistfully eating grass and wondering why Cat had deserted him.

In the middle of the night, he had a strange dream.

It started with something tapping at his

biggest window. Cat turned over in his sleep and tried to take no notice, but the tapping grew more and more insistent, until he dreamed that he woke up and shambled across the room to open the window. He could see a face through the glass, upside down, looking at him with shining purple-blue eyes. But he never saw it clearly, because a great white moon was directly behind it, dazzling him.

"Enchanter," it said, muffled by the glass. "Enchanter, can you hear me?"

Cat put his hand on the catch and slowly pushed the window open. The face retreated upward to give the window room to open. Cat heard its feet shuffle on the roof and what were probably its wings flap and spread for balance. By the time he had the window wide open, he knew that a great shadowy dragonlike thing was sitting on the round turret roof above him.

"What do you want?" he said.

The face came down again and put itself through the window upside down. It was huge. Cat backed away from it, feeling a faint, dream-like brush of what seemed to be feathers against his ear.

"You have my child in there," the creature said.

Cat looked over his shoulder to where the moonlight gleamed softly off the strange object nestling in his scarf. He had no doubt that this was what the creature was talking about. "Then it's an egg?" he said.

"My egg," the great pointed mouth said.

With a dreadful feeling of loss and desolation, Cat said, "You want it back?"

"I can't take it," the creature answered sadly. "I'm under a sundering spell. I can only get free at full moon nowadays. We put the egg outside the spell, and I wanted to be sure that my child was in safe hands. It should be buried in warm sand."

There was no difficulty about that. Cat turned toward the gleaming egg and converted his warmth spell into a warm sandy one. "Is that right? What else should I do?"

"Let it live free when it hatches," the creature

replied. "Give it food and love and let it grow."

"I'll do that," Cat promised. Even in his dream he wondered how he would do it.

"Thank you," the great beast said. "I will repay you in any way I can." It withdrew its head from the window. There was a slight shuffling overhead. Then a great shadow dropped past the window on enormous outspread wings and wheeled away across the moon as noiselessly as an owl.

Cat staggered sleepily toward the egg, wondering how else he could fulfill the creature's trust. In his dream, he doubled the amount of warm sand, made trebly sure that no one could knock it down or disturb it and, as an afterthought, covered it all over with love and friendship and affection. That should do it, he thought, wriggling down into his bed again.

He was quite surprised in the morning to find the window wide open. As for the egg, he could warm his hands on it from a yard away. It must have been one of those real dreams, Cat thought as he went off for his shower. Chrestomanci had said that they happened to enchanters.

When Cat came back, the redheaded maid, Mary, was in his room, glaring at the egg. "You expect me to dust that thing?" she said angrily.

"No," Cat said. "Don't touch it. It's a dragon's egg."

"Mercy me!" Mary said. "As if I'd go near it! I've enough to do with the place in this uproar as it is."

"Is Chrestomanci still missing?" Cat asked.

"Not a sign of him," Mary said. "They've all been sitting in the main office doing spells to find him all night. The cups of tea and coffee I've taken in there for them, you wouldn't believe! Lady Chant looks like death this morning."

Cat was sorry that Millie was so upset. In the middle of the morning, when there had been no further news, he went along to the main office to tell Millie that Chrestomanci was all right— or, not *quite* all right, he thought, feeling around in the distance as he went. There was a bit of something wrong, but no danger.

Millie was not in the office when he got there. "She's gone to lie down," they told him. "You mustn't disturb her, dear, not when she's so worried."

"Then could you tell her that Chrestomanci's more or less all right?" Cat said.

He could tell that they did not believe he could possibly know. "Yes, dear," they said, humoring him. "Run along now."

Cat went away, feeling sad, as he always did when this kind of thing happened. As he went, he remembered that "Run along" was exactly what Marianne's two great-uncles had said to her. And he had told Marianne that this was undermining her— Cat stopped short halfway along one of the Castle's long pale green corridors. He realized that he knew how Marianne was being made to feel unsure of herself because exactly the same thing was always happening to him. He wondered if he should go back to the office and *insist* on being allowed to find Chrestomanci for them.

But why should they *allow* him to do something they couldn't do for themselves?

Cat stood and thought. No, if he insisted or even asked, someone would forbid him to try. The obvious thing was to go and *get* Chrestomanci and bring him back, without any fuss or bother or asking. And why not do it straightaway? Cat stood until he had fixed in his mind precisely where in the dim distance Chrestomanci was. Then he launched himself and shot over to the place.

He hit a barrier that was like an old, wobbly fence. The fence swayed and shot him back with a *twang*. The next second, he was back in his own tower room with all the breath knocked out of him.

Cat sat on his carpet and gasped. He was truly indignant. He *knew* he should have gotten to Chrestomanci. And that barrier was so shoddy. It was made of magic, but it was like rusty barbed wire and old chicken netting. It ought to have been a pushover.

All the same, his next thoughts were for the

dragon's egg sitting on his chest of drawers. He could have hurt it or cracked it, arriving back with such violence. He got up and anxiously put his hands on it.

It was not cracked. It was warm and peaceful and comfortable, basking in the hot sand spell, enfolded in the spells of affection. Cat could feel the life in it through his fingers. It was almost purring, like Nutcase in Irene's arms. So *that* was all right. Now he had to get to Chrestomanci. He sat on his bed and considered.

The mistake had been to dive straight at the barrier, straight at Chrestomanci, he decided. It must have been designed to throw you off if you did that. Yes, it *was*. It had been made to throw you off and throw you off the scent too. But Cat now knew the barrier was there, and he knew Chrestomanci was somehow behind it. That ought to mean he could sneak up to it and perhaps slip through it sideways. Or it was so shoddy that he could even break it, if that was the only way to get through. And he was fairly sure that being a left-handed enchanter gave him an advantage. That barrier felt as if it had been constructed by right-handed people who had been—rather long ago—very set in their ways. He could take them by surprise if he was clever.

Cat got up and sauntered out of his room and down the spiral stair. Keeping his mind deliberately vague, in case the barrier people expected him to try again, he made his way down through the Castle and out beside the stables. Here he had a wistful moment when he longed to go and talk to Syracuse, but he told himself he would do that afterward, whatever Chrestomanci said, and sauntered on toward the hut where Roger and Joe met to talk machinery. They were in there at that moment. He heard Roger say, "Yes, but if we patent *this*, everyone will try to use it." Cat grinned and sidled in among their "Don't Notice" spells. Now it was not even his own magic that was hiding him. Then he launched himself again.

This time, he went quite gently and left side

first. Holding his strong left hand out in front of him, he felt at the barrier as he floated up to it, until he found a weak place. There, quite quietly, he bent a section of what seemed to be chicken wire aside and popped through the space.

He felt a thump as his feet hit a roadway and he opened his eyes.

He was standing on a road that was more of a mossy track than a road. The huge trees of an old wood stood on either side of it, making an archway where the road vanished into distance.

He smelled bacon cooking.

Cat thought of Marianne's bacon spell and grinned as he looked for where the scent was coming from. A few yards on, there was an old man in a squashy felt hat sitting by a small fire on the grass verge, busily frying bacon and eggs in an old black frying pan. Beyond the old man was an ancient, decrepit wooden cart, and beyond that, Cat could just see an old white horse grazing on the bank. All his pleasure and triumph at fooling the barrier vanished. This was not Chrestomanci. What had happened?

"Excuse me, sir," he said politely to the old man.

The old man looked up, revealing a little fringe of gray-white beard, a brown seamy face, and a pair of very wide, shrewd brown eyes. "Good afternoon to you," the old man said pleasantly, and he gave Cat a humorous look because it *was* by now after midday. "What can I do for you?"

"Have you seen an enchanter anywhere around here?" Cat asked him.

"The only one I've seen is you," the old man said. "Care for some lunch?"

It was early for lunch, but Cat found that launching himself at the barrier had made him ravenous, and the smell of that bacon made him even hungrier. "Yes, please," he said. "If you can spare it."

"Surely. I'm just about to put in the mushrooms," the old man said. "You like those? Good. Come and sit down then."

As Cat went over to the fire, the horse beyond

the cart raised its head from grazing to look at him. There was something odd about it, but Cat did not properly see what, because he went to sit down then and the old man said, quite sharply, "Not there. There's a thriving clump of milk-wort there I'd like to keep alive, if you please. Move here. You can miss the strawberries, and silverleaf and cinquefoil never mind being sat on much."

Cat moved obediently. He watched the old man fetch out a knife that had been sharpened so much that it was thin as a prong and use it to slice up some very plump-looking mushrooms.

"You have to put them in early enough to catch the taste of bacon, but not so early that they go rubbery," the old man explained, tossing the mushrooms hissing into the pan. "A fine art, cooking. The best mushrooms are sticky buns, the ones the French call cèpes, and best of all are your truffles. It takes a trained dog or a good pig to find truffles. I've never owned either, to my sorrow. Do you know the properties of the milk-wort I stopped you sitting on?"

"Not really," Cat said, somewhat surprised. "I know it was supposed to help mothers' milk, but that's not true, is it?"

"With the right spell done, it's perfectly true," the old man said, turning the mushrooms. "Your scientific herbalists nowadays always neglect the magics that go with the properties, and then they think the plants have no virtue. A great waste. Change the spell from womanly to manly, and your milkwort does wonders for men too. Pass me over those two plates there beside you. And what's the special virtue of the small fern beside your foot?"

Cat picked up the two wooden plates and passed them over while he inspected the fern. "Invisibility?" he said doubtfully. Now he came to look, the grassy verge was a mass of tiny plants, all different. And the wild strawberries almost underneath him were ripe. He felt as he often did with Syracuse, as if he was being given a whole new way of looking at the world.

The old man, pushing bacon, eggs, and mushrooms onto the plates with a wooden spatula, said, "Not invisibility so much as a very good 'Don't Notice.' You can be a tree or a passing bird with some of this under your tongue, but you have to tell it what you need it to do. That's mostly how herb magic works. Tuck in and enjoy it."

He passed Cat a full plate, still sizzling, with a bent knife and a wooden fork lying across it. Cat balanced the plate on his knee and ate. It was delicious. While he ate, the old man went on telling him about the plants he was sitting among. Cat learned that one plant made your breath sweet, another cured your cough, and that the small pink one, ragged robin, was very powerful indeed.

"Handled one way, it slides any ill-wishing away from you," the old man said, "but if you pick it roughly, it brings a thunderstorm. It's not good to be rough with any living thing. Handle it the third way, and ask for its help, it can bring strong vengeance down on your enemy. Has the egg hatched yet?"

"No, not yet," Cat said. Somehow it did

not surprise him that the old man knew about the egg.

"It will soon, once it's warm and being loved," the old man said. He sighed. "And its poor mother can set her mind at rest at last."

"What—what's it going to be?" Cat asked. He found he was quite nervous about this.

"Ah, it will bring its own name with it," the old man answered. "Something weak and worried and soft, it will be at first, that's certain. It'll need all your help for a while. Finished?" He held out his big brown hand for the plate.

"Yes. It was really good. Thank you," Cat said, passing the plate, knife, and fork over.

"Then you'd better be going after your Big Man," the old man said. Cat, in the middle of standing up, stared at him. The old man looked slightly ashamed. "My fault for distracting you," he said. "I was very desirous of meeting you, you see. Your Big Man's not far away."

Cat could feel Chrestomanci quite near. He thought the old man must be pretty powerful to have distracted him from knowing until now. So he thanked him again and said good-bye, rather respectfully, before he set off along the mossy road.

As he passed the cart, the old white horse once more raised her head to look at him. Cat found himself facing a most unhorselike pair of interested blue eyes with a tumble of white mane almost across them. Sticking out from that swatch of white horsehair was quite a long pointed horn. It was pearly colored, with a spiral groove around it.

He turned to the old man incredulously. "Your horse has got—your horse is a unicorn!" he called out.

"Yes, indeed," the old man called back, busy with his fire.

And the horse said, "My name is Molly. I was interested to meet you too."

"How do you do," Cat said respectfully.

"Not so bad, considering how old I am," the unicorn said. "I'll see you." She went back to grazing again, tearing up mouthfuls of grass and tiny flowers.

Cat stood for a moment, sniffing the smell of her. It was not quite like a horse. She smelled of incense, almost, together with horse smell. Then he said, "See you," and went on his way.

About a hundred yards down the road, he found he needed to turn off and plunge into the wood to the right. He waded through bracken and crunched across thorny undergrowth, until he came to clearer ground under some bigger trees. There he found an open space, knee-deep in old leaves. As Cat waded into the leaves, Chrestomanci came wading out into the space as well from the opposite direction. They stopped and stared at one another.

"Cat!" said Chrestomanci. "What a relief!"

He was wearing clothes Cat had never seen him in before, plus fours with thick knitted socks and big walking shoes, and a sweater on his top half. Cat had never seen Chrestomanci in a sweater before, but as he was also carrying a walking stick, Cat supposed that these were what Chrestomanci thought of as clothes for walking in. He had never seen Chrestomanci in need of a shave before, either. It all made him look quite human.

"I came to get you," Cat said.

"Thank heavens!" Chrestomanci replied. "There seemed no reason why I should ever get out of this wood."

"How did you get in?" Cat asked him.

"I made a mistake," Chrestomanci admitted wearily. "When I set off, my aim was simply to check up on what you told me about the roads, by walking to Ulverscote Wood if I could. But when I found myself repeatedly walking back to the Castle, whatever direction I took, I got irritated and pushed. I got to the wood with a bit of a fight, but then I couldn't get *out*. I must have been walking in circles for twenty-four hours now."

"This isn't really Ulverscote Wood," Cat told him.

"I believe you," Chrestomanci said. "It's a sad, lost, empty place whatever it is. How do we get home?"

"There's a funny sort of a barrier," Cat told

him. "I think they put you behind it if you break their turn-you-back-to-the-Castle spell, but I'm not sure. It's pretty old and rusty. Just start a slow teleport to the Castle and I'll try to get us through."

"I've tried that," Chrestomanci said wryly.

"Try again with me," Cat said.

Chrestomanci shrugged, and they set off. Almost at once, they were up against the barrier. It seemed much more real from this side. It looked almost exactly like chicken wire and old corrugated iron that was grown all over with brambles, goosegrass, and thickly tangled honeysuckle. In among the tangle Cat thought he saw swags of bright red briony berries and the small pink flowers of ragged robin. Aha! he thought, remembering what the old man had told him. A slide-you-off spell. He turned himself left side foremost and scratched about among the creepers to find a join. While he groped, he felt Chrestomanci being slid away backward. Cat had to seize hold of Chrestomanci's walking stick with his other hand and drag him forward to the place where he *thought* he could feel two pieces of corrugated iron overlapping. Luckily, before they were both swept away backward again, Chrestomanci saw the overlap too and helped Cat force the two pieces apart. It took all the strength of both of them.

Then they squeezed through. They arrived, panting and strung with creepers, halfway up the Castle driveway, where Cat found he still had hold of Chrestomanci's walking stick.

"Thank you," Chrestomanci said, taking his stick back. He needed it to walk with. Cat saw he was limping quite badly. "Lord knows what that barrier was really made of. I refuse to believe such strong magic can be simply chicken fencing."

"It was the creepers, I think," Cat said. "They were all for binding and keeping enemies in. Have you hurt your ankle?"

"Just some of the biggest blisters of my life," Chrestomanci said, pausing to pull a long strand of clinging goosegrass off his sweater. "I've been walking for a day and a night, in shoes I'm beginning to hate. I shall throw the socks away." He limped on a few steps and started to say something else, in a way that seemed quite heartfelt, but before he could begin, Millie came dashing down the driveway and flung her arms round Chrestomanci.

Millie was followed by Julia, Irene, Jason, Janet, and most of the Castle wizards. Chrestomanci was engulfed in a crowd of people, welcoming, exclaiming, asking where he had been, congratulating Cat, and wanting to know if Chrestomanci was all right.

"No I am *not* all right!" Chrestomanci said, after five minutes of this. "I have worldwide blisters. I need a shave. I'm tired out and I haven't had anything to eat since breakfast yesterday. Would *you* feel all right in my position?"

Saying this, he vanished from the driveway in a cloud of dust.

"Where's he gone?" everyone said.

"To have a bath, I imagine," Millie said. "Wouldn't *you*? Someone go and find him some foot balm while I go and order him something to eat. Cat, come with me and explain how on earth you managed to find him."

An hour later, Chrestomanci summoned Cat to his study. Cat found him sitting on a sofa with his sore feet propped on a leather tuffet, shaved and smooth again and wearing a peach satin dressing gown that put Cat in mind of a quilted sunset. "Are you all right now?" Cat said.

"Perfectly, thank you, thanks to you," Chrestomanci replied. "To continue the conversation we were about to have when the welcoming hordes descended, I can't stop thinking about that barrier. It's a real mystery, Cat. Twenty-odd years ago, when I was around your age, I was dragged off on the longest, wettest walk of my life up to then. Flavian Temple marched me right across Hopton Moor almost to Hopton. I set Hopton Wood on fire. There were no turn-you-round spells then and no kind of barrier. I know. I would have welcomed either of them heartily. Temple and I walked miles in a straight line, and nothing stopped us."

"The barrier looked quite old," Cat said.

"Twenty years can grow a lot of creepers," Chrestomanci said, "and a lot of rust. Let's take it that the barrier is no older than that. The real puzzle is, why is it *there*?"

Cat would have liked to know that too. He could only shake his head.

Chrestomanci said, "It may only apply to Ulverscote Wood, of course. But I see I shall have to investigate the whole thing. The real reason I asked you in here, Cat, is to tell you that I can't, after the way you rescued me, keep you apart from that wretched horse any longer. The stableman tells me its feet are sounder than mine are. So off you go. There's just time for a ride before supper."

Cat hurtled off to the stableyard. And there would have been time for a ride, except that Syracuse saw Cat coming and hurdled the paddock gate, and hurdled Joss with it as Joss tried to open the gate. Syracuse then dashed several times round the yard and jumped back into the paddock, where he spent a joyous hour avoiding the efforts of Joss, Cat, and the stableboy to catch him. After that, there was no time left before supper.

Chapter Ten

"No she is *not*!" Gammer shouted, so loudly that the Dell's crowded little living room rang all over with the noise. "Pinhoes is Pinhoes and make sure you look after Nutcase for me, Marianne."

"I don't understand you, Gammer," Marianne said boldly. She thought Cat had been right to say she was downtrodden, and she had decided to be brave from now on.

Gammer chomped her jaws, breathed heavily, and stared stormily at nothing.

Marianne sighed. This behavior of Gammer's would have terrified her a week ago. Now she was being brave, Marianne felt simply impatient. She wanted to go home and get on with her story.

Since her meeting with Irene, the story had suddenly turned into "The Adventures of Princess Irene and Her Cats," which was somehow far more interesting than her first idea of it. She could hardly wait to find out what happened in it next. But Aunt Joy had sent Cousin Ned down to Furze Cottage to say that Gammer wanted Marianne *now*, and Mum had said, "Better see what she wants, love." So Marianne had had to stop writing and hurry round to the Dell. Uselessly, because Gammer was not making any sense.

"You *have* got Nutcase, have you?" Gammer asked anxiously.

"Yes, Gammer." Marianne had left Nutcase sitting on the drainboard, watching Mum chop herby leaves and peel knobby roots. She could only hope that he stayed there.

"But I'm not having it!" Gammer said, switching from anxiety to anger. "It's not true. You're to contradict it whenever you hear it, understand?"

"I would, but I don't know what you're talking about," Marianne said.

At this, Gammer fell into a real rage.
"Hocum pocum!" she yelled, beating the floor
with her stick. "You're all turned against me! It's
insurpery, I tell you! They wouldn't tell me what
they'd done with him. Put him down it and pull
the chain, I told them, but *would* they do it?
They lied. Everyone's *lying* to me!"

Marianne tried to say that no one was lying to
Gammer, but Gammer just yelled her down. "I
don't *understand* you!" Marianne bawled back.
"Talk *sense*, Gammer! You know you can if
you try."

"It's an insult to Pinhoes!" Gammer
screamed.

The noise brought Aunt Dinah striding
cheerfully in. "Now, now, Gammer, dear. You'll
only tire yourself out if you shout like that. She'll
fall asleep," Aunt Dinah said to Marianne, "and
when she wakes up she'll have forgotten all
about it."

"Yes, but I don't know what she's so angry
about," Marianne said.

"Oh, it's nothing, really," Aunt Dinah said,

just as if Gammer was not sitting there. "It's only that your aunt Helen was in here earlier. She likes to have all your aunts drop in, tell her things, cheer her up. You know. And Helen was telling her that the new lady that's just bought Woods House is a Pinhoe born and bred—"

"She is *not*!" Gammer said sulkily. "*I'm* the only Pinhoe around here."

"Are you, dear?" Aunt Dinah said cheerily. "And where does that leave the rest of us?"

This seemed to be the right way to treat Gammer. Gammer looked surprised, ashamed, and amused, all at once, and took to pleating the clean, clean skirt that Aunt Dinah had dressed her in that morning. "These are not my clothes," she said.

"Whose are they, then?" Aunt Dinah said, laughing. She turned to Marianne. "She'd no call to drag you over here for that, Marianne. Next time she tries it, just ignore it. Oh, and could you ask your mum for more of that ointment for her? She gets sore, sitting all the time."

Marianne said she would ask, and walked

away among the chickens and the ducks, taking care to latch the gate behind her. Joe was always forgetting to shut the gate properly. Last time Joe forgot, the goats had gotten out into everyone's gardens. The things Aunt Joy had said about Joe! Marianne discovered herself to be missing Joe far more than she had expected. She wondered how he was getting on.

"Mum," Marianne asked, as she came into the herby, savory steam of the kitchen in Furze Cottage. Nutcase, to her relief, was still there, sitting on the table now, among the jars and bottles waiting to be filled with balms and medicines. "Mum, *is* Mrs. Yeldham a Pinhoe born and bred?"

"So your great-uncle Lester says," Mum said. Her narrow face was fiery red and dripping in the steam. Wet curls were escaping from the red-and-white checked cloth she had wrapped round her head. "Marianne, I could use your help here."

Marianne knew how this one worked: help Mum, or she would get no further information.

She sighed because of her unfinished story and went to find a cloth to wrap her hair in. "Yes?" she said, once she was hard at work beating chopped herbs into warm goose grease. "And?"

"She really is a Pinhoe," Mum said, carefully straining another set of herbs through a square of muslin. "Lester went up to London and checked the records in case he did wrong to sell her the house. You remember those stories about Luke Pinhoe, who went to London to seek his fortune a hundred years ago?"

"The one who turned his Gaffer into a tree first?" Marianne said.

"Only overnight," Mum said, as if that excused it. "He did it so that he could get away, I think. There must have been quite a row there, what with Luke refusing to be the next Gaffer, and his father crippling both his legs so that he'd have to stay. Anyway, they say that Luke stole his father's old gray mare and rode all night until he came to London, and the mare made her way back here all on her own. And Luke found an enchanter to mend his legs—and that must be true, because Lester found out that Luke set up as an apothecary first, which would have been hard to do as a cripple. He'd have been more likely to have been begging on the streets. But there he was, dealing in potions because he was herb-cunning, like me. But Luke seems to have found out quite soon that he was an enchanter himself. He made himself a mint of money out of it. And his son was an enchanter after him, and *his* son after that, right down to this present day, when William Pinhoe, who died this spring, had only the one daughter. They say he left his daughter all his money and two servants to look after her, and *she's* the Mrs. Yeldham who bought Woods House."

While Mum paused to spoon careful measures of fresh chopped herbs into the strained water, Marianne remembered that Irene had talked about someone called Jane James, who must have been her cook. It did seem to fit. "But why is Gammer so angry about it?"

"Well," Mum said, rather drily, "I *could* say it's because she's lost her wits, but between you and me and the gatepost, Marianne, I'd say it's because Mrs. Yeldham's more of a Pinhoe than Gammer is. Luke was his Gaffer's eldest son. Gammer's family comes down from the second cousins who went to live in Hopton. See?" She covered her bowl with fresh muslin and went to put it in the cold store to steep.

Marianne started to lick goose grease from her fingers, remembered in time that it was full of herbs you shouldn't eat, and felt rather proud of being a Pinhoe by direct descent—or no! *Her* family descended from that Gaffer's *second* son, George, who had been by all accounts a meek and rather feeble man, and did just what his father told him. So Irene was more Pinhoe than Marianne— "Oh, what does it *matter?*" she said aloud. "It was all a hundred years ago!" She looked round for Nutcase and was just in time to catch him sneaking through the window Mum had opened to try to get rid of the steam. Marianne grabbed him and shut the window. "No, you mustn't," she told Nutcase as she put him on the floor. "Some of them move into

Woods House today. They won't want *you*."

As everyone in Ulverscote somehow knew—
without anyone's precisely being *told*—Irene's
two servants arrived that morning. They came
in a heavy London van that took two cart horses
to pull it, bringing some basic furniture to put
into the house. The good furniture was supposed to arrive later, when the Yeldhams moved
in. Uncle Simeon and Uncle Charles went up
there in the afternoon to see what alterations
were going to be required.

They came away chastened.

"Massive job," Uncle Simeon said, in his
untalkative way, when the two of them arrived
in Furze Cottage to report to Dad and drink
restorative tea. "And the new stove and water
tank to come from Hopton before we can even
start."

"That Jane James!" Uncle Charles said feel-
ingly. "You can't put a foot wrong there. Proper
old-time servant. All I did was think the two of
them was married and—ooh! And there was he,
little trodden-on-looking fellow, but you have to

call him *Mister* Adams, *she* says, and show proper respect. So then I call her *Miss* James, showing proper respect like she told me, and she shoots herself up and gathers herself in like an umbrella and 'I'm Jane James, and I'll thank you to remember it!' she says. After that we just crawled away."

"Got to go back, though," Uncle Simeon said. "The Yeldhams come to see what's needed tomorrow, and *she* wants you to start on the whitewash, Charles."

Irene and Jason were indeed due to set off to confer with Pinhoe Construction Limited in Woods House that next day. Irene took a deep breath and invited Janet and Julia to go with them. "Do come," she said. "Whatever Jane James has done to it, I know it's going to look a depressing mess still. I need someone to tell me how to make it livable in."

Janet looked at Julia and Julia looked at Janet. It was more a sliding round of eyes than a proper look. Irene seemed to hold her breath. Cat could see Irene knew the girls did not like her for some reason, and it obviously worried her. At length, Julia said, not altogether politely, "Yes. Please. Thank you, Mrs. Yeldham," and Janet nodded.

It was not friendly, but Irene smiled with relief and turned to Cat.

"Would you like to come too, Cat?"

Cat knew she was hoping he would help make the girls more friendly, but Syracuse was waiting. Cat smiled and shook his head and explained that Joss was taking him for a ride beside the river in half an hour. And Roger was not to be found. Irene looked a little dashed, and only Janet and Julia went with Jason and Irene to Ulverscote.

In the normal way, all Ulverscote would have come out to stare at them. But that day only a few people—who had all had the presence of mind to call on the Reverend Pinhoe in order to stare over the vicarage wall—caught sight of the four of them getting out of Jason's car. They all told one another that the fair-haired girl looked as sour as Aunt Joy, and what a pity, it just showed you what they were like at That Castle, but Mrs. Yeldham did credit to the Pinhoe family. A real lady. She was born a Pinhoe, you know. .

The rest of the village was in the grip of a mysterious wave of bad luck. A fox got into the chick pen at the Dell and ate most of the baby chicks that Nutcase had not accounted for. Mice got into the grocer's and into the pantry at the Pinhoe Arms. The wrong bricks were delivered to mend the Post Office wall.

"Bright yellow bricks I am *not* having!" Aunt Joy screamed at the van men. "This is a Post Office, not a sandcastle on a beach!" And she made the men take the bricks away again.

"Before I could even take a look at them too!" Uncle Simeon complained. He was in Dr. Callow's surgery when the bricks were delivered, with a sprained ankle. He had been forced to send his foreman, Podge Callow, to consult with the Yeldhams in his place. Besides Uncle Simeon, the surgery was crowded with sprains, dislocations, and severe bruises, all to Pinhoes and all of them acquired that morning. Uncle Cedric was there, after falling from his hayloft, and so was Great-Uncle Lester, who had shut his thumb in his car door. Almost all of Marianne's cousins had had similar accidents, and Great-Aunt Sue had tipped boiling water down her leg. Dr. Callow had to agree with her that this spate of injuries was not natural.

Down at Furze Cottage, Mum was trying to deal with further cuts and scrapes and bruises, working under great difficulty, as she said to Marianne. Half of her new infusions had got mildew overnight. Marianne had to sort the bad jars out for her before they infected the rest. Meanwhile, Uncle Richard, carefully carving a rose on the front of a new cabinet, let his gouge slip somehow and plowed a deep bloody furrow in the palm of his other hand. Mum had to leave her storeroom yet again and sort him out with a wad of cobwebs and some lotion charmed to heal.

"I don't think this is natural, Cecily," Uncle Richard said while Mum was bandaging his hand. "Joy shouldn't have cursed Gammer like that."

"Don't talk nonsense," said Dad, who had come in to make sure his brother was all right. "I stopped Joy before she started. This is something else."

Dad was about the only person who believed this. As the bad luck spread to people who were only distantly related to Pinhoes, and then to people who had no witchcraft at all, most of Ulverscote began to blame Aunt Joy. Aunt Joy's face, as Mum said, would have soured milk from a hundred yards away.

The bad luck extended to Woods House too. There, to Jane James's annoyance, the man installing the new stove dropped it on his foot and then mystified her by limping away into the village saying, "Mother Cecily will fix me up. Don't touch the boiler till I get back."

While Mum was dealing with what she suspected was a broken bone in this man's foot, Marianne discovered—mostly by the severely bad smell—that the whole top shelf of jars in the storeroom had grown fuzzy red mold. And Nutcase disappeared again.

Nutcase reappeared some time later in the hall of Woods House, just in time to trip Uncle Charles up, as Uncle Charles crossed the hall carrying a ladder and a bucket of whitewash. Uncle Charles, in trying to save himself, hit himself on the back of the head with the ladder and dropped the bucket of whitewash over Nutcase.

The clang and the crash fetched Jane James and Irene from the kitchen and Janet, Julia, and Jason from what was going to be the dining room. Everyone exclaimed in sympathy at the sight of the house painter lying under a ladder in a lake of whitewash, while beside him the desperate white head of a cat stuck out from under the upturned whitewash pail.

Uncle Charles stopped swearing at the sight of Jane James's face, but continued telling the world at large just what he would like to do to Nutcase. As he told Marianne later, a bang on the head does that to you. And those two girls *laughed*.

"But are you all right?" Jason asked him.

"I'd be better off if that cat was dead," Uncle Charles replied. "I didn't chance to kill him, did I?"

Janet and Julia, trying—and failing—not to laugh too much, tipped the pail up and rescued Nutcase. Nutcase was scrawny, clawing, and mostly white. Whitewash sprayed over everyone as Nutcase struggled. Janet held him at arm's length, with her face turned sideways, while Irene and Jason dived to help Uncle Charles. "Oh, it's a *black* cat!" Julia exclaimed as the underside of Nutcase became visible. Jason's foot skidded in the whitewash. He tried to save himself by grabbing Irene's arm. The result was that Jason fell flat on his face in the whitewash and Irene sat in it. Janet's opinion of Irene changed completely when Irene simply sat on the floor and laughed.

"All their good clothes ruined," Uncle Charles told Marianne. He arrived, a trifle dizzily, at Furze Cottage with Nutcase clamped under one arm. "It just goes to show that even an enchanter can't avoid a bad-luck spell. That fellow's a full enchanter, or I'm a paid-up Chinaman. Don't tell Gammer he is. She'd take a fit. He had me standing up while his face was still in the matting. Take your cat. Wash him. *Drown* him if you like."

Marianne took Nutcase to the sink and ran both taps on him. Nutcase protested mightily. "It's your own fault. Shut up," Marianne told him. Dad was sitting at the table assembling the flowers and frondy leaves of ragged robin in the careful overlapping pattern of a counter-charm, and Marianne was trying to listen to what he was saying to Uncle Charles about the bad-luck spell.

"It's an ill-chancing. Positive," Uncle Charles was saying. "I knew that as soon as that damn ladder hit my head. But I don't know whose, or—"

Mum interrupted by bawling from the front room, where she was treating a small boy for a sudden severe cough. She wanted to know if Uncle Charles was concussed.

"Just a bit dizzy like," Dad bawled back.

"He's fine. Yes," he said to Uncle Charles. "It feels like a nudge job to me. One of those that lies in wait for all the things you *nearly* get wrong, like you *nearly* trip and you *nearly* drop a pail of whitewash, and it gives those a nudge so that you do it *really*. It doesn't have to be strong to have a big effect."

"That doesn't account for the fox," Uncle Charles objected. "Or they're saying a lot of little ones have got the whooping cough. It can't account for that."

"Those could be separate," Dad said. "If they *were* a part of it, then I'd have to say, to be fair, that it's stronger than a nudge—and nobody's dead yet."

Meanwhile, Jason's whitewash-spattered party was leaving Woods House in order to get some clean clothes. Jason looked particularly spectacular, as not only the front of him, but the tip of his nose and the fringe of his hair were white. He was annoyed enough to shout with rage when his car refused to start. He called the car more

names than Uncle Charles had called the cat.
Janet's theory was that the car eventually started
out of pure shame. Julia told her that Jason had
used magic, a lot of magic.

When the car was finally chugging, they
drove out into the road and out beyond the last
small houses of the village. There Jason stopped,
with a screech and a violent jerk. He jumped out
of the car and stood in the middle of the road,
glaring around at the hedges.

"What's he *doing*?" Janet said.

They all looked anxiously at Jason's clownlike
figure.

"Magic," Julia said, and got out too.

Janet and Irene followed Julia just as Jason
made a dive for a clump of plants growing on
the verge. "*And* right in the middle of the
artemisia to lend it power!" they heard him say.
He hacked into the clump with the heel of his
boot. "Come out, you!"

A little black lump with trailing strings came
out of the plants. It looked like a dirty lavender
bag that someone had not tied up properly. Jason

hacked it out of the grass and down the bank to the road. "*Got* you!" he said. Irene took one look at the thing and went back to the car, looking white and ill. Julia felt queasy. Janet wondered what was the matter with them both. It was only a greasy gray bag of herbs. "Keep back," Jason said to her. He kicked the bag into the center of the road and bent over it warily. "Someone's been very nasty here. This is a brute of an ill-wishing—it's probably infecting the whole village by now. Get in the car while I get rid of the thing."

By this time even Janet was feeling something wrong about the bag. She stumbled and nearly fell over as Julia pulled her back to the car. "I think I'm going to be sick," Julia said.

They watched from inside the car while Jason levitated the bag fifteen feet into the air and made it burst into flames. It burned and it burned, with improbably long crimson flames, and gave off a whirl of thick black smoke. Jason kept collecting the smoke and sending it back to the flames to burn again. They all, even Janet, had the feeling that the bag was trying to fall on Jason and burn him too. But Jason made it stay in the air with batting motions of his left hand, the way you make a balloon stay in the air, batting and batting, while his other hand collected smoke and fed it back to the flames, over and over, until at last there was nothing left of it, not even the smallest flake of ash. He was sweating through the whitewash when he came back to the car.

"Phew!" he said. "Someone around here is not nice at all. That thing was designed to get worse by the hour."

All this while, Cat was trotting blissfully on Syracuse along the bank of the river, following Joss on his big brown horse. Syracuse was drawing Cat's attention to the smells of the river valley—the mildly churning river on one side with its rich watery smells, and the damp grassiness from the plants on its banks, and the way the scents from the rest of the valley were those of late summer. Cat sniffed the dry incense smells from the fields and thought he would know it was the end of August even if he suddenly went blind. Syracuse, who was feeling quite as blissful as Cat, helped him sense the myriad squishy things in the river going about their muddy lives, all the hundreds of creatures rustling about on its banks, and the truly teeming life of birds and animals in the meadows above.

Cat set a spell to keep off the midges and horseflies. They were teeming too. They came pouring out of the bushes in clouds. While he set the spell, he had the feeling that he always had now when he rode out, the same feeling he had first had in Home Wood, that despite the thronging of living things, there ought to have been *more*. Behind the bustle of creatures, and behind the flitting and soaring of birds, there was surely an emptiness that should have been filled.

Cat was once again trying to track down the emptiness, when everything stopped.

Birds stopped singing. Creatures stopped

rustling among the rushes. Even the river lost its voice and seemed to flow milklike and silent. Joss stopped too, so suddenly that Syracuse nearly shot Cat off into the water, going sideways to avoid the rear end of Joss's horse.

Mr. Farleigh stepped into sight beyond a clump of willows, with his long gun under his arm.

"Morning, Mr. Farleigh," Joss said respectfully.

Mr. Farleigh ignored the politeness, just as he ignored Cat too, sitting slantwise across the path behind Joss. His grim eyes fixed accusingly on Joss. "Tell the Pinhoes to stop," he said.

Joss clearly had no more idea than Cat did what this meant. He said, "Sorry?"

"You heard me. Tell them to stop," Mr. Farleigh said, "or they'll be having more than a bit of ill-chancing coming down on them. Tell them I told you."

"Of course," Joss said. "If you say so."

"I do say," Mr. Farleigh said. He shifted a little, so that he was now ignoring Cat more than ever. Pointedly and deliberately ignoring him. "And you've no business letting Castle people out all over the place," he said. "Keep the Big Man's nose out of things, do you hear me? I had to take steps over that myself the other day. Do your job, man."

In front of Cat, Joss was making helpless movements. Cat could feel Syracuse, underneath him, making movements that suggested it would be a good plan to barge past Mr. Farleigh and tumble him into the river. Cat entirely agreed, but he knew this was not wise. He made movements back at Syracuse to tell him not to.

"My job's not to *stop* things, Mr. Farleigh," Joss said apologetically. "I only report."

"Then report," Mr. Farleigh said, "or I don't know where it will all end. Take some steps, before I have to get rid of the lot of them." He swung round on the heel of his big boot and plodded away down the river path.

When Mr. Farleigh had vanished ahead of them behind the willows, Joss turned to Cat. "Got to go up through the meadows now," he said. "It won't do to shove Mr. Farleigh off the path."

Cat longed to ask Joss what was going on here, but he could tell Joss was hoping that Cat had not understood a word of what had been said. So he said nothing and let Syracuse follow Joss up through the fields at the side of the valley. Around them, birds flew and creatures rustled, and the river behind them went back to churning again.

Chapter Eleven

The egg started hatching that night.

Cat was not really asleep when it did. He was lying in bed thinking. That night at supper, Julia had told everyone about the greasy gray lavender bag. Chrestomanci had not said anything, but he had looked unusually vague. When Chrestomanci looked vague, it always meant that he was attending particularly closely. Cat was not surprised when Chrestomanci took Jason away to his study afterward to ask him all about it. An ill-chancing was a bad misuse of magic, and it was, after all, Chrestomanci's job to stop such things. The trouble was, Cat knew he should have told Chrestomanci about Mr. Farleigh too, because he was fairly sure that bag was one of the things Mr. Farleigh had been talking about by the river.

He tried to work out why he had said nothing. One good reason was that Joss Callow was obviously some kind of spy, and telling Chrestomanci would give Joss away. Cat liked Joss. He did not want to get Joss into trouble—and it would be very bad trouble, Cat knew. But the real reason was because Mr. Farleigh had said these things while Cat was sitting there on Syracuse, hearing every word. It was as if Mr. Farleigh had no need to worry. If he was powerful enough to lock Chrestomanci himself away behind a barrier of chicken wire, then he had enough sour, gnarled power to get rid of everyone in the Castle if he wanted to. He had more or less said so.

Let's face it, Cat thought. It's because I'm scared stiff of him.

It was then that Cat began to hear a muffled tapping.

At first he thought it was coming from the window again, but when he sat up and listened, he knew the noise was coming from inside his room. He snapped the light on. Sure enough, the big mauve-speckled egg was rocking gently in its nest of winter scarf. The tapping from inside it was getting faster and faster, as if whatever was in there was in a panic to get out. Then it stopped, and there was an exhausted silence.

Oh, help! Cat thought. He jumped out of bed and quickly took off the safety spell and then the warm-sand spell, hoping this would make things easier for the creature. He bent anxiously over the egg. "Oh, don't be dead!" he said to it. "*Please!*" But he knew the thing must have been for years in a cold attic. It was surely at the end of its strength by now.

To his huge relief, the tapping started again, slower now, but quite strong and persistent. Cat could tell that the creature inside was concentrating on one part of the egg in order to make a hole. He wondered whether to help it by making the hole for it, from outside. But he was somehow sure this was a bad idea. He could hurt it, or it could die of shock. The only thing he could do was to hang helplessly over the egg and listen.

Tap, *tap*, TAP, it went.

And a hair-fine crack appeared, near the top of the egg. After that, there was another exhausted silence. "Come *on*!" Cat whispered. "You can do it!"

But it couldn't. The tapping started again, weaker now, but the crack did not grow any bigger. After a while, the tapping was going so fast that it was almost a whirring, but still nothing happened. Cat could feel the creature's growing panic. He began to panic too. He didn't know what to *do*, or what would help.

There was only one person in the Castle that Cat knew could help. He rushed to his door, opened it wide, and then rushed back to the egg. He picked it up, scarf and all, and raced away down his winding stair to find Millie. He could feel the egg vibrating with terror as he ran. "It's all *right*!" he panted to it. "Don't panic! It'll be all right!"

Millie had her own sitting room on the next

floor. She and Irene were sitting there, chatting quietly over mugs of cocoa before bed. Millie's big gray cat, Mopsa, was on her knee, filling most of it, and Irene had two more of the Castle cats, Coy and Potts, wedged into her chair on either side. All three cats sprang up and whirled to safe, high places when Cat slammed the door open and rushed in.

"Cat!" Millie exclaimed. "What's wrong?"

"It won't break! It can't get out!" Cat panted. He was almost crying by then.

Millie did not waste time asking questions. "Give it to me, here on the floor. Gently," she said, and kneeled quickly on the furry hearth rug. Cat, shaking, panting and sniffing, passed her the egg at once. Millie put it carefully down on the rug and carefully unwrapped the scarf from it. "I see," she said, running her finger lightly along the thin, almost invisible crack. "Poor thing." She put both hands around the egg, as far as they would reach. "It's all right now," she murmured. "We're going to help you."

Cat could feel calmness spreading into the egg, along with hope and strength. He always forgot that Millie, apart from Chrestomanci and himself, was the strongest enchanter in the country. People said she had been a goddess once.

Irene came to kneel on the hearth rug too. "The shell seems awfully thick," she said.

"I don't think that's the problem—quite," Millie murmured. Her hands moved to either side of the crack and began gently, gently trying to spread it wider. Mopsa edged in under Millie's elbow and stared as if she were trying to help. She probably was, Cat realized. All the Castle cats descended from Asheth temple cats and had magic of their own. Coy and Potts, on the mantlepiece, were staring eagerly too. "Ah!" Millie said.

"What?" Cat asked anxiously.

"There's a stasis spell all round the inside of the shell," Millie said. "I suppose whoever put it there was trying to preserve the egg, but it's making things really difficult. Let's see. Cat, you and Irene put your hands where mine are, while I try to get rid of the spell. Hold the split as wide as you can, but very gently, not to crack it further."

They kneeled with their heads touching, Cat and Irene—Irene rather timidly—pulling at the crack, while Millie picked at the tiny space they made. After a moment, Millie made an annoyed noise and grew the nails on her thumb and forefinger an inch longer. Then she picked again with her new long nails, until she succeeded in pulling a tiny whitish piece of something through.

"Ah!" they all said.

Millie went on pulling, slowly, steadily, gently, and the filmy white something came out farther and farther, and finally came out entirely, with a faint whistling sound. As soon as it was free, it vanished. Millie said, "Bother! I'd like to have known whose spell it was. But never mind." She leaned down to the egg. "Now you can get to work, my love."

The creature inside did its best. It tapped and

hammered away, but so feebly by then that Cat could scarcely bear to listen.

Irene whispered, "It's very weak. Couldn't we just break the shell for it?"

Millie shook her head, tangling her hair into Irene's and Cat's. "No. Much better to feed it strength. Put your hands on mine, both of you." She took hold of the egg, with her fingernails normal length again. Cat laid his hands over Millie's, and Irene doubtfully did the same. Cat could tell that Irene had no notion of how to give strength to someone else, so he did it for her and pushed Irene's strength inside the egg, along with his own and Millie's.

The creature inside now hammered away with a will. Tap, tap, taptaptap, *taptaptap*, BANG. *CRACK*. And a thing that might have been a beak—anyhow, it was yellowish and blunt—came out through the mauve shell. There it stopped, seeming to gasp. It looked so tender and soft that Cat's nose and mouth felt sore in sympathy. Fancy having to break this thick shell with *that*! he thought. Next second, the beak had been joined by a small, thin paw with long pink nails. Then a second paw struggled out, tiny and weak like the first.

The cats were all on the alert now. Mopsa's nose was almost on the widening dark crack.

"Is it a dragon?" Irene asked.

"I'm—not sure," Millie said.

As she spoke, the weak claws found the edges of the crack, scrabbled, and then shoved. The egg split into two white-lined halves, and the creature rolled loose. It was much bigger than Cat expected, twice the size of Mopsa at least, and it was desperately thin and scrawny and slightly wet, and covered with pale, draggled fluff. It opened two round yellow eyes above its beak and looked at Cat imploringly. "Weep, weep, weep!" it went.

Cat did what it seemed to want and gathered it up into his arms. It snugged down against him with an exhausted sigh, beak and front paws draped over his right arm, and hind claws quite painfully hooked on his left pajama sleeve. It had a tail like a piece of string that hung down on his knee. "Weep," it said.

It was much lighter for its size than Cat thought it should be. He was just about to ask Millie what on earth kind of creature it was, when the door of Millie's sitting room opened and Chrestomanci hurried in, looking anxious, with Jason behind him. "Is there some kind of crisis?" Chrestomanci asked.

"Not exactly," Millie said, pointing to the creature in Cat's arms.

Chrestomanci looked from the two broken eggshell halves on the hearth rug to the creature Cat was holding. He said, "Bless my soul!" and came over to look. He ran a finger down the creature's back, from soft beak to stringy tail, and picked up the tail to look at the tuft on its end. Then he went to the other end of it and examined the long pink front claws. Finally, he spread out one of the two funny little triangular things that grew from the creature's shoulders. "Bless my soul!" he said again. "It really is a griffin. These are its wings. Look."

They did not look much like wings to Cat.

They had no feathers and were covered with the same pale fluff as the rest of it, but he supposed that Chrestomanci knew. "What do they eat?" he asked.

"Blowed if I know," Chrestomanci said, and looked at Jason, who said, "Me neither."

As if it had understood, the baby griffin promptly discovered that it was starving. Its beak opened like a fledgling bird's, all pink and orange inside. "*Weep!*" it said. "Weep, weep, weep, weep! *Weep. WEEP, WEEP, WEEP!*" It struggled about in Cat's arms so painfully that he was forced to put it down on the hearth rug, where it lay spread-eagled and weeping miserably. Mopsa rushed up to it and began washing it. The baby griffin seemed to like that. It hunched itself toward Mopsa, but it did not stop its shrill, miserable "Weep, weep, weep!"

Millie stood up and did some quick conjuring. When she kneeled down again, she was holding a jug of warm milk and a large medicine dropper. "Here," she said. "Most babies like milk, in my experience." She filled the dropper with milk and gently squirted some into the corner of the gaping beak.

The baby griffin choked and most of the milk came out on to the hearth rug. Cat did not think it liked milk. But when he said so, Millie said, "Yes, but it's got to have *something*, or it'll die. Let's get some milk into it for now—it can't do any *harm*—and in the morning we'll rush it down to the vet—Mr. Vastion—and see what he can suggest."

"Weep, weep, weep," went the griffin, and choked again when Millie squeezed some more milk into it.

There followed three hours of hard work, during which they all five tried to feed the baby griffin and only partly succeeded. Irene was best at it. As Jason said, Irene had a knack with animals. Cat was next best, but he thought that by the time his turn came, the baby griffin had gotten the hang of being fed from a dropper. Cat got most of a jugful into it, but that seemed to do very little good. He had barely laid it down looking contented, when it raised its beak and went

"Weep, weep, weep!" again. And it was the same for the other four. Eventually, Cat was so exhausted that he only stayed awake because he was so desperately sorry for the baby griffin. It needed a parent.

Chrestomanci yawned until his jaw gave out a sort of *clop*. "Cat, if you don't mind my asking, how did you come by this insatiable beast?"

"It hatched," Cat explained, "from the egg in Jason's attic. A girl called Marianne Pinhoe said I could have it. The house belonged to her father."

"Ah," Chrestomanci said. "Pinhoe. Hmm."

"It was under a stasis spell," Millie said. "It must have been in that house for years."

"But Cat somehow succeeded in hatching it. I see," Chrestomanci said, sighing. It was his turn to feed the baby griffin. He sat on the hearth rug, a very strange sight in a frilly apron that Millie had conjured for him, over his dark crimson velvet evening dress, and aimed the dropper at the griffin's open beak. The griffin choked again and most of the milk dribbled out.

Diana Wynne Jones

Chrestomanci looked resigned. "I think," he said, "that the only way to deal with this poor creature is to cast a four-hour sleep spell over it and get it to the vet as soon as it wakes up."

Everyone wearily agreed. "I'll conjure a dog basket for it," Millie said.

"No," Cat said. "I'll have it in bed with me. It needs a parent."

He set off back to his room with the sleep-bespelled griffin draped on his arms. Millie went with him to make sure they got there safely, and Mopsa followed them. Mopsa seemed to have decided to be the griffin's mother. No bad thing, as Millie said. Cat fell asleep with the baby griffin snuggled against him, snoring slightly, and Mopsa snuggled against the griffin. Between them, they had nearly pushed Cat out of the bed by the morning.

He woke to find that the griffin had wet his bed. That was scarcely surprising after all that milk, Cat supposed. And here the poor thing was, going "Weep, weep" again.

Millie arrived on the third "Weep!" as anxious

as Cat was. "At least it's still alive, poor little soul," she said. "I've telephoned Mr. Vastion, and he says he can only see it this morning if we bring it down to his surgery now. He's got to go and see to a very sick cow after that. You get dressed, Cat, and I'll see if it will drink some more milk."

Cat climbed over the griffin and Mopsa and got out of his somewhat smelly pajamas, while Millie once more aimed the dropper at the griffin's desperate beak. It spat the milk out. "Oh, well," Millie said. "They're going to have to change your bedding anyway. I've told Miss Bessemer. It's lucky I thought to bring it a clean blanket. Are you ready yet?"

Cat was just tying his boots. He had dressed all anyhow, in his old suit trousers and the red sweater he wore to ride in. Millie had done much the same. She was in a threadbare tweed skirt and an expensive lace blouse, and too worried about the griffin to notice. She spread out the fluffy white blanket she had brought and Cat tenderly lifted the griffin onto it. It was shivering. And it continued shivering even when it was wrapped in the blanket.

They left Mopsa finishing the milk Millie had brought and hurried down to the main door of the Castle. Millie had not bothered to wake the Castle chauffeur. She had brought the long black car round to the front of the Castle before she came to wake Cat. The griffin was still shivering when Cat got into the passenger seat with it, and it went on shivering while Millie drove the short distance down into Helm St. Mary and along to the vet's surgery on the outskirts of the village.

Cat liked Mr. Vastion at once. He wore glasses like little half-moons well down on his nose and looked humorously at Cat and Millie over them. "Now what have we here?" he said. His voice was a gloomy kind of moan, with a bit of a grunt to it. "Bring it in, bring it in," he told them, waving them through to his consulting room, "and put it down here," he said, pointing with a thick finger at a high, shiny examining table. When Cat carefully dumped the bundle of blanket on the table, Mr. Vastion unwrapped it in a resigned way, moaning, "What a parcel. Is this necessary? What have we in here?"

To Cat's surprise, the griffin seemed to like Mr. Vastion too. It stopped shivering and looked up at him with its great golden eyes. "Weep?"

"And *weep* to you too," Mr. Vastion grunted back at it, unwrapping. "You shouldn't coddle them, you know. Not good for any animal. Now— Oh, yes. You have a fine boy griffin here. Small still, but they grow quite quickly, you know. Does he have a name yet?"

"I don't think so," Cat said.

"Quite right," Mr. Vastion moaned. "They always name themselves. Fact. I read up about griffins before you got here. Just in case this wasn't a complete hoax. Very rare things in this world, griffins. First one I've ever seen, actually. Just a moment."

He paused, holding the griffin down with one expertly spread hand, while, with the other hand, he picked up a frog that had somehow appeared on the table and threw it out of the window.

"Damn nuisance, these frogs," he moaned, while he turned the griffin this way and that, feeling its stomach and its ribs and its legs and examining both sets of claws. "They've got a plague of frogs here," he explained. "Came to me and asked me to get rid of them. I asked them what I was supposed to do—poison the duck pond? Told them to get rid of the things themselves. They're Farleighs. Should know how. But there's no doubt too many frogs are a pest. They get in everywhere. And they strike me as half unreal anyway. Some magician's idea of a joke, I'd say." He held the griffin's beak open and looked down its throat. "Fine voice in there, by the look of it. Now let's have you over, old son."

Mr. Vastion set the griffin on its feet and unfolded the little triangular stubs of its wings. He felt round the bottom of them. "Plenty of good flight muscles here," he grunted. "Just need a bit of growing and fledging. The feathers will come, along with the proper coat at the back end. You'll find this fluff will drop out as he grows. Just what were you worrying about?"

"We don't know what to give him to eat," Cat explained. "He doesn't like milk."

"Well, he wouldn't, would he?" Mr. Vastion moaned. "The front half of him's bird. Look."

He turned the griffin deftly over on its side, where it lay peacefully. Cat could see that it liked this firm handling. Mr. Vastion slid his hand over the creature's beak, and then upward, so that its small tufty ears were flattened.

"Now you've got the contours," he grunted. "Reminds me of nothing so much as an osprey. Or a sea eagle, even more. Magnificent birds. Huge wingspan. Take that as your guide, but chop the food up small or he'll choke. Sea eagles do take fish, but they take rabbits even more. Easier to catch. I expect this fellow will be quite happy with minced beef. But he'll want raw veg etables chopped into it too, to keep him healthy. I'd better show you. Hold him for me a minute, Lady Chant."

Millie put both hands on the peacefully lying griffin. "He's so thin and weak!"

Mr. Vastion gave out a long moan. "Of *course* he is. Just hatched. All newborn creatures are like this. Skinny. Feeble. Bags under their eyes. Excuse me a moment. I'll get him some puppy food." He left the room in the sort of shuffling plod that seemed to be his way of walking.

Another frog landed on the table while they waited. Cat picked it up and, like Mr. Vastion had done, threw it out of the window. A flopping feeling on his feet showed him two more frogs that had somehow landed on his boots. In the dim light down there, parts of them glowed transparent green, with touches of red. Cat saw Mr. Vastion had been quite right. These frogs were only partly real. He bent down and collected both frogs in his left hand, just as Mr. Vastion shuffled back into the room. The baby griffin leaped up from under Millie's hands with its beak wide open, going, "Weep, weep, weep!" in such excitement that it seemed about to leap right off the table. Cat quickly sent all the frogs back to where they came from and dived to catch the griffin.

"That's right," Mr. Vastion grunted. He was holding a large handful of raw mince mixed with shredded carrot. They watched him put the meat into his bunched-up fingers, so that his hand was roughly beak shaped. "Like this, see," he moaned, and popped the handful expertly down the griffin's throat. "Think you can do that?"

The griffin swallowed, clapped its beak, and looked soulfully up at Mr. Vastion. "Weep?"

"In a bit, fellow. Lady Chant will take you home and give you a square meal there," Mr. Vastion moaned. "Bring him back again if you're worried. That will be ten and sixpence, Lady Chant."

They got back into the car again, Cat carrying the griffin without the blanket. Millie tossed the blanket into the backseat, saying, "I think we were worrying too much, Cat. Raw meat! Thank goodness he told us!" She drove off, around the village green and up the long driveway to the Castle, where she did not stop at the main door; she drove on around to the kitchen door and stopped outside that.

Cat was surprised at how many people were crowded into the kitchen to meet them. Mr. Frazier, the butler, opened the kitchen door to them. Mr. Stubbs, the head cook, met them as they came in, surrounded by his apprentices, and asked anxiously just what it was that griffins ate.

"Raw mince," Millie said, "with grated carrots—and chopped parsley, I think, for clean breath."

"I rather thought that might be it," Mr. Stubbs said. "Eddie, fetch out that minced rabbit. Joan and Laurie, grate us some carrots, and Jimmy, you chop parsley. And you'll be wanting breakfast yourselves while you feed him, I guess. Bert, coffee, toast."

Miss Bessemer the housekeeper was there too, hurrying to spread newspaper on a table for Cat to put the griffin down on. "A basket in your room?" she asked Cat. "I've found you a nice roomy one. And we'll bespell the lining until he's house-trained, dear, if you don't mind."

As the mince arrived, the baby griffin stood

up on wobbly legs, whirling its stringlike tail and going "Weep!" again. A crowd surrounded the table to watch. Cat saw Joe the boot boy, Mary, Euphemia and two other maids, several footmen, all the kitchen staff, Mr. Frazier, Miss Bessemer, nearly all the Castle wizards, Roger, Janet, Julia, Irene, Jason, and Mopsa, looking possessive. He even caught a glimpse of Chrestomanci, in a purple dressing gown, at the back of the crowd, watching over people's heads.

"We don't get a griffin every day," Millie said. "You feed him, love. He came to you, after all."

Cat took up a fistful of meat, made his fingers into a beak, and posted the lump down the griffin's expectant throat. "Oh, bless!" someone murmured as the griffin swallowed, looked pleased, and looked up for more. "Weep?" That plateful went in no time. Cat had only time to snatch a piece of toast before there was a further, louder "Weep, *weep*!" and Mr. Stubbs had to fetch more meat. The baby griffin ate all the rabbit there was, followed by a pound of minced steak, and then went "Weep!" for more. Mr.

Stubbs produced smoked salmon. It ate that. By this time its scrawny stomach was round, and tight as a drum.

"I think that will do," Millie said. "We don't want him ill. But he obviously needs a lot."

"I sent an order down to the butcher, ma'am," Mr. Stubbs said. "I can see it's going to be quantities. Every four hours, if you ask me, if he's anything like a human baby."

"Oh, help!" Cat said. "Really?"

"Pretty certainly," Mr. Frazier said, suddenly revealing himself as a bird fancier. "Your fledgling bird eats its own weight in food daily, and often more. Better weigh it, Mr. Stubbs. You may need to increase your order."

So the kitchen scales were fetched and the griffin was discovered to weigh over a stone already, sixteen pounds, in fact. It objected to being weighed. It wanted to go to sleep, preferably in Cat's arms. While Cat carried it away upstairs, with its beak contentedly resting on his shoulder and Mopsa following watchfully, Mr. Stubbs did sums on the back of an old bill. The total came to so much that he sent Joe down to the butcher's to double his first order.

Joe stopped to exchange an urgent look with Roger before he left. "I'll wait," Roger said. "Promise."

"Get *going*, Joe Pinhoe!" Mr. Stubbs said. "You lazy layabout, you!"

Chapter Twelve

Over in Ulverscote there was suddenly a plague of frogs.

Nobody had seen the like before. There were thousands of them, and there was a sort of green-redness to them if you saw them in the shade. They got in everywhere. People trod on them when they got out of bed that morning and found them in the teapot when they tried to make tea. About the only inhabitant of the village who enjoyed the plague was Nutcase. He chased frogs all over Furze Cottage. His favorite place to hunt them into was Marianne's bedroom. Then he killed them on Marianne's bedside rug.

Marianne picked up the strange, small black

remains. The frogs seemed to shrink when they were dead and die away into something dark and dry with holes in. Not real, she thought. There was a smell coming off them that she knew. Where had she smelled that particular odor before? She knew Joe had been there when she smelled it. Was it when they stole the stuffed ferret? No. It was before that. It was when Gammer had sent that blast of magic at the Farleighs.

That's it, Marianne thought. These are Gammer's.

She went downstairs and put the dry remains into the waste pail. "I'm going round to see Gammer," she told Mum.

"Does she want you *again*?" Mum said. "Don't be too long. I'm still finding jars with mildew in them. We're going to have to scald the lot out."

Though the wave of bad luck had stopped as suddenly as it had begun, the effects of it were still there, in the mildew, in half-healed cuts, sprained ankles, and—this seemed to be the final thing the spell had done—an outbreak of whooping cough among the smaller children. Dismal coughing came from most of the houses Marianne passed on her way to the Dell. But the right kind of red bricks were just now being delivered at the Post Office as she went by.

Aunt Joy was standing on her lawn above the broken wall, watching the delivery. "I may have my bricks," she grumbled to Marianne, "but that's as far as it goes. Your uncle Simeon's too busy doing the renovations at Woods House, hobbling around with a stick, if you please! All for that new woman who says she's a Pinhoe. If he can do it on one leg for *her*, why not for *me*? As if my money wasn't as good as hers!"

There was a lot more on these lines, but Marianne only smiled at Aunt Joy and went on. As Dad often said, if you stayed to listen to Aunt Joy, you'd be there a week and she still wouldn't have finished grumbling.

There were frogs in the lane all the way to the Dell, and the pond in front of the cottage was a seething, hopping mass of them. The ducks had given up trying to swim and were sitting grumpily on the grass.

"I don't know what we've done to deserve this," Aunt Dinah said, opening the door for Marianne. "Anyone would think we'd offended Moses or something! Go on in. She's been asking for you."

Marianne marched into Gammer's crowded living room. "Gammer," she said.

Gammer's ruined face turned up to her. "I'm not in my right mind," Gammer said quickly.

"Then you shouldn't do magic," Marianne retorted. "There's frogs all over the village."

Gammer shook her head as if she were saddened by the way people behaved. "What's this world becoming into? Those shouldn't be there."

"Where should they be, then?" Marianne challenged her.

Gammer shook her head again. "No need to take on. Little girls shouldn't worry their heads over such things."

"*Where?*" Marianne said.

Gammer bent her face down and pleated her freshly starched skirt.

"*Where?*" Marianne insisted. "You sent those frogs somewhere, didn't you?"

Very reluctantly, Gammer muttered, "Jed Farleigh should have left me alone."

"Helm St. Mary?" Marianne said.

Gammer nodded. "And all over. There's Farleighs in all the villages over there. I forget the names of those places. I don't remember so well these days, Marianne. You have to understand."

"I do," said Marianne. "You sent frogs to Helm St. Mary, right outside Chrestomanci Castle, so that they were almost bound to notice, and you made the Farleighs so angry that they ill-wished us and sent the frogs right back. Aren't you ashamed, Gammer?"

"That's Jed Farleigh all over," Gammer said. "Hides out over there, thinks he's safe from me. And they're spying on me all the time, spying and lurking. It wasn't me, Marianne. It was Edgar and Lester. I didn't tell them to do it."

"You know perfectly well that Edgar and Lester would *never* send anyone frogs!" Marianne said. "I'm disgusted with you, Gammer!"

"I have to defend myself!" Gammer protested.

"No, you don't, not like *this*!" Marianne said, and stormed out among the frogs, down the lane and past the stack of new bricks. Feeling angrier and braver than she had ever been in her life, she stormed on down Furze Lane and into the shed behind Furze Cottage. There, Dad and Uncle Richard were trying to saw wood without cutting frogs in half. "Gammer did these frogs," she told them.

"Oh, come now, Marianne," Dad said. "Gammer wouldn't do a thing like that!"

"Yes, she would. She *did*!" Marianne said. "She sent them to Helm St. Mary, but the Farleighs sent them back here and did an ill-wishing on us because Gammer made them so angry. Dad, I think we're in the middle of a war with the Farleighs without knowing we are."

Dad laughed. "The Farleighs are not that

uncivilized, Marianne. These frogs are just someone's idea of a joke—you can see they're creatures bewitched from the way they glow. Run along and don't worry your head about them."

Whatever Marianne said after that, Dad simply laughed and refused to believe her. She went indoors and tried to tell Mum.

"Oh, *really*, Marianne!" Mum said, holding a kettle with a cloth round the handle, amid clouds of steam. "I grant you Gammer's mad as a coot these days, but the Farleighs are sane people. We *cooperate* with them around the countryside. Just get your hair tied up and give me a hand here and *forget* about the beastly frogs!"

Marianne spent the rest of the day boiling kettles in a sort of angry loneliness. She did not trust Gammer simply to stop at frogs. She knew she had to get someone to believe her before the Farleighs got so angry that they did something terrible, but Dad and Mum seemed to have closed their minds. Some of the time, she was tempted just to keep quiet about Gammer and let bad things happen. But she had started being brave now, and she felt she had to go on. She wondered who else might believe her. Someone who might stop Gammer and explain to the Farleighs. Apart from Uncle Charles, she could think of no one, and Uncle Charles was working up at Woods House with Uncle Simeon. I'll talk to him when he gets off work, she decided. Because I think it really is urgent.

By that afternoon, the frogs had become such a nuisance that Uncle Richard took action. He harnessed Dolly the donkey to the cart and filled the cart with bins and sacks. Then he called in all Marianne's cousins, all ten of them, and the troop of them went round the houses collecting frogs. They were handed frogs by squirming fistfuls everywhere. For those people who were too old or too busy with the whooping cough to collect frogs for themselves, the boys went in and tipped frogs out of tea caddies and scooped frogs out of cupboards, shoes, and toilets, while the rest hunted frogs in the gardens. They came joyfully out again with squirming, croaking sacks and dumped them in the cart. Then they went on to the next house. They caught two hundred frogs in the vicarage and twice that number in the church. The only place with more frogs was the Dell.

"Stands to reason," Uncle Richard said, refusing to believe a word against Gammer. "There's a pond at the Dell."

When, finally, the cart was piled high with bulging sacks and croaking bins and there was hardly a loose frog to be seen, they took Dolly down Furze Lane to the river and tipped all the frogs in. Uncle Richard scratched his head over what happened then. Every frog, as it hit the running water, seemed to dissolve away to nothing. The cousins could not get over it.

"Well, they say running water kills the craft," Uncle Richard told Mum and Marianne, when he came to Furze Cottage for a cup of tea after his labors, "but I'd never believed it until now. Melted away into black like foam, they did. Astonishing."

Here, Marianne looked round and noticed that Nutcase was missing again. "Oh, *bother* him!" she wailed, and hurried to the table to set the knife spinning. It was still whirling round and round when there was a knock at the front door.

"See who that is, Marianne!" Mum called out, busy pouring hot water on the tea.

Marianne opened the door. And stared. A very tall, thin woman stood there, carrying a basket. She had straight hair and a flat chest and she wore the drabbest and most dust-colored dress Marianne had ever seen. Her face was long and severe. She gazed at Marianne, and Marianne was reminded of a teacher about to find fault.

Before Marianne could ask what this stranger wanted, the woman said, "Jane James. From Woods House. Wrong way to make your acquaintance, I know, but did you know your cat walks through walls? He was in my kitchen eating the fish for Mr. Adams's supper. Doors all shut. Only explanation. Don't know how you'll keep him in."

"I don't either," Marianne said. She looked up at the grim face and found it was full of hidden humor. Jane James evidently found the situation highly amusing. "I'm sorry," she said. "I'll come and fetch him back at once."

"No need," said Jane James. She opened the basket she was carrying and turned Nutcase out of it like a pudding onto the doormat. "Pleased to meet you," she said, and went away.

"Well I'll be—!" Uncle Richard said, as Marianne shut the front door. "Quite a touch of the craft in that woman, if you ask me!"

"And no *wonder* we can't keep that cat in!" Mum said, putting the teapot on the table.

Nutcase sat on the doormat and glowered at Marianne. Marianne glowered back. They can believe Jane James that Nutcase walks through walls, but they can't believe *me* about Gammer, she thought. "You," she said to Nutcase, "you're as bad as Gammer! And I can't say worse than that!"

Meanwhile, back at the Castle, Cat was trying to get used to the way he had to feed a baby griffin every four hours—at least, it was usually only about three and half hours before the griffin woke, with its stomach all flat and thin again, and went "Weep, weep, weep!" for more food. He was carrying it to the kitchen yet again—and it felt a good deal heavier than it was when it first hatched—when Julia stopped him on the stairs.

"Can I help you feed him?" she asked. "He's just so sweet! Janet wants to help too."

Cat realized that this was exactly what he needed. He said quickly, "We can have a feeding rota, then. You can feed him in the day, but I'll have to look after him at night."

In fact, as he soon discovered, a surprising number of people wanted to help feed the griffin. Miss Bessemer wanted to, and so did Mr. Stubbs and Euphemia. Millie wanted to, having, as she said, a personal interest in this griffin. And Irene, when she was not over in Ulverscote seeing to the alterations to her new house, begged to have a turn as well.

At first Cat found himself sitting over the person feeding the griffin as possessively as Mopsa did. He knew it was happier when he was beside it. But when the griffin seemed perfectly used to somebody else putting lumps of meat into its beak, Cat—rather guiltily—sighed with relief and went off to ride Syracuse. Before long, he only had to feed the griffin during the nights.

He went up to his room every night carrying two large covered bowls of meat, each with a stasis spell on it to keep it fresh. By the third night he was—well, *almost*—used to being woken at midnight and again at four in the morning by the griffin's "Weep, weep, weep!" If this did not wake Cat, then Mopsa did, pushing her cold nose urgently into Cat's face and treading heavily on his stomach.

What he never seemed to get used to was how sleepy he was during the day.

On the third night, Mopsa as usual woke him at midnight. "All right. I know, I *know*!" Cat said, rolling out from under Mopsa's nose and feet. "I'm coming." He sat up and switched on the light.

To his surprise, the griffin was still heavily asleep, curled in its basket with its yellow beak propped on the edge, making small whistling snores. But there was something tapping on his big window. It was exactly like that strange dream he had had. I think I know what that is! Cat thought. He got out of bed and opened the window.

An upside-down face stared at him, but it was human.

Cat stared back, finding this hard to believe.

"Can you give us a bit of help?" the face asked, rather desperately. "It's raining."

Because it was upside down, it took Cat a moment or so to recognize that the face belonged to Joe the boot boy. "How did you get *there*?" he said.

"We made this flying machine," Joe explained, "but we didn't get it right. It crashed on your roof. Roger's up here too, wedged like."

Oh, my lord! Cat thought. *That's* what they've been up to in that shed! "All right," he said. "I'd better bring you in here. Let yourself go loose."

By using a spur-of-the-minute mixture of conjuring and levitation, Cat managed to pull Joe off the roof and bend him around through the window and into his room. Unfortunately, this seemed to dislodge the crashed flying machine. As Joe flopped heavily onto Cat's carpet, there was a set of long sliding sounds from above, followed by a cry of horror from Roger. Cat was only just in time to catch Roger as he fell past the window and to levitate him inside too.

"Thanks!" Roger gasped.

Both of them stood by the window, panting, pale, and speckled with rain. Instead of doing as Cat would have expected and crawling away to bed, the two of them went into an anxious conference. Joe said, "Where do you reckon we went wrong, then? Think it was the rain?"

Roger answered, "No. I think we got the wiring wrong on the stuffed eagle."

Joe said, "May have to start again from scratch, then."

"No, no," Roger said. "I'm sure we've got the basics. We just need to refine it some more."

They're mad! Cat thought. He looked past them at the wreckage. It was now hanging down across the window, growing wetter by the second. As far as Cat could see, it was a number of interlocked pieces of tables and chairs, with a three-legged stool in there somewhere, and dangling upside down in the midst of it a forlorn and draggled stuffed golden eagle. The eagle had wires coming out of it, together with a few damp tufts of herbs.

"I belong to Chrestomanci Castle," the eagle remarked sadly. Everything in the Castle was bespelled to say this if it was taken more than a few feet from the castle walls.

"Where did you get the eagle?" Cat asked.

"It was in one of the attics," Roger said. "We have to insulate the dandelion seeds, for a start."

"We might try using willow herb instead," Joe replied.

The griffin woke up. Instead of screaming for food, it sat up and stared at the two wet boys and the dangling wreckage with interest. Mopsa sat on Cat's bed and stared, too, disapprovingly.

"You can't leave all that stuff hanging there," Cat said.

"We know," said Roger. "Or we could use both kinds of seeds."

"And gear up the bikes a bit," Joe replied.

"It's a real nuisance," Roger said, "having to do things at night in order not to be found out. Cat, we'll go down into the garden. When we whistle, can you levitate the flying machine down to us? Gently, mind, in order not to break it any more."

"I suppose so," Cat said.

Joe went down on one knee to pet the griffin as if it were a dog. "Aren't you *soft*!" he said to it. "All that fluff. Where have I seen one of you before? It'll come down in bits, you know. Part of it got hooked on your turret."

Cat giggled. If he had been Chrestomanci, he knew he would have said, The *griffin* got hooked on the turret? "All right," he said. "I'll send it up first, to unhook it, before I send it down. You two get down to the garden before someone notices it."

The two aviators hurried off, both limping slightly. The griffin opened its beak.

"All right," Cat said. "Don't say it!"

He had time to feed the griffin a square meal before a soft whistle came from the garden below. Cat put the bowl away and leaned out of the window to levitate the wreckage.

"I belong to Chrestomanci Castle," the stuffed eagle said piteously.

"I know," said Cat. "But this is difficult."

The remains of the flying machine were wedged onto the turret. Cat had to spread the various bits of it apart and send them downward piece by piece. He had no idea what most of the bits were. He simply floated them away from his roof and down to the ground. Another soft whistle and a faint chorus of voices singing "I belong to Chrestomanci Castle!" told him when all the parts had landed safely under the cedar trees. Wooden clatterings and the occasional soft *clang* showed that the two aviators were now hauling the stuff away, protesting that it belonged to the Castle.

"They're *mad*!" Cat told Mopsa and the griffin. "Quite mad." He went back to bed.

The griffin did not wake him again that night. In the morning, it climbed out of its basket and woke Cat by nudging him with its beak. Cat opened his eyes to find two yellow griffin eyes staring into his, interested and friendly. "Oh, I do like you!" Cat said, before he had had time to think. Then he felt guilty, because Syracuse was bound to be jealous.

Still, there was nothing to be done about Syracuse just then. Cat got dressed, while the griffin staggered around the room investigating everything Cat owned. There was no doubt that it had grown again in the night. The dark beginnings of feathers were showing on its neck and on its absurd, stubby wings.

"Isn't it growing too quickly?" Cat asked Millie anxiously, when he had gotten it down to the kitchen. The griffin was now far too heavy for Cat to carry. The two of them came downstairs in a mixture of staggering and levitating— and some flopping—and the griffin looked very pleased with himself for getting there.

Millie pursed up her mouth and studied the griffin. "You have to remember," she said, "that griffins are strongly magical creatures, and this one must have spent years inside that stasis spell in the egg. I think it's making up for lost time. I wonder how big it's going to be."

Only about the size of Syracuse, Cat hoped. Any bigger would be really awkward. He was about to say so, when Millie added, "Cat, I'm worried about Roger. He seems so tired today."

"Um," Cat said. "He could have been up all night reading."

"He must have been," Millie agreed. "He had six books by his bed when I went in, all from other worlds. They were all about flying. I do hope he's not going to do anything silly."

"He won't," Cat said, because he knew Roger already had.

He left Millie shoving mince into the griffin and went to muck out Syracuse, soon done by enchanter's methods. While Cat was grooming Syracuse, wishing that there was some magical method to do this too, Joss Callow came in.

"It's my day off today," Joss said. "If you want a ride, you'd better make it now before break-fast."

"Yes, please," Cat said.

He had Syracuse out in the yard and saddled up, and Syracuse was bouncing, tugging, and dancing as usual, too glad to be ridden to let Cat get up and ride him, when Syracuse abruptly stopped dead and flung his head up. Cat looked round to see the griffin staggering enthusiasti-cally toward them. Cat could only stare at it. He could not think what to do.

Syracuse stared, too, down his upheld nose. It was hard to blame him. The griffin was such a plump, scrawny, unfinished-looking creature. It still had not gotten the hang of walking. It rolled from side to side, scratching the stones of the yard with its long pink claws, and whirling its stringy tail behind it. Cat could see it was terri-bly proud at having found him.

"It's only a baby," he said pleadingly to Syracuse.

As the griffin staggered near, Syracuse swayed backward on all four feet, snorting. The griffin stopped. It stared upward at Syracuse. Its beak fell open with what seemed to be admiration. It made a whirring noise and stretched its face up. And Syracuse, to Cat's relief and astonishment, lowered his own shapely head and nosed the griffin's beak. At this, the griffin's little wings worked with excitement. It cooed, and Cat could have sworn that a grin grew at the sides of its beak. But he had to stop it when it put out a clumsy front paw that was obviously meant to be friendly but threatened to scratch Syracuse's nose.

"That'll do. So you like one another. That's good," Cat said. "How did you get out here anyway?"

Millie came dashing across the yard. "Oh, I only turned my back for a minute when Miss Bessemer came to ask about towels! And off he went. Come on, come back with Millie, little griffin. Oh, I wish he had a name, Cat!"

"Klartch," said the griffin.

"*That's* a new noise," said Millie. "Whatever it means, you've got to come in, griffin."

"No—wait," Cat said. "I think it's his name. *Is* your name Klartch, griffin?"

The griffin turned its face up to him. It was definitely smiling. "Klartch," it said happily.

"Mr. Vastion *said* they named themselves," Millie said, "but I didn't realize that meant they *talked*. Well, Klartch, that goes two ways. If you can talk, you can understand too. Come indoors with me at *once* and finish your breakfast. Now."

The griffin made a small noise like "Yup" and followed Millie obediently back to the kitchen. Well, well! Cat thought.

Joss, who had been standing looking utterly dumbfounded, said, "That creature—where did it come from?"

"A girl called Marianne gave me his egg," Cat said.

"*Marianne* did?" Joss said. "Marianne *Pinhoe*?" Cat nodded. Joss said dubiously, "Well, I suppose in a way she had a right to. But you'd better not let Mr. Farleigh get a sight of the thing. He'd go spare."

Cat could not really see why the sight of a baby griffin should annoy Mr. Farleigh, but he was sure Joss knew. *Everything* seemed to annoy Mr. Farleigh anyway.

Chapter Thirteen

Marianne did catch Uncle Charles on his way home from Woods House, but he refused to believe that Gammer could do any wrong. He laughed and said, "You have to be older to understand, my chuck. None of us Pinhoes would do a thing like that. We *work* with the Farleighs."

Though this seemed to show that no one was going to believe her, Marianne went on trying to make *someone* understand about Gammer. Almost everyone she spoke to over the next few days said, "Gammer wouldn't do a thing like that!" and refused to talk about it anymore. Uncle Arthur gave Marianne a pat on the head and a bag of scrittlings for Nutcase. "She was a good mother to me and a good Gammer to all of us," he said. "You never knew her in her prime."

Marianne wondered about this. She supposed that a mother with seven sons had to be a good one, but she went and asked Mum about it all the same.

"Good mother!" Mum said. "What gave you that idea? When I was your age, my mother and her friends were always looking out cast-off clothes for your dad and his brothers, or they'd have been running round in rags. She said those boys were too scared of Gammer to tell her when they'd grown out of their things."

"But didn't Gammer notice their clothes?" Marianne said.

"Not that I ever saw," Mum said. "She left the younger ones to Dad to look after."

But Mum had never liked Gammer, Marianne thought, trying to be fair. Uncle Arthur truly believed what he had said. In many ways Uncle Arthur was very like Dad, though, always believing the best of everyone. Mum snorted whenever Dad said kind and respectful things about Gammer, and called it "rewriting history." So where did the real truth lie? Somewhere in the middle? Marianne sighed. The facts seemed to be that no one, even Mum, was going to believe that Gammer had sent the Farleighs a plague of frogs or—Marianne stopped on her way upstairs to go on with her story of Princess Irene.

Oh, heavens! she thought. Suppose it wasn't *only* frogs!

She turned and went downstairs again. "Just going down to the Dell!" she called to Mum, and went straight there to talk to Aunt Dinah.

As she passed the Post Office, she was glad to see that some of Uncle Simeon's people were now working on the ruined wall. They were working in that deceptively slow way that witchcraftly workmen did such things, and the wall was nearly waist high already. That must mean that the alterations up at Woods House were almost finished, with the same deceptive, witchcraftly speed.

And here was an example of the way no one would believe any ill of Gammer, Marianne thought. Gammer had broken that Post Office wall. But everyone was treating it as an accident, or an act of God.

She had half a mind to go into the Post Office. Aunt Joy would believe her. But Aunt Joy always believed the worst of everyone. And, more importantly, no one believed Aunt Joy. Marianne went on down the lane toward the Dell. There were still a few of the charmed frogs jumping about in the hedges there. It had been impossible to catch every single one.

Aunt Dinah had surprise all over her square blond face, when Marianne said she wanted to talk to *her* and not Gammer. But she led the way into her little, dark kitchen, where there were fresh-cooked queen cakes on wire trays all over the table. Aunt Dinah pushed them aside, telling Marianne to eat as many as she wanted, and made them both a cup of coffee. "Now, dear. What is it?"

Marianne had decided to approach this very

carefully. Sniffing the lovely smell of new cake, she said, "Does Gammer do any magic at all these days?"

Aunt Dinah looked perplexed, and a little worried. "Why do you want to know, dear?"

"Well," Marianne said. "It looks as if I might have to be the next Gammer, doesn't it? And I don't really know enough." This was perfectly true, but the next bit wasn't. She said, in a bit of a rush, "I wondered if she was up to giving me some lessons, seeing her mind isn't quite right these days. Does she do any workings? Does she get them wrong at all?"

"You have a point," Aunt Dinah agreed. "But I don't see how she *can*, dear. You'd be better off asking your dad to teach you. Gammer just sits these days. Of course she mutters a bit."

"Don't tell me," Marianne said artificially, "that she's still going on about the Farleighs!"

"Well, you've heard her," said Aunt Dinah. "I admit she can sound quite abusive at times, but it doesn't mean a thing, bless her!"

"Does she do anything else at all?" Marianne

asked, trying to sound disappointed.

Aunt Dinah smiled and shook her head. "Nothing. She just sits and plays with things like a child. The other day she'd got hold of a rose hip and a bit of sneezewort, and she was taking them apart and twiddling them for hours." (Oh dear! That's itches and rashes and colds in the head! Marianne thought.) "Lately," Aunt Dinah said, "she's been asking for water all the time. I've watched her pour it from one glass to another and smile—" (What's *that* for? Marianne wondered. It *has* to be another spell, if she smiled!) "And she mixed soot with some of it," Aunt Dinah went on, "and made it so dirty I had to take it away from her." (So some of it's a filth spell, Marianne thought.) "Oh, and the other day," Aunt Dinah admitted, lowering her voice because this was disgraceful, "she caught a *flea*. I was *so* ashamed. I don't mind her catching ants, the way she does, but a *flea!* I try to keep her clean as clean, but there she was, holding it and saying, 'Look, Dinah, here's a flea!' I offered to kill it for her, but she did it herself."

So now she's done a plague of ants and a plague of fleas! Marianne thought. Right under Aunt Dinah's nose, too! Those poor Farleighs! No wonder they ill-chanced us! Nerving herself up to say such a thing to a grown-up aunt, Marianne asked, "But don't all those things seem to be spells of some kind, Aunt Dinah?" Particularly the water, Marianne thought. If she's poisoned their water, that's wicked!

"Oh, no, dear," Aunt Dinah said kindly. "She's just amusing herself, bless her. She's left the craft behind her now."

Marianne drew in a deep, cake-scented breath and said boldly, "I don't think she has."

Aunt Dinah laughed. "And I know she has. Don't worry your head, Marianne, and get your dad to teach you. You can trust Isaac and I to look after Gammer for you."

So here was another person who would only believe the best of Gammer, Marianne thought sadly as she got up to go. It was almost as if they were under a spell. "I'll let myself out. Thanks for the coffee," she told Aunt Dinah.

She strode straight through the hall and ignored Gammer's voice, raised from behind the door of the front room. "Is that you, Marianne?" Gammer always seemed to know when Marianne was in the Dell.

"No, it *isn't!*" she muttered with her teeth clenched.

As she marched off down the lane between the rustling, croaking hedges, Marianne considered Gammer's spells and wished she knew how to cancel them. They would be strong. If she had any doubts about *how* strong, she only had to remember the blast of magic Gammer had sent at the Farleighs. That wasn't just a plain blast, either. It was meant to send the Farleighs away, certainly, but it was also intended to make them believe that Gammer was upright and innocent and in her right mind. Gammer was an expert at interwoven spells.

"Oh!" Marianne said out loud, and almost stopped walking.

Of *course* Gammer had laid a spell on everyone. She didn't want anyone to stop her getting her revenge on the Farleighs and she didn't want to be blamed when the Farleighs fought back. So she had bespelled every single Pinhoe in the village to think only the best of her. The thing that had confused Marianne was the way she herself seemed to be immune to the spell.

Or not quite immune. Marianne walked slowly on, remembering the day they had moved Gammer out of Woods House. It had been perfectly reasonable to her then—if annoying—that Gammer should have rooted herself to her bed, and not at all unreasonable that Gammer should have chased Dolly with the kitchen table and knocked the Post Office wall down. Now she looked back on it, she saw that it was *dreadful* behavior. Gammer must have been pouring on the ensorcellment that day.

But she had probably started setting the spell before that, probably while she was poltergeisting those poor nurses. None of the aunts and uncles had blamed Gammer for that—but then they almost never did blame Gammer for anything she did—

Marianne's eyes went wide as she realized
that Gammer might have been setting this spell
all of Marianne's own life. No one *ever* blamed
Gammer. She had only to look at the Farleighs
to realize how unlikely that was. The Farleighs
certainly obeyed old Mr. Farleigh, because he
was their Gaffer, but they grumbled that he
was set in his ways and very few of them *liked*
him. But the Pinhoes treated Gammer as if she
was something natural and precious, like rain
in April that was good for the crops—and
people grumbled about rain, but never about
Gammer.

It puzzled Marianne why she herself seemed
to be mostly immune to Gammer's spell. She
thought it must be that Mum was always saying
sour things about Gammer—even though Mum
was not immune to the spell herself. Mum was
not going to help Marianne deal with Gammer.
Marianne wondered, rather desperately, if anyone could. Then it occurred to her that the spell
almost certainly only applied to people who
actually lived in Ulverscote. There were Pinhoes

who lived in other places, outside the village. Who could she ask?

The nearest and most obvious person was Great-Uncle Edgar. He and his wife, Great-Aunt Sue, lived a couple of miles out, along the Helm St. Mary road. It was no good expecting Great-Uncle Edgar to believe anything bad about Gammer. He was her brother, after all. But, when she thought about it, Marianne had hopes of Great-Aunt Sue. Aunt Sue had come from a wealthy family on the other side of Hopton, according to Mum, and might be expected to take a more outside view of things— and she surely couldn't see Gammer as blameless after nearly getting squashed to death between Gammer's bed and the doorpost. Mum had been taking Aunt Sue jars of her special balm for her bruises ever since.

"Shall I take Aunt Sue another jar of your balm?" Marianne asked Mum as soon as she got back to Furze Cottage.

"Oh, *would* you!" Mum said. "I'm so busy making up tinctures to help whooping cough, you wouldn't believe! They say little Nicola's really poorly with it. She could hardly fetch her breath last night, poor little mite!"

Marianne took off her pinafore and went to fetch her bike from the shed. The first thing she saw there was Mum's new broomstick. Marianne eyed it, wondering whether to borrow that instead. The stick was white and fresh and the bristles thick and stiff and pinkish. She could see it would fly splendidly. But Mum might object, and Aunt Sue was more likely to look kindly on Marianne if she arrived on an ordinary bicycle. She sighed and wheeled out her bike instead.

It felt strange to be doing this. Last time Marianne had ridden her bike, she had been on her way to school, with Joe pedaling beside her. Joe always made sure Marianne got safely to the girls' school, although Marianne was not sure that he always went on to the boys' school after that. Joe was not fond of school.

Joe would have believed me about Gammer! Marianne thought. He said worse things about

Gammer than Mum did. And he was surely outside the spell, ten miles away at the Castle. Now
there was a thought! But try Aunt Sue first.

As Mum came to the front door with the jar of
balm, the bicycle obviously put her in mind of
school too. "Remind me to beg us a lift to
Hopton from your uncle Lester," she said, putting the jar of balm into Marianne's bike basket.
"We have to get there for your school uniform
sometime this week. School starts again the
week after this, doesn't it? Goodness *knows* how
I'm to get Joe *his* new uniform, with him away
working. He'll have grown a foot, I know."

This gave Marianne a sad feeling of urgency
as she rode away up the hill. There would be no
time for anything once she went back to school.
She would have to get someone to believe her
about Gammer *soon*, she thought, standing on
her pedals to get up the steep part of the road by
the church.

She saw the Reverend Pinhoe out of the corner of her eye as she puffed upward. He was in
the churchyard by one of the graves, talking to

someone very tall and gentlemanly. A stranger, which was odd. Pinhoes didn't exactly welcome strangers in the village. But Marianne was distracted then, by two furniture vans up ahead of her, each labeled PICKFORD & PALLEBRAS. Each van was pulled by two dray horses, and both drivers were cracking whips and shouting as they made the difficult turn in through the gates of Woods House. It looked as if the Yeldhams were moving in already.

Marianne put one foot on the ground when she came level with the gates—saying to herself it was not curiosity: she had to stop to get her breath—and watched men in green baize aprons spring down and unlatch the backs of the vans. The van she could see into best had some very nice Londonish furniture stacked inside it. She saw chairs with round backs and buttons, covered in moss green velvet, and a sideboard that Dad would have put his head on one side to admire greatly. Good old work—she could almost hear Dad saying it—beautiful marquetry.

She inherited that from Luke Pinhoe, Marianne thought. It somehow brought home to her that Irene really was a Pinhoe. And she's coming back home to live! Marianne thought, getting back on her bike. That's good.

She pedaled past the last few houses and came between the hedges, where the road bent. And there, coming toward her, were six other cyclists, all girls. As soon as they saw Marianne, they stopped and swung their cycles sideways in a herringbone pattern, blocking the road. Marianne recognized the one in front as Margot Farleigh and the next one as Margot's cousin Norma. She didn't know the names of the others, but she knew they were all Farleighs too, and probably best friends with one another because they all had the same hairstyle, very smooth and scraped back, with one little thin dangling plait down one cheek. Oh dear! she thought. She could smell, or feel—or whatever—that each girl had a spell of some kind in the basket on the front of her bike.

"Well, look who's here!" Margot Farleigh

said jeeringly. "It's Gammer Pinhoe's little servant!"

"Off to Helm to put another ill-chancing on us, are you?" Norma asked.

"No, I'm not," Marianne said. "I never put a single ill-chance on anyone."

This caused a chorus of jeering laughs from all six girls. "Oh, didn't you?" Margot said, pretending to be surprised. "My mistake. You didn't bring us frogs, then, or fleas, or nits?"

"Or the rashes, or the flu and the whooping cough, I suppose?" Norma added.

At this, the rest began calling out, "Nor you didn't put ants in our cupboards, did you?" and "What about all the mud in our washing?" and "What made Gammer Norah swell up, then?" and "So you didn't make Dorothea fall in the pond—like hell you didn't!"

Marianne sagged against her bicycle, thinking, Oh lord! Gammer *has* been busy! "No, honestly," she said. "You see, Gammer's not right in her head, and—"

"Oh? Really?" Margot drawled.

"Excuses, excuses," said Norma.

"She's right enough in her head to flood all Farleigh houses knee deep in water!" Margot said. "*All* our houses, from Uphelm to Bowbridge. Not anyone else's, mark you. Our Gammer Norah's in a raving rage about it, let me tell you."

"She's not sent us the stomachache so far," Norma said. "Is that what you're bringing us now?"

Marianne knew they had a right to be angry. She began to say, "Look, I'm sorry—"

That was a mistake. But then anything she said would have been, Marianne knew. Margot said, "*Get* her, everyone!" and all the girls threw down their bicycles and went for Marianne.

She was kicked and punched and had her hair pulled, agonizingly. She tried to defend herself by making a bull-like rush at Margot, and went floundering among bicycles, tripping, crashing and being hit and pinched and scratched by any girl who could lay hands on her. Spell bags fell out of bicycle baskets and got trodden on. The air from hedge to hedge filled with strong white powder. Everyone was sneezing in it, but too angry to notice. Marianne threw punches in all directions, some of them magical, some with her fists, but this only made the Farleigh girls angrier than ever. She ended up crouching half underneath her own bicycle, while Margot jumped on it.

"That's *right*!" screamed the others. "Squash her! *Kill* her!"

"Here, here, *here*!" Joss Callow said loudly, riding up behind the fight. "Stop that at *once*, you girls! You hear me?"

Everyone turned round guiltily and stared at Joss Callow parking his bike meaningly against the hedge. Marianne stood up from under her bent bike. Her hair was all over her face and she could feel her lips swelling.

"Now what was this all about?" Joss said. "Eh?"

"*She* started it!" Margot said, pointing at Marianne. "The hateful little *slime*!"

"Yes, look what she did to me!" Norma

said, holding out a torn sleeve.

"And she's *ruined* my bike!" said another girl. "She's *disgusting*!"

They all knew Joss because his mother lived in Helm St. Mary. He knew them too. He was not impressed. "Funny thing," he said. "I never see you girls except you're making trouble. Six to one is cowards' work in my book. Ride away home now."

"But we've got an errand to run—" Norma began, and stopped in dismay, looking at the burst spell bag under her feet. "Just look what she did to this!"

"I don't care what you think you're doing here," Joss said. "Go home."

"Who are you to tell us that?" Margot asked rudely.

"I mean what I say," Joss said. He nodded to each girl in turn and, as he nodded, each girl's hairstyle writhed on her head and stood itself straight up in the air. Hairgrips and rubber bands pinged off into the road. In instants, the hairstyles had become long, upright bundles on the top of heads, with the little pigtails waving off to one side like feelers.

All the girls clutched their heads. Several of them screamed. "I can't go home like *this*!" Norma wailed.

"People'll laugh!" Margot screeched. She took a double handful of her bushy Farleigh hair and tried to pull it down. It sprang upright again through her fingers.

"Yes," Joss said. "Everyone who sees you will laugh like a drain. And serve you right. It'll go down when you go into your own house, and not before. Now get going."

Sullenly, the girls picked up their bicycles and mounted them, snarling and complaining to one another when most of the mudguards proved to be loose. Norma said, among the clanking and clattering, "Why has he left *her* hair alone?"

As they rode off, looking long headed and decidedly peculiar, Margot answered loudly, "He's a mongrel half-Pinhoe, that's why."

She meant Joss to hear, and he did. He was not pleased. When Marianne said, "Joss, they were angry because Gammer's been putting spells on the Farleighs," he simply scowled at her.

"I'm not standing here to listen to accusations, Marianne," he said. "I don't care what it was about. I'll straighten your bike for you, but that's your lot."

He picked up Marianne's bicycle and, with a few expert twists and bangs and the same number of well-directed stabs of witchcraft, he straightened the bent frame and twisted pedals and made the wheels round again. Tears in Marianne's eyes distorted the sight of him putting the chain back on. Gammer has been *so* thorough! she thought. *No one* believes a word I say!

"There," Joss said, handing her the restored bike. "Now get wherever you were going, get your face seen to, and don't try insulting any Farleighs again." He picked up his own bike, swung his leg swiftly across the saddle, and rode away into the village before Marianne could think of what to say.

She stood in the road for a moment, softly weeping in a way she thoroughly despised. Then she pulled herself together and took a look at the little burst bags and the white powder from them lying in a trail across the road and dusting the hedges on either side. Those girls had been bringing some fierce stuff to wish on the Pinhoes. From the sore feeling down her back, Marianne was sure it was another illness of some kind. Luckily, it was so fierce that whoever sent it had made it so that it did not work until someone said the right word, but, even so, Marianne knew she ought not to leave it here. Someone could say the right word accidentally at any time.

Sighing, she laid her bike down and wondered how to deal with it. This was something Mum would have been better at than she was.

There was one thing she could do that might work. Marianne had not tried it very often because Mum had been so alarmed when she discovered Marianne could do it.

Marianne took a deep breath and, very carefully and gently, summoned fire. She summoned it to just the surface of the road and very tops of the leaves in the hedges. And in case that was not enough, she instructed it to burn every scrap of the powder wherever it was.

Little blue flames answered her, flickering an inch high over road, grassy banks, and hedges. Almost at once, the flames filled with tiny white sparks, hissing and fizzing. Then the powder underneath caught fire and burned with a most satisfactory snarling sound, like a bad-tempered dog. The six little bags went up with six soft powdery *whoomps* and made clumps of flame that were more green than blue and sent up showers of the white sparks. Like a fireworks display, Marianne thought, except for the strong smell of dragon's blood. When she called the flames back, every scrap of the powder was gone and there was no sign of the bags.

"Good," Marianne said, and rode onward.

She must have been an alarming sight when she arrived at Great-Uncle Edgar's house, what with her swollen mouth, scratched face, and wild, pulled hair. Her knees were scraped too, and one of her arms. Great-Aunt Sue exclaimed when she opened the door.

"Good gracious, dear! Did you fall off your bicycle?"

Aunt Sue was so crisp and starched and orderly and looked so sympathetic that Marianne found she was crying again. She held out the jar of balm and gulped, "I'm afraid it got cracked."

"Never mind, never mind. I haven't finished the last one yet," Aunt Sue said. "Come on in and let me see to your scrapes." She led Marianne through to her neat and orderly kitchen, surrounded by Great-Uncle Edgar's five assorted dogs, all of them noisily glad to see Marianne, where she made Marianne sit on a stool and bathed her face and knees with some of Mum's herbal antiseptic. "What a mess!" she said. "Surely a big girl like you knows enough charms by now not to fall off a bike!"

"I didn't fall off." Marianne gulped. "There were some Farleigh girls—"

"Oh, come now, dear. You just told me you fell off," Aunt Sue said. And before Marianne could explain, Aunt Sue hurried to fetch her a glass of milk and a plate of macaroons.

Aunt Sue's macaroons were always lovely, pale brown and crusty outside and softly white and luscious inside. Biting into the first one, Marianne discovered that one of her teeth was loose. She had to concentrate hard for nearly a minute to get it fixed back in again. By then she had completely lost her chance to point out to Aunt Sue that she had *not* said she had fallen off her bike, and that Aunt Sue had just assumed she had.

Nothing could make it clearer that Aunt Sue was not going to listen to her properly. But Marianne tried. "I met six Farleigh girls," she said carefully, when the tooth was firm again. "And they told me that Gammer has been sending them ill-chance spells. They've had frogs and nits and ants in their cupboards, and now they've got whooping cough too."

Great-Aunt Sue looked disgusted. She passed

both hands down her crisply flounced skirt and said, "There's no believing how superstitious some of these country girls can be! It's amazed me ever since I came to live in Ulverscote. Anything that's caused by their own dirty habits—and the Farleighs are not a clean clan, dear—they try to blame on somebody's use of the craft. As if anyone would *stoop*—and certainly not your poor grandmother! She can barely walk these days, so Dinah tells me."

Marianne knew it was no good then, but she said, "Gammer sits there and does spells, Aunt Sue. Little cunning things that Aunt Dinah doesn't notice. The latest one was water."

"And what does she do with that? Cause a flood?" Aunt Sue asked, brightly and disbelievingly.

"Yes," Marianne said. "In all their houses. And mud in their washing."

Aunt Sue laughed. "Really, dear, you're as credulous as the Farleighs. Anyway, this whooping cough is simply a natural epidemic. It's all over the county now. Edgar tells me they have cases from Bowbridge to Hopton."

Spread by the widening rings of an ill-chance spell, before someone put a stop to the spell, Marianne thought. But she did not say so. There was no point, and she felt tired and sore and shaken. She sat quietly and politely on the stool and listened to Aunt Sue talking about all the things Aunt Sue always talked about.

Aunt Sue's two sons first, Damion and Raphael. Aunt Sue was very proud of them. They were both in Bowbridge, doing very well. Damion was an accountant and Raphael was an auctioneer. It was a pity they were both going bald so young, but baldness was in Aunt Sue's family and it always came from the female, didn't it?

Then the dogs. Mr. Vastion said they were all too fat and needed more exercise. But, said Aunt Sue, how were they to get walked properly with Edgar so busy and the boys not at home anymore? Aunt Sue had enough to do in the house.

Then the house. Aunt Sue wanted new wallpaper. It was a lovely house, and Aunt Sue had never stopped being grateful to Gammer for giving it to them when Gaffer died. Gammer was so generous. She had given Uncle Arthur the Pinhoe Arms, Uncle Cedric the farm, and let Isaac have the smallholding. But truly, Marianne, this place was almost as run-down as Woods House.

Marianne looked round the bright, empty, efficient kitchen and wondered how Aunt Sue could think that. And for the first time, she wondered if all this property had been Gammer's to give away. If Dad was the one the property came to, shouldn't it have been *Dad* who gave it away? She thought she must ask Mum.

Aunt Sue said that she had booked Uncle Charles, over and over, to redecorate the house, but Uncle Charles always seemed to have something more urgent to do. And Aunt Sue was not going to employ anyone else, because Uncle Charles used the craft in his work, which made him quicker and neater than anyone in the county. But now he had gone to redecorate

Woods House. Why should a newcomer, even if she was a Pinhoe born, have the right to take up Uncle Charles's time?

By this time, Marianne had had enough. She did not want to hear either Uncle Charles or the lovely Princess Irene being gently criticized by Aunt Sue. She stood up, thanked Aunt Sue politely, and said she had to be going now.

Meanwhile, Joss Callow arrived at the Pinhoe Arms, ready to report to Marianne's father. As he was parking his bike in the yard, little blue flames broke out all over the front of him, hissing and fizzing and sending out small white sparks. They squirted from under his boots and even sizzled for a moment on the front wheel of his bicycle. Joss beat at them, but they were gone by then.

"Have to do better than that, girls," he said, naturally thinking it was a revenge from Margot Farleigh and her friends.

Then he forgot about it and went into the Snug, where Harry Pinhoe was waiting for him and Arthur Pinhoe leaning through the hatch. "Search me what the Big Man's up to just now," he said, when he was comfortably settled with beer and pickled eggs. "He's very busy with something, but I don't know what. They've got all the old maps and documents out in their library and you can feel the magic they're using on them, but that's all I can tell you."

"Can't Joe tell you?" asked Joe's father, puffing at the pipe he allowed himself at these times.

"That Joe," said Joss, "is bloody useless, excuse my French. He's never *there*. I don't know what he does with his time, but I'm not the only one to complain. Mr. Frazier was about ready to blow his top yesterday when Joe went missing. And Mr. Stubbs was fit to kill, because he wanted an order taken to the butcher and Joe had vanished off the face of the earth."

Harry Pinhoe and Joe's uncle Arthur exchanged sad shrugs. Joe was always going to be a disappointment.

"Oh, that reminds me," Joss said. "Young Cat Chant—Eric, the nine-lifer, you know—has hatched an abomination somehow. Griffin, I think. I saw it this morning. I hardly knew what it was at first. It was all fluff and big feet, but it's got wings and a beak, so that's what it must be."

Uncle Arthur shook his head. "Bad. That's bad. We don't want one of those out."

"Not much we can do, if it's living in the Castle," Harry Pinhoe observed, puffing placidly. "We'd have to wait to catch it in the open."

"And when I asked him, this young Eric said your Marianne gave him the egg," Joss added.

"*What?!*" Harry Pinhoe was disturbed enough to let his pipe drop on the floor. Groping for it, red in the face, he said, "That egg was stored safe in the attic. It should have been safe there till Kingdom Come. I put the workings on it myself. I don't know what's got into Marianne lately. First she goes round telling everyone that poor Gammer's setting spells on the Farleighs, and now she does *this*!"

"She said that about Gammer to me too," said Joss. "She was in a hen fight with some Farleigh girls about it, out on the Helm road just now."

"Let her just wait!" Harry said. His face was still bright red. "I'll give her what for!"

All unknowing, Marianne free-wheeled down past the Pinhoe Arms, more or less at that moment. At the bottom of the hill, she braked, put one foot down, and stared. The expensive taxi from Uphelm was standing throbbing outside the house where Nicola lived. As Marianne stopped, Nicola's dad, who ought to have been working on the Post Office wall, hurried out of the house carrying Nicola wrapped in a mass of blankets and got into the taxi with her. Marianne could hear the wretched, whooping, choking breathing of Nicola from where she stood.

"Taking her to the hospital in Hopton," old Miss Callow said, standing watching. "Doctor says she'll die if they don't."

Nicola's mother, looking desperately anxious, hurried out of the house in her best hat, calling instructions over her shoulder to Nicola's eldest sister as she left. She climbed into the taxi too, and it drove away at once, faster than Marianne had ever seen it go.

Marianne rode on to Furze Cottage, almost crying again. It might have been the Farleighs who sent the whooping cough, but it was Gammer who had provoked them. As she wheeled her bike into the shed, she decided she would *have* to have another talk with Mum.

But that all went out of her mind when Dad—red faced and furious—burst in through the front door as Marianne came through the back and began shouting at her at once. He began with, "What do you mean, giving away that egg?" and went on to say that Marianne was a worse disappointment than Joe was and, having torn her personality to shreds, accused her of spreading evil talk about Gammer. Finally he sent her to her room in disgrace.

Marianne sat there with Nutcase, doing her best to stop the tears trickling off her face onto Nutcase. "I was only trying to be brave and truthful," she said to Nutcase. "Does this happen to everyone who tries to do the right thing? Why does no one believe me?" She knew she would have to talk to Joe. He seemed to be the only person in the world who might listen to her.

Chapter Fourteen

The griffin became very lively that day. He was also growing an odd small tuft of feathers on his head, like an untidy topknot.

"I think that is going to be his crest," Chrestomanci said when Janet asked. "I believe all griffins have one." Chrestomanci seemed to be taking as much interest in Klartch as everyone else. He came into the playroom—in a more than usually embroidered dressing gown—while Janet, Julia, and Cat were finishing breakfast, and kneeled down to inspect Klartch all over. "Accelerated growth," he said to Klartch. "You have a lot of magic, don't you? You've been held up in your egg for years, and you're trying to make up for lost time, I imagine. Don't overdo it, old fellow. By the way, where is Roger?"

Cat knew Roger was in that shed with Joe by now. Roger had snatched a piece of toast and raced away eating it, to get on with rebuilding the flying machine. But he had not *said* that was what he was going to do. Cat held his tongue and let Julia and Janet tell Chrestomanci that they had no idea where Roger had gone. Luckily Chrestomanci seemed satisfied with this.

As soon as Chrestomanci had sailed away again, Klartch invited everyone for a romp. Cat was not sure how Klartch did this, but it was not long before all four of them were rolling about on the floor and leaping from the sofa to the chairs in a mad game of chase. This was when they discovered that griffins could laugh. Klartch laughed in small, chuckling giggles when Julia caught him, rolled him over, and tickled him, and he laughed in long hoots when Cat and Janet chased him round the sofa. Then Janet jumped on him and Klartch dodged. His long front claws caught in the carpet and tore three large strips out of it.

"Oh—oh!" they all said, Klartch included.

"And just look what that creature's done!" Mary the maid said, coming in to clear away the breakfast. "That's what comes of having a wild beast indoors."

Cat guiltily put the carpet back together. They collected three balls and a rubber ring from the cupboards and took Klartch out into the gardens instead. As soon as they came out onto the great smooth lawn, gardeners appeared from all directions and hurried toward them.

"Oh, they're not going to let us play!" Janet said.

But it was not so. They all wanted to see Klartch. "We heard no end about him," they explained. "Odd-looking beast, isn't he? Does he play?"

When Julia explained that playing was what they had come out to do, a gardener's boy ran and fetched a football.

Klartch pounced on it. All six of his front claws sank into it. The football gave out a sad hiss and went flat. Klartch and the gardener's boy both looked so miserable about it that Cat picked up the football and, after thinking hard, managed to mend it, blow it up again, and make it griffin-proof in future.

Then everyone, even the head gardener, joined in a game that Janet called Klartchball. The rules were a little vague and mostly involved everyone running about, while Klartch galloped and rolled and tripped other players up. It was such fun that Roger and Joe emerged from their shed and joined in for a while. The game only stopped when Klartch suddenly stood still, hunched himself, and rolled over on his side in the middle of the lawn.

"He's dead!" Julia said, appalled. "Daddy *told* him not to overdo things!"

They all raced over to Klartch, fearing Julia was right. But when they reached him, Klartch was breathing steadily and his eyes were shut. "He's asleep!" Cat said, hugely relieved.

"We forgot how young he really is," Janet said.

The gardeners put Klartch in a wheelbarrow

and trundled him to the kitchen door. Klartch did not stir the entire time. They trundled him indoors and parked him in a pantry, where he slept until Mr. Stubbs had his lunch ready. Then he woke up eagerly and, instead of opening his beak and going "Weep!" he said, "Me!" and tried to eat the mince by himself.

"You *are* coming on well," Millie said to him admiringly. "Cat, at this rate, he won't be needing you to feed him in the night for much longer."

Cat did hope so. He was so sleepy most of the time that he was sure he would never manage to stay awake during lessons, when lessons started again.

The holidays were indeed almost over. The children's tutor, Michael Saunders, arrived back in the Castle that evening, keen and talkative as ever. He talked so much over supper that even Jason could hardly get a word in, let alone anyone else. Jason wanted to tell everyone about the changes they were making to Woods House, but Michael Saunders had been to the worlds in

Series Eight to take the young dragon he had been rearing back into the wild, and he had a longer tale to tell.

"I had to take the wretched creature to Eight G in the end," he said. "We tried Eight B, where he came from, and all he would do was shiver and say the cold would kill him. Eight A's colder, so we went to C, D, and E, and C was too wet for him, D was too empty, and it was snowing when we got to E. I skipped F. There are more people there, and I could see he was itching for the chance to eat a few. So we went on to G, and he didn't like it there either. It began to dawn on me that the wretch was so pampered that nothing less than tropical was going to suit him. But G has equatorial forests, and I took him down there. He liked the climate all right, but he refused to catch his own food. All he would say was 'You do it.' I thought about it a bit, and then I trapped him one of the large beasts they call lumpen in that Series, and as soon as he was eating it, I left him to it and came away. If he wants to eat again, he'll have to hunt now—"

Here Michael Saunders noticed the way Roger, Janet, Julia, and Cat were all looking at him. He laughed. "Never fear," he said. "I don't intend to start giving you lessons until next Monday. I need a rest first. Nursemaiding a teenage dragon has worn me ragged."

In Cat's opinion, nursemaiding a baby griffin was quite as bad. He gave Klartch a large meal before he went to bed that night and fell asleep seriously hoping that Klartch would not wake up until the morning. It seemed a reasonable hope. When Cat put the light out, Klartch was lying on his back in his basket, with his tight, round stomach upward, snoring like a hive of bees.

But no. Around one o'clock in the morning, Mopsa's dabbing nose and treading paws woke Cat up. When he groaned and put the light on, there was Klartch, thin as a rake again, standing on his hind legs to look into Cat's face. "Food," he told Cat mournfully.

"All right." Cat sighed and got up.

It was a very messy business. Klartch insisted

on feeding himself. Cat's main job seemed to be to scoop up dropped dinner and dump it back into Klartch's bowl for Klartch to spill again. Cat was sleepily scraping meat up from the carpet for the thirtieth time, when he heard a sharp tapping on the window. This was followed by a thump.

What have Roger and Joe done with their flying machine *this* time? he thought. Mad. They are quite *mad!* He went and opened the window.

A broomstick swooped inside with Marianne riding sidesaddle on it. Cat dodged it and stared at her. Seeing Cat, Marianne gave a cry of dismay, slipped off the broom, and sat down hard on the carpet. "Oh, I'm *sorry!*" she said. "I thought this was the attic!"

Cat caught the broomstick as it tried to fly away through the window again. "It's a tower room, really," he said as he shut the window to stop the broom escaping.

"But your light was on, and I thought it was bound to be Joe in here!" Marianne protested. "Which is Joe's attic, then? He's my brother, and I need to talk to him."

"Joe has one of the little rooms down by the kitchen," Cat told her.

"What—downstairs?" Marianne asked. Cat nodded. "I thought they always put servants in the attics," Marianne said. "*All* the way down?"

Cat nodded again. By this time he was awake enough to be quite shocked at how pale and miserable Marianne looked. One side of her face was bruised and she had a big, sore-looking scrape across her mouth, as if someone had beaten her up recently.

"So I'd have to go down past all your wizards and enchanters to get to Joe?" she said dismally.

"I'm afraid so," Cat said.

"And I'm not sure I *dare*," Marianne said. "Oh, dear, why do I keep doing everything *wrong* just lately?"

Cat thought she was going to cry then. He could see her trying not to, and he had no idea what to say. Fortunately Klartch finished his meal just then—all of it that was in the bowl anyway—and came bumbling across the room to see why this new human was sitting dejectedly on the floor. Marianne stared, and stared more when Klartch caught one of his front talons on the carpet and fell on his beak beside her knees.

"Oh, I thought you were a dog! But you're *not*, are you?" Marianne put her hands under Klartch's face and helped him struggle to his feet. Then she helped him unhook his claw from the carpet. "You've got a beak," she said, "and I think you're growing wings."

"He's a griffin," Cat told her, glad of the interruption. "He's called Klartch. He hatched from that egg you gave me."

"Then it really *was* an egg!" Marianne was distracted from her troubles enough to kneel up and stroke Klartch's soft fluffy coat. "I wonder if they had that egg because we've got a griffin on the Pinhoe Arms. And a unicorn. My uncle Charles painted both of them on the inn sign when he was young. Mind you," she told Klartch, "you've got a long way to go before you look like *our* griffin. You need some feathers, for a start."

"Growing some," Klartch said, rather offended.

At this Marianne said, just like Millie, "I didn't know they *talked*!"

"Learning," said Klartch.

"So perhaps it was worth it, giving the egg away," Marianne said sadly. "I don't think you were going to hatch where you were." She looked up at Cat, and a tear leaked its way down the swollen side of her face. "I got into terrible trouble for giving you his egg," she said. "And for trying to do what you said and tell the truth. Be confident, you know, how you said to me. No one in Ulverscote is speaking to me now."

Cat began to feel a slow, guilty responsibility. "I was saying it to myself too," he confessed. "What did I make you do?"

Marianne put her face up and pressed her scratched lips together, trying not to cry again. Then she burst into tears anyway. "Oh, drat it!" she sobbed. "I hate crying! It wasn't my fault, or yours. It was Gammer. But no one will believe me when I say it was her. Gammer's lost her mind, you see, and she keeps sending the

Farleighs frogs and nits and things, and dirtying their washing and flooding their houses. So the Farleighs are furious. And *they* sent *us* bad luck and whooping cough. My distant cousin Nicola's been taken to hospital with it and they think she'll *die*! But Gammer's cast this spell on everyone so that no one will blame *her* for any of it."

Marianne was sobbing in such earnest now that Cat conjured her a pile of his handkerchiefs.

"Oh, *thanks*!" Marianne wept, pressing at least three of them to her wet face. She went on to describe the fight with the Farleigh girls and the way she had gotten rid of the white powder. "And that was silly of me," she sobbed, "but it was really *strong* and I had to do something about it. But Joss Callow had told Dad about the fight, and Dad shouted at me for insulting the Farleighs, and I *didn't*! I told Dad about the powder they were bringing, and he went up there this evening to see it and of course there wasn't any, because I'd burned it all, and he came back and shouted at me again for trying to stir up trouble—"

"What *was* the powder?" Cat asked.

"A bad disease with spots and sores," Marianne said, sniffing. "I think it may have been smallpox."

Ouch! Cat thought. He did not know much about diseases, but he knew *that* one. If it didn't kill you, it disfigured you for life. Those Farleigh girls had not been joking. "But wouldn't they have caught it too?"

"They must have made some immunity spells, I suppose," Marianne said. "But those wouldn't have stopped it spreading all over the county to people who haven't done a thing to the Farleighs. Oh, I don't know what to *do*! I want to ask Joe if he can think of a way to stop Gammer, or at least take off the spell she's got on everyone. I want *someone* to believe me!"

Cat thought about Joe, who had rather impressed him on the whole. Joe had brains. Marianne was probably right to think Joe would know what to do, except—there was this mad flying machine. Joe's head was, at the moment, literally in the clouds. "Joe's pretty busy just now," he said. "But I believe you. My sister was a witch who got out of hand like your Gammer. If you like, I could go and tell Chrestomanci."

Marianne looked up at him in horror. Klartch yelped as her hand closed on a fistful of his fluff. "Sorry," Marianne said, letting go of Klartch. "No! No, you can't tell the Big Man! Please! They'd all go *spare*! Pinhoes, Farleighs, Callows, everyone! You don't understand—we all keep hidden from him so he won't boss us about!"

"Oh," said Cat. "I didn't know." It seemed a bit silly to him. This was the kind of problem Chrestomanci could solve by more or less simply snapping his fingers. "He doesn't boss people unless they misuse witchcraft."

"Well, we *are* doing," Marianne said. "Or Gammer is. Think of something else."

Cat thought. He was so tired, that was the problem. And the more he cudgeled his sleepy brain, the more responsible he felt. There was no doubt that he had said just the one thing to Marianne likely to start her getting into the mess she was now in. He ought to help her, even though what he said had really been to tell himself something instead. But how was he to stop a witch war among people he didn't even know? Walk up to this Gammer person and put her in a stasis spell? Suppose he got the wrong old lady? He wanted to tell Marianne that it was hopeless, except that she was so upset that she had come miles at night on a broomstick. She must have sneaked off from her angry father to do it too. No, he had to think of something.

"All right," he said. "I'll think. But not now. I'm too sleepy. Klartch keeps needing to be fed in the night, you see. I'll have a real, serious think in the morning. Is there anywhere I can meet you to tell you any ideas I get?"

"Tomorrow?" Marianne said. "All right, as long as it's secret. I don't want Dad to know I talked to you—you're as bad as the Big Man to him. He says you're a nine-lifed enchanter too. I didn't know. I thought you were Irene's son. Can you get Irene to bring you to Woods House again? People from the Castle have to be with a Pinhoe to get there, you see. Otherwise they stop you and send you back here."

"I think so," said Cat. "She goes there most days with Jason. And I tell you what—I'll try to get Joe to come too if he's free. Meet me around midday. I have to think first, and exercise Syracuse."

Marianne looked puzzled. "I thought his name was Klartch."

"Syracuse," Cat explained, "is a horse. Klartch is this griffin. The cat sitting on my bed staring at you is Mopsa."

"Oh," said Marianne. She almost grinned. "You do seem to be surrounded in creatures. That's a dwimmer-thing, I think. I can tell you have quite strong dwimmer. See you tomorrow at midday, then." Looking much more cheerful, she scrambled up and stared round for her broomstick.

Cat plucked the broomstick away from the window and handed it politely to Marianne. "Will you be all right?" he asked, trying not to yawn. "It's pretty dark."

"As long as the owls miss me," Marianne said. "They never look where they're going. But if you had any idea how uncomfortable it is riding a broomstick, you wouldn't ask. I suppose one more set of bruises won't notice. See you." She sat herself sideways on the hovering broomstick. "Ouch," she said. "This is Mum's broom. It doesn't like me riding it."

Cat opened the window for her and Marianne swooped out through it, away into the night.

Cat stumbled back to bed. He had not a clue how to solve Marianne's problems. He simply hoped, as he pushed Mopsa out of the way, that a good idea came into his head while he was asleep. He was asleep the next second. He forgot to turn out the light. He did not see the offended way Mopsa jumped down and joined Klartch in his basket.

He woke—much too soon, it seemed—when Janet barged cheerfully into his room, saying, "Breakfast, Klartch. Come on down to the kitchen. I'm going to start house-training him today," she told the yawning Cat. "It *should* be all right if we can get downstairs fast enough."

When Janet and Klartch had crashed out of

the room, Cat sat up, searching his sleepy brain for any ideas that might have landed in it during the night. There was one, but it struck him as very poor and stupid indeed, one only to be used if nothing else occurred to him. He got up and went along to have a shower, hoping that might liven his brain up a little. The water in the Castle was bespelled, and Cat had hopes of it.

But nothing happened. With only the poor, thin idea in his head, Cat got dressed and went downstairs. He met a strong disinfectant spell on the next flight down. This was followed by the angry clattering of a bucket and Janet's raised voice. "Purple nadgers, Euphemia! He's only a baby! And he's terribly ashamed. Just look at him!" It sounded as if Klartch had not gotten downstairs quite fast enough after all.

Cat grinned and galloped down the other set of stairs that led to the stable door. They came out past the cubbyhole where Joe was supposed to clean shoes. Rather to Cat's surprise, Joe was actually there, busily blacking a large boot.

Cat leaned into the little room. "Your sister

was here last night, trying to find you," he said. "She's got troubles. She says your Gammer is secretly putting spells on the Farleighs."

"Our Gammer?" Joe said, calmly rubbing away at the boot. "You must know she is. You saw me on my way to set the first spell for her, didn't you?"

"The tadpoles?" Cat said.

"Frogs," said Joe.

"Oh," Cat said. "Um. *Those* frogs. In Helm St. Mary?"

"That's right," Joe said. "Gammer said if I could get the one spell out for her, then she could follow the thread with a load of others, and if she did, it would work her free of the containment my dad had put on her. By-product, she called it. She pointed her stick at me to make me do it. And I didn't want to have rode all the way to Ulverscote for nothing and I knew Gaffer Farleigh did put an addle spell on her— Marianne swears he did, and she knows—so I took the jar to Helm St. Mary and tipped it into their duck pond there for her."

Cat was hugely relieved. He had no need to use his poor, thin idea. Joe could solve Marianne's problems with a word. "Then do you think you could come to Ulverscote with me this morning and tell your father? Marianne says Gammer's set a spell on everyone so that they don't believe her and the Farleighs are sending them plagues in revenge."

Joe's head went sulkily down as he pondered. He shrugged. "If Gammer's done that, then they won't believe me neither, not if they don't believe Marianne. She's strong in the craft, Gammer is, and I'm no one. Besides, Mr. Frazier says he'll have me up before the Big Man if I don't stay here where I'm paid to be. *And* just when we've got our machine near perfect! No. Sorry. Can't oblige you."

And, to prove that Joe was not just making excuses, Mr. Frazier came along the kitchen corridor just then, saying, "Joe Pinhoe, are you working? Master Cat, I'll trouble you not to interrupt Joe in his work. We're privileged today. Master Pinhoe has actually cleaned a boot."

"Just going," Cat told Mr. Frazier. He leaned farther into the cubbyhole and asked, "Is Mr. Farleigh the gamekeeper any relation to the Farleighs who got the frogs?"

"Jed Farleigh," said Joe. "He's their Gaffer." Hearing Mr. Frazier treading closer, he picked up two more boots and tried to look as if he was cleaning all three at once.

Cat said "Thanks" to him and hurried toward the stables, thinking. If he understood rightly, these Gammers and Gaffers were the heads of these tribes of witchy people, and if Mr. Farleigh the gamekeeper was one, the whole thing was much more frightening than Cat had realized. No wonder Marianne had been so upset. And here was he, Cat, with only one poor, second-rate idea to put against it all. Joe was no help. Cat hurried out into the yard, feeling small and weak and heartily wishing he had not agreed to help Marianne.

As Cat crossed the yard, Jason came out of his herb shed with a stack of flat wooden boxes. Cat went over to him. Jason, by the time Cat reached him, was standing on one leg, holding the boxes on one knee while he locked the shed. He spared Cat a harried smile. "What can I do for you, young nine-lifer?" The smells of many kinds of herbs, faint and sweet or rich and spicy, swam round the pair of them.

"Can you give me a lift to Woods House today?" Cat asked.

"Well, I *could*," Jason said, "but you'd have to find your own way back. We're moving in there for good today. Irene's busy packing."

Cat had not realized that things had moved on so quickly. He was quite taken aback. But he supposed that when an enchanter did things, he did them more swiftly than other people. And he was going to miss Irene. "Not to worry, then," he said. "Thanks."

He stood aside and watched Jason carry the boxes away across the yard. That did it, then. He was let off. But somehow that did not make him terribly happy. Marianne would be expecting him. He would have let her down. No, he would have to find a way to get to Ulverscote on his own. It was a pity that he had such a poor, thin idea to take there.

He could teleport, he thought, there and back. That ought to have been easy, but for the mis-direction spell—and then there was that barrier. If he tried it without one of the Pinhoes, he could end up caught behind the barrier like Chrestomanci. Better think of some other way. Cat walked slowly over to Syracuse's stall to tell it to muck itself out, considering.

Joss Callow met him as he got there. "When you're ready, we'll ride out over the heath," he told Cat. "Half an hour?"

Cat's mind had this way of making plans without Cat knowing it was. "Can you make it later than that?" he asked, without having to think. "Jason and Irene are leaving today and I'll need to say good-bye."

"Suits me," Joss said. "I've plenty to do here. Eleven o'clock, then?"

"Fine," Cat said gratefully. While he cleaned the stall and gave Syracuse his morning pepper-mint, he found out what he meant to do. His mind had it all neatly worked out. He was going to ride to Ulverscote on Syracuse, and the way to make sure he got there was to follow the river. He was fairly sure the same river ran past the Castle and through Ulverscote. And, surely, even the most secretive of Pinhoes and the angriest of Farleighs could not change the way a river ran. They might deceive him into *thinking* it ran the other way, but Cat was fairly sure he could guard against that if he kept his witch sight firmly on the way it was *really* flowing.

Cat gave Syracuse a pat and a strong promise to ride him later and went indoors. Before he went upstairs to the playroom for breakfast, he dodged into the library where, much to the surprise of old Miss Rosalie, the Castle librarian, he asked for a map of the country between the Castle and Ulverscote.

"I don't understand this," Miss Rosalie grumbled, spreading the map out on a table for him. "*Everyone* seems to want this map at the moment. Jason, Tom, Bernard, Chrestomanci, Millie, Roger. Now you."

Miss Rosalie always grumbled. She thought all books and maps should be on shelves. Cat paid no attention to her. He leaned over the map and carefully followed the wavy blue line of the river as it snaked through its steep valley beside the Castle. Sure enough, the valley, and the river with it, curved its way on, around the hill with Ulverscote Wood on it, and ran along the bottom of the slope where Ulverscote village was. By that stage, the valley was a simple dip, but it was the same river. Cat's brain had gotten it right. He thanked Miss Rosalie and raced away.

In the schoolroom, Klartch was sitting on the sofa trying very seriously to eat a banana. "He's in disgrace," Euphemia snapped, banging toast and coffee down in front of Cat. "Don't you go and be nice to him."

While Janet was loudly protesting that Klartch was only a baby and that the way to teach babies was to be nice to them, Julia said to Cat, "Jason and Irene are moving out today, did you know? Are you coming down to the hall to say good-bye to them?"

Cat nodded. His mind was busy with the problem of how to get rid of Joss without making Joss suspicious. He thought he had it.

Julia said, "Roger?"

Roger just grunted. He was busy making diagrams on scraps of paper. He had been doing this at every meal for weeks now. Julia looked at the ceiling. "Boys! Honestly!"

Here Chrestomanci sailed in, wearing a kingly red dressing gown with ermine down the front. He took a long stride and got the banana skin away from Klartch just as Klartch tried to eat it. "I think not," he said. "We don't want any more accidents on the stairs."

"Good morning, Daddy," Julia said. "Why does everyone always have their minds on something *else*?"

"A good question," Chrestomanci said, tossing the banana skin into the air. It disappeared. "I suppose it must be because we all have a lot to think about. Roger." Roger looked up guiltily. The scraps of paper had somehow disappeared, like the banana skin. "Roger, I need to talk to you," Chrestomanci said, "on a matter of some urgency. Can you come with me to my study, please."

Roger got up, looking pale and apprehensive. Chrestomanci politely ushered him out of the schoolroom ahead of himself and gently closed the door behind them both. The other three looked at one another, glanced at Euphemia, and decided to say nothing.

Roger had still not come back when everyone gathered in the hall to say good-bye to Irene and Jason. He and Chrestomanci were almost the only people missing.

"Never mind," Jason said, shaking hands with Millie. "We'll see him when we give our house-warming party."

"I'll make sure he's there," Millie said. "Jason, it's been a pleasure having you."

Jason went round shaking hands with every-one. Irene followed, hugging people. Cat stood a little back from the throng. He was engaged in the most delicate piece of long-distance magic he had ever done, trying to make Joss's big brown horse lose a shoe in a way that looked completely natural, without hurting the horse. He took its off hind foot up in imaginary hands and gently prized at the long iron nails that held the shoe on, going round them each several times, easing them out a bit at a time, until the horseshoe was hanging away from the hoof. Then he gave the horseshoe a sharp sideways push. It flew off. At least Cat thought it did. He certainly felt the horse give a jump of surprise. He let its foot carefully down. Then he picked the shoe up in imaginary hands and looked at it with imaginary eyes. Good. All the nails were most satisfactorily bent, as if the horse itself had twisted the horseshoe off. He tossed the shoe into a corner of the stall so that the horse was less likely to tread on it and injure itself.

He came back to himself to find Irene hugging him. "You're very quiet, Cat. Is something wrong?" she asked. There were scents around Cat of spice and flowers. Irene always smelled lovely.

"I shall miss you," Cat said truthfully. "May I

come and visit you later today, or will you be too busy?"

"Oh, what a nice idea!" Irene said. "Be our first visitor, Cat. I'm longing to show off what we've done to the house. But make it after midday so that we can unpack a little first."

Cat grinned a trifle anxiously as he shook hands with Jason. How soon would Joss notice that missing horseshoe? He hadn't yet. Perhaps the shoe hadn't really come off. It was often quite hard to tell if magic had worked or not.

He came to the door with everyone else and watched as Jason and Irene climbed into the small blue car. They could not have fitted Cat into it anyway. There was luggage strapped all over it and more piled into the backseat, with Jason's herb boxes on top of that. They drove off in a waft of blue smoke, herb scent, and Irene scent, waving joyously as they vanished down the drive.

"I think they'll be very happy," Millie said. "And I'm longing to see their house. I think I shall drive over there as soon as they're settled in."

She won't get there, Cat thought, without a Pinhoe to take her. I wonder what will happen then. He was edging away as he thought, wondering more about that horseshoe than about Millie. As soon as no one was looking at him, he turned and ran for the stables. It was nowhere near eleven yet, but he had to know.

He got there just as Joss was leading the big brown horse out through the stableyard gate. "Cast a shoe," Joss called over his shoulder to Cat. "I have to get him down to the blacksmith before we can ride out. So don't hold your breath. We could be gone hours if the forge is busy. I'll send someone to tell you when I'm back. All right?"

"All right," Cat said, trying not to look as relieved and joyful as he felt.

Chapter Fifteen

Marianne was having even more difficulty getting away than Cat was. She was in such disgrace at home that Mum was making her do all sorts of chores in order to keep Marianne under her eye.

"I'm not having you going round spreading any more tales," Mum said. "If you've cleaned your room, you can come and sort these herbs and worts for me now. Throw out any leaves and berries that look manky. Then put worts in this bowl and just the fresh tips of the leaves in that one. And I want it done right, Marianne."

As if I was four years old again! Marianne thought. *I know how to sort herbs, Mum!* It looked as if she was *never* going to get out of the house today. The only good thing about today was that, thanks to Mum's lotions, Marianne's bruises and scrapes had almost disappeared in the night. But what was the good of that when she was a prisoner? Marianne sighed as she spread the fresh green bundles of plants apart on the table. Nutcase jumped up beside her and rubbed sympathetically against her arm. Marianne looked at him. Now *there* was an idea. If she could persuade Nutcase to wander off again . . .

"Go and visit Woods House, Nutcase," she whispered to him. "Why don't you? You *like* going there. Go on. As a favor to me? Please?"

Nutcase moved his ears and twitched his tail and stayed sitting on the table. But I live *here* now, he seemed to be saying.

"Oh, I *know* you do, but pay a visit to Woods House anyway," Marianne said. She opened the side window and put Nutcase out through it.

Two minutes later, Nutcase came in through the back door with Mum when she brought in an armful of plants and unloaded them in the sink to be cleaned. He jumped onto the drain-board and gave Marianne a smug look.

As soon as Mum had gone out into the garden again, Marianne picked Nutcase up and carried him through the house to the front door. She opened the door and dumped him on the path outside. "Go to Woods House!" she whispered fiercely to him.

Nutcase's reply was to sit in the middle of the tiny front lawn, stick a leg up, and wash. Marianne shut the front door, hoping he would leave when he was ready.

Five minutes later, Nutcase came in through the back door again, with Mum and another bundle of herbs.

This is *hopeless*! Marianne thought, while Mum ran water in the sink. I shall just have to walk off without an excuse and get into worse trouble than ever. Wasn't there *any* way she could tempt Nutcase to Woods House? Could she do something like the bacon spell she had tempted him with, the time she gave Cat the egg? But I can't do that from *here*, she thought, right at the other end of the village. Or could she? When she looked at Woods House in a special, witchy way, she could feel that the bacon spell was still there. It only needed reactivating. But could she manage to start it up again from here, strongly enough to tempt Nutcase all the way from Furze Cottage? No, I'm not strong enough, she thought.

But Cat had said she *was*. He had said she had nearly enchanter-strength magic but just didn't trust herself. He had made her bold enough to get into this trouble. Surely she could be bold enough to get herself out of it.

All right, she said to herself. I'll try.

Marianne nipped the last fresh leaf tips into the bowl and concentrated. And concentrated. And trusted herself and concentrated some more. It was odd. She felt as if each new push she gave herself spread her mind out, wider, and then wider still, until she almost seemed to be hovering beside the faded remains of the bacon spell in the hall of Woods House. She gave it a flip and brought it to life again, and then a further flip to make it stronger—or she hoped she did. It was so hard to tell for sure.

But look at Nutcase!

Nutcase's head went up and then went up farther, until he was nose upward, sniffing. Marianne watched him, hardly daring to breathe. Nutcase gave himself a shake and got up and stretched, front legs first, then back legs. Then, to Marianne's acute amazement, Nutcase really did walk through the kitchen wall. He trod toward the wall, steadily and deliberately, but when his head touched the whitewashed bricks, he didn't stop. He didn't even slow down. He walked on. His head disappeared into the wall, then his shoulder ruff, then most of his body, until he was just a pair of black, walking hind legs and a tail. The legs walked out of sight and left only the bushy, waving tail. Then there was only the tip of the tail, which vanished with a jerk, as if Nutcase had given a pull to fetch it through. Marianne was left staring at the bricks of the wall. There was no sign of the place where Nutcase had gone through. Well, well! she thought.

She gave Nutcase ten minutes to get on his way. Then, when Mum came in from the garden again, she said, "Mum, have you got Nutcase?" She was surprised how natural she sounded.

Mum said, "No. I thought he was with you. Oh—*bother*!"

They searched the house as they always did, then Dolly's stall, because Dolly and Nutcase seemed to have struck up a friendship, and then they went to Dad's work shed and asked if Nutcase was there. Of course Nutcase was in none of these places. Mum said, "Better go after him quick, Marianne. If he gets down to the Dell again and your uncle Isaac finds him, there'll be hell to pay. Hurry. Get a wiggle on, girl!"

Marianne shot out of Furze Cottage, delighted.

At the top of Furze Lane, the men building the Post Office wall all pointed uphill with their thumbs, grinning. "Off again. Went that way."

It was a relief that Nutcase had not suddenly decided to visit the Dell instead. Marianne turned uphill. There was no Nicola to shout to her where Nutcase had gone, but Nicola's mum was standing in her doorway. She pointed uphill and nodded to Marianne.

Marianne hovered backward on one foot for a second. "How's Nicola?"

Nicola's mother put one hand out and made swaying motions with it. "We're hoping."

"Me too!" Marianne said, and went on, past the grocer, past the Pinhoe Arms and then the church.

The big gates to Woods House, when she came to them, seemed really strange, newly mended, newly painted, and shut. Marianne had never known those gates to be shut since Gaffer died. It felt odd to have to open one half of the gates and slip round it into the driveway. The overgrown bushes there seemed to have been cut back a bit. They gave Marianne a sight of the front door long before she was used to seeing it. A small, battered blue car was parked outside.

Oh, they're here! Marianne thought. She suddenly felt a total trespasser. This was not one of the family houses anymore. She had had no business arranging to meet Cat here. And she would have to knock at the front door—which was now painted a smooth olive green—and ask for Nutcase.

Marianne found she could not face doing this. She sheered away round the house into the garden, hoping Nutcase had gone to sun himself there. She could always say, quite truthfully, that she was looking for Gammer's cat if anyone asked, and it was always possible that Cat would see her out of one of the windows—always supposing Cat was here, of course.

The garden was transformed.

Marianne stood for a moment in amazement, looking from the smoothly trimmed square shape of the beech hedge to the lawn that was almost a lawn again. Someone had scythed and then mowed the long grass. It still had a stubbly gray look, but green was pushing through in emerald lines and ovals, showing where there had once been flower beds. Marianne went along the trim hedge, pretending to look into it for Nutcase, and marveling. The gooseberry bushes at the end, where the wood began, had been cleared and pruned, along with the old lilac trees behind them. No sign of Nutcase there. But there had been currant bushes there all these years, and Marianne had never known, and a stand of raspberry canes that still had raspberries on them. When she turned alongside the canes—keeping to the edges just like a cat might—she saw that the long flower bed against the wall that hid the vegetable garden actually had flowers in it now: long hollyhocks, asters, dahlias, and montbretia mostly at this time of year, but enough to make it look like a flower bed again.

She slipped guiltily round the end of the wall and found that the vegetable garden was most transformed of all. It was like Uncle Isaac's professional market garden. Everything was in neat rows in moist black earth, pale lettuces, frilly carrots, spiky onions. A lot of the beds were plain black earth with string stretched along, where seeds had not yet come up. And— Marianne stared around—she had not known that the walls had roses trained along them.

They had always seemed a mass of green creeper. But this had been pared away and the roses tied back, and they were just now coming into bloom, red and peach colored and yellow and white, as if it were June, not nearly September.

Marianne crunched her way timidly down a newly cindered path toward the house. I'm looking for my cat when somebody asks. When she reached the archway beside the conservatory, she peered cautiously through.

The little man energetically digging in Old Gaffer's herb patch drove his spade to a standstill beside the tall mugwort and smiled at her. "Made a bit of a change here," he remarked to her. "How do you like it?"

Marianne could not help staring at him, even while she was smiling back. He was so small, so bandy, and so brown. His hair grew in tufts round his bald head and his wrinkly face had two tufts of beard on it, just under his large ears. If there were such things as gnomes, Marianne thought, she would be sure he was one. But his smile was beaming, friendly, and full of pride in his gardening. Her own smile enlarged to beaming in reply. "You've done so *much*! In no time at all!"

"It was the dream of my life," he said, "to work in a country garden. Mistress Irene, bless her, promised me that I should, and she kept her promise as you see. I've hardly started yet. August's not the best time to dig and sow, but I reckon that if I can get it all in good heart by the autumn, then when spring comes, I can *really* begin. They call me Mr. Adams, by the way. And you are?"

"Marianne Pinhoe," said Marianne.

"Oh," said Mr. Adams, "then you're quite a personage around here, as I read it."

Marianne made a face. "Not so's you'd notice. I—er—came looking for my cat."

"Nutcase," said Mr. Adams. "In the house. He went past me into the conservatory five minutes ago. Before you go in, come and look how your grandfather's herb bed's coming along. It went against the grain with me to leave it till last, when it's so near the house, but I had to wait for

Mr. Yeldham to come and tell me which were the weeds. Awful lot of strange plants here."

He beckoned to Marianne so imperiously that she came nervously out from the archway, to find the big plot looking almost as she remembered it from Gaffer's time: low cushions of plants round the edges, tall gangly ones near the middle, and medium-sized ones in between, each one carefully placed in sun or shade as it needed, and growing in different-colored earths that were right for them. The spicy whiffs of scent made her throat ache, remembering her Old Gaffer.

She smiled down at Mr. Adams. She was a lot taller than he was. "You've made this almost how it should be, Mr. Adams. It's wonderful."

"For my pleasure," he said. "And to be worthy of Princess Irene."

Thoroughly surprised, Marianne said, "I call her that too!"

Cat rode quite slowly along the river path, so that Syracuse waltzed and bounced, wanting to go faster. Even after galloping round the paddock before they set out, Syracuse was still bored by walking.

They were going the same way that the river flowed, and Cat kept firmly remembering this. The water had already tried to deceive him twice by seeming to flow the other way. Last spring, when Mr. Saunders had been teaching him how you used witch sight, Cat had been rather bored. It had seemed so obvious. Now he was glad of those lessons. The lessons had not been so much about how you saw things truthfully when they were bespelled—Cat could do that standing on his head—but about how to *keep* seeing them when other spells were trying to distract you. Mr. Saunders, being the keen, fierce kind of teacher he was, had invented a dozen fiendish ways to take Cat's mind off what he was seeing. Cat had hated it. But now it was paying off.

Cat kept that river firmly under his witch sight and did not allow it to get away once. He did not look at the surrounding valley at all.

Now he was warned, he could feel it swirling about, trying to suggest he was going the wrong way.

Thanks to Syracuse, he could attend to the valley by smelling it instead of looking. The scents of water, rushes, willows, and the tall meadows had changed quite a lot in the short time since he had last come this way with Joss. The spiciness was damper, sadder, and smokier and smelled of summer giving way to autumn. Cat surprised himself by thinking that a year was really a short time. Things changed so *fast*. Which was silly, he thought, almost getting distracted, because you could do so much in a year.

Mr. Farleigh was suddenly standing in front of them in the path.

He was there so abruptly and unexpectedly— and so solidly—that Syracuse was startled into trying to rear. There was a difficult few seconds when Cat nearly fell off and Syracuse's back hooves walked off the path and squelched among the rushes. Cat managed to keep himself in the saddle and Syracuse right way up, but only with a frenzy of magic and of spells he had no idea he knew. Mr. Farleigh watched his struggles sarcastically.

"I told you not to come here," he said, as soon as Syracuse's front hooves were on the ground again.

Cat was quite angry by then. It was an unusual experience for him. Up to now, when things happened that would have made most people angry, Cat had just felt bewildered. But now, he faced Mr. Farleigh's pale-eyed glare and was surprised to find himself filled with real fury. The man could have hurt Syracuse. "This is a public bridle way," he said. "You've no right to tell me not to use it."

"Then use it to go home on," Mr. Farleigh said, "and I'll not turn you back."

"But I don't want to turn back," Cat said with his teeth clenched. "How do you think you can stop me going on?"

"With the weight of this whole county," Mr. Farleigh said. "I carry it with me, boy."

He did, too, in some odd way, Cat realized.

Though Syracuse was trampling and sidling, highly disturbed by the magic Cat had used, Cat managed a small push of power toward Mr. Farleigh. He met a resistance that felt as old as granite, and as gnarled and nonhuman as a tree that was petrified and turned to stone. The stony roots of Mr. Farleigh seemed to have twined and clamped themselves into the earth for miles around.

Cat sat back in his saddle wondering what to do. He was *not* going to go tamely back to the Castle, just because a bullying witchmaster with a gun told him to.

"*Why* don't you want me to ride this way?" he asked.

Mr. Farleigh's strange pale eyes glowered at him from under his bushy brows. "Because you mess up my arrangements," he said. "You have no true belief. You trespass and you trample and you unveil that which should be hidden. You try to release what should be safely imprisoned."

It sounded religious to Cat. He bent forward to pat Syracuse's tossing head and wondered how to say that he had not done any of these things. As to Mr. Farleigh's arrangements, he should just make them some other way! People should be allowed to ride where they wanted.

He was just deciding that there was no way to say this politely, and he had opened his mouth to be rude, when he was interrupted by a most unusual set of sounds coming from somewhere behind his right shoulder. There were voices, chattering, singing, and murmuring, as if quite a large crowd of people were walking along the top of the meadows. This noise was mixed with a strange, shrill whispering, which was combined with creakings and clatterings and a wooden thumping. Cat's head swiveled to see what on earth it was.

It was the flying machine. It was coming slowly across the top of the meadow about a hundred yards away and about twenty feet in the air. And it was the most peculiar object Cat had seen in his life. To either side of it, a jointed set of broken tables slowly flapped. Something that looked like a three-legged stool whirled furiously on its nose. The rest of it looked like a tangle of broken chairs all loosely hooked together, with each bit of it working and waving and making little flaps of wood go in and out. It had a long feather duster for a tail. In the midst of it, Cat could just see the dismantled frames of two bicycles and two people on them, pedaling madly. And every bit of this strange contraption was calling out as it came, "I belong to Chrestomanci Castle, I belong to Chrestomanci Castle!" high, low, shrill, and steady.

Mr. Farleigh said, in a voice that was almost a groan, "The very air is not safe from them!" Cat's head whipped back to find Mr. Farleigh staring up at the machine in horror. As Cat looked, Mr. Farleigh pulled something on his gun and raised it.

The gun barrel moved to track the flying machine and, before Cat could do more than put one hand out and shout, "*No!,*" Mr. Farleigh fired.

Cat thought there was a yell from the machine. But the *crack-bang!* of the shot sent

Syracuse into a panic. He squealed and reared in earnest. Cat found himself clinging to a vertical horse and fighting to keep Syracuse's trampling back hooves from going into the river. He saw everything in snatches, among flying horsehair and clods of mud and grass splashing into the water, but he saw Mr. Farleigh slam another cartridge into his gun and he saw, uphill, the flying machine tipping to one side so that one set of flapping tables almost brushed the grass.

Then Syracuse came down, quivering with terror. Cat saw the flying machine right itself with a clap and a clatter. Then it was off, with astonishing speed, tables flapping, feather duster wagging, boys' feet flashing round and round. It had slipped over the top of the hill and vanished from sight before Mr. Farleigh could raise his gun again.

While Mr. Farleigh lowered his gun, looking grim and frustrated, Cat patted Syracuse and pulled his ear to quiet him. He said to Mr. Farleigh, "That would have been murder." He was surprised that his voice came out firm and angry and hardly frightened at all.

Mr. Farleigh gave him a contemptuous look. "It was an abomination," he said.

"No, it was a flying machine," Cat said. "There were two people in it."

Mr. Farleigh paid no attention. He looked beyond Cat and seemed horrified again. "Here is another abomination!" he said. He lowered his gun farther and aimed at the path behind Cat.

Cat snatched a look behind him. To his terror, he found that Klartch had followed them. Klartch was standing in the path with his beak open and his small triangular wings raised, obviously paralyzed with fear. Without having to think, Cat put out his left hand and rolled the barrel of Mr. Farleigh's gun up like a party whistle or a Swiss roll.

"If you fire now, it'll blow your face off!" he said. He was truly angry by then.

Mr. Farleigh looked grimly down at his rolled-up gun. He looked up at Cat with his bushy eyebrows raised and gave him a sarcastic stare. The gun, slowly, started to unroll again.

Behind Cat, Klartch went "Weep, weep, weep!" Syracuse shook all over.

What shall I do? Cat thought. He knew, as clearly as if Mr. Farleigh had just said so, that after he had shot Klartch, Mr. Farleigh would shoot Syracuse and then Cat, because Cat was a witness and Syracuse was in the way. He had to do something.

He pushed at Mr. Farleigh with his left hand out and came up against flinty, knotty power, like an oak tree turned to stone. Cat could not move it. And the gun steadily unrolled. Mr. Farleigh stared at Cat across it, immovable and contemptuous. He seemed to be saying, *You can do nothing.*

Yes, I *can*! Cat thought. I must, I *will*! Or Klartch and Syracuse will be dead. At least I've still got three lives left.

The thought of those three lives steadied him. When Mr. Farleigh shot him, Cat would still be alive, on his eighth life, just like Chrestomanci was, and he could do something then. All the things he had been taught by Chrestomanci surged about in his head. There must be *something* Chrestomanci had said— Yes, there was! After Cat had sent Joe to the ceiling, Chrestomanci had said, "Even the strongest enchanter can be defeated by using his own strength against him." So instead of pushing *against* Mr. Farleigh's heavy, stony power, suppose Cat pushed *with* it? And quick, because the gun was nearly unrolled.

Then it was not difficult at all. Cat pushed out hard with his left hand and made Mr. Farleigh into a petrified oak tree.

It was a weird thing. It stood nine feet high, made of bent and twisted gray rock, and it had huge and knotty roots that had somehow delved and gouged their way into the earth of the path where it stood. It had a broken-looking hump at the top, which had probably been Mr. Farleigh's head, and three lumpy, writhen branches. One branch must have been the gun, because the other two had stone oak leaves clinging to them, each leaf with a glitter of mica to it.

Syracuse hated it. His front feet danced this

way and that, trying to take him away from it. Klartch gave out another frightened "Weep, weep!"

"It's all right," Cat said to both of them. "It won't hurt you now. Honestly." He got down from Syracuse and found he was shaking as badly as the horse was. Klartch crept up to him, shaking too. "I *wish* you hadn't followed me," Cat said to him. "You nearly got killed."

"Need to come too," Klartch said.

Cat had half a mind to take them all back home to the Castle. But he had promised to meet Marianne and they were well over halfway by now. And he could tell, by the sound of the river and the feel of the meadow, that Mr. Farleigh had been the center that held the misdirection spells together. They were so weak now that they were almost gone. It would be easy to get to Woods House, except for— Cat looked up at the ugly stone oak, looming above them. There would be no getting Syracuse past that thing, he knew. Besides, it was right in the path and a terrible nuisance to anyone trying to go this way.

Cat steadied his trembling knees and sent the stone oak away somewhere else, somewhere it fitted in better, he had no idea where. It went with a soft rumble like thunder far off, followed by a small breeze full of dust from the path, river smell, and bird noises. The willows rattled their leaves in it. For a moment, there were deep trenches in the path where the stone roots had been, but they began filling in almost at once. Sand and earth poured into the holes like water, and then hardened.

Cat waited until the path was back to the way it had been and then levitated Klartch up into Syracuse's saddle. Klartch flopped across it with a gasp of surprise. One pair of legs hung down on each side, helplessly. Syracuse craned his head round and stared.

"It's the best I can do," Cat said to them. "Come on. Let's go."

Chapter Sixteen

Marianne looked up gladly as Cat came across the stubbly lawn, leading Syracuse. She was sad to see that Joe was not with him, but at least Cat was here. She had begun to think he was not coming.

"Friend of yours?" asked talkative Mr. Adams. "That's a fine piece of horseflesh he's got there. Arab ancestry, I shouldn't wonder. What's he got on the saddle?"

Marianne wondered too, until Cat came near. She saw that Cat stared at Mr. Adams much as she had done herself. "Oh, you've brought Klartch!" she said.

"He followed me. I had to bring him," Cat said. He did not feel like explaining how lethal that had nearly been.

"I love your horse," Marianne said. "He's beautiful." She went boldly up to rub Syracuse's face. Cat watched a little anxiously, knowing what Syracuse could be like. But Syracuse graciously allowed Marianne to rub his nose and then pat his neck, and Marianne said, "Ah, you like peppermints, do you? I'm afraid I—"

"Here you are," Mr. Adams said, producing a paper bag from an earthy pocket. "These are extra strong—he'll like these. They call me Mr. Adams," he added to Cat. "Been in Princess Irene's family for years."

"How do you do?" Cat said politely, wondering how he would get a private word with Marianne with Mr. Adams there. While Marianne fed Syracuse peppermints, he hauled Klartch off the saddle and dropped him in the grass—with a grunt from both of them: Klartch was heavy and landed heavily. Mr. Adams stared at Klartch in some perplexity.

"I give up," he said. "Is it a flying bird-dog, or what?"

"He's a baby griffin," Cat explained. He tried

to smile at Mr. Adams, but the word *flying* made him terribly anxious suddenly about Roger and Joe, and the smile was more of a grimace. He didn't think that Mr. Farleigh's bullet had hit either of them, but it had certainly hit the flying machine somewhere, and one of them had yelled. Still, there was nothing he could do.

"Shall I look after the horse for you while you go indoors?" Mr. Adams offered. "Second to gardening, I love tending to horses. He'll be safe with me."

Cat and Marianne exchanged relieved looks. Marianne had been wondering how they were going to talk in private too.

"I'll look after this griffin fellow too, if you like," Mr. Adams offered.

"Thanks. I'll take Klartch with me," Cat said. He did not feel like letting Klartch out of his sight just then. He handed Syracuse over to Mr. Adams and managed to thank him, although he was nervous again, knowing what Syracuse could be like. But Syracuse bent his head to Mr. Adams and seemed prepared to make a fuss of him, while Mr. Adams murmured and made little cheeping whistles in reply.

It seemed to be all right. Marianne and Cat went to the open door of the conservatory, with Klartch lolloping after them. "Is something the matter?" Marianne said as they went. "You look pale. And you only talk in little jerks."

Cat would have liked to tell Marianne all about his encounter with Mr. Farleigh. He was almost longing to. But that strange thing happened in his head that made him so bad at telling people things, and all he could manage to say was, "I had a—a turn up with Gaffer Farleigh on the way." And as soon as Marianne was nodding in perfect understanding, Cat was forced to change the subject. He leaned toward her and whispered, "Is Mr. Adams a *gnome*?"

Marianne choked on a giggle. "I don't *know*!" she whispered back.

Cat was feeling much better and they were both trying not to laugh as they entered the conservatory. It was transformed. When Cat had last been here, the glass of the roof and walls had been too dirty to see through, and the floor had been coconut matting with dead plants standing about on it. Marianne could hardly remember it any other way. Now the glass sparkled and there were big green frondy plants, some of them with huge lilylike flowers, white and cream and yellow, which Jason must have brought here from his store. The floor that the plants stood on was a marvel of white, green, and blue tiles, in a gentle eye-resting pattern. There were new cane chairs. Best of all, a small fountain—that must have been covered up by the old matting—was now playing, making a quiet chuckling and misting the fronds of the plants. The smell this brought out from the flowers reminded them both of Irene's scent.

Marianne said wonderingly, "This must all have been underneath! How *could* Gammer have kept it all covered up?"

Thoroughly curious to know what the rest of the house was like now, they went on into the hall. The same tiles were here, blue, white, and green, making the hall twice as light. To

Marianne's surprise, the tiles went on up the walls, to about the height of her shoulders, where she had only known dingy, knobbly cream paint before. Above the tiles, Uncle Charles had painted the walls a paler shade of the blue in the tiles. Marianne wondered if Uncle Charles had chosen it, or Irene. Irene, certainly. There were plants here too, one of them a whole tree. The stairs had been polished so that they gleamed, with a rich, moss-colored strip of carpet down the middle.

Klartch had difficulty walking on the tiles. His front talons clattered and slid. His back feet, which were more like paws, skidded. Cat turned and waited for him.

Marianne, watching Klartch, said, "I suppose Gammer covered the tiles with matting because they were slippery. Or was it in case they got spoiled? What was your idea for helping me?"

Cat turned back to her, wishing it was a bigger, better idea. "Well," he began.

But Jason came out of one of the rooms just then. "Oh, hello!" he said. "I didn't hear you arrive. Welcome to the dez rez, both of you!"

And Irene came racing down the moss-carpeted stairs, crying out in delight. She seized Marianne and kissed her, hugged Cat, and then kneeled down to lift Klartch up by his feathery front legs so that she could rub her face on his beak. Klartch made little crooning noises at her in reply. "This is splendid!" Irene said. "Not many people can say that their very first visitor was a griffin!" She lowered Klartch down and looked anxiously up at Marianne. "I hope you don't mind what we've done to the house."

"Mind?" Marianne said. "It's wonderful! Were these tiles always up the walls like this?" She went over and rubbed her hand across them. "Smooth," she said. "Lovely."

"They were painted over," Irene said. "When I discovered them under the paint, I just had to have it scraped off. I'm afraid the painting Mr. Pinhoe wasn't very pleased about the extra work. But I cleaned the tiles myself."

Uncle Charles was an idiot then, Marianne thought. "It was worth it. They glow!"

"Ah, that's Irene's doing," Jason said, with a proud, loving look toward his wife. "She's inherited the dwimmer gift. Dwimmer," he explained to Cat, "means that a person is in touch with the life in everything. They can bring it out even when it's hidden. When Irene cleaned those tiles, she didn't just take the paint and dirt of ages off them. She released the art that went to making them."

A slight noise made Marianne look up at the stairs. Uncle Charles was standing near the top of them, in his paint-blotched overalls, looking outraged. None of the adult Pinhoes liked to hear the craft openly spoken of like this. Not even Uncle Charles, Marianne thought sadly. Uncle Charles was becoming more of a standard Pinhoe and less of a disappointment every day. Oh, I *wish* they'd let him go and study to be an artist, like he wanted to after he painted our inn sign! she thought.

Uncle Charles coughed slightly and came loudly down the wooden part of the stairs. Marianne knew that, although it looked as if

Uncle Charles was trying to keep paint off the mossy carpet, what he was really doing was making a noise in order to stop Jason talking about dwimmer. "I've finished the undercoat in the small bathroom, madam," he said to Irene. "I'll be off to my lunch while it dries and come back to do the gloss this afternoon."

"Thank you, Mr. Pinhoe," Irene said to him.

Jason said, trying to be friendly, "I don't know how you do it, Mr. Pinhoe. I've never known paint to dry as quickly as yours does."

Uncle Charles just gave him a fixed and disapproving look and clumped across the tiles to the front door. The look, and Uncle Charles's head with it, jerked a little when he saw Klartch. For a fraction of an instant, delight and curiosity jumped across his face. Then the disapproving looked settled back, stronger than ever, and Uncle Charles marched on, and away outside.

He left a slightly awkward silence behind him.

"Well," Jason said at length, a bit too heartily, "I think we should show you all over the house."

"I only came to find my cat, really," Marianne said.

"Jane James has got him," Irene said. "He's quite safe. *Do* come and see what we've done here!"

It was impossible to say no. Jason and Irene were both so proud of the place. They swept Cat and Marianne through into the front room, where the moss green chairs, new white walls, and some of Irene's design paintings on it in frames, made it look like a different room from the one where Gammer had shouted at the Farleighs. Then Cat and Marianne were swept to Jason's den, full of books and leather, and Irene's workroom, all polished wood and a sloping table under the window, with an antique stand for paints and pencils that Marianne knew Dad would have admired: it was so cleverly designed.

After this they were whirled through the dining room and then on upstairs, into a moss green corridor with bedrooms and bathrooms opening off it. Irene had had some of the walls moved, so that now there were bedrooms, sunny and elegant, which had not been there when Marianne last saw the house. The trickling cistern cabinet had become a white warm cupboard that was full of towels and made no noise at all. Uncle Simeon, Marianne thought, had done wonders up here, sprained ankle and all.

"We're still thinking what to do with the attics," Irene said, "but they need a lot of sorting out first."

"I want to check all those herbs for seeds. Some of them are quite rare and may well grow, given the right spells," Jason explained as he swept everyone downstairs again.

Marianne sent Cat an urgent look on the way down. Cat pretended to be waiting for Klartch in order to look reassuringly back. They had to let Jason and Irene finish showing them the house. It was no good trying to talk before then.

Down the passage from the hall, which turned out to be lined with the same blue, green, and white tiles, Jason flung open the door to the kitchen. More of those tiles over the sink, Marianne saw, and in a line round the room; but mostly the impression was of largeness, brightness, and comfort. There was a rusty red floor, which the place had always needed, in Marianne's opinion, and of course the famous table, now scrubbed white, white, white.

Nutcase leered smugly at her from Jane James's bony knees. Jane James was sitting in a chair close to the stove, stirring a saucepan with one hand and reading a magazine she held in the other.

"I've taken the scullery for my distillery," Jason said. "Let me show—"

"Lunch in half an hour," Jane James replied.

"I'll tell Mr. Adams," Irene said.

Jane James stood up and put the magazine on the table and Nutcase on the magazine. Nutcase sat there demurely until Klartch shuffled and clacked his way round the door. Then Nutcase stood up in an arch and spat.

"Don't be a silly cat," Jane James said, as if she saw creatures like Klartch every day. "It's only a baby griffin. Will he eat biscuits?" she asked Cat. She seemed to know at once that he was responsible for Klartch.

"*I'll* eat biscuits," Jason said. "She makes the best biscuits in this world," he told Marianne.

"Yes, but not for you. You'll spoil your lunch," Jane James said. "You and Irene go and get cleaned up ready."

Cat was not surprised that Jason and Irene meekly scurried out of the kitchen. Nor was he surprised when Jane James gave a secret smile as she watched them go. He thought she was quite certainly a sorceress. She reminded him a lot of Miss Bessemer, who was.

Her biscuits were delicious, big and buttery. Klartch liked them as much as Cat and Marianne did and kept putting his beak up for more. Nutcase looked down from the table at him, disgustedly.

After about her tenth biscuit, Marianne found herself searching Jane James's face for the humor she was sure was hidden there. "That time you brought Nutcase home in a basket," she said curiously, "you weren't cross about him, really, were you?"

"Not at all," Jane James said. "He likes me

and I like him. I'd gladly keep him here if he's too much trouble for you. But I kept seeing you chasing around, worrying about him. Did you get *any* holiday to yourself this year?"

Marianne's face crumpled a little as she thought of her story of "Princess Irene and her Cats," still barely started. But she said bravely, "Our family likes to keep children busy."

"You're no child. You're a full-grown enchantress," Jane James retorted. "Don't they *notice*? And I don't see any of your cousins very busy. Riding their bikes up and down and yelling seems to me how busy *they* are." She stood up and planted Nutcase into Marianne's arms. "There you are. Tell Mr. Adams to come for his lunch on your way out."

You had to go when Jane James did that, Cat thought. She was quite a tartar. They thanked her for the biscuits and went out into the passage again. As they turned left toward the hall, they nearly collided with a person who appeared to come out of the tiled wall.

"Ooops-a-la!" that person said.

They stared at him. Both of them had a moment when they thought they were looking at Mr. Adams and that Mr. Adams had shrunk. He had the same tufts of hair and the same wrinkled brown face with the big ears. But Mr. Adams had not been wearing bright green, blue, and white checkered trousers and a moss green waistcoat. And Mr. Adams was about the same height as Cat, who was small for his age, where this person only came up to Cat's waist.

Klartch clacked forward with great interest.

The little man fended him off with a hand that appeared to be all long, thin fingers. "Now, now, now, Klartch. I'm not food for griffins. I'm only a skinny old househob."

"A *househob*!" Marianne said. "When did you move in here?"

"About two thousand years ago, when your first Gaffer's hall was built in this place," the little man replied. "You might say I've always been here."

"How come I've never seen you before, then?" Marianne asked.

The little man looked up at her. His eyes were big and shiny and full of green sadness. "Ah," he said, "but I've seen *you*, Miss Marianne. I've seen most things while I've been sealed inside these walls these many long years, until the dwimmer-lady, Princess Irene, let me out."

"You mean—under the cream paint?" Marianne said. "Did Gammer seal you in?"

"Not she. It was more than paint and longer ago than that," the househob said. "It was in those days after the devout folk came. After that, the folks in charge here named me and all my kind wicked and ungodly, and they set spells to imprison us—all of us, in houses, fields, and woods—and told everyone we were gone for good. Though, mind you, I never could see why these devout folk could believe on the one hand that God made all, and on the other hand call us ungodly—but there you go. It was done." He spread both huge hands and brought his pointed shoulders up in a shrug. Then he bowed to Marianne and turned and bowed to Cat. "Now, if you'll forgive me, dwimmer-folk both, I believe Jane James has my lunch ready. And she doesn't hold with me coming in through her kitchen wall. I have to use the door."

Amazed and bemused, Cat and Marianne stepped back out of the househob's way. He set off at a crablike trot toward the kitchen. Then turned back anxiously. "You didn't eat all the biscuits, did you?"

"No, there's a big tinful," Cat told him.

"Ah. Good." The househob turned toward the kitchen door. He did not open it. They watched him walk through it, much as Marianne had watched Nutcase walk through the wall in Furze Cottage. Nutcase, at the sight, squirmed indignantly in Marianne's arms. He seemed to think he was the only one who should be able to do that sort of thing.

Cat and Marianne looked at each other, but could think of nothing to say.

It was not until they were halfway across the hall that Marianne said, "You think you have an idea for what I can do about Gammer?"

"Yes—I hope," Cat said, wishing it was a

better idea. "At least, I think I know someone you could ask. I met a man in your wood here who I think could help. He was awfully wise."

Marianne felt truly let down. "A man," she said disbelievingly. "In the wood."

"*Really* wise," Cat said rather desperately. "Dwimmer wise. And he had a unicorn."

Marianne supposed Cat was speaking the truth. If he *was*, then a unicorn did make a difference. If househobs were real, then might not unicorns be real too? A unicorn was part of the Pinhoe coat of arms and could—surely?—be expected to be on her side. And they were in such a mess, she and the Pinhoes and the Farleighs, that anything was worth a try.

"All right," she said. "How do I find them?"

"I'll have to take you," Cat said. "There was a queer barrier in the way. Do you want to come now?"

"Yes, please," Marianne said.

Chapter Seventeen

Outside, beyond the conservatory, Mr. Adams was leaning against Syracuse with his arms round Syracuse's neck, amid a strong smell of peppermint. Positively canoodling, Cat thought, rather jealously. But then, Cat thought, looking at Mr. Adams closely, besides seeming as if he had gnome in his ancestry—or was it househob?—Mr. Adams had more than a little of this strange thing called dwimmer. He was bound to get on with Syracuse, because Syracuse had it too.

Mr. Adams, however much he was enjoying Syracuse, was only too ready to hand Syracuse over and go in for his lunch. "There's no doubt," he said, in his talkative way, "that working a

garden gives you an appetite. I've never *been* so
hungry as I am since I moved here."

He went on talking. He talked all the time he
was helping Cat heave Klartch up across
Syracuse's saddle. He talked while he checked
the girths. He talked while he carefully cleaned
his spade. But eventually he talked his way
through the archway in the wall and round to
the kitchen door. They could hear him begin
talking to Jane James as he opened it. As soon as
the door shut, Marianne put Nutcase secretly
down in the beech hedge. "You go on home to
Furze Cottage," she told him. "You know the
way."

"Not happy," Klartch said plaintively from
the saddle.

Cat could see Klartch was uncomfortable, but
he said, "It's your own fault. You *would* follow
me. You can't walk fast enough to keep up, so
stay up there and I'll let you down when we find
the road."

He and Marianne set off, Cat leading
Syracuse, across the stubbly lawn to the row of

lilacs at the back. There they found the small rickety gate Cat had come in by. It was green with mildew and almost falling apart with age, and they had to shove it hard to get it open again.

"I'd forgotten this was here," Marianne said, as they went through into the empty, rustling wood. "Gaffer used to call it his secret escape route. Which way do we go?"

"Keep straight on, I think," Cat said.

There was no path, but Cat set his mind on the whereabouts of that barrier and led the way, over shoals of fallen leaves, past brambles and through hazel thickets, deeper and deeper among the trees. Some of the time he was dragged through bushes by Syracuse, who was getting very excited by the wood and wanted to throw Klartch off and run. Poor Klartch was jogged and jigged and bounced and was less happy than ever. "Down!" he said.

"Soon," Cat told him.

They came to the barrier quite unexpectedly on the other side of a holly bush. It stretched as far as either of them could see in both directions, rusting, ramshackle, and overgrown. Marianne looked at it in astonishment.

"What's this? I never saw *this* before!"

"You didn't know to look for it, I expect," Cat said.

"It's a *mess*!" Marianne said. "Creepers and nettles and rusty wire. Who put it up?"

"I don't know," Cat said. "But it's made of magic, really. Do you think you could help me take it down? We won't get Syracuse past it the way I got in last time."

"I can *try*, I suppose," Marianne said. "How do you suggest?"

Cat thought about it for a moment and then conjured the nearest clothesline from Ulverscote. It came with a row of someone's underpants pegged on it, which made them both struggle not to give shrieks of laughter. Each of them had the feeling that loud laughter might fetch the person who had made the barrier here. From then on, they spoke in low voices, to be on the safe side.

While Marianne carefully unpegged the pants and put them in a pile by the nearest tree, Cat fastened each end of the rope to the back of the saddle on Syracuse, using a thick blob of magic to fix it there. Klartch reared up and watched with interest as Cat took the rest of the clothesline and stretched high to loop it along the ragged top of the barrier. Klartch was an actual help here. Because Klartch was attending to the barrier, Cat somehow knew that it was mostly unreal. It had been made out of two small pieces of chicken wire and one length of corrugated iron, plus a charm to make the weeds grow over it, and then stretched by magic to become the long, impenetrable thing it was now. This meant that the clothesline was going to slide straight through it and come loose, if Cat was not careful.

"Thanks, Klartch," Cat said. As soon as the rope was jammed in along the ragged spikes of rusty iron, he fixed it there with a truly enormous slab of magic. He jerked it to test it. It was quite solid. "You take one side and pull hard when I say," Cat murmured to Marianne, and took hold of the rope on the other side.

"What charm do I use when I pull?" Marianne asked.

"Nothing particularly," Cat said, surprised that she should ask. Ulverscote witchcraft must be very different from enchanter's magic. "Just think hard of the barrier coming down."

Marianne's eyebrows went up, but she obediently took hold of the rope on her side. She was terribly obedient, Cat thought. He remembered Janet once telling him that *he* was too obedient, and he knew that had been the result of the way his sister always despised him. He was suddenly, firmly, decided that, however much Marianne protested, he was going to tell Chrestomanci about her.

"Right," Cat said to Syracuse in a low voice. "Work, Syracuse. Walk on."

Syracuse turned his head and stared at Cat. Me, *work*? said every line of him. And he simply planted himself and stood there, whatever Cat said.

"You can have another peppermint," Cat said. "Just walk. We need your strength."

Syracuse put his ears back and simply stood.

"Oh, lord!" Marianne said. "He's as bad as Nutcase. You go and lead him, and I'll pull on both halves of the rope." She collected Cat's side of the rope and stood in the middle, holding both lengths of clothesline.

If Syracuse decided to kick out, he could hurt Marianne there. Cat hurried round to Syracuse's head and took hold of his bridle. He found a slightly furry peppermint in one of his pockets and held it out at arm's length in front of Syracuse's nose, before he dared pull on the bridle. "Now come *on*, Syracuse! Peppermint!"

Syracuse's ears came up and he rolled an eye at Cat, to say he knew exactly what Cat was up to.

"Yes," Cat said to him. "It's because we really need you."

Syracuse snorted. Then, when Cat was ready to give up, and to his huge relief, Syracuse started to trudge forward, stirring up clouds of broken dead leaves that got into Cat's eyes and his mouth and down his boots and even some-how down his neck. Cat blinked and blew and urged Syracuse and encouraged him and willed at the barrier. He could feel Marianne behind them, willing too with surprising power, as she pulled on the clothesline like someone in two tug-of-wars at once.

The barrier rustled, grated, groaned, and keeled slowly over in front of Marianne. When Cat turned to tell Syracuse he was a good horse and to feed him the peppermint, he could see the long line of metal and creepers in both directions, slowly falling flat, piece by piece, rather like a wave breaking on a beach. He could hear metal screaming and branches snapping, off into the distance both ways. Cat was rather surprised. He had not expected to bring the whole thing down. But he supposed it must be because the barrier had been made out of just the one small piece, really.

"Hooray!" Marianne said quietly, letting go of the rope.

Though the barrier now looked like a pile of nettles, brambles, and broken creepers, there was still jagged metal underneath. Cat flicked the rope loose from it and undid the fastenings from Syracuse and, while Marianne busily pegged the pants back onto the rope, he tried growing a mat of ivy over the barrier, to make it safer for Syracuse to walk on. Chrestomanci was always telling him that he should never waste magic, so Cat fed the slab of magic that had fastened the rope back into the fallen creepers.

This was quite as startling as the way the whole barrier had come down. Ivy surged and spread and gnarled and tangled, a mature and glossy dark green, in a whispering rush, that put out yellowish flowers and then black fruits in seconds, not just in one place as Cat had intended, but off along the fallen barrier in both directions. By the time Marianne had turned round with the pants pegged back on the clothesline, the barrier was a long mound of ivy as far as she could see both ways. It looked as if it had been growing there for years.

"My!" she said. "You do have dwimmer, don't you!"

"It may be the magic in this wood," Cat said. He sent the clothesline back where it had come from, then he turned Syracuse round and led him carefully over the ivy bank and down into the mossy road beyond. While Marianne crunched her way across after them, Cat stopped and got Klartch down. Klartch immediately became hugely happy. He gave out whistling squeaks and went lolloping off toward the nearest bend in the road. The mossy surface seemed perfect for his clawed feet. Syracuse felt it was perfect for hooves too. He bounded and waltzed and tried to take off after Klartch so determinedly that Cat was dragged along in great hopping bounds, with Marianne pelting after them.

They whirled round the bend in the road with Klartch in the lead. The old cart was there, parked in a new place on the verge, with the seeming old white mare grazing beside it. Beyond that, the old man looked up in amazement from his panful of mushrooms and bacon. He just managed to let the pan go and brace himself, before Marianne rushed up and hurled herself on him.

"Gaffer!" she screamed. "Oh, Gaffer, you're not dead after all!" She pushed her face into the old man's tattered jacket and burst into tears.

Syracuse stopped dead when he saw the old unicorn. She raised her head from the grass and looked at him inquiringly. A ray of sun, slanting between the trees, caught her horn and lit it into pearly creams and greens and blues. Or was that blue and green and white, like the tiles in Woods House, Cat wondered. Syracuse tiptoed respectfully toward her and put out his nose. Graciously, the old unicorn touched her nose to his.

"He's got unicorn blood in him somewhere," she remarked softly to Cat. "I wonder how that happened."

Beyond her, Klartch was creeping toward the pan of mushrooms and bacon with his beak out. Cat thought he ought to go and drag him away. But Marianne was kneeling in the old man's arms, sobbing out what seemed to be private

things, and Cat was embarrassed about inter-
rupting. However, while Cat hesitated, the old
man swiveled himself around and spared an arm
from Marianne in order to tap Klartch firmly on
the beak. "Wait," Cat heard him say. "You shall
have some presently." And he went back to lis-
tening attentively to Marianne.

"Do you understand a little more about
dwimmer now?" the unicorn said conversation-
ally to Cat.

"I—think so," Cat said. "Irene has it.
Marianne keeps saying I've got it too. Have I?"

"You have. Even more strongly than my old
Gaffer," the unicorn told him. "Didn't you just
grow several miles of ivy?"

Nearly a year ago now, Cat had been forced to
accept that he was a nine-lifed enchanter. That
had been hard to do, but he supposed it made it
easier to accept having dwimmer too. He
grinned, thinking of himself stuffed full of every
kind of magic—except, he thought, Joe Pinhoe's
kind. But then, when he thought about it, he
knew that Joe had been using dwimmer to ani-

mate that stuffed ferret of his. How muddling. "Yes," he said. "Can you tell me what I ought to be doing with it?"

"We all hoped you might ask me that," said the unicorn. "You can do many thousands of folk the same favor that Irene did for her house-hob, if you want."

"Oh," said Cat. "Where are these people?"

Syracuse nudged up to the unicorn and snorted impatiently.

"I'll have a long talk with you in a moment," she said to him. "Why don't you graze on this tasty bank for a while?"

Syracuse looked at her questioningly. She stumped forward a step or so and flicked her horn affectionately along his mane. All his tack vanished, saddle, bit, reins, everything, leaving him without so much as a halter. He looked much better like that to Cat's eyes. Syracuse twitched all over with relief, before he bent his head and started tearing up mouthfuls of grass and little fragrant plants.

"If you can taste it through all the peppermint

you've eaten," the unicorn remarked drily. She said to Cat, "I'll put it all back later. The folks are here. Hidden behind. Imprisoned for no fault that I can see, except that they scare humans. Can't you feel this?"

Cat examined the wood with his thoughts. It was quiet, too quiet, and the silence was not peace. It was the same emptiness that he had felt whenever he rode out with Syracuse, by the river and on the heath, and behind the emptiness was misery, and longing. It was the same thing that he had felt in Home Wood when he first encountered Mr. Farleigh. As for this wood, he remembered Chrestomanci saying, rather irritably, what a dreary, empty place it was. But here there seemed to be no rack of dead animals to act as a gate between the emptiness and the misery in the distance behind.

"I don't know what to do about it," he told the unicorn. He had not managed to do anything in Home Wood, even with a gate. What did you do here, against complete blankness? "You can't clean a wood the way Irene cleaned those tiles."

"You can make an opening, though," the unicorn suggested quietly. "Make a road between the background and the foreground. That's how roads usually go."

"I'll try." Cat stood and thought. If he thought of it as like stage scenery, he supposed he could make the empty wood seem like a solid sort of curtain that had been drawn across the real scenery, the blue distance behind, and then tightly fixed. "Draw it like a curtain?" he asked the unicorn.

"If you want," she answered.

The trouble was, it was only the *one* curtain. There was no opening, the way there was with window curtains, where you take hold of the two sides and pull them apart. Cat could not see himself tearing trees and grass and bushes in two. Even if he *could*, it would kill everything. No. The only thing to do seemed to be to find the edge of the curtain, wherever that was, and pull it from there.

He looked for the edge. There was *miles* of this curtain. Like a sheet of rubbery gauze, it stretched and stretched, out across the country, out across the continent, over the oceans, right to the edges of the world. He had to stretch and stretch himself to get near it, and the rubbery edge kept slipping away from his imaginary clutching fingers. Cat clenched his teeth and stretched himself more, just that little bit further. And at last his reaching left hand closed on the thin, slippery edge of it. He put both hands to it and hauled. It would hardly budge. Someone had pegged it down really firmly. Even when the unicorn came and rested her horn gently on Cat's shoulder, Cat could only move the thing an inch or so.

"Try asking the prisoners to help," the unicorn murmured.

"Good idea," Cat panted. Still hanging on to the distant end of the curtain, he pushed his mind into the empty blue distance behind it, and it was not empty. The ones inside were all swarming, drifting, and anxiously clustering toward the other side of the curtain. "Pull, pull!" he whispered to them. "Help me *pull!*" It was so like making Syracuse pull down the barrier that he almost offered them peppermint.

But they needed no bribery. They were frantic to get out now. They swooped on the place where Cat's imaginary hands were clutched, in a storm of small, fierce strangenesses, and fastened on beside Cat and heaved. Beside Cat, the unicorn put her horn down and heaved too.

The curtain tore. First it came away in a long strip across the middle, making Cat stagger back into the unicorn. Then it tore downward, then diagonally, as more and more eager creatures inside clawed and hauled and pulled at it. Finally it began flopping down in wobbly dead heaps, which folded in on themselves and melted. Cat could actually smell it as it melted. The smell was remarkably like the disinfectant spell Euphemia had used on the stairs. But this smell was overwhelmed almost at once by a sweet, wild scent from the myriad beings who came whirring out past Cat's face and fled away into the landscape. Cat thought it was, just a little, like the incense smell from the meadows by the river.

"Done it, I think!" he gasped at the unicorn. He slid down her hairy side and sat on the bank with a bump. He was weak with effort. But he was glad to see that the trees of the wood were still there. It would have been a mistake to have tried to tear the wood in half.

"You have," the unicorn said. "Thank you." Her horn gently touched Cat's forehead. It smelled like the meadows too.

When Cat recovered and sat up properly, he saw that the old man was still talking earnestly with Marianne. But he knew what had been going on. His bright brown eyes kept turning appreciatively to the woods, although he now had the pan on his knees and was feeding a soothing mushroom to Marianne and then some bacon to Klartch, as if there was no difference between them.

"But, Gaffer," Cat heard Marianne say, "if you've been trapped here all these years, where do you get your bacon from?"

"Your uncle Cedric puts it through the barrier for me," Gaffer said. "And eggs. They all know

I'm here, you know, but Cedric's the only one who thinks I might need feeding."

While they talked, the wood was making a great rustling and heaving. Like a sail filling with wind, it seemed to be filling with life around them. Cat looked down and saw, almost between his knees, a multitude of tiny green beings milling and welling out of the ground. Other, bigger ones flitted at the corners of his eyes. When he looked across the road, he could see strange gawky creatures stalking among the trees and small airborne ones darting from bush to bush. There seemed to be a tall green woman walking dreamily through a distant patch of sunlight. Someone came up behind Cat—all he could see of him or her was a very thin brown leg—and bent over to whisper, "Thank you. None of us are going to forget." He or she was gone when Cat turned his head.

Hooves sounded on the mossy road. The unicorn, who was now standing head to tail with Syracuse, presumably having the talk she had promised, looked up at the sound. "Ah," she said. "Here comes my daughter, free at last. Thank you, Cat."

Cat and Marianne both found themselves standing up as a splendid young unicorn dashed along the road and stopped beside the old man's cart. She was small and lissome and silvery, with quantities of white mane and tail. Cat could see she was very young because her horn was the merest creamy stub on her forehead. Syracuse, at the sight of her, began to prance and sidle and make himself look magnificent.

"Ah, no," the old unicorn said. "She's still only a yearling, Syracuse. She's been a yearling for more than a thousand years. Give her a chance to grow up now."

The small unicorn ignored Syracuse anyway and trotted lovingly up to her mother.

"Beautiful!" Gaffer said admiringly. He put the food down on the grass for Klartch and leaned over to concentrate on the young unicorn.

Klartch, to Cat's surprise, turned away from the food and went shambling and stumbling across the road, making squeaks and hoots and long quavering whistles. The sounds were answered from inside the wood by a deeper whistling, like a trill on an oboe. A blot of darkness that Cat had taken for a holly brake stirred and stretched and moved out into the road, where she lifted great gray wings and put her enormous horn-colored beak down to meet Klartch. Cat knew it was the creature that had landed on his tower before Klartch was hatched. She was surprisingly graceful for something that huge, gray and white from her sleek feathered head to her lionlike furry body and swinging tufted tail. She lifted a feathered foot with six-inch talons on the end and gently, very gently, pulled Klartch in under one of her enormous wings.

She was Klartch's mother, of course. For the first time in his life, Cat knew what it was like to be truly and wretchedly miserable. Before, when he had been miserable, Cat had mostly felt lost and peevish. But now, when he was going to lose Klartch, he felt a blinding heartache that not only devastated his mind but gave him a real, actual pain somewhere in the center of his chest. It was the hardest thing he had ever done, when he heaved up a difficult breath and said, "Klartch ought to go with you now."

The mother griffin drew her beak back from Klartch squirming and squeaking under her wing and turned her enormous yellow eyes on Cat. Cat could see she was as sad as he was. "Oh, no," she said in her deep, trilling voice. "You hatched him. I'd prefer you to bring him up. He needs a proper education. Griffins are meant to be as learned and wise as they are magical. He ought to have teaching that I never had."

Gaffer said, rather reproachfully, "I did my best to teach you."

"Yes, you did," the mother griffin replied. She smiled at Gaffer with the ends of her beak. "But you could only teach me when I got out at full moon, Gaffer man. I hope you can teach me all the time now, but I'd like Klartch to have an enchanter's upbringing."

"So be it," Gaffer said. He said to Cat, "Can you do that for her?"

"Yes," Cat said, and then added bravely, "It depends what Klartch wants, though."

Klartch seemed surprised that anyone should question what he wanted. He dived out from under the griffin's big wing and scuttled over to Cat, where he leaned heavily against Cat's legs and wiped his beak against Cat's riding boots. "Mine," he said. "Cat mine."

The pain lifted from Cat's chest like magic. He smiled—because he couldn't help it—across at Klartch's mother. "I really will look after him," he promised.

"That's settled, then," Gaffer said, warm and approving. "Marianne, my pet, would you do me the favor of running down to the village and telling your dad I'll be along shortly to sort things out? He won't be too pleased, I'm afraid, so tell him I insisted. I'll follow you when I've tidied up here."

Chapter Eighteen

Now that Marianne was leaving, Cat realized that he ought to be going too. Joss Callow would have complained to Chrestomanci by this time. He went up to the big griffin and held his hand out politely. She rubbed it with her great beak. "May I visit Klartch from time to time?" she asked.

"Yes, of course," Cat said. "Any time." He hoped Chrestomanci wouldn't mind too much—he hoped Chrestomanci wouldn't mind too much about all of it. He would have to confess what he had done to Mr. Farleigh sometime soon. He decided not to think about that yet.

When he turned round, Syracuse was stamping irritably because his saddle and bridle were back. Marianne was staring at the two unicorns.

"Gaffer," she said, "when did old Molly turn into a unicorn?"

Gaffer looked up from cleaning out his pan. "She always was one, pet. She chose not to let people see it."

"Oh," Marianne said. She was very quiet, thinking about this, as she walked along the mossy road with Cat and Syracuse. The old gray mare who took Luke Pinhoe to London and then came back on her own—had that been Molly too? Unicorns lived for hundreds of years, they said. Marianne wished she knew.

Cat was letting Klartch bumble along behind them since the surface suited his feet so well. Around them, the woods were full of green distances that had not been there before and alive with rushings, rustlings, and small half-heard voices. There was laughter too, some of it plain joyful, some of it mean and mocking.

Marianne said to Cat, "You've let all the hidden folk out, haven't you?"

Cat nodded. He was not going to apologize, even to Chrestomanci, about that.

Marianne said, "My family are going to be furious with you. They fuss all the time that it's their sacred task to keep them in."

A particularly mocking and malevolent laugh rang out among the trees as Marianne said this. "Some of them don't sound very nice," she added, looking that way uneasily.

"Some humans aren't very nice either," Cat said.

Marianne thought of Great-Uncle Edgar and Aunt Joy and said, "True."

The road ran out into strong daylight a moment later. They found themselves on a rocky headland, looking down on Ulverscote across a long green meadow. They were above the church tower here and could see down into the main street over the roof of the Pinhoe Arms. It was quiet and empty because everyone was indoors having lunch.

This rocky bit, Cat thought, was the part of Ulverscote Wood that he and Roger had kept seeing when they tried to get to it before. While they waited for Klartch to catch up, he looked out the other way, across the wide countryside, over humping hills, hedges, and the white winding road, wondering if he could see the Castle from here.

He saw a most peculiar bristling black cloud coming across the nearest hill. It spread across a stubble field on one side and a pasture on the other, and it appeared to be trickling and wobbling along the road too. It was rushing toward them almost as fast as a car could go. An angry buzzing sort of sound came with it.

"What on earth is that?" he said to Marianne. "A swarm of huge wasps?"

Marianne looked, and went pale. "Oh, my lord!" she said. "It's the Farleighs. On broomsticks and bicycles."

Cat could see it was people now: angry, determined women of all ages whizzing along on broomsticks and equally angry men and boys pedaling furiously along the road.

Marianne said, "I must go down and warn everyone!" and set off at a run down the meadow.

But it was too late. Before Marianne had gone three steps, the horde of Farleighs had swept down into Ulverscote and the place was black with them. Yelling with fury and triumph, the broomstick riders sprang off onto their feet, lofted their brooms, and began smashing windows with the butt ends. The cyclists arrived, braking and howling, and threw powdered spells in through the smashed windows. Inside the houses, Pinhoes screamed.

At the screams, a whole crowd of Pinhoe men, who must have been having lunch in the inn, came swarming out of the Pinhoe Arms, carrying stools and chairs and small tables. Marianne saw Uncle Charles there, brandishing a chair leg, and Uncle Arthur charging in front with a coatrack. They all fell on the cyclists, whacking mightily. More Pinhoes poured into the street from the houses, and others leaned out of upstairs windows and threw things and tipped things upon the Farleighs.

Round the smashed windows of the grocer's and the chemist's, there were instant battles.

Feet crunched in broken glass there, cheeses and big bottles were hurled. Broomsticks walloped. In almost no time, the main street was a fighting tangle of bent bicycles and shouting, screaming people. Marianne could see Gammer Norah Farleigh at the back of the fight, yelling her troops on and cracking an enormous horsewhip.

Down the hill at the other end, Aunt Joy raced out of the Post Office carrying a long bar of scaffolding like a lance and screaming curses. Uncle Isaac and Uncle Richard were pelting up behind her. Marianne saw her parents running behind them. Mum was carrying her new broom, and Dad seemed to be waving a saw. Nicola's mother came out of her house dressed in her best, on her way to visit Nicola, screamed, went in and slammed her door. Up the hill at the other end, Great-Uncle Lester, who was coming in his car to give Nicola's mother a lift to the hospital, bared his teeth and drove straight at the back of Gammer Norah. She saw him coming in time and levitated to the roof of his car, where she rode screaming, cracking her whip and trying to break his windscreen with her broomstick. Uncle Lester drove slowly on regardless, trying to run over Farleighs, but mostly running over bicycles instead.

Behind the car, Great-Uncle Edgar and Great-Aunt Sue, who must have been out exercising their dogs, were arriving at a tired trot. They were surrounded by exhausted dogs, who were mostly too fat and tired to bite Farleighs, although Great-Aunt Sue shrieked at them to "Bite, bite, bite!" They settled for barking instead.

The Reverend Pinhoe appeared on the churchyard wall, waving a censer of smoking incense on a chain and making prayerful gestures. When that made no difference to the struggling mayhem in the street below him, he swung the censer at any Farleigh head he could reach. There were clangs and terrible cries. And down near the Post Office, Marianne's parents had entered the fray, Mum batting with her broom and Dad swinging the flat of the saw at any Farleigh near. Even above the noise of the rest, Marianne could hear the dreadful *ker-blatt SWAT* from Dad's saw. And she and Cat both winced at what Aunt Joy was doing with her scaffolding pole.

They both turned their eyes away to the upper end of the village again. There, behind the row of yelping dogs, the long black car from the Castle edged cautiously out of the gates of Woods House and crawled to a halt at the back of the battle, as if Millie, who was driving it, was at a loss to know what to do. Nearly a thousand fighting witches seemed a bit much even for an enchantress as strong as Millie.

"Do something! *Do* something!" Marianne implored Cat.

Nearly a thousand fighting witches were a bit much for Cat too. And he was not going to take Syracuse and Klartch in among that lot. But someone was going to be killed soon if he didn't do *something*. That man with the saw down the hill was starting to hit people with the edge of it. There was blood down that end of the street. A giant stasis might stop it, Cat thought. But what happened when he took the stasis *off*?

All the same, Cat drew in his power, as he had been taught, in order to cast the stasis. He almost had enough when, with a violent clattering and screams of "I belong to Chrestomanci Castle!" the flying machine swept in from above the Post Office. The faces of the fighters turned upward in alarm as it clapped and flapped and shouted its swift way over their heads.

A giant voice, magically amplified and accompanied by a steady chant of "I belong to Chrestomanci Castle!" shouted, "OUT OF THE WAY! We're CRASHING!"

Everyone dived to the sides of the street. The machine did not so much crash as simply keep on in a straight line. It seemed to get lower with every flap of the jointed tables, but in fact it was the street that got steeper and the flying machine just flew into it. It landed with a great clatter and a tremendous crunching of bicycles underneath, exactly opposite the Pinhoe Arms. The chanting from the broken furniture faded to a murmur. Joe and Roger sat back gasping. Joe was without his shirt, and both were covered with sweat. Roger's hair was so dark with perspiration that, for a moment, he looked quite strikingly like his father.

Every person there was able to make that comparison quite easily. Chrestomanci stood up among the tangle of chairs at the back of the machine. Chrestomanci's left arm was in a bloodstained sling that seemed to have been Joe's shirt, and his smooth gray jacket was torn. He looked very unwell, but no one had any doubt who he was. Pinhoes and Farleighs, panting, with hair hanging over their faces and, in some cases, blood running down among the hair, stopped fighting and said to one another, "It's the Big Man! That's torn it!"

Cat sighed and sent his gathered magic off as a goodwill spell. "Mr. Farleigh shot him!" he said to Marianne.

Marianne merely nodded and went running off down the meadow, making for the alleyway beside the Pinhoe Arms. As she ran, she could hear tinny bongings as Gammer Norah trampled up and down the roof of Great-Uncle Lester's car, shouting, "Don't you dare interfere! We don't need you from the Castle! These Pinhoes turned our Gaffer into a stone tree! So keep out of it!"

"I believe you have made a serious error there, ma'am," Chrestomanci replied.

When Marianne hurtled out of the other end of the alley into the street, Gammer Norah was still shouting. Her hair had come down from its bun into a sort of wad on one shoulder. What with that, and her long eyes narrowed with rage, she looked as menacingly witchy as a person could. But Chrestomanci was just standing there, waiting for her to stop. The moment Gammer Norah had to pause to take a breath, he said, "I suggest you join me in the Pinhoe Arms to discuss the matter."

Gammer Norah drew herself up to her full squat height. "I will not! I have never been inside a public house in my life!"

"In the inn yard, then," Chrestomanci said. He climbed out of the flying machine, which seemed to settle and spread once he was out of it. As Marianne rushed up to it, she could hear all the chairs, stools, tables, and even the feather duster at the tail, still whispering that they belonged to Chrestomanci Castle.

"Are you all right?" she asked Joe. He looked almost as pale as Chrestomanci.

Joe stared up at her as if she was a nightmare. "He *shot* him!" he said hoarsely. "Gaffer Farleigh shot the Big Man! We had to land on Crowhelm Top and do first aid. He was bleeding in *spurts*, Marianne. I'd never done a real healing before. I thought he was going to die. I was *scared*."

Marianne said soothingly, "But he's got nine lives, Joe."

Roger looked up at her. "No, he hasn't. He's only got two left, and he could have been down to just the one. I was scared too."

Meanwhile, all around them, Farleighs were sullenly separating from Pinhoes, picking up bicycles and broomsticks and kicking them into working order. Two particularly hefty Farleigh men came and stood beside the flying machine. "You're on top of our bikes," one of them said, in a way that suggested trouble.

At this Chrestomanci came and put his hand on Joe's shoulder. He gave Marianne a long, vague look as he said, "You two get yourselves back to the Castle now." Joe and Roger both groaned at the thought of further effort. "Well, you *are* blocking the main road," Chrestomanci said, "and these gentlemen need their bicycles."

"Who are you calling gentlemen?" the Farleigh man demanded.

"Not you, obviously," Chrestomanci said. "Roger, tell Miss Bessemer to give you both hot, sweet tea and then lunch, and ask her to send Tom and Miss Rosalie here to me at once. Miss Rosalie is to bring the folder from my study, the blue one." His bright dark eyes met Marianne's, making her jump. "Young lady, would you mind very much giving them a strong boost to get them airborne? I see you have the power. And you," he added to the Farleigh men, "please stand clear."

Marianne nodded, highly surprised. As the Farleigh men grudgingly moved back, Joe and Roger exchanged a look of misery and Joe said, "Right. One, two, three." The two of them began pedaling. The three-legged stool revolved on the front and the machine trembled all over.

Help! Marianne thought. How do you boost? There was no charm for this any more than there was for pulling the barrier down. She supposed she had better do it the way Cat had told her, by willing.

She willed, hard and ignorantly. The flying machine went straight upward, with a mighty clattering and a scream of "I belong to Chrestomanci Castle!" It tipped left wing downward, and the bent bicycle that had been caught in the woodwork clanged out of it, almost on top of the Farleigh it belonged to.

"Straighten her out!" Joe shrieked.

Marianne did her best, Roger did *his* best, and Joe swayed himself madly to the right. Marianne realized what to do and gave them another boost, forward this time. The pieces of table began to flap at last and the machine sailed forward up the hill, forcing Gammer Norah to slide quickly off Uncle Lester's car or be smacked on the head. The machine then swayed sideways the other way, to only just miss the Castle car as it crept downhill toward the Pinhoe Arms, and then pitched the other way to skim across the heads of Uncle Cedric and Aunt Polly, who were arriving too late, both perched on the same cart horse. After that it straightened out and went majestically flapping, creaking, and whispering over the chimneys of Woods House. Most of Aunt Sue's dogs decided it was the real enemy and went off up the road after it, yapping fit to burst.

"Oh, I wish it hadn't gone!" one of Marianne's smaller cousins wailed. "I wanted a go in it!"

Marianne shuddered. The thing looked even chancier than riding Mum's broomstick at night. She watched the Castle car stop by the Pinhoe Arms. It had all four tires thickly coated in spells against the broken pieces of glass in the road. Clever, she thought. Uncle Lester's car had three flat tires and several bicycles sticking out from underneath it. Millie got out from the driver's seat and hurried toward Chrestomanci, horrified at the state he was in. Jason sprang out from the other side. The back door opened to let out Joss Callow, to Marianne's surprise. Joss turned to help out Irene, who was holding Nutcase in her arms.

I think Nutcase really is going back to Woods House to live, Marianne thought, not sure whether she was sad or relieved. And really, some of my uncles are so *slow*! she added to herself, as Uncle Cedric and Aunt Polly clopped massively downhill and Uncle Simeon came thundering uphill in his builder's van, both of them far too late to do any good.

There was almost a quiet moment after this, while Chrestomanci conferred quickly with Jason and Millie and Millie seemed to be trying to patch Chrestomanci up. Marianne looked up at the sign on the Pinhoe Arms that Uncle Charles had painted the year she was born. The unicorn was definitely Molly, and the griffin facing her was, equally definitely, Klartch's mother. Uncle Charles had *known*. Then why had he always pretended that things like unicorns and griffins didn't exist?

And where was Gaffer? Marianne wondered anxiously. He said he would come.

Chrestomanci looked round, checking up on everybody. "I need all the principals in this matter in the inn yard with me now," he said.

The words caught Cat as he was halfway down the meadow. Chrestomanci was using Performative Speech, the enchanters' magic Cat had been wrestling with after he put Joe on the ceiling. He recognized it as he arrived with a jolt in the inn yard with Syracuse. Klartch, draped across the saddle, was shot off backward as Syracuse made his usual objections to people using magic on him. Cat was carried off his feet for a moment, and it was Marianne who rescued Klartch with a quick levitation spell, and lowered him gently to the cobbles.

"Thanks!" Cat gasped, and then had to turn the other way as, to his dismay, Joss Callow dodged up and grabbed Syracuse from the other side.

"I'll walk him back home for you if you like," Joss said breathlessly, searching in his pocket for a peppermint.

Joss was not angry with him, Cat realized. Joss was extremely anxious to get away from here. Cat did not blame him. The people Joss spied *for* and the people Joss spied *on* were all here in the yard, and most of them were strong magic users.

"Thanks. Would you?" he said, and gave Syracuse over to Joss gladly, wishing he had the same excuse to leave. But Chrestomanci's eye was now on Cat, bright and vague. Cat looked back, appalled at all the blood on Chrestomanci and at how unwell Chrestomanci looked. He knew he should have stopped Mr. Farleigh firing that gun at all.

Chapter Nineteen.

Chrestomanci turned to have a word with Uncle Arthur, who had a black eye again. "Yes," he said. "Find her something as much like a throne as you can. That may calm her down. And drinks all round on the Castle, if you please." Cat could see Chrestomanci was feeling dreadful, but holding himself together by magic.

As Joss led Syracuse out of the inn yard, things settled down into a sort of open-air conference. Gammer Norah was given a mighty carved wooden chair from the Snug—where she sat and glared round aggressively—and sour Dorothea was given a smaller chair next to her. Various Farleigh cousins sat on barrels around them, trying to look dignified. Cat and

Marianne sat on crates with Klartch between them. Everyone else pulled around the weatherbeaten benches and settles from beside the inn walls to sit in a rough circle, while Uncle Arthur hurried out again with a cushioned chair from the saloon bar for Chrestomanci. Chrestomanci sank into it gratefully.

Drinks began arriving then. Chris Pinhoe and Clare Callow came out with trays of mugs, followed by Aunt Helen and most of her boys with trays of glasses. But they were not the only ones giving out drinks. Cat saw a thin green nonhuman hand reach round Gammer Norah's chair to present her with a foaming mug.

"Not for me. I never drink anything but water," Gammer Norah said, loftily pushing the mug aside.

The hand drew back so that it was out of Gammer Norah's sight, and the mug it held changed to a straight glass full of transparent liquid, which it held out to Gammer Norah again. A very quiet titter of laughter came from behind the chair as Gammer Norah seized the glass and took a hearty swig from it.

Cat was wondering what it really was in that glass, when two brownish purple hands pushed themselves between himself and Marianne, invitingly holding out glasses of something pink. Cat was going to take one, but Millie caught his eye and shook her head vigorously. "No, thank you," Cat said politely.

Marianne looked at him and said, "No, thank you," too. The hands drew back in a disappointed way. "Look what you did!" Marianne whispered to Cat. "They're *everywhere*!"

They were too, Cat realized, as he gratefully took a glass of real ginger beer from the tray Marianne's cousin John held out to him. The brownish purple hands were now offering what looked like beer to Uncle Charles and Marianne's dad. Marianne could not help giggling while she sipped her lemonade, when both men took the not-beer. Sour Dorothea was swigging from an enormous glass of not-water. At the gate of the yard, where a crowd of Pinhoes and Farleighs stood looking on, small half-seen shapes were flitting among legs and peering round skirts, and hands of strange colors were passing people glasses and mugs. Things that were almost like squirrels skipped along the walls of the yard. Up on the inn roof someone invisible was playing a faint skirling tune behind one of the chimneys.

"Oh, well," Cat said.

"I can't think what this Big Man thinks he's got to say to us," Gammer Norah said to Dorothea, loudly and rudely. "*We* did nothing wrong. It was all those Pinhoes' fault." She held out her empty glass. "More, please." The green hand obligingly filled it with not-water again.

Chrestomanci watched it rather quizzically. "I am not," he said, "in a very forgiving state of mind, Mrs.—er—Forelock. Your Gaffer did his best to shoot me this morning, when all I was doing was testing from the air the extent of your quite unwarranted misdirection spells. Let me make this clear to all of you: those spells are a misuse of magic that I am not prepared to treat lightly. It makes it worse that the fellow who

shot at me—I presume to prevent me investigating—appears to be my own employee. My gamekeeper." He turned to Millie in a bewildered way. "Why do we need a gamekeeper, do you know? Nobody at the Castle shoots birds."

"Of course not," Millie said, quickly taking up her cue. "According to the records, the last people to go shooting were wizards on the staff of Benjamin Allworthy, nearly two hundred years ago. But the records show that, when the next Chrestomanci took over, everyone quite unaccountably forgot to dismiss Mr. Farleigh."

Jason leaned forward. "More than that," he said. "They increased his salary. You must be quite a wealthy lady these days, Mrs. Farleigh."

Gammer Norah tossed her head, causing her bun to unroll even further. "How should I know? I'm only his wife, and his third wife at that, I'd have you know." She pounded her broomstick on the cobbles of the yard. "None of that alters the fact that the poor man's turned into a stone tree! I want justice! From these Pinhoes here!" Her long eyes narrowed, and she glared along the row of Marianne's uncles and aunts.

All of them glared back. Uncle Arthur said, "We. Did. Not. Do. It. Got that, Gammer Norah?"

"We wouldn't know how," Dad added in his pacific way. "We're peaceful in our craft." He looked down and noticed the saw he was still carrying and became very embarrassed. He bent the saw about, boing *dwang*. "We always cooperated," he said. "We've lent Gaffer Farleigh our strength for the misdirections for eight years now. We lent him strength for one thing or another as long as I've been alive."

"Yes, and what did your Gaffer *do* with it? That's what *I* want to know!" Marianne's mother asked, leaning forward fiercely. "If you ask me, he had the whole countryside under his thumb, doing what *he* wanted. And now I hear he's been at it for nearly two hundred years! Using *our* craft to lengthen his days, wasn't he?"

"Go it, Cecily!" Uncle Charles murmured.

"Never mind that!" Gammer Norah shouted,

pounding with her broom again. "He's still unlawfully turned to stone! If you didn't do it, who *did*? Was it *you*?" she demanded, turning her long-eyed glare on Chrestomanci.

"I wonder what you mean by 'unlawfully,' Mrs. Farlook," Chrestomanci told her. "The man tried to kill me. But it was not my doing. When one has just been shot, it is very hard to do anything, let alone create statues." He gazed around the inn yard in his vaguest way. "If the person who did it is here, perhaps he would stand up."

Cat felt Chrestomanci using Performative Speech again and found himself standing up. His stomach felt as if it was dropping out of his body, ginger beer and all. "It was me, Mrs. Farleigh," he said. His mouth was so dry he could hardly speak. "I—I was riding by the river." The frightening thing was not so much that they were all witches here. It was the way they were all people he didn't know, gazing at him in accusing amazement. But behind Gammer Norah's chair, green and purple-brown hands were punching the air in joy. The ones like squirrels were bounding about on the walls. And behind the inn chimneys, the music changed to loud, glad, and triumphant. This helped Cat a great deal. He swallowed and went on, "I wasn't quick enough to stop him firing at the flying machine—I'm sorry. But after that he was going to shoot Klartch, then Syracuse, then me. It was the only way I could manage to stop him."

"*You?*" said Gammer Norah, leaning incredulously on her broom. "A little skinny child like *you*? Are you lying to me?"

"Deep in evil," Dorothea said. "They're all like that."

"I was born with nine lives," Cat explained.

"Oh, you're *that* one, are you?" Gammer Norah said venemously. She was going to hurl a spell at him, Cat knew she was. But Millie made a small, quick gesture and Gammer Norah's attention somehow switched back to the Pinhoes. "I don't see any of *you* looking very sorry!" she yelled at them.

This was true. Grins were spreading across most of the Pinhoe faces. Cat sat down again, hugely relieved, and gave Klartch's head a comforting rub.

Gammer Norah screamed, "And what about the rest of it? Eh? What about the rest?"

"What rest is this?" Chrestomanci asked politely.

"The frogs, the ill-wishing, the fleas, the nits, the ants in all our cupboards!" Gammer Norah yelled, pounding with her broomstick. "Deny all that *if* you can! Every time we sent a plague back on you, you did another. We sent you whooping cough, we sent you smallpox, but you still didn't stop!"

"Bosh. We never sent you anything," Uncle Richard said.

"It was *you* sent *us* frogs," Uncle Charles added. "Or is *your* mind going now?"

Cat felt his face grow bright and hot as he remembered sending those frogs away from Mr. Vastion's surgery. He was wondering whether to stand up and confess again, when Marianne spoke up, loudly and clearly. "I'm afraid it was Gammer Pinhoe sending all those things on her own, Mrs. Farleigh."

Cat realized she was a lot braver than he was. She was the instant target of every Pinhoe there. The aunts glared at her, even more fiercely than they had glared at Gammer Norah. The uncles looked either contemptuous or reproachful. Dad said warningly, "I *told* you not to spread stories, Marianne!"

Mum added, "How *could* you, Marianne? You *know* how poorly Gammer is."

And from the back, Great-Uncle Edgar boomed, "Now that's enough of that, child!"

Marianne went pale, but she managed to say, "It *is* true."

"Yes," Chrestomanci agreed. "It *is* true. We at the Castle have been checking up on all of you rather seriously for the last few weeks. Ever since young Eric here pointed out to me the misdirection spells, in fact, we have had you under observation. We noted that an old lady called Edith Pinhoe was sending hostile magics to

Helm St. Mary, Uphelm, and various other villages nearby, and we were preparing to take steps."

"Though we did wonder why none of you tried to stop her," Millie put in. "But it's fairly clear to me now that she must have bespelled all of you as well." She smiled kindly at Marianne. "Except you, my dear."

While the Pinhoes were turning to one another, doubtful and horrified, Gammer Norah kept beating with her broomstick. "I want justice!" she bellowed. "Plagues and stone trees! I want justice for both! I want—" She broke off with a gurgle as a green hand clapped itself over her mouth. A purple-brown hand firmly took away her broomstick.

Cat thought that most people there decided that Chrestomanci had shut her up. He was fairly sure only a few of them could see the hidden folks. But Chrestomanci could.

Chrestomanci swallowed a slight grin and said, "Presently, Mrs. Farago, although you may not like the justice when you have it. There are a few serious questions I have to ask first. The most important of these concerns the *other* Gaffer in the case, the Mr. Ezekiel Pinhoe who was said to be dead eight years ago. Now a short while ago, I visited Ulverscote—"

"But you couldn't!" quite a number of Pinhoes protested. "You're not a Pinhoe."

"I took the precaution of getting a lift with Mr. and Mrs. Yeldham here," Chrestomanci said. "As you may know, Mrs. Yeldham was born a Pinhoe." Beside him, Irene colored up and bent over Nutcase on her knee, as if she were not sure that being a Pinhoe was altogether a good thing. Chrestomanci looked over to where the Reverend Pinhoe was quietly sipping lemonade over by the inn door. "I called on your vicar— Perhaps you could explain, Reverend."

Oh, it was *him*! Marianne thought. The day I met the Farleigh girls. He was in the church-yard.

The Reverend Pinhoe looked utterly flustered and extremely unhappy. "Well, yes. It is a most terrible thing," he said, "but most impressive magic, I must admit. But appalling, quite appalling all the same." He took an agitated gulp of lemonade. "Chrestomanci asked me to show him Elijah Pinhoe's grave, you see. I saw no harm in that, of course, and conducted him to the corner of the church where the grave was—is, I mean. Chrestomanci then most politely asked my permission to work a little magic there. As I saw no harm in that, I naturally agreed. And—" The vicar took another agitated gulp from his glass. "You can judge my astonishment," he said, "when Chrestomanci caused the coffin to emerge from the grave—without, I hasten to say, disturbing a blade of grass or any of the flowers you Pinhoe ladies so regularly place there—and then, to my further surprise, caused the coffin to open, without disturbing so much as a screw."

The Reverend Pinhoe tried to take another gulp from his glass and discovered it was empty. "Oh, please—" he said. A blue-green hand emerged from behind the rain barrel beside him and passed him a full glass. The Reverend

Pinhoe surveyed it dubiously, then took a sip and nodded.

"I thank you," he said. "I think. Anyway, I regret to have to inform you that the coffin contained nothing but a large wooden post and three bags of extremely moldy chaff. Gaffer Pinhoe was not inside it." He took another sip from his new glass and turned a little pink. "It was a great shock to me," he said.

It was a great shock to some of the aunts too. Aunt Helen and Great-Aunt Sue turned to each other and gaped. Aunt Joy said, "You mean someone *stole* him? After all we spent on flowers!"

Chrestomanci was looking vaguely around the yard. Cat knew he was checking to see who was surprised by the news and who was not. The Farleighs looked a little puzzled but not at all surprised. Most of the Pinhoe cousins were as surprised as Aunt Joy was and frowned at one another, mystified. But to Marianne's dismay, none of her uncles turned a hair, though Uncle Isaac tutted and tried to pretend he was upset.

Dad took it calmest of all. Oh, dear! she thought sadly.

"A very strange thing," Chrestomanci said. Cat could feel him using Performative Speech again. "Now who can explain this odd occurrence?"

Great-Uncle Edgar cleared his throat and looked uneasily at Great-Uncle Lester. Great-Uncle Lester went gray and seemed to get very shaky. "*You* tell them, Edgar," he quavered. "I—I'm not up to it after all this time."

"The fact is," Great-Uncle Edgar said, looking pompously around the inn yard, "Gaffer Pinhoe is not—er—actually dead."

"What's this?" Gammer Norah cried out, catching up rather late. "What's this? Not *dead*?" She's drunk! Marianne thought. She's going to start singing soon. "What do you mean, not dead? I *told* you to kill him. Gaffer Farleigh *ordered* you to kill him. Your own Gammer, his *wife*, said you had to kill him. Why didn't you?"

"We felt that was a little extreme," Great-Uncle Lester said apologetically. "Edgar and I simply used that spell that was used on Luke Pinhoe." He nodded at Irene. "Your ancestor, Mrs. Yeldham. We disabled both his legs. Then we put him in that old cart he loved so much and drove him into the woods."

Irene looked aghast.

"It had been our intention," Uncle Edgar explained, "to stow him beyond and behind with the hidden folks. But, upon experiment, we found we couldn't open the confining spell. So we made another confining spell by building a barrier and left him behind that."

"Please understand, Gammer Norah," Great-Uncle Lester pleaded. "Gaffer Farleigh knew all about it, and he didn't object. It—it seemed so much *kinder* that way."

Chrestomanci said, so softly and gently that both great-uncles shuddered, "It seems to *me* exceedingly cruel. Who else knew about this *kind* plot of yours?"

"Gammer knew, of course—" Great-Uncle Edgar began.

But Chrestomanci was still using Performative Speech. Dad spoke up. "They told all of us," he said, bending his saw about. "All his sons. They needed to, because of dividing out his property. We weren't surprised. We'd all seen it coming. We arranged for Cedric and Isaac to leave him eggs and bread and stuff behind the barrier." He looked earnestly up at Chrestomanci. "He must be still alive. The food goes."

Here, Great-Aunt Sue, who had been sitting holding the collar of the one fat dog that had come back from chasing the flying machine, quite suddenly stood up and slapped her hands down her crisp skirt. "Alive in the woods," she said. "For eight years. Without the use of his legs. And all of you lying about it. *Nine* grown men. I'm ashamed to belong to this family. Edgar, that does it. I'm leaving. I'm going to my sister outside Hopton. Now. And don't expect to hear from me again. Come on, Towser," she said, and went striding briskly out of the yard, with the dog panting after her.

Great-Uncle Edgar sprang up despairingly.

"Susannah! Please! It's just—we just didn't want to upset anyone!"

He started after Great-Aunt Sue. But Chrestomanci shook his head and pointed to the bench where Great-Uncle Edgar had been sitting. Great-Uncle Edgar sank back onto it, purple faced and wretched.

"I must say I'm glad Clarice isn't here to hear this," Great-Uncle Lester murmured.

I wish *I* wasn't here to hear it! Marianne thought. Tears were pushing to come out of her eyes, and she knew she would never feel the same about any of her uncles.

Aunt Joy, who seemed to have waited for this to be over, stood up too, and folded her arms ominously. "Eight years," she said. "Eight years I've been living a lie." She loosed one arm in order to point accusingly at Uncle Charles. "Charles," she said, "don't you expect to come home tonight, because I'm not having you! You spineless layabout. They do away with your own father, and you don't even mention the matter, let alone object. I've had enough of you, and that's final!"

Uncle Charles looked sideways at Aunt Joy, under her pointing finger, with his head down, rather like Joe. Marianne did not think he looked enormously unhappy.

Aunt Joy swung her pointing finger round toward the rest of the aunts. "And I don't know how you women can sit there, *knowing* what they've all done and lied about. I'm ashamed of you all, that's all I have to say!" She swung herself round then and stalked out of the yard as well. The invisible person on the roof played a march in time to Aunt Joy's banging shoes.

Marianne looked at her other aunts. Aunt Polly had not turned a hair. Uncle Cedric had obviously told her everything years ago. They were very close. Aunt Helen was staring trustingly at Uncle Arthur, sure that he had good reasons for not telling her; but Aunt Prue was looking at Uncle Simeon very strangely. Her own mother looked more unhappy than Marianne had ever seen her. Marianne could tell Dad had never said a word to her. She looked at Uncle Isaac's grave face and wondered what—

if anything—he had told Aunt Dinah.

"I hope no one else wishes to leave," Chrestomanci said. "Good." He turned his eyes to Dad. Though his face was pale and pulled with pain, his eyes were still bright and dark. Dad jumped as he met those eyes. "Mr. Pinhoe," Chrestomanci said, "perhaps you would be good enough to explain just *what* you had seen coming and *why* everyone felt it was necessary to— er—do away with your father."

Dad laid the saw carefully down by his feet. The brownish purple hand at once obligingly offered him another tankard of drink. Harry Pinhoe took it with a nod of thanks, too bothered by what he was going to say to notice where the drink had come from. "It was that egg," he said slowly. "The egg was the last straw. Anyone had only to look at it to know Gaffer had fetched it from behind the confinement spell. Everything else led up to that, really."

"In what way?" Chrestomanci asked.

Harry Pinhoe sighed. "You might say," he answered, "that Old Gaffer suffered from too much dwimmer. He was always off in the woods gathering weird herbs and poking into things best left alone. And he kept on at Gammer that the hidden folk were unhappy in confinement and ought to be let free. Gammer wouldn't hear of it, of course. Nor wouldn't Jed Farleigh. They had rows about it almost every week, Gammer saying it has always been our *job* to keep them in, and Gaffer shouting his nonsense about it was high time to let them out. Well, then—"

Harry Pinhoe took a long encouraging pull at his strange drink and made a puzzled face at the taste of it before he went on.

"Well, then, the crisis came when Gaffer came out of the woods with this huge, like egg. He gave it to Gammer and told her to keep it warm and let it hatch. Gammer said why should she do any such thing? Gaffer wouldn't tell her, not until she put a truth spell on him. *Then* he told her it was his scheme to let the hidden folks out. He said that when this egg hatched, he would be there to watch the bindings on the hidden folks undone." Harry Pinhoe looked unhappily over at Chrestomanci. "That did it, see. Gaffer said it like a prophecy, and Gammer couldn't have that. *Gammer's* the only one that's allowed to prophesy, we all know that. So she told her brothers Gaffer was quite out of hand and ordered them to kill him."

Marianne shivered. Cat found he had one hand protectively on Klartch, gripping the warm fluff on his back. Klartch, luckily, seemed to be asleep. Chrestomanci smiled slightly and seemed entirely bewildered. "But I don't understand," he said. "*Why* is it necessary to keep these unfortunate beings confined?"

Dad was puzzled that he should ask. "Because we always have," he said.

Gammer Norah came abreast of the talk again. "We always have," she proclaimed. "Because they're abominations. Wicked, ungodly things. Sly, mischievous, wild, and *beastly*!"

Dorothea looked up from her enormous glass. "Dangerous," she said. "Evil. Vermin. I'd destroy every one of them if I could."

She said it with such venom that a desperate,

terrified shiver ran round all the half-seen and invisible beings in the yard. Cat and Marianne found themselves clutched by unseen, shaking hands. One half-seen person climbed into Marianne's lap. A hard head with whiskers—or possibly antennae—butted pleadingly at Cat's face and, he was fairly sure, another person ran up him and sat on his head for safety. He looked at Chrestomanci for help.

Chrestomanci, however, looked at Dorothea and then, sternly, at Harry Pinhoe. "I regret to have to tell you," he said, "that Gaffer Pinhoe was quite right and the rest of you are quite, quite wrong."

Dad jerked backward on his bench. There was an outcry of shocked denial from Pinhoes and Farleighs alike. Dad's face turned red. "How come?" he said.

Millie glanced at Chrestomanci and took over. "We've been finding out all about you," she said. "We've traced Pinhoes, Farleighs, and Cleeves right back almost to the dawn of history now."

There was another shocked muttering at this,

as everyone realized at last that their secrecy was truly at an end. But they all listened attentively as Millie went on.

"You've always lived here," she said. "You must be some of the oldest witch families we know about. We found you first almost like clans, most of you living in tiny houses round the chief's great hall, and the rest of you living *in* the hall as followers of the chief. Woods House is certainly built on the exact spot where the Pinhoe hall was—and that was built a surprisingly long time ago too. Before the church, in fact. The Farleigh hall seems to have been destroyed in the trouble that came, but the Cleeves still have theirs, although it's the Cleeve Arms now, over in Crowhelm."

This caused some interest. Pinhoes and Farleighs turned to one another and murmured, "I never knew that. Cleeve Arms *is* old, though."

Heads turned back to Millie as she continued. "Now there are at least three important things you should know about those early days. The first is that your chief, who was known as Gaffer from quite early on, was chosen from among the old chief's family, and he was always chosen for having the most dwimmer. And he wasn't just chief, he was a prophet and a foreteller too. Your Old Gaffer was behaving just as he should, in fact. *He* was the one who chose the Gammer— and she wasn't always his wife, either. She was the woman with the most dwimmer. And the pair of them not only governed the rest, they worked in *partnership* with the hidden folks. These folks were cherished and loved and guarded. You shared magics with them, and they repaid you with healings and—"

This was too much for everyone. Millie was drowned out with cries of "That *can't* be!" and "I never *heard* such twaddle!"

Millie smiled slightly, and her voice suddenly came out over and above the objections, clear as a bell and, seemingly, not very loud. But everyone heard when she said, "Then comes the awful gap, with all sorts of horror in it." Everyone hushed to hear what this horror was.

"A new religion came to this country," Millie

said, "full of zeal and righteousness—the kind of religion where, if other people didn't believe in it, the righteous ones killed and tortured them until they did. This religion hated witches and hated the hidden folk even more. They saw all witches and invisible folks as demons, monsters, and devils, and their priests devised ways of killing them and destroying their magic that really worked.

"All three Gaffers at this time prophesied, as far as we can tell, and all of you, Pinhoes, Farleighs, and Cleeves, at once made sure that no one knew you were witches. What craft you used, you used in utmost secrecy, and because the hidden folk were even more at risk than you were, you all combined to keep them safe by locking them away behind the back of the distance. It was only intended to be a temporary measure. The Gaffers were all quite clear that the bloodthirsty righteous ones would go away in time. And so they did. But before they did, their priests became even more skillful and learned to conceal their plans even from the

Gaffers. Even so, the Gaffer Farleigh of the time started to prophesy disaster. But that was the night the bloodthirsty ones attacked.

"They came with fire and swords and powerful magics, and they killed everyone they could." Millie looked round the yard and at the people clustering at the gate. "When they had finished," she said, "the only people left were children, all of them younger than any of the children here. We think the bloodthirsty ones took all the children they could catch and educated them in their own religious ways, and some children escaped to the woods. The gap lasts about fifteen years, so those children had time to grow up. Then, thank goodness, the bloodthirsty ones were conquered themselves, probably by the Romans, and you all came together again, those from the woods and those who had been captured, and started to rebuild your lives."

Chrestomanci took a deep breath as Millie finished and steadied himself on the arms of his chair. He was looking awfully ill, Cat thought anxiously. "But you see what that means,"

Chrestomanci said. "These children had been too young to understand properly. They only knew what their anxious parents had impressed on them before the slaughter. They thought they had to keep their craft secret. They believed it was their duty to keep the hidden folks confined— and they had a vague notion that danger would come if they didn't. And they all knew that if a Gaffer prophesied, horrible things would happen—so they chose Gaffers that were good at giving orders, rather than those with dwimmer or the gift of foresight. And," Chrestomanci said ruefully, "I am afraid to say that the bloodthirsty doctrines of the religious ones had rubbed off on quite a lot of them, and they saw it as their religious duty to do things this way."

A long, thoughtful silence followed this. While it lasted, Cat watched a spidery hand, a new one that was a silvery white color, reach from behind Chrestomanci's chair to pass Chrestomanci a small glass of greenish liquid. Chrestomanci took it, looking rather startled. Cat watched him sniff it, hold it up to the light, and then cautiously dip a finger into it. His finger came out sparking green and gold like a firework. Chrestomanci examined it for a moment. Then he murmured, "Thank you very much," and drank the glassful off. He made the most dreadful face and clapped his hand to his stomach for a moment. But after that he looked a good deal better.

Everyone stirred then, except for Gammer Norah and Dorothea, who seemed to be asleep. Dad looked up and said, "Well, it makes a good story."

"It's more than a story," Chrestomanci said. He turned to a piece of the air beside him and asked, "Have you got a record of all this, Tom?"

Chrestomanci's secretary, Tom, was unexpectedly standing there, holding a notepad. Beside him stood old Miss Rosalie, the Castle librarian. She had her glasses down her nose and her nose almost inside the large blue folder she held, which she seemed to be reading avidly.

Tom said, "Every word, sir, right from the start."

Miss Rosalie looked up from the folder and, in her usual tactless, downright way, declared, "I've never met such flagrant misuse of magic, not *ever*. Not to speak of conspiracy to misuse. You can prosecute the lot of them."

Chrestomanci and Millie looked as if they had rather Miss Rosalie had kept her mouth shut. There was an outcry of anger and dismay from all round the yard. The Pinhoe uncles stood up threateningly and so did most of the Farleigh cousins. Gammer Norah woke up with a jump, glaring.

Unfortunately, that was the moment when Klartch woke up too, and staggered inquiringly out across the cobbles.

Chapter Twenty

Cat was sure that either Chrestomanci or Millie—or possibly both of them—had caused Klartch to wake up. It was otherwise hard to understand how Klartch slipped so easily between Cat's clutching fingers, or how Marianne missed her grab for his tail.

Dad said, "What the hell is *that*?"

"It's what came out of the egg," Uncle Charles told him. "Didn't I mention it to you? I know I told Arthur."

Their voices were almost drowned in Dorothea's screams. "It's an abomination! Kill it, Mother! Oh, the folks are loose! We're all dead meat! *Kill* it!"

Gammer Norah sprang to her feet and

pointed at Klartch, who turned his head toward her inquiringly. "Death," Gammer Norah intoned. "*Die*, you misbegotten creature of night."

To Marianne's embarrassment and Cat's heartfelt relief, nothing happened. Klartch just blinked and looked wondering. Dorothea pointed a finger at him and shrieked, "*Melt! Die! Begone!*" Klartch stared at her, while a crowd of hard-to-see beings rushed to him and hovered round him protectively. Quite a number of people could see these. Everyone began shouting, "The folks are loose! The folks are loose!" Some of those gathered by the gate screamed as loudly as Dorothea.

Rather shakily, Chrestomanci stood up. "Do be quiet, all of you," he said wearily. "It's only a baby griffin."

The noise died down, except for Gammer Norah, who said angrily, "Why didn't I kill it? Why is it not dead?"

"Because, Mrs. Furlong," Chrestomanci said, "while we were talking, my colleague Jason

Yeldham here has been busy removing your magic."

Gammer Norah gaped at him. "*What?*"

Dad said, "That *has* to be nonsense. Magic's an inborn part of you. And, Marianne, you had no business at all giving that blasted boy that egg. You've betrayed our sacred trust and I'm very angry with you."

Chrestomanci sighed. "You didn't listen to a word we said, did you, Mr. Pinhoe? There *is* no sacred trust and the hidden folks were only confined as a temporary measure for their own safety. And magic may be inborn, but so are your appendix and your tonsils. They can be removed too. Better show them, Jason."

Jason nodded and made a gentle pushing motion. A huge ball, made up of half-transparent green-blue strands, all wound up like a vast ball of knitting wool, rolled away from beside Jason's knees. In a light, drifting way it rolled to the middle of the yard and came to a stop there. "There," Jason said. "That's all the Farleigh magic. Every bit of it."

Gammer Norah, Dorothea, and the Farleigh cousins stared at it. One cousin said, "You'd no right to do that to us."

"I not only have the right," Chrestomanci said, "but as a government employee it's my duty to do this. People who use their magic to give a whole village a dangerous disease like smallpox are not to be trusted with it."

"That was just Marianne telling stories," said Dad.

Chrestomanci nodded at Tom, who flipped back pages in his notebook and read out, "'We sent you whooping cough, we sent you smallpox, and you still didn't stop!' Those are Mrs. Farleigh's exact words, Mr. Pinhoe."

Dad said nothing. He picked up his saw again and bent it about, meaningly.

Irene nudged Jason and whispered to him. Jason grinned and said, *"Yes!"* He turned to Chrestomanci. "Irene thinks the wood folks ought to have this magic as compensation for wrongful imprisonment."

"A very good idea," Chrestomanci said.

Irene stood up to make happy beckoning movements to the walls, forgetting that Nutcase was asleep on her knee. Nutcase thumped to the ground, looked irritably around, and saw all the half-seen creatures leaving Klartch in order to dive delightedly upon the ball of magic. He was off like a black streak. He got to the ball of magic first and plunged into it, straight through and out the other side. Trailing long strings of blue-green, with a crowd of angry beings after him, he raced up across Dorothea, up the pile of barrels behind her, and from there to the top of the wall.

There will be no holding Nutcase now, Marianne thought, watching Nutcase jump off the wall into the alley and Dorothea resentfully licking scratches on her arm. She was depressed and worried. Dad was never going to understand and never going to forgive her. And Gaffer had still not turned up. On top of that, school started on Monday week. Though look on the bright side, she thought. It'll keep me away from my family, during the daytime at least.

Meanwhile, the hard-to-see people were helping themselves enthusiastically to the rest of the ball of magic. The ball shrank, and tattered, and seemed to dissolve away like smoke in a wind. There were a lot more of the folks than Cat or Marianne had realized. Some of them must have been completely invisible.

Cat conjured a sausage roll from somewhere inside the Pinhoe Arms and set out to coax Klartch away from the middle of the yard. He did not like the way Gammer Norah and some of the Pinhoes were looking at Klartch. He found himself, with the sausage roll held out in front of Klartch's beak, backing away past a row of Marianne's aunts.

"Strange-looking creature, isn't he?" said one.

"You can see it's a baby from the fluff. Rather sweet in a yicky way," said a second.

The third one said, "What are you doing with one of my sausage rolls, boy?"

And the one who Cat was sure was Marianne's mother said, thinking about it, "You know, it's going to look just like Charles's painting on the inn sign when it's grown. And it's going to be vast. Look at the size of the feet on it."

Before Cat could think of anything to say in reply, the Farleighs were leaving, trudging sullenly out of the yard, muttering murderously about having to walk home now they had no magic.

"It isn't exactly like tonsils," Chrestomanci remarked as they tramped past him. "It can grow back in time if you're careful." He was standing with Tom on one side of him and Miss Rosalie on the other, and it is doubtful if any of the Farleighs heard him, because Miss Rosalie was saying brightly at the same time, "I make that forty-two charges of misuse of magic, sir, in Ulverscote alone. Shall I read them out?"

"No need," Chrestomanci said. "Yet." He said to all the Pinhoes, "You all understand, do you, that I can take your magic too, or have nearly all of you arrested? Instead of doing that, I am going to ask for your cooperation. You have a whole new set of magics here, and one of my duties is to study unknown magic. I would particularly like to know more about the kind you call dwimmer." His eyes flicked to Cat for a moment. "I think I need to know more of dwimmer as soon as possible. We would like as many of you as feel able to visit the Castle and explain your working methods to us."

He got eight outraged glowers from Marianne's uncles and great-uncles for this. Dad twanged his saw disgustedly. Millie bustled happily up to the aunts, who all turned their backs on her, except for Marianne's mother, who folded her arms and stared, rather in Aunt Joy's manner.

"You're the famous herb mistress, aren't you, Mrs. Pinhoe?" Millie said. "I really would be grateful if you'd come and give me a lesson or so—"

"What, give away all my secrets?" Mum said. "You've got a hope."

"But, my dear, why ever do you need to keep things secret?" Millie asked. "Suppose you'd been killed in the fight just now."

"I've tried to bring Marianne up to know herbs," Mum said. She gave Marianne an irritated look. "Not that it seems to have taken very well."

"Well, of course it wouldn't," Millie said, smiling at Marianne. "Your daughter's an enchantress, not a witch. She'll have quite a different way of doing things."

While Mum was staring at Marianne as if Marianne had suddenly grown antlers and a trunk, Millie sighed and whirled away to Chrestomanci, saying, "Get in the car, love. You look wiped."

"I need to have a word with Gammer Pinhoe first," Chrestomanci said.

"I'll drive you down to the Dell, then," Millie said.

This caused Cat to have to tempt Klartch all the way back across the yard to the car. They went rather slowly because both Cat and Klartch were constantly turning to watch strings of blue-green magic fluttering along the walls, or being dragged into barrels, or flying in tatters from chimneys, as the half-seen folk carried it away. Millie waited for them, and Jason held the rear door open and helped Cat heave Klartch in beside Irene. Klartch instantly ramped upright to look out of the window. There were loud popping sounds as his talons went into the expensive leather upholstery.

By that time, the Pinhoes had gathered that Chrestomanci was going down to the Dell. They were not going to let him loose on Gammer on her own. Cat found himself between Marianne and Miss Rosalie, inside a crowd of Pinhoes, all of them trotting, jogging, and crunching broken glass behind the car as it glided down the hill.

"Gaffer must be *somewhere*," Marianne said miserably as they passed Great-Uncle Lester's ruined car.

Dad answered her by giving vent to his feelings. "Look what you brought us to, Marianne! This is all your fault for thinking you know better than the rest of us. The good old ways are not good enough for you. No. You had to get us noticed by the Castle. And see where we are now, at the mercy of these jumped-up, jazzy know-it-alls in good suits, who'll have us arrested if we don't do—"

He was interrupted for a second here by Nicola's mother, swooping uphill past them on her broomstick. "I can't wait, Lester!" she called out. "I'll miss visiting hours."

As Great-Uncle Lester gave her a dismal wave, Dad took up his diatribe again. "Them and their threats! How can they say we've misused magic and then want to know what it is we do? It makes no sense. But they think they have the right to give us a going-over with their newfangled stuck-up ways and their stupid stories about slaughter in history and children misunderstanding—I don't believe a word of it. We're just ordinary folk, doing what we've always done, and they come along—"

Miss Rosalie, who had been looking increasingly annoyed, snapped, "Oh, shut *up*, man! Of *course* you can go back to your good old ways. We want to *study* them."

This simply set Dad off again. "Poking and

prying. Going on about craft things nobody should talk about. Letting out the hidden folk. That's just what I'm complaining about, woman! What are we, a flaming *fish tank*?"

"I refuse to argue with you!" Miss Rosalie panted haughtily.

"Good!" said Dad, and went on with his diatribe in an increasingly breathless mutter as the car gathered speed down the hill. He did not stop, even when the car was turning the corner at the bottom of the hill, where they encountered Aunt Joy standing on her half-built wall.

"I meant what I said!" Aunt Joy shouted, and hurled a suitcase at Uncle Charles. "You're not coming back, and here's your things, wedding suit and all. I jumped on it."

Uncle Charles did not try to answer. He simply picked up the battered suitcase and trotted on, smiling sheepishly at Uncle Richard. "Staring at us," went Dad. "Thinking they're so clever. Fish tank. All Marianne's fault."

At the Dell, they found Gammer outside the front door, surrounded by hard-to-see flying folk. They did not appear to love Gammer. They darted in, pulled her hair, tweaked and scratched at her, and darted back away. Gammer beat at them with a rolled-up newspaper. "Shoo!" she shouted. "Gerroff! Shoo!"

Aunt Dinah, who could not seem to see the flying ones at all, was dodging helplessly in and out, ducking under the newspaper and saying, "That's enough now, Gammer dear. Come inside now, dear."

"Fish tank," said Dad, and ran down in a kind of moaning sound as he saw how easily Gammer had managed to walk out through his careful containment spells.

Gammer stared at Chrestomanci as he climbed stiffly and shakily out of the car. She seemed to know at once who he was. "Don't you dare!" she shouted at him as he walked toward her round the duck pond. "You've only come to interferret me. I didn't do it. It was Edgar and Lester."

The half-seen ones knew who Chrestomanci was too. They flew up from Gammer in a body and roosted on the cottage roof to watch.

"I know about Edgar and Lester, ma'am," Chrestomanci said. "I want to know why you were persecuting the Farleighs."

"Jedded my head," Gammer said. "My mouth is porpoised."

"Means her lips are sealed," Uncle Charles translated from among the crowd.

"Utterly dolphined," Gammer agreed.

"And possibly whaled as well," Chrestomanci murmured. "I think you had better unwalrus them, ma'am, and—"

The gate from the back way, through Uncle Isaac's vegetable acres, clicked quietly open to let Molly and Gaffer through.

Not everyone saw them straightaway, because the corner of the cottage was in the way. But Marianne saw. And she knew why Gaffer had been so long on the way. His legs were bent and bowed and his feet twisted so that it was all but impossible for him to walk. He had both arms across the unicorn's back. She was walking one careful step at a time, and then stopping so that

Gaffer could swing himself along beside her. Each time his legs had to take his weight, Marianne saw him shudder with pain.

She turned and screamed at her great-uncles. She was so angry that both of them recoiled from her, almost into the hedge at the back. "That is the cruelest thing I ever saw! Uncle Edgar, I shall never speak to you again! Uncle Lester, I shall never go *near* you!" She raced toward Gaffer and tore the ensorcellment off him. It was a bit like clearing weeds and creepers off a struggling overgrown tree in Mum's garden. Marianne clawed and pulled and dragged, and the spell fought back like thorns and nettles, but she finally hauled it all away, panting, with stinging hands and tears in her eyes, and threw it to the hard-to-see folk to get rid of. They swooped on it and took it away gladly.

Gaffer slowly and creakily stood to his proper height, the same height as Chrestomanci. He smiled at her. "Why, thank you, pet," he said.

Molly turned her head to say sadly, "I can heal wounds of the flesh, but that was magic." She added to Gaffer, "Keep your arm over me. You won't walk easily straightaway."

They moved on, around the corner of the cottage. Chrestomanci, now leaning beside Cat on the long black bonnet of the car, could see them perfectly, but Gammer, with Aunt Dinah dodging around her, was too busy screaming insults at Chrestomanci to notice.

"Inkbubble chest of drawers!" she yelled. "Unstuck bog!"

Cat thought that both the unicorn and the tall old man had a curious, unreal, silvery look as they came round into the sunlight at the front of the cottage.

There was a long murmur from the Pinhoes. "It's old Gaffer!" and "Isn't that his old mare, Molly?" they said.

This alerted Gammer. She swung around, with dismay all over her ruined face. "You!" she said. "I told them to kill you!"

"There were times when I wished they had," Gaffer answered. "What have you been up to, Edith? Let's have the truth now."

Gammer shrugged a little. "Frogs," she said. "Ants, nits, fleas. Itching powder." She giggled. "They thought the itching was more fleas and washed till they were raw."

"Who did?" Gaffer asked. He took his arm off Molly and stood looking down at her on his own. The unicorn backed herself round and stepped across to Chrestomanci. There she stretched her neck out and gave Chrestomanci's ragged, bleeding arm the merest flick with her horn.

Chrestomanci jerked and gasped. Cat could feel the warm rush of health from the horn, even though it was not aimed at him. "Thank you," Chrestomanci said gratefully, looking into the unicorn's wise blue eyes. "Very much indeed." He was a better color already and, although the blood was still there, all over Joe's shirt, Cat was fairly sure that there was now no bullet wound in Chrestomanci's arm.

"My pleasure," replied the unicorn. She winked a blue eye at Cat and stepped around again toward Gaffer.

"*Who* did?" Gaffer was repeating. "Who have you been tormenting now?"

Gammer looked mulishly down at the grass. "Those Farleighs," she said. "I hate the lot of them. That Dorothea of theirs met a griffin by the Castle gates and they said I let it out."

"The griffin was only looking for her egg, poor creature," Gaffer said. "She thought it might have arrived at the Castle by then. What had you done with it?"

Gammer scrubbed at the grass with one toe. She giggled a little. "It wouldn't break," she said, "not even when I threw it downstairs. I made Harry stick it in the attic with a binding on it and hoped it would die. Nasty thing."

Gaffer pressed his lips together and looked down at her with great pity. "You've gone like a wicked small child, haven't you?" he said. "No thought for others at all. But your spells on them are stronger than ever, and they still all do your bidding."

The unicorn softly approached.

Gammer looked up and saw the long,

whorled horn coming toward her. "No!" she said. "It wasn't me! It was Edgar and Lester."

Gaffer shook his head, floppy old hat and all. "No, it was *you*, Edith. Let go now. You've gone your length."

He stood aside and let Molly gently touch the tip of her horn to Gammer's forehead. Cat felt the warm blast of this too, but this time it seemed to be blowing the other way. Gammer gave out a small noise that was horribly like Klartch's "Weep!" and crumpled slowly down on the grass, where she lay curled up like a baby.

Aunt Dinah charged forward. "What has that monster done?"

Gaffer looked at her with tears running on his withered cheeks and into his beard. "You wouldn't wish to be forced to obey madness for the next ten years, would you?" he said. His pleasant voice was all hoarse. He coughed. "She'll last three days now," he said. "You'll have time to choose your new Gammer before she dies."

Aunt Dinah looked helplessly at the other

Pinhoes crowded around the car and the pond. "But there's only Marianne," she said. Marianne's heart sank.

"Ah no," Gaffer said. "Marianne has her own way to go and her own race to run, bless her. You mustn't lumber anyone with this who hasn't found her own way in life first." He looked toward the rear door of the car, where Irene and Jason were trying to shove Klartch back inside. Klartch wanted to get out and examine the ducks. "My friend Jason's lady has more dwimmer than I've known for many years," Gaffer said. "Think about it."

Irene looked up into the massed stares of the Pinhoes and turned bright, warm red. "Oh, my goodness!" she said.

Chapter Twenty-one

Uncle Richard and Uncle Isaac walked carefully around the edge of the pond, and the Reverend Pinhoe followed them. Warily, giving the unicorn a very wide berth, the two uncles picked Gammer up and carried her away indoors. Aunt Dinah rushed in after them. Dad watched them with a scowl. "I wouldn't have Marianne anyway," he said. "She's not suitable."

"No indeed," Chrestomanci agreed. "She can override any of your spells any time she pleases. Awkward for you. Tell me, Marianne, how do you feel about being educated at the Castle? As a weekly boarder, say, coming home every weekend? I've just made the same arrangement with your brother Joe. Would you like to join him?"

Marianne could hardly think, let alone speak, for huge, nervous delight. She felt her face steretching into a great smile. Looking up at Gaffer, she saw his eyes twinkling encouragement to her, even though he was busy mopping his cheeks on his ragged sleeve.

Before either of them could say anything, Dad burst out, "*Joe*, did you say? What do you want with *him*? He's even more of a disappointment than Marianne is!"

"On the contrary," Chrestomanci said. "Joe has immense and unusual talent. He has already invented three new ways of combining magic with machinery. A couple of wizards from the Royal Society are coming down to interview him tomorrow. They're very excited about him. So what do you say, Marianne?"

"I see!" Dad burst out, again before Marianne could speak. "I see. You're going to take them off and make them think they're too good for the rest of their family!"

"Only if you make it that way," Chrestomanci replied. "The surest way to make them think they're too good for you is to keep telling your-self that and then telling them that they are."

Dad looked a trifle dazed. "I can't get my head around this," he said.

"Then you have a problem, Mr. Pinhoe," Chrestomanci said, and then turned away to Gaffer. "Are you going to be taking your former place again as Gaffer, sir?" he asked.

Gaffer slowly shook his head. "Molly and I are not really with this world anymore," he said. The twinkle with which he was looking at Marianne began to glow. "I was always one for walking the woods," he said. "Now I can walk again, I'll be going far and wide with Molly, bringing young Jason more odd herbs than he's seen in his life, I reckon. Besides," he added, and the glow blazed into humor now, "if you're wanting them all to go on the way they always did, then Harry will do you a fine stout job at that. Let him carry on." He bent and kissed Marianne, a soft, tickly brushing with his beard. "Bye, pet. You go and find who you really are, and don't let anyone stop you."

He and Molly turned to go. Chrestomanci went striding back to the car, where Tom was standing with Miss Rosalie. "Tom, take Miss Rosalie back with you," Cat heard him say. "Make a list of her forty-two misuses of magic and send a copy to each of the Pinhoe brothers and both their uncles. I want them all to know what trouble they could be in if they don't cooperate with us." Tom nodded and took hold of Miss Rosalie's skinny arm. Both of them vanished. Chrestomanci turned to tell Cat to get into the car.

But there was a frantic, pattering, yelling disturbance at the back of the crowd. Marianne's uncles and aunts scattered this way and that, and the Reverend Pinhoe, who was still only halfway round the pond, was dislodged into the water with a splash. He stood up to his knees in green weeds, staring as Dolly the donkey came racing past. She was somehow not Dolly as Marianne had always known her. She was taller and slenderer, and her ears were not so big. Her usual yellowish color was now silvery, almost silver gilt. And a small, elegant spire of horn grew from her forehead.

"My other daughter!" Molly said, and turned round to lay her head across Dolly's back.

"I thought I'd missed you!" Dolly panted. "It's been such years. I had to break the door down."

Uncle Richard, who was just coming out through the cottage door, stood astonished. "Dolly!" he said. "Why did I never know—how didn't I know?"

"You never looked," Dolly said, rubbing herself against Molly's shaggy side.

Chrestomanci said impatiently to Cat, "Get in. Let's go."

But Klartch had decided he wanted to meet Dolly. Jason had to grab him around his wriggling body and dump him in the backseat of the car, where he somehow covered Irene in green pond weed. And now Millie was climbing out of the driver's seat to help the Reverend Pinhoe out of the pond and offer him a lift back up the hill. More pond weed arrived in the car.

Chrestomanci looked exasperated. He went back to Marianne. "The car will come for you at eight thirty on Monday," he said to her. "I hope it will be cleaner by then. Pack for five days."

I see how Dad feels, Marianne thought. He *does* expect everyone to do what he says. And she thought, I'll miss school. Suppose they throw me out of the Castle after a week? Will school have me back? But I'll learn all sorts of new magic. Do I want to? She gave Chrestomanci a nervous and slightly indefinite nod.

"Good." Chrestomanci strode back to the car. Cat was now packed in beside everyone else, with Klartch across their knees. Nothing would possess Klartch to get down on the floor. He wanted to look out of the window. "Thank *goodness*!" Chrestomanci said, throwing himself in beside Millie. "I really *must* have a word with Gaffer Farleigh before all the other Farleighs get back!"

The Pinhoes stood aside and watched unlovingly while Millie turned the car and drove out of the Dell. She drove along the lane, where a few enchanted frogs still croaked in the hedges, and then on up the hill, past groups of mournful people sweeping up broken glass, past Great-Uncle Lester's stranded car, and stopped by the vicarage to let the Reverend Pinhoe squelch away, along with Irene and Jason, all of them covered in green weed. After that, Cat and Klartch expanded in the backseat and Millie put on speed.

It was not long before they began passing Farleighs. Gammer Norah and Dorothea first, since they had been the last to leave, shot the car poisonous looks as it purred past them. After that came a whole line of Farleighs, trudging along the side of the road pushing bent bicycles or carrying useless broomsticks. Some of them made rude gestures, but most of them dejectedly ignored the car as it whispered by. When they had passed the last Farleigh, still only about halfway home, Chrestomanci seemed to relax. "How come you turned up so providentially?" he asked Millie.

"Oh, I only went down to the village to post a

letter," Millie said, "and the first thing I saw was a really *peculiar* statue of a tree, standing in the middle of the green. Norah Farleigh was stamping about beside it, haranguing people. As I walked past, I heard her say something like 'and we'll do for those Pinhoes!' and I saw there was going to be trouble. Then while I was posting the letter and wondering what to do, I recognized one of our horses outside the smithy. So I hurried over there and found Joss Callow. I said, 'Leave the horse and come with me at *once*. We may be in time to stop a witches' war in Ulverscote.' I knew I had to have a Pinhoe with me, you see, or their spells would stop me getting there. And Joss was only too glad to come with me. He was afraid someone was going to get killed—he kept saying so. But we hadn't reckoned on the Farleighs being so *quick*. By the time we'd gone back to the Castle and I'd gotten the car out, they were already on the way. The road was blocked by bicycles and the air was thick with broomsticks. We had to crawl behind them the whole way. So I went to Woods House and picked up the Yeldhams, in case they got hurt—I knew I could keep them safe in the car—but when we came out into the village they were fighting there like mad things and none of us could think of how to stop them. I don't know what would have happened if you hadn't come along in that flying machine."

"I was *not* happy to be there," Chrestomanci said. "I'd only persuaded Roger to take me in order to get an overview of the misdirection spells."

"I'm glad the boys survived it," Millie said. "I *must* remind Roger that he has only one life."

They purred on for another couple of miles. They were almost in Helm St. Mary when they saw a man in the distance wrestling with a horse. The man was being bounced and dangled and dragged all over the road.

Cat said, "It looks as if Joss has run out of peppermints."

"I'll handle it," said Chrestomanci.

Millie crept up behind Joss and whispered to a stop far enough away not to outrage Syracuse any further. Chrestomanci rolled down his window and held out a paper bag of peppermints. More of Julia's, probably, Cat thought.

"*Thank* you, sir!" Joss said gratefully.

Cat said sternly, "Syracuse, *behave*!"

Chrestomanci said, "By the way Mr.—er— Carroway—"

"Callow," Joss managed to say. He was hanging on to the reins with both hands, with the paper bag between his teeth.

"Callow," Chrestomanci agreed. "I do hope you are not considering giving in your notice at all, Mr. Carlow. You are by far and away the best stableman we have ever had."

Joss flushed all over his wide brown face. "Thank you, sir. I—well—" He spat the bag into his hand and waved it enticingly under Syracuse's nose. "It's a job I'd be glad to keep," he said. "My mother lives in Helm St. Mary, see."

"She was born a Pinhoe, I take it," Chrestomanci said.

Joss flushed redder still and nodded. Chrestomanci did not need to say he knew that

Joss had been planted in the Castle as a spy. He gave Joss a gracious wave as Millie drove on.

Very soon after this, the car was scudding round the village green of Helm St. Mary, just below the Castle. There, slap in the middle of the green, stood the stone oak tree, looking like a twisty, granite, three-armed memorial of some kind. Hard for Gammer Norah to miss it there, Cat thought guiltily. He'd had no idea he had sent it here.

"Dear me," Chrestomanci murmured as the car crunched to a halt beside the green. "What a very ugly object." He climbed out. "Come on, Cat."

Cat scrambled out and persuaded Klartch to stay inside the car. He was not looking forward to this, he thought, as he followed Chrestomanci over to the stone tree.

"Uglier than ever, close to," Chrestomanci said, looking up at the thing. "Now, Cat, if you could turn at least his head back, I'd be glad of a word with him. You can leave the gun as granite, I think."

Cat was somehow very much aware of Klartch watching anxiously through the car window as he put his hands on the cold, rough granite. And because Klartch was watching, Cat knew there was also a ring of half-seen beings watching quite as anxiously from behind every tuft of grass on the green. In fact, Klartch made him see that they were everywhere, swinging on the inn sign, sitting on the roofs, peering out of hedges, and perched on chimneys. Cat saw that he had let them all out, all over the country. They would always be everywhere now.

"Turn back into Mr. Farleigh," he said to the stone oak.

Nothing happened.

Cat tried again with his left hand alone, and still nothing happened. He tried putting both hands on the rough, knobby place that must have been Mr. Farleigh's face, and then pushing both hands apart to clear the stone away. Still nothing happened. Chrestomanci moved Cat aside and tried himself. Cat knew that this was unlikely to work. Chrestomanci almost never could turn anything back once Cat had changed it: their magic seemed to be entirely different. And he was right. Chrestomanci gave up, looking exasperated.

"Let's try together," he said.

So they both tried, and still nothing happened. Mr. Farleigh remained a gray, faintly glistening, obdurate oak made of stone.

"It comes to something," Chrestomanci said, "when two nine-lifed enchanters together can make no difference whatsoever to this thing. What did you *do*, Cat?"

"I told you," Cat said. "I made him like he really was."

"Hmm," said Chrestomanci. "I really must learn more about dwimmer. It seems to be your great strength, Cat. But it's very frustrating. I wanted to tell him what I thought of him—not to speak of asking him how he managed to be a gamekeeper we didn't need for all those years." He turned discontentedly away to the car.

A flitting half-seen being drew Cat's attention to Joss's bored horse, still hitched up outside the smithy. "I'd better bring Joss his horse back," Cat said. "You go on."

Chrestomanci shrugged and got into the car.

Cat ran over to the horse. It had all four shoes again. "All right if I take him?" he called to the blacksmith, deep inside his coaly cave of a shed.

The blacksmith looked up from hammering and called back, "About time. I'll send the bill up to the Castle."

Cat mounted the horse from the block of stone beside the smithy. It was much taller than Syracuse. Otherwise, it had no character at all. He got no feelings from it, not even a wish to go home. This felt very strange after Syracuse. But at least its dull mind left Cat free with his own thoughts. As he clopped round the green in the early evening light, Cat wondered if he had left Mr. Farleigh as a stone tree because he *wanted* him that way. Mr. Farleigh had scared him. He had scared the half-seen beings even more. As Cat turned up through the Castle gates, the beings skipped and skittered among the trees lining the driveway, laughing in their delight that Mr. Farleigh was no longer a threat. Cat wondered if they had helped him leave Mr. Farleigh as he now was.

He had had no lunch, and he was starving. Klartch would be hungry too. Cat made the lumpish horse go faster and—because it was now thinking dimly of home and food—he took it the short way he was not supposed to go, along the gravel in front of the newer part of the Castle. The flying machine was spread out on the lawn there, in front of four deep brown skid-marks in the grass. It looked as if Roger and Joe had had a rough landing.

Janet and Julia were cautiously inspecting the machine. Janet called out, "Cat, I can't find Klartch anywhere!"

Julia called out, "What have you been up to without *us*? It isn't fair!"

"You wouldn't have enjoyed it," Cat called back. "Millie's got Klartch."

"I don't care," Julia shouted. "It still isn't fair!"

* * *

Marianne arrived very apprehensively the next Monday. She found she was in for ordinary lessons at first with Joe, Roger, Cat, Janet, and Julia, taught by a tall, keen man called Michael Saunders. She was impressed by Mr. Saunders. No one else had ever made Joe do any schoolwork at all. But Joe had been promised a big new work shed where he and Roger could experiment with all their new ideas, provided he pleased Mr. Saunders. So Joe sat at a desk and worked, and very soon proved to be quite extraordinarily good with figures.

Marianne began to enjoy herself. She made friends instantly with both the other girls, and she liked Cat anyway, although she was shy of Roger. Roger *would* talk about machinery or money.

Most afternoons, Marianne and Cat had a lesson with Chrestomanci. At first, Marianne could hardly speak for nerves. Enchanter's magic was all so strange, and Cat knew so much more than she did. But she discovered on the second afternoon that Cat was slow with Magic Theory, whereas Marianne found it so easy that she almost felt she knew most of it already. Anyway, the next half of the lesson was always more like a conversation, with Cat and Chrestomanci asking her interested questions about the craft and dwimmer and herb lore. After the first terrifying afternoon, Marianne felt entirely at ease and talked and talked.

She had brought her story with her, of "Princess Irene and Her Cats," but she never got very far with it, because she was always being roped in for games with the girls or with Klartch and half the people in the Castle, and these were all so much fun that she never seemed to have time for anything else.

By the end of the week, she was enjoying herself so much that it was a real wrench when she and Joe had to go home to Ulverscote. They found they had missed Gammer's funeral. But at least they arrived in time to welcome Nicola home from hospital, pale and skinny but no longer seriously ill. As they walked back from the welcome party, Joe and Marianne talked all the time about Chrestomanci Castle. In fact, they talked of nothing else all weekend. Dad was morose about it, but Mum listened, doubtfully but intently. When the car came and fetched Joe and Marianne away again the next Monday, their mother went thoughtfully along to Woods House to talk to Irene.

Irene had never been officially named as the next Gammer, but people were always going to talk to her as if she was. Irene would lay her pencil down across her latest delicate design work and listen seriously with Nutcase on her knee. Nutcase was now able to get into any cupboard or at any food he fancied, and only Jane James could control him. Mum told Marianne it was a blessing that Irene liked that cat so much.

Irene's advice was always considered to be excellent—though Irene told Marianne that all she did was to tell people what they were really trying to say to her. One of the first people to consult her was Uncle Charles. He put on his badly crumpled wedding suit and went up to Woods House as an official visitor, where he told

Irene many things. Shortly after that, he enrolled as an advanced student at the Bowbridge College of Art. Mum told Marianne that Uncle Charles was intending to go to London to seek his fortune in a year or so.

"There's another who's above his own family now," Dad said.

Mum's own visit to Irene resulted in her sharing the car that came for Joe and Marianne on the third Monday and arriving at Chrestomanci Castle too. Millie welcomed her with delight. Mum spent a most enjoyable morning talking to Millie over coffee and biscuits—good, but not as good as Jane James's, Mum said, but then whose were?—talking about everything under the sun, including the deep mysteries of herbs. After a bit, she agreed to let Chrestomanci's secretary, Tom, come in and take notes, because, as Millie said, she was saying things that even Jason had never heard of. Marianne's mum enjoyed this visit so much—including the chance to have lunch with both her children—that she went back to the Castle many times. It annoyed Dad, but, Mum said, there you go, that's Dad.

After this, the car going to the Castle on a Monday was often quite crowded with Pinhoe ladies—and their broomsticks for the return journey—visiting various people in the Castle. Mr. Stubbs and Miss Bessemer were busy learning from the craft too. Amazing new chutneys and tangy pickles made their way into the Castle, along with certain magical embroideries for sheets, clothes, and cushions. The Castle gave them spells in return, but most Pinhoe ladies were agreed that Castle spells were not a patch on the spells of the craft. It made them feel pleasantly useful and superior.

The men mostly went over by bicycle. They were even more superior, particularly Uncle Richard and Uncle Isaac, when they found themselves giving lessons in woodworking and the craft of growing things to a ring of earnest gardeners and footmen.

"Bah!" said Dad. "Letting them pick your brains!"

By this time, it was all round the country,

beyond Bowbridge in one direction and Hopton the other way, that Edgar and Lester Pinhoe had done away with Gaffer Pinhoe. Both of them lost clients. In the end, neither of them could stand the gossip anymore. They moved away to Brighton, where they lived together in a bachelor flat. Great-Aunt Clarice moved in with Great-Aunt Sue, where they lived in the house just outside Ulverscote among more fat, lazy dogs than anyone could count. Dad called the house The Fleapit from then on.

Gammer Norah and her daughter Dorothea naturally bore a grudge. They were the ones who spread the gossip about Edgar and Lester. When Marianne's two great-uncles left, Gammer Norah and Dorothea took to standing on the green of Helm St. Mary, where they scowled so at any Pinhoes visiting the Castle that, as Mum said, it made you nervous in case they still had the evil eye. But that stopped when Gammer Norah won a lottery ticket for two to go to Timbuktu, and both Norah and Dorothea went. "We can't have them festering away on our doorstep," Millie said, with a wink at Mum. "They had to go before their magic grew back."

"Typical interference," Dad said.

Klartch continued to grow. By Christmas he was developed enough to join the others in the now crowded schoolroom and learn to read and write. Even Janet began to realize that Klartch was a friend and not a pet. Games of Klartchball still got played on the lawn, but the rules changed with Klartch's size. Klartch was a team on his own by the New Year.

Often, usually around dusk, the Castle staff got used to seeing a huge female griffin come ghosting down to the lawn. This was sometimes confusing, because Joe's latest flying machine was also liable to arrive home at dusk, whereupon it usually crashed. The way to tell the difference, Mr. Frazier explained, was that if it was the griffin, you got knocked down in the corridor by Klartch rushing out to see his mother. If Klartch did not appear, then *you* rushed out with healing spells and mending crafts the Pinhoes had taught you.

And sometimes, sometimes, when Cat rode out on Syracuse into the more distant woods, they would see a tall old man striding along in the distance with his hand on the back of a glimmering white unicorn.